||PUBLISHING||

Copyright © 2011 by Frances Dyanne Davis
Published by WD Publishing
P.O. Box 1218
Bolingbrook IL. 60440
WDPublishing@aol.com

This book is a work of fiction. Characters, names, locations, events and incidents (in either a contemporary and/or historical setting) are products of the author's imagination and are being used in an imaginative manner as a part of this work of fiction. Any resemblance to actual events, locations, settings, or persons, living or dead, is entirely coincidental.

ISBN: 978-0-9844348-3-1
Manufactured in the United States of America
First Edition
Cover Design
A.M. Wells

THE AFFAIR

BY

DYANNE DAVIS

Dyanne Davis TITLES:

The Critic
Another Man's Baby
Many Shades of Gray
Two Sides to Every Story
Forever And A Day
Let's Get It On
Misty Blue
The Wedding Gown
The Color of Trouble

Anthologies:

Continental Divide (Lotus Blossoms Chronicles 11) Anthology
On My Knees (Destination Romance) Anthology

Titles under F.D. Davis:

In The Beginning
In Blood We Trust
The Good Side of Evil (Carnivale Diabolique) Anthology
Lest Ye Be Judged

Dedication:

To David Abrahamson: Thank you so much for sharing your journeys with me. I don't think I would have felt Jeremy and Dimitra's story so deeply had it not been for you. You didn't believe me when I told you it might take years to see the book in print, did you? (smile) It's been years since we communicated but you are often in my thoughts and more so during the editing of this book. Here's wishing you light to guide you on future journeys.

Acknowledgements:

As always, thanks and glory to God for allowing me without censure to tell the stories of the voices in my head.

To Jeremy and Dimitra, thank you for choosing me to tell your story. I'm honored

Mary O'Gara, a great psychic and teacher. The years of studying with you will no doubt be reflected in this and future work. Thank you for telling me of your own experiences to offer validity to a scene contained in this book that felt so real to me that I knew it had to be true. You confirmed that not only is the unbelievable possible, but happens each moment of every day.

To Debbie Pfeiffer for putting me in touch with people who were willing to talk to me. Even fiction requires research and were it not for you I would not have been able to do such a thorough job.

To Peggy Scolan and Patricia Smith: Thank you both for being so willing to share your impressions with me.

Sidney Rickman, I wonder if you've goggled your name. I don't think I go a month without mentioning you somewhere in the cyber regions. I know you can't help wondering what's next and groaning when you see another mss arrive for you with my name on it. I promise you it's the characters that like talking so much, not me. (smile) As always, Sidney, I couldn't do this without the world's best editor.

A shout out of course to the members of my Yahoo family. Hello family!

Starting and ending with the best. Bill and Bill Jr. My prayer is that God continue to bless the three of us with a long and healthy life together

THE AFFAIR

Blood was everywhere. The smell of copper filled my nostrils and I gagged. My hands were covered with the warm sticky substance and my eyes burned with tears from the pain of leaving my beloved. One look at my husband Jeremy and the truth was evident. I was dying. His fear wiped away my own. I had to be brave for him. My dear sweet husband, my soul mate forever and ever.

He was holding me in his arms, his own hands covered in my blood. His tears ran freely down his brown cheeks as he struggled with what he knew but couldn't accept. And he obviously ached from the knowledge, determined to heal me, unwilling to let me go. It was apparent our gifts would not help. In all of the world there was but one mystic with powers great enough to combat the inevitable, but he was too far away and my link with him was weakened by the loss of blood. I gazed on my husband. His pain was more than I could bear. I listened for sounds of the baby I'd just given birth to and didn't hear him.

"Jeremy, the baby," I said with all the strength that was left in me. "I want to see our son. He's not crying. Bring him to me, please."

For the longest time Jeremy didn't move. He was holding me so tightly that the bones in his hands were pressing into the small of my back, revealing his desperation. He seemed determined to link with me, have me take from his life force to sustain my own. He would die for me. I knew that as surely as I knew I would never allow it.

"Jeremy, bring me our son," I said, pushing him away from me. "Get the baby," I cried, desperate to hold our son.

I waited, praying for just another breath. I couldn't die before I touched my son, made sure he knew he was loved. I passed my hand over his limp little body. "Breathe, little one," I urged, "breathe, and live."

I stuck my bloody fingers into his small, silent mouth, pulling out the remnant of the hard birth he'd endured. "I love you, my son," I cried. "I love you." Then I gave him the only thing I had left to give, his birthright. My gifts.

"Love him," I urged my husband, pulling him toward me, laying his hand on the son I knew he no longer wanted. "Promise me you'll love him. It wasn't his fault. I wanted to give you a son. Love him as I do, Jeremy, and take care of him. Do you promise, Jeremy?"

"I promise," he said with a steady stream of tears cascading down his brown cheeks. My heart broke anew for my husband's pain. I clutched his hand, kissed it with lips that even I knew were chilled and I placed his hand on the back of our son. I blessed them both, loving them, pledging to love them always, to find them in the next life.

With my lips pressed firmly to my baby's, I breathed the last of my life's breath into my son. I could feel my spirit leave my body. Blood filled my lungs and I choked.

I woke gasping for breath, tears streaming down my face.

"Are you alright? Did you have the dream again?" Larry asked.

"Yes," I answered, looking at my husband Larry, feeling dazed that one moment I was with a man I knew I was married to, the other part of my soul, and the next I was in bed with this man I'd been married to for an entire lifetime. I trembled, shaken by the intensity.

"Larry, it didn't feel like a dream." I wanted to explain but he shushed me as he usually did.

"It has to be," he asserted. "You're not crazy enough to think it means anything. Go back to sleep, honey. It was just a dream."

"Larry, it was real." I pleaded with him to listen. "I don't know how, but it was real. I lost my son, I lost my baby."

"Your son is alive and well, Mick. Derrick is fine. Now stop this nonsense and go back to sleep. You need your rest."

His voice was stern, a bit of the anger, the disappointment he felt at my continuing to have the dream coming through in his words to me. In the beginning of our marriage, he'd comforted me. Now he merely wanted me to stop the dreams. As if I could.

I lay back down afraid to sleep. I'd had some version of this dream for most of my life. Even as a child I'd dreamt of my husband with hair the color of night and our baby son, and my heart ached for both of them. I wanted to find them.

My mother had taken me to a shrink, demanding that I stop my nonsense, stop my obsession with the voices I heard calling to me. So I had. At least that was what I told her. But it hadn't mattered; when my parents' marriage fell apart my mother blamed the collapse on me, on what she called my craziness.

For a while the dreams came less often and were less vivid. My life was so busy, consumed with everyday problems, a husband, children and a job. I had no time for the lover in my dreams, no time for a child I'd held for only a moment, a child to whom I'd given my dying breath. Still, I grieved, but I grieved alone, afraid to have Larry call me crazy as my mother had.

Eventually I slept again, and the next day my husband and I woke at the same moment. It was the day of our twenty-sixth anniversary. I could tell in his eyes, in his kiss, that the memory of the dream lingered with him and it hurt him.

I felt that he blamed me for having the dream and I knew that for the rest of the day I would walk on eggshells doing everything in my power to make him happy. Denying my own truths would do that. I was very aware of that fact and I resented it. But like everything else in my life, I would shove my own feelings aside. Larry's wishes would come first. They always did.

We gave each other several kisses and wished each other a happy anniversary. I knew my husband was still upset over this part of me that he wished he could banish. I couldn't blame him. I had no business dreaming of another man, real or imagined.

"Michelle, I'm thinking maybe you should see someone. Those dreams of yours are becoming more frequent. I don't understand why you're having them. Maybe you're not happy with me, with us. There has to be something going on."

I looked at Larry, about to tell him that I wasn't happy, hadn't been happy for a long time. His next words stopped me before I could arrange the words I wanted to say.

"Of course you're happy," Larry declared. "Who wouldn't be? We have a good solid marriage, four beautiful daughters, a handsome son and wonderful grandchildren. You'd be crazy not to be happy."

And that was what stopped me. I'd be crazy not to be happy. I'd be crazy to keep thinking of this dark-haired lover, this child that had never existed.

"Anything special you want to do for our anniversary?" Larry asked, giving me the look that said he did. He wanted to make love and I knew it was in part because he loved me, in part because he wanted to drive the thoughts of another man from my mind and my heart.

So we did. We made love and I clung to my husband as memories rolled over me, memories I couldn't shake. A supreme knowing filled me. This time I could not push it away. Something was going to happen to tear apart our home. I could feel it with every atom of my being and I didn't know if I could stop it. I didn't even know if I wanted to stop it.

We exchanged no gifts, no cards for our anniversary. We simply made love, made that our declaration. Larry thought we had everything that we needed; he thought we should save our money for the kids, help them out, not waste it on useless gifts when we already had everything that we wanted.

The only problem was that I didn't have everything that I wanted. The home and cars meant nothing. I wanted to feel validated. I wanted to stop feeling dead inside as if I'd lost something very special to me and would never find it. I wanted to talk about this with my husband without fear that he would want to commit me. I wanted to find one person who understood what I was saying, who didn't think I was crazy.

Larry had an entirely different view of our marriage. He was happy. We were friends, we enjoyed each other's company and we had sex regularly. The only fly in the ointment was my dreams, and those he dealt with by reprimanding me, advising me to get more rest, to stop watching romantic movies that were putting crazy ideas in my head.

I suppose that was our main difference. He felt my dreams were something I needed help for, and I felt they were more. There were many times I felt that if Larry would simply talk with me about the dreams I could put them into proper focus. But he either couldn't or wouldn't. And what I felt in the end was cheated.

There are times I can't imagine my life without my husband Larry at my side. Then there are other times that I don't know how I can continue another day, another minute of the sameness.

Thoughts of Jeremy and our son haunted me constantly. I tried hard to keep it from Larry. I had to. I wanted to keep it from myself. I wanted it to end. Sometimes I wanted my very life to end.

The day after our anniversary, I had an eerie, weighted down feeling. At the time it didn't seem exactly like depression, but now I'm not so sure. I had to fight to remain in my own body. I continually felt a tugging of my spirit to leave. I'm not sure anyone can understand this unless they've lived through it, but that's the only way I can describe it.

I truly believe that if I had not fought against the sensations that day, I could have closed my eyes and died.

I knew this. I was fully aware of my feelings. I knew it the same way I knew many things in my life. And like the other things that I knew, this too I shoved away from me.

I decided to make a short run to the local grocer for a few things I didn't really need. I felt a sense of urgency, that if I didn't connect with other living, breathing humans, my husband would come home to a cold wife, stiff with rigor mortis. So, I grabbed my bag and left.

The brightly lit store did little to lift my spirits. I was randomly picking out items, trying to prolong my time there, not wanting to go home alone to an empty house. I thought of Viola, the old woman I'd hit with my car six months before when I was leaving the grocery store. I'd seen her for only a nanosecond before she bounced off my car. Instantaneous guilt filled me. Why hadn't I seen her? I gripped the handle of my cart, trying desperately to keep the memories at bay, knowing it was to no avail.

I shivered, the sensation going all the way to my spine. I again saw the blood, heard the fragile bones as they broke. I stopped in the middle of an aisle and wiped away the tears that always accompanied the memory.

"Don't move, don't try to talk." I whispered, *going down on my knees beside the limp body, grasping the elderly woman's hand. "I'm so sorry, I didn't see you in time. I'll get help," I said, reaching in the pocket of my jacket for my phone.*

"What's your name?" I asked after finishing the call, wanting to keep the woman as calm as possible.

"Viola."

"Viola, you're going to be fine. Help will be here soon. They'll get you to the hospital."

"I don't have money for a hospital," Viola answered grasping my hand. "I don't have insurance."

"Ill take care of everything, I'll make sure your bills are paid. I'll come visit you, make sure you have what you need. I promise," I said, clutching the woman's hand in mine meaning every word that I spoke.

It had seemed an eternity before the paramedics wrapped Viola up and carried her away on a stretcher. I'd stayed behind to talk to the police. And then I called Larry, frantic for him to meet me at the hospital. Larry told me to stay where I was, that I was too distraught to drive and at that point I was. So I waited for him to come.

When he did, I began babbling almost incoherently, so glad to have him at my side. "Larry, they took her to St. Mary's."

I managed to get those words out before collapsing against him. Overwhelming guilt filled me. Why hadn't I seen her, why hadn't I at least sensed her? I had always been good at sensing danger. There were too many questions I didn't have the answers to. So I closed my eyes and prayed for the woman to be all right.

I didn't open my eyes again until the car stopped and Larry turned off the ignition. Again I prayed for the strength to go into the hospital and see the old woman. When I opened my eyes, I blinked several times in disbelief, then looked at Larry. He'd taken me home.

"Larry, why did you bring me home?" I asked, dumbfounded as to his reasons.

"Come in the house, Mick. We have to talk." He answered me in a tight voice, alerting me that something was wrong.

As an attorney, Larry was concerned with our legal liabilities, I wasn't. We fought about my wanting to keep my promise and go to the hospital. At one point, he physically held me down. That surprised the hell out of me. In all our years of marriage, Larry had never attempted to use brute force against me. For weeks, we fought about my going to see Viola, until at last out of sheer exhaustion I gave up, and then gave in.

I knew Viola was part of the reason that I was feeling disconnected. I had hoped that I could escape thoughts of her by running away from my home. No such luck.

I wished I'd had appointments, doctors to call on, but my calendar was clear. I had the day off. There wasn't even a reason for me to go into the office. But regardless of that I found myself wishing that I had gone to work just to be around people. I didn't need to be alone. I thought about calling Larry and asking him to come home, but right then, his was the last face I wanted to see. No, I'd have to wait out the feeling of dread alone.

I hated this position I'd willingly placed myself in when I married the handsome go-getter who'd promised to protect me always. At nineteen, that had been exactly what I wanted to hear, what I'd always dreamed. Larry was my black knight.

Somewhere along the way my dreams changed. I no longer wanted to be protected or to have my decisions made for me, but I'd failed to notify my husband of the change. So, I unjustly blamed him for a situation I could have taken control of at any time. The problem was that I hadn't learned that lesson soon enough.

It was only when I hit the dreaded forty mark that I really became aware of my growing resentment toward my life, my family, my husband and most of all, toward myself.

I'd turned into my mother. I didn't want to rock the boat, to fight, to have it escalate into divorce as my parents' marriage had. No, I wanted my marriage to Larry to be forever. I didn't want to be crazy and alone so I kept my feelings bottled inside.

If it had not been for that little old woman darting out into the path of my car, maybe I could have lived out the remainder of my life this way. But it had happened. I was being haunted by a woman still alive.

The smell of the blood that oozed from her body assaulted my senses on a daily basis. Her pitiful cries, the look of pain and shock in her pale blue eyes never left me. And with the memory, the dreams returned in full force.

Viola's clothes spoke of poverty, and her words had confirmed it. Her main worry, despite my continued reassurance, was how she could afford a hospital visit. My promise that I would be there for her had brought a weak smile to her pale lips.

"It wasn't your fault," she'd said, squeezing my hands, her wrinkled flesh covering my own. It was only then that I noticed the trembling in my hands.

It was Viola's touch that I felt now as I stood in the store trying to control the bizarre feelings taking over my body. I felt as if I'd betrayed the old woman by never following through on my promise. I'd left her thinking I would be there for her. I'd failed her and I'd failed myself.

I needed something to chase away the thought of Viola and her raggedy coat and the sight of cans of tomato sauce flying up in the air and landing on my car, eggs breaking and pooling into a gooey mess.

I couldn't shake the memory. I looked down at my own cart filled with only the best the store had to offer, things I gave no thought to purchasing.

It hit me how hard it must have been for Viola to scrape money together for the meager groceries in her bag.

"My food." I thought I'd heard her say those words but I was never sure.

Michelle, think of something else, I scolded myself. *Viola is in the past. Keep her there.* So, I thought of my children, all grown and moved away and I thought briefly of my grandchildren. I knew this wasn't an empty nest feeling, because the kids got on my nerves and I was glad when they finally left. As for the grandkids, my rule was two hours, then back home they went. Nor did I encourage spending holidays with us.

Larry had laughed at me when I shared my feelings with him. He thought I was teasing. Why, I don't know. I told him in the most serious fashion. But he couldn't accept my feelings, I suppose because he loved them so much and enjoyed their company. Several times a year he always planned trips for us to see the kids but at the last instant I usually told him I had an emergency at work and couldn't go but that I'd make it up to him when he returned.

In my job as a medical sales representative that excuse was as flimsy as the nightgown I'd always wear for Larry on his return.

The kids enjoyed having their father to themselves and I enjoyed not having to visit them. Funny thing, as much as I wished for time alone, I couldn't wait for Larry to come home. Maybe I was a bit crazy.

Chapter Two

I met Chance when I was shopping for my husband's dinner. Can you imagine the irony in that? In his name? Anyway, when I could malinger no longer, I at last paid for my groceries and made my way toward the exit.

The sky had been a beautiful cerulean blue when I went in, but now it was an angry gray. Fat drops of water began to plop down as I left the store and by the time I was halfway to my car, the rain was pouring down in buckets. The paper bag I'd opted for in the store quickly became saturated and collapsed, spilling my groceries under cars and into the greasy puddles.

I stood for a moment, soaked to the bone, watching my dinner scatter like so many pearls from a broken strand. I started to cry. It wasn't so much the food or the wasted money, but in that moment those scattering groceries represented my life and my emotions.

I saw tomato sauce flying in the air, eggs breaking, though I had bought neither. I could no more escape my feelings of guilt for not going to see Viola than I could escape my own flesh.

So I did the only thing I could. I cried harder than I ever had in my life, in the rain, in the parking lot, my arms outstretched to the heavens. At first I didn't notice the man retrieving my items and placing them in a double plastic bag.

When he handed the plastic bag filled with my groceries back to me, I saw sympathy in his face and his eyes and cried harder. For a moment he looked confused. Then he put his arms around me and held me, pressing my head into his chest.

I held on to him as if my very life depended on it. Despite the cold rain, I felt an electrical energy emanating from his body and twining around me. I felt as if I had come home at last. Strange, but it was how I felt.

For long minutes the rain poured down over us. I truly wanted to stop crying, but the fact that I was crying in the rain, in the parking lot, with a strange man comforting me, made me cry more.

At last I gained control and lifted my head from his chest and looked at him. There was an expression of awe on his face, of wonderment. "Do I know you?" I attempted to smile, but the intensity of his look prevented it.

"I'm sorry about this." I waved my hand around attempting to convey to him that I was not usually a woman given to hysterics.

"Are you better now?" he asked.

"I think so, but I don't want to be alone."

I forced myself to look, really look, at the man standing in front of me. He was tall, almost as tall as Larry. That would make him close to six feet.

His hair was jet black, like a raven's, and had the tiniest sprinkling of gray around the temples. The rain had plastered his shirt flat against his chest and abdomen, revealing that he was lean and muscular.

I examined his face. Strong chin, a mouth that was firm and inviting, tiny laugh lines etched into the contours.

But it was his eyes that gave me pause. I'd been attracted to Larry because of the beauty of his golden brown eyes. This man standing before me possessed without a doubt the most captivating blue eyes God had ever bestowed on a human. I'd never seen that particular color on any living being. I gazed into their depths and became lost. I pulled back to get a better look at the total man. His skin was the color of heated gold from his obvious tan. In spite of the cold rain his touch was hot and inviting. But none of those things were the reason behind my actions. There was something familiar about him and it frightened me.

I closed my eyes against the rush of unexpected emotions. I knew I needed to get a grip, yet my head was spinning and for no known reason, I felt a surge of pure joy overtake me. I was relieved when he spoke.

"You look as if you could use some company. Would you like to go somewhere and have a cup of coffee…maybe talk…a little?"

"You're right, I could use some company." I was no longer sobbing, just crying quietly now. I took a good look at this man who'd taken the time to comfort me.

For the first time I noticed something behind the intense look in his eyes. He was in pain. I wanted to do something to help, anything to take away this stranger's own pain and sorrow.

I wanted only to comfort this man. He felt familiar to me, this stranger who'd shown me such compassion. This time there would be no call to ask my husband what I should do. I would do what I wanted.

I felt him pulling away from me and I backed away also. Maybe I'd only imagined the intense heat searing me. Despite the chill of the rain I could feel heat rush to my cheeks and was glad of my olive complexion. My blush would only be internal for feeling stupid in mistaking a stranger's kindness. We gazed into each other's eyes for maybe five seconds.

"Do you believe in fate?"

He asked me this only a moment before I found myself in his arms again, his lips covering my own, tasting the rain on his tongue and the sweet mint of his breath.

His mouth filled me with a heat that I knew but had abandoned long ago. It was as if I had found my life again. I no longer wanted to die.

I don't remember putting my groceries in my car, but I must have, because later I took them out. What I do remember is the man silently holding out his hand to me. I knew what he wanted. He wanted me. And I wanted him.

I do remember him opening the door of his Jeep Cherokee to let me in. That was the first moment I became conscious that I was soaked. I worried about ruining his seats. He smiled at me and kissed my hand.

I truly wish I could say that I was so overcome with passion that I was unaware of what I was doing, but that wasn't the case. I thought about the book and later the movie, *The Bridges of Madison County*, and how I had argued that the woman had no right to cheat on her husband, that he'd done nothing wrong, that she just wanted to have an affair.

Well, I was now that woman. My husband by the usual standards is the ideal mate. He loves me, of that I'm sure. He provides a good living for us and he's the perfect father. In fact, I think the only thing about our life that bothers Larry is my "flights of fancy," as he calls them. He's teasingly told me on several occasions that he would never commit me, that he'd take care of me himself. I know he means it as a joke but the possibility of it happening is always with me. Now I no longer cared. It didn't matter.

While I was sitting in a Jeep with a man whose name I didn't know, I knew it didn't make any difference. I was going through with it.

The thought of asking him to get condoms crossed my mind. I briefly thought of AIDS, then how irresponsible I was being. I could be driving away with a serial killer. I just wanted for once to do something that had not been pre-approved by my husband. Besides, I knew instinctively that this man wouldn't hurt me. There was some connection to him that I felt in my being.

If one of my daughters had done something so incredibly dumb I would have read her the riot act, and I did attempt to do so for myself. The hotel was only a couple of blocks away, right in my own small town where anyone could walk in and see me, but I truly didn't care.

I didn't care at that point that my thick, cinnamon- colored dyed hair was soaked and tangled and falling in heavy curls down my back and over my face. I didn't care that I was a total mess and that the desk clerk looked at us curiously.

I knew the stranger had signed us in as Mr. and Mrs. and I got a tingle. I might as well have stepped in front of a moving train. That was the impact this stranger was having on me. For some idiotic reason, though, it felt right. I felt as if I were truly his wife, his mate, and that this was a proper thing I was about to do. I wasn't about to commit adultery. I was only going to make love with my husband, my true husband whose name I did not know.

Inside the room I sat on the edge of the bed in my wet clothes. He went into the bathroom and returned with a stack of towels. He held out his hand to me and I stood, again knowing what he wanted. I lifted my arms as though I were a child and allowed him to undress me.

He toweled my body dry so gently that I would have thought I was in a dream if not for the surge of desire filling my entire being. I wanted him physically and spiritually, not in a religious sense. I mean that I wanted his spirit to mate with my own.

I admit I felt better dry, and I smiled at him. He smiled back, took another towel, and began drying my hair strand by long strand. He kissed each blotted strand, touching it as though he was remembering doing it before.

He moved from my hair to my ears, drying them, kissing them, touching them. He did this over every inch of my body.

"I was beginning to think I would never find you again," he whispered against the small of my back, but I heard him. I didn't question what he meant. I knew.

I was trembling so hard that he pulled away to look at me. "You're not afraid, are you?"

"A little."

His smile was my reward. My fears drained away, leaving me feeling wild, decadent, and free. I took a towel and did for him what he had done for me, drying his body, kissing him tenderly.

My fingers searched his body furiously for landmarks and craters I evidently knew existed. I had made love with this man many times before. I shivered, wondering how that could be possible.

One of us pulled the covers back from the bed. I'm not sure which of us, only that suddenly we were under the covers holding each other, touching, and we were both crying softly.

"I've been waiting for you," he said to me.

"And I've been trying to find you," I answered.

When we came, it was together. I knew then what it was I'd been missing, what my husband who I knew without a doubt loved me could never give me. He could never give me this supreme feeling of connection, but it wasn't his fault.

We lay together for the longest time, still touching. "I've never done anything like this before," I said to him. I didn't want him to think I was some kind of tramp.

I started to pull away and he tightened his arm around me. He had a strange look in his eyes. "This is not the first time we've made love," he said authoritatively.

"What are you talking about?" I turned so that I could look in his eyes. These were my feelings, my thoughts. How was it possible that he was having them?

"What are you talking about?" I asked again. I don't know you. I don't even know your name." Yet the feel of his skin under my fingers called me a liar. I knew every cell in his body. Intimately.

"Can't you feel it?" he responded. "Our meeting was not an accident."

The strange thing was that I knew it wasn't an accident, but to admit to what I thought it really was would mean that my life would now take on a different meaning. I had to do something to pretend that my life hadn't just changed forever. I wanted to believe that his words gave me reason to worry, that perhaps I had just slept with a stalker, no matter how incredible it was. Maybe I had better think of some way to escape. I had to believe that the words this stranger spoke made him sound like a nut. If I didn't, it would mean that I was nuts.

"Are you saying you planned this, that you've done this type of thing before?" I was offended and wondered how it was that he happened to have plastic bags.

He stared at me a moment before answering. "I didn't plan today. In fact, standing in the rain getting soaked was the last thing I had on my mind."

"I sat in my car watching you. I saw you coming out of the store and your bags break. I never intended to get involved, but when you stood there crying, I watched people walking away from you, looking at you strangely. Before I knew it, I was out of the car, running into the store to grab plastic bags."

He looked me over, his voice sounding insulted. "No, I don't remember having done this, if you mean by this, our meeting in the rain." There was a slight shift in his body. His eyes softened and his lips stretched into a smile.

"It was fated for us to meet. I've been waiting years for you." His eyes were smiling at me yet his words to any sane person were those of a person that definitely belonged on Prozac. And I was trying to the best of my ability to be a sane person.

"What's your name?" It was a little late to think of getting acquainted, but I still needed to know who I'd slept with, so that when I went to confession I could tell on him also.

"Chance."

I looked at him. "You've got to be kidding."

He hopped out of the bed and walked across the room, lean and muscular. I feasted my eyes on his beauty, on his strength, not feeling ashamed, not minding that I was a middle-aged woman with not so firm breasts and an extra twenty pounds on my five-five frame. I didn't care. I felt beautiful and I knew he found me beautiful as well.

Chance brought me back his wallet. I examined the picture and the name. Chance Morgan? I held my left hand out for him to examine. "I should have told you this sooner but I'm married." He merely smiled. *Okay,* I thought, *this joker has more problems than I do.*

"I've been married twenty-six years. Yesterday was my anniversary."

"And today you wanted to die. You came to the store because you could feel yourself giving in to the sweet invitation of death. You had no idea that you were searching for me until you found me, but then you knew. I saw the recognition in your eyes. I felt it in your touch, in your response to me."

Oh God, what was happening to me? "What the heck are you talking about?" I asked.

"Tell me you don't believe me."

"I do believe you, but you're scaring me."

"What would you like for this to be?"

"I'd like for you to be just a little bit crazy maybe. It would make all of this easier for me. Listen, are you…are you on any kind of medications?"

"No medications, anything else you want to know?"

"I was going to ask if you're nuts, but thought maybe I shouldn't, just in case. Perhaps I should be nice to you until I return to my home, my life, and the safety of my husband's arms."

"Is that really what you want after all the time we've wasted not being together in this life, to just leave me and return to your home?"

His eyes suddenly looked so sad. I felt I had betrayed him, and in a way that hurt more than what I had done to my husband. I had denied the life that Chance seemed to be remembering.

"Deny that you wanted to die."

I got out of the bed then, keeping a wary eye on Chance. It was time for me to end this fantasy.

"Listen, Chance, thank you for this afternoon."

I once again felt shame snaking through my body warming my skin, making me feel flushed and vulnerable. I gazed at him, seeing something that I could swear was love in his eyes and rushed to finish the statement I'd started. "I mean, for picking up my groceries, and for letting me cry on your shoulder, but I really have to go now. My husband is waiting for me."

I replaced my still damp clothing and glanced at my watch. Ten P.M. I couldn't believe it. Where had the time gone? Had I really made love to a stranger in a hotel room only a few miles from my own home? A stranger that now claimed we'd done this very thing countless times?

I didn't know what to say. What does one say to a lover they don't quite know?

"Listen, it was nice meeting you."

I made my way to the door, for the first time wondering if Chance were married, if he had a wife who could be waiting for me in some hidden corner of the room. I shivered at the thought until it became real in my mind. I was thinking at any moment she could spring up, grab me, and plunge a knife into my body. I imagined my husband's shock. The newspaper would spread the news for days. Our town didn't have very much action. A woman murdered by the hands of a stranger she'd picked up in the parking lot of the grocery store would be very big news.

My husband didn't deserve this. He didn't deserve the snickers of having to bury an unfaithful wife. I knew it would worry him that I'd been unhappy enough to do this. I didn't want him to think that this had been going on for months or years. I had reached the door when I felt the tears starting up again.

"Dimitra," he called out to me. "What's your name this time?" he asked. His voice was pleasant, not threatening in the least.

I turned around sharply. "My name's Michelle. Michelle Powers."

As I was looking at him, a strange sensation laid claim to my soul. Dimitra, the name he'd called me gave me pause. I rolled it around on my tongue. That name was familiar to me.

I wanted to back away from Chance, yet at the same time I wanted never to leave him. I felt what he was saying was true. This stranger had a claim on me.

"Well, Michelle, I'm sorry I made you cry. I can tell you're frightened and have no idea what I'm talking about. I also know you're wondering what you've done and if I'm going to stop you from leaving."

He smiled then. A sadness that broke my heart filled his eyes. I remembered him holding me in the rain and suddenly it was crystal clear. There was no way this man Chance would ever hurt me, or had ever hurt me.

"I have to go," I said to him, then remembered that my car was still in the parking lot.

"If you'll close the door so I can get dressed, I'll take you back." He offered.

I closed the door rather sheepishly. I had been about to make a grand exit without transportation. "I should call my husband." I looked at him as though for approval before reaching for the phone. I dialed, waiting impatiently for Larry to answer.

"Hi, Larry." My voice sounded low and muffled as if my mouth were stuffed with cotton. I breathed easier as Larry didn't seem to notice anything out of the ordinary.

"Hey, where are you?"

"My friend Peaches is having some trouble with her husband. She needed to talk."

The lie slid out of my mouth so easily that I almost thought it was true, until I looked at the rumpled sheets.

"Is she okay?"

"She's been better."

The concern in Larry's voice was not making me feel the guilt I should be having right about now. I was only glad that there was no Peaches. No one to bring into my lie. No one that Larry would ever see, or talk to, to either confirm or deny my tale.

"Did you eat?" I didn't know what else to say to him.

"No. I was waiting for you. I didn't see anything on the stove."

I felt a flush of anger. *Couldn't he do anything without me there?* "Why don't you make yourself a sandwich?"

"What do we have?"

"There's ham and turkey in the fridge."

"Do we have any soda?"

"Yes."

"What kind?"

I had gone past annoyed at this point, but as I watched Chance dressing, I subdued my tone. "Larry, why don't you check?"

"I could just wait for you to come home."

"I may not be home for hours."

"I'll wait."

"Are you waiting for me to make you a sandwich?"

"Well, I like the way you do it. Plus, I was thinking maybe we could have some desert. You know the kind I mean."

He laughed then and I lost the last vestige of control. I was in a hotel room liberating my spirit with a stranger. I didn't want to consider having mundane chores waiting for me at home.

"I'll be home as soon as I can."

I glanced at Chance underneath my lashes. He was pretending not to hear my conversation. I said a hurried goodbye to my husband and hung up the phone.

"I think you might want to take a shower."

Chance's gaze found mine. I didn't know what to say, how to answer him. I'd completely forgotten that I undoubtedly smelled of sex.

I started for the shower, then paused. "Chance, is this the first time you've made love to a woman of color?"

"A woman of color? What in the world does that mean? Like I said, I've made love to you a million times before, in many skins. Surely you're aware that in each incarnation it's our soul that returns. Our bodies are merely vessels for our souls."

"So your answer would be yes?"

Chance laughed. "My answer would be yes. I have loved you in all your glorious skins and I have loved you in every corner of the globe."

"Were we ever in India?" I don't know why I asked but the words just slipped out.

"Yes, we lived several incarnations in India. Our bodies never bothered either of us before. Does the difference in the color of our skin bother you in this incarnation?"

A flash of my dark-haired husband came to me and the poverty of India. Could it have been that country I'd seen in my many dreams? "No, Chance, it doesn't bother me." He was eyeing me strangely.

"You'd better go ahead and take your shower. I'll dry your clothes with the blow dryer," he offered.

Half of me wanted him in there with me. The other half wondered if he would toss the dryer into the shower and kill me in that fashion.

He laughed aloud. "Michelle, I'm not an ax murderer and I've never done anything like this before. I promise, I'm not going to do anything to you."

I didn't want to take my clothes off for two reasons. I wanted Chance again and I was afraid of my feelings. Never in my entire life had lust ruled. I had never really known lust until now. *God*, I prayed, h*elp me please. Something is happening and I can't control it.*

I didn't look at Chance, but went instead to the bathroom, removed my clothing and called out to him to come and dry them. The sound of the dryer made me pause and for a moment I peered over the shower curtain at this man, Chance, drying my clothes.

I watched as he held my blouse in his hand, running the hair dryer along the creases of the soft material. He was using his fingers to push away the wrinkles. I smiled to myself at his actions.

He held my blouse to his cheek and I saw him close his eyes for a moment. He had a dreamy look as though he was reliving a very pleasant memory. When he reached for my pants, I closed the curtain. I felt like an intruder on his life.

Suddenly it was more important to me than ever that he not think me a slut. But how could he not, when I'd done things with him that it had taken Larry years to persuade me to do. And with Chance I was the initiator. I'd wanted him and all the things we'd done. Sure I'd done them with my husband but I'd never really wanted to. I glanced at Chance once more, wanting him so badly I ached inside. Think I was a slut? I knew I had just become one.

"Chance…," I stammered, "I swear, I've never done this before."

"What? Taken a shower?" He chuckled low and I realized he was trying to put me at ease.

"I've never cheated on my husband, nor have I wanted to."

I continued applying the bath gel liberally to my body. I had to keep my hands busy in order to talk. I had to make him understand what I'd done was so unlike me, to simply walk away with a stranger and make love with him. Even my fantasies had never included anything so decadent or dangerous.

"Chance, I'm a prude."

For a moment I thought of all the things I'd done to him, with him, and I blushed crimson beneath the hot water. The heat my brown skin usually kept buried combined with the hot water and covered my body inside and out. My explanation was wrong and so was my reasoning, but something was beginning to take hold, some knowledge of who this man Chance might be. I couldn't stop the loud sigh that escaped my lips.

"If anyone else had done this, I would be the first to condemn their behavior. I can't believe I acted with such random disregard for my very life, or for my husband's."

"How do you mean that?"

I heard the hurt in his voice, hurt that I recognized. I didn't want to say it, but it was truly what I was feeling. "You could have some disease that I have now gotten. For all I know you could even have AIDS."

There were other things I wanted to say to him, but I managed to keep my mouth closed. What was I going to do for the next few months when my husband wanted to touch me? How was I supposed to get him to wear a condom for his own protection?

I heard the curtain being pulled away. Chance was standing there, a frown on his face.

"Do you think I hop into bed with every woman I meet in a parking lot?"

"I don't know. I know nothing about you."

"Michelle, you don't have to worry. I don't have anything."

"How do I know you're telling me the truth?"

"I guess you're just going to have to trust me, aren't you. You really don't remember me, do you?"

There was sadness in his eyes and in his voice. The combined forces struck fear once again in the marrow of my being. I wondered why he kept saying that. I had never met him. Yet on some level I felt I had. But if I so much as gave the thought a chance to grow, I feared I would go insane.

"Michelle, I assumed you came with me because you remembered. I never thought you were a slut."

I started to interrupt when he held up a hand to stop me.

"I'm not talking about this life, but a past life. We've spent many lifetimes together. You've been calling to me and I've been searching for you. For my wife."

Okay, now it was time for me to end this madness, to get my wet, naked body out of the shower. It was time for me to return to my home, to my husband and my life.

"Chance, what you're talking about doesn't make any sense. I would have to be crazy to believe that," I said and shivered, thinking of what Larry would say to me if he ever found out. He would definitely have more than enough evidence to commit me.

I dared a glance at Chance. "This is crazy," I repeated. Besides, I'm not sure I believe in past lives."

"Are you saying you felt no connection to me, that there's nothing about me that appears familiar?"

The answer required no thought. Yes, of course I felt a connection to him. I don't think I would have been able to make love with him if I hadn't. I was hoping that knowledge would allow me to be able to sleep at night. Maybe then I'd be able to forgive myself for walking away with a perfect stranger.

"No, Chance. Nothing."

"Then why did you come with me?"

He was staring intently at me, his blue eyes warm, his face curious. I wanted to lie, had planned on it. Then a picture of the two of us together in the motel lobby flashed before me. I remembered the way I'd felt when I saw him sign us in as Mr. and Mrs.

"You want the truth?" I stared back into those blue eyes that appeared to be penetrating my soul. He didn't answer. What was he going to say? *'No, tell me a lie.'*

"I felt disconnected there in the parking lot, and somehow going with you felt like the lifeline I needed." I reached for the towel and wrapped myself in it, moving as far away from Chance as I could get in the small bathroom.

"Do you mind if I dress in private?"

I held my hands out for my now dry clothing and put them on in the cramped bathroom. I was an adult. Playtime was over. No matter how I sugar coated this, I had committed adultery. My sins would follow me, of that I was sure. I couldn't remember the last time I'd blatantly lied to my husband.

I wanted to tell myself that telling him I was with a friend was far kinder than telling him the truth. Surely that little lie shouldn't count. But what of the bigger lie, the one I didn't want to acknowledge. It hung at the back of my mind fighting to get out as I attempted to fight the overpowering feeling I was having for Chance. I couldn't deny the hunger raging in my veins and in my heart for this man. When he'd closed the bathroom door in order for me to dress, I'd felt an undeniable loss followed by a sense of love as powerful as I've ever felt for Larry, maybe even more so.

Chance was no longer the danger. I was. And I didn't know what to do other than leave. Loving a man I didn't know, that was crazy I tried to tell myself as the ache in my heart grew. I was acting like a love struck prepubescent girl. I needed to rationalize this out. This had nothing to do with my feelings of familiarity concerning Chance or his talk of reincarnation. It was simply because in such a fragile emotional state he'd been there when I'd desperately needed a way to live, a reason. Of course I would form an attachment. After all, how many strangers would take the time to comfort a hysterical woman and hold her to them while she cried in the rain? That was all there was to it, a romanticized gratitude.

Now dressed, I entered the bedroom grateful that Chance had dressed while I was in the bathroom. I wondered if he had anyone at home waiting for him since he'd not bothered washing our combined smells from his body.

"Are you ready?" I asked. He looked at me before smiling and answering me.

"Yes, didn't you think I'd be? Or did you think perhaps I'd try and convince you to stay?"

"It wouldn't have mattered, I wouldn't have. I was prepared to call and ask my husband to come for me if you weren't going to take me back to my car."

"Why not a taxi?"

"I hadn't thought of that."

"Are you telling him where you were tonight?"

"Why hurt him? I never plan on seeing you again." I noticed the smile creasing his handsome face. He didn't believe me. He walked toward the door, then turned and held his hand out to me. "You never answered my question. Do you believe in fate, Michelle?"

"Not necessarily."

"Well, I do."

Chance tilted my chin upwards, his gaze locked on mine, and he kissed me slowly. Energy fused us together. I wanted to sob, 'Oh my God, I found you.' But I didn't. I held those words in as the electrical charge filled me. His touch, his look, his love, I knew it. I needed to back away from him now, or I'd never be able to leave him. I could feel the sorrow welling upwards in my being. Sorrow that seemed to date back farther than I'd been alive. Instead of moving from him as his arms wrapped around me I held on to him for dear life, until I was finally able to plead softly in a whisper in his ear, "Please release me."

His fingers trailed over my back, each touch igniting another part of my soul that had been dead. Tears streamed from my eyes as he slowly moved away. From somewhere the knowledge came that I'd not been asking him to release me from his embrace but from something much larger. Nothing in me wanted to leave him, everything screamed out the knowledge that was finally staring me in the face, the knowledge that I knew I was not ready or able to accept.

"I believe we were meant to be together in this lifetime as we were in the past." Chance leaned into me and whispered. "I don't believe I found you in order for you to leave my life."

We walked from the room together. I felt safer now out in the corridor hearing other people's voices, couples maybe. Or could there perhaps be other strangers behind the doors making love in abandon with people they didn't know, as I had done? I prayed there weren't as many fools out there as I'd been.

We were both silent as he drove me back to the parking lot. It was only as I put my hand on the handle to open the door that he stopped me.

"Michelle, we will see each other again. It's our destiny."

"I'm not giving you my number."

"I don't need it. Just as you appeared in my life today you'll reappear."

He attempted to brush his lips across mine, but I moved away. In a matter of seconds I was in my car ignoring him staring after me. I had to race home while I was able. It was only my head that wanted to return home.

My heart and soul wanted to remain with this man Chance. My spirit wanted to run as far away from my husband and family as I could get.

Chapter Three

"Hon, is that you?"

It was Larry, his voice so cheerful that I was suddenly depressed. I wasn't when I went away with a stranger and made love, but the sound of my husband's voice filled me with a bone chilling dread.

"It's me," I answered him as I glanced hastily at the sink to tell if he'd eaten. He hadn't. There were no dishes. And God forbid that he would have washed them after he was done. *Where had that thought come from?* I wondered. My husband had cheerfully done the dishes for twenty-six years. So had I. Washing dishes together had always been a time of bonding for us. Besides thinking of it as one of our chores it was something I liked doing. Immersing my hands in hot soapy water while Larry dried, I always felt that I was cleansing something more important than dishes.

Now it puzzled me that the thought of doing dishes was enough to bring about irritation. Of course it was easier thinking that than thinking about what I'd just done. That I'd just committed adultery. It was then that I took in a deep breath and released it. Well at least I hadn't had an affair. A one night stand didn't make an affair, did it?

"How's your friend, Peaches? I don't recall hearing you mention her before." Larry asked me with concern in his voice.

"There's a good reason for that." I turned toward him wanting to tell him the truth, wondering what he would say. Of course I was aware that in part what I would be doing would be transferring my guilt to my husband. It was then I wondered if I'd done what I had in order to punish my husband.

"Did you make yourself a sandwich?" I finally asked.

"Nah, I wasn't too hungry. I thought I'd wait for you. You know I don't like eating alone."

With my head in the refrigerator I sighed, knowing there was a lot of truth in Larry's statement. Like I said, we needed each other. But I had needed him six months ago to help me keep my promise to an old lady. He hadn't. Now I was tired of being needed to fulfill my husband's wants. "Larry, you're used to me taking care of you. What if I were dead? What would you do?"

"Stop talking crazy, nothing's going to happen to you. You're just still thinking about that nightmare. Hey, do we have any pickles?"

I reached back in and grabbed the pickles, opened the jar, stuck my fingers in without benefit of a fork and handed the pickle to my husband, who looked at me as if I'd suddenly grown two heads.

"Are you all right?" Larry asked.

"Why, because I didn't use a fork?" I almost smiled at him then.

"Well, you're acting funny, like maybe I've done something to you. Are you angry with me about something, or are you just angry at men in general because of your friend's husband?"

I decided to ignore that question. "I thought I was going to die today."

I noticed he took exactly two bites out of the sandwich I had placed in front of him before he acknowledged my statement.

"You weren't in another accident, were you?" He perused my body as though it were a legal brief. "Couldn't have been too bad, you look fine to me." He dismissed my statement and continued eating.

His lack of concern only served to irritate me further. "No, I wasn't in an accident. I was sitting at home wondering what to make for dinner, when this feeling came over me that I had the power to die. All I had to do was will it and it would be so."

Larry took a drink of soda and another bite of his sandwich. He had a smile on his face.

"I don't think you have any control over when you die, Mick. It's not in your hands."

There now, I'd been firmly put in my place. As an attorney his thinking was practical and analytical and I'd always succumbed. Now I wanted him to listen, to give some credence to my feelings.

"You're wrong. I believe we all have that power. I'm sure others have willed themselves to die. I'm telling you, today I had that control. All I had to do was will it. I had to will myself not to."

"Then do it now. Let me see."

I knew he was teasing me, but he hurt my feelings just the same. "Larry, would you like to know what I really did today?" I asked.

"I already know. You were with your friend Peaches."

"I don't have a friend named Peaches."

"Okay, where were you?"

He was laughing at me now. "I went to the store and got rained on. Then I met a stranger in the parking lot. I went to a hotel and made love with him."

"Oh? And what was this stranger's name?"

I looked at him, anger filling me, knowing that he didn't believe me. "His name is Chance."

"And his last name?"

"I don't remember."

I wasn't stupid. I was only going so far with this. I knew Larry wouldn't believe me, but just in case I didn't want him armed with the information to find my afternoon lover.

Larry started laughing then. "That's great. You go to bed with a stranger you met by chance, named Chance. Am I supposed to believe that?"

Curiosity got the better of me then. Was I so predictable that my husband didn't believe it was possible for me to commit the act? Did he think no one could possibly want me?

"Larry, are you laughing because you don't think another man would find me attractive?"

"No, honey, I'm talking from twenty-six years on the job experience. You with another man? I don't think so. And I'm damn sure you wouldn't go to bed with a stranger. If you don't want me asking questions about Peaches, just say so, but something so ridiculous I don't believe."

"I told you, I wasn't with Peaches. In fact, she doesn't exist. I made her up."

"No, I don't think so. Now that I think about it, I'm sure I've met her."

"You did not, she doesn't exist."

"Honey, what's wrong with you? Don't let your friend's problem wreck our night. We have a perfect marriage. Be thankful. Don't try and invent problems. Stop talking crazy."

"Why don't you ever hear me?"

"Why are you trying to start a fight? I always listen to you."

I thought about the five kids we'd had that I hadn't wanted. "Sure, you listen the same way you listened when I told you I didn't want kids." He sobered instantly, his laughter stilled by the memory of my last pregnancy.

"That was post-partum depression. You're as happy as I am that we have a large family."

"Larry, I'm not. I never was," I all but shouted.

"Yes, you are. You're just saying that because I didn't take you seriously when you said you had the ability to close your eyes and die."

"They're all adults now. Have you ever heard me say I miss them?"

"Of course you miss them. You're their mother."

"Have you ever heard me say it?"

"I don't remember, but it doesn't matter. I know you miss them."

"How do you know that?"

"Experience."

He took his last bite of the thick ham sandwich and smacked loudly. As he came to hug me, the smacking sound amplified in my ear.

"I know everything about you, dear wife. You are my love and my life. We're one."

Yeah, you know me, I thought. *You know me so well that you don't know that for the past six months I've been dying inside from having broken my promise to Viola. You know me so well that you've forgotten how important it is for me to keep a promise. And you know me so well, that you've never asked me why I never wanted children. I don't know why, but one of my greatest fears was that if I had children that something would happen to them. You know me so well that you don't believe I almost died today. You don't believe I cheated on you and somewhere in your world, I'm this paragon of virtue, this perfect mother. Oh yeah, Larry, you know me.*

My head felt as if it were about to split wide open. For a senior medical sales rep, it sure didn't seem as if I was being treated that way.

This was the third shift in territories in the past year and once again, my load had increased.

A quick inspection of the new maps and new doctors I had to call on made me groan. This added territory would add at least another hour to my already busy day, maybe more.

For a nanosecond, I thought of quitting. Larry had been pushing me to quit for the last five years. As a prominent attorney, he made more than enough money to take care of our needs and our wants.

So why did I work? To preserve my sanity? Even when the kids were small, I worked. The idea of staying home cooped up with crying babies and their constant demands was not my idea of fun. I had been determined that even if it took every dime I earned to get someone else to care for them at least eight hours a day, I would do it.

My job gave me more than enough freedom to be able to take off for every school trip, every kindergarten play. For every scrape and bruise they received I ran home immediately. I never felt I cheated them out of anything. But for my own mental well-being, I needed to work.

My mother couldn't believe that I'd rather work than remain at home. I remember the thousands of times as a child that I had wished she worked. Then I would not have had to hear her continuous complaints about my father, complaints she never had the courage to voice to him. She never spoke up, never rocked the boat.

I knew what she thought of me, of my working. She was from a generation where the woman stayed home. She had done it. She thought I should also.

Despite my feelings of having been forced into motherhood, I always played my part to perfection. I did everything that was expected of me and then some. What did it matter if my heart wasn't in it? I was the only one that knew. No one had to know the fear that was in my heart with each new pregnancy; how it almost paralyzed me when I first held my babies, thinking they would die in the night. My one clear memory of joy at being a mother was when my eldest, Erica was a baby and I was breastfeeding her. Then being a mother had made me happy until I remembered that if God knew how happy I was she would be taken away. And with each subsequent birth I'd successfully shut those happy feelings away. Those times had almost made me deliver myself into the hands of the doctors with their lab coats and electrical shock treatment. What happened to me during and after pregnancy wasn't normal and I knew that.

Anyway, I looked down the list at the five new doctors, dreading having to pass first an interrogation by the receptionist, then the nurses. I've been a sales rep long enough to know that if you're not nice to the staff you'll never be allowed in to see the doctor.

This meant I would have to stock up on treats from the grocery store, probably Hershey's kisses. They always worked. I stocked my bag with what felt like a ton of pens and notepads, grateful the bag was on wheels.

Today would be mostly courtesy calls for me to feel out the doctors and staff. My regular clients I could push back. Larry and I had dinner plans. I'd promised him I would be home early.

Dr. Morgan's name was the last one on the list. I could feel the tension begin in my shoulders. I sat for twenty minutes waiting. The staff, cordial but not overly friendly, had directed me to a chair then dismissed me. I was beginning to wonder if they'd forgotten to give the doctor my card. That happened a lot.

Then the smiling face of a plump nurse ushered me to the doctor's office.

His head was bent over papers. It had been almost a month since I'd made love with Chance, but I knew the moment I entered the room it was him. I glanced behind me for the nurse who had already left. I stood there waiting until he finally looked up and smiled at me, not looking in the least surprised.

"Hi, Michelle."

"Chance, I didn't know you were a doctor."

"You didn't ask. You ran away too fast to ask me anything."

My cheeks were burning. Never in my entire life had I ever been more embarrassed. Chance had gotten up and was walking toward me smiling. I started praying. *God, don't let him touch me.*

He walked past me to the door, closed it gently, then came back to me. "Do you believe in fate now?"

His eyes were teasing. I didn't want to be teased. I'd almost convinced myself that I had dreamt of meeting him. That I'd never done the things I had. Now here he was standing before me. Real.

"Do you mind if I sit?" I didn't wait for an answer. My legs were so spongy that I couldn't have remained standing if I had wanted to.

He perched his hip on the corner of his desk, waiting for me to answer. "I'm married, Chance. I told you that. If you're looking for an affair, I can't. I love my husband."

The sound echoed inside my head and I wondered if I had shouted. "I have a good marriage. I'm not about to ruin it." My hands were hurting from gripping the arms of the chair. I forced myself to look into his eyes with a defiance I didn't feel.

"I don't recall asking you to have an affair. I merely asked if you believed in fate."

"How can you believe in all this nonsense? You're a man of science." As I asked, I was fighting to still the pounding of my heart.

"How can you not?" His response was automatic, as if he'd been waiting for me to ask him just that question. So I answered him with what I hoped would put an end to this conversation.

"Because I'm over twenty-one, married with five kids and a paid off mortgage. I don't have time to indulge in foolishness."

"Is your little speech intended to scare me off? I don't scare easily. If you remembered anything at all about me it should be that. That and the fact that I've loved you forever. I vowed that no matter where or when, I would always find you and reclaim you. And I have. This lifetime took a little longer, that's all."

I sat watching him, a feeling of fullness in my head. He was sounding like a guru. The things he was saying, the way he was looking at me, touched the core of my being and I believed him. I not only believed him, but I knew who he was and the knowing scared me more than the thought that I could at last be going crazy. I shivered and pulled my arms around my body.

"Could I have a drink of water?" My throat suddenly felt parched. Hopefully, something tangible, like water, would help to ground me. He picked up the phone and asked someone to bring in a glass of water.

There was a soft knock on his door. I expected him to move from his perch on his desk, but he didn't.

He called out for the person to come in and one of the secretaries entered and extended the water to him. He thanked her, nodded his dismissal, then relinquished the glass to my trembling fingers.

"Are your patients aware that you believe in all this hocus pocus?" I asked, curious to know the answer.

"Why should they be? They're aware that I'm the best cardiologist in the field and that's all they care about."

"And your wife and family?" I saw him grinning at me.

"I'm not married. I was once, for almost two years to a beautiful woman that I thought I loved. We've been divorced for twenty years. No children."

I allowed some of the droplets of water to linger on my tongue and moistened my chapped lips. "Why did you get a divorce?"

"I realized I was playing a part," he continued, "There was too much missing. Her touch was foreign, her kisses, her loving me. It all felt so wrong. I didn't want to go on like that for thirty or forty years so I ended it."

"Is that a shot at me?"

"It wasn't intended to be. I was merely telling you what happened. I always had a sense that I was waiting for the woman who would complete me. A year after I was married I knew it was a mistake. I started having dreams of another life, of another woman I had loved, loved still. Then something happened to confirm it."

He was waiting for me to ask what had happened. I couldn't, I didn't want to know. I glanced at my watch. I didn't want the staff thinking anything was going on with the door closed and us in there so long. I knew he was watching me. I brought my eyes up quickly and stared into his.

"This is my office. I pay their salaries. It's not the other way around."

How did he always seem to know exactly what I was thinking? I was almost afraid to continue looking at him.

"I don't have patients waiting."

"Can you read minds?"

"With you it's not necessary. Your thoughts are so transparent." He smiled then. "Just as when you thought I was an ax murderer. That was an easy one to get."

How could he be smiling, talking about our having lived many lifetimes together? What was he expecting from me now? What did he want me to do?

A long, sad sigh filled the room before he spoke again. "I'm sorry to have sprung all this on you. I assumed you'd been waiting for me also. I heard you calling me. I thought maybe you already knew."

A flash of my hands searching his body, as though in remembrance, replayed in my mind. And I remembered it had felt as if he were my true husband when he'd registered us as Mr. and Mrs. at the hotel

"Aren't you curious, just a little?"

I had to admit I was curious. "Chance, how can you be so sure that even if this is true, I'm the one?"

His hand reached out for my face and I pulled away. I was thinking of Larry and knew that if Chance Morgan touched me again I would be convinced of his statement and my marriage would be over.

He stopped, his hand in midair, and smiled. "When I held you in my arms in the parking lot I knew. When we made love there was no doubt in my mind that we had a history, that you were the one I'd been waiting for.

"When I tasted your skin it was just as I remembered and your smell…I could feel my soul rejoicing at the scent of you. How could I not know? How could you not?"

I didn't answer him. Instead I stood to leave. My good sense was failing me. I wanted nothing more than to allow Chance to wrap me in his arms, to feel what I'd felt that night, that I'd found my way home. Instinctively I knew he was right. I felt the connection.

"I bought you something."

I stopped and waited at the door. "How could you know I was coming?" This time it was Chance who didn't answer. I watched him as he went back to his desk and pulled open a drawer.

He handed the heavy package to me and stood away. His eyes connected with mine and I knew he was aware of my need for space. He wasn't going to crowd me, and for that I was grateful. I saw my name on the card.

"I don't know if I should accept gifts from you, Chance."

He started toward me, laughing, his face glowing with amusement. "Michelle, it's no big deal. It's not like I'm giving you a contract for your soul"

He was teasing me, his smile warm and inviting. "Come on, please. Open it."

I tore away the wrapping and spotted a bundle of books dealing with reincarnation and other psychic topics. The one that caught my eye seemed to deal with regression therapy.

"Have you read all of these?" I asked in amazement.

"Yes, and many more. I've been through regression therapy a number of times. Now I don't need it. The memories come to me as clearly now as what I had for breakfast this morning."

I saw him hesitate. I was wondering why. So far he'd done nothing to prove he wasn't some middle-age hippie. Then for some reason I thought of Jim Jones, that preacher from the seventies who'd led all those poor people out of the country to a supposedly better life and forced them to commit mass suicide. Would this thing with Chance end with my death?

"What is it, Chance? Why are you looking at me like that?" I was more than curious now.

"Would you like me to take you through a regression?"

"No, I don't think so."

"I can fill you in on our lives. Would it be possible for us to have dinner together tonight?"

"I'm having dinner with my husband." I glanced at the wedding ring fitting snugly on my finger, a symbol of my life and the choice I had made. "It was nice seeing you again, Dr. Morgan. Thanks for the books."

"Larry, do you believe in past lives?" I waited as my husband paused long enough in his eating to give me a quizzical look.

"What is all this talk with you lately?"

He was watching me intently. I could tell he wanted only to eat and go home, maybe make love and watch a little television. I could be opening up a conversation that I wouldn't know how to handle, yet I still wanted to pursue this avenue of thought.

I glanced around the crowded restaurant wondering if there were any other conversations going on that paralleled what I wanted to discuss with Larry.

"I've just been thinking about fate and our lives. I was just wondering if this life we have… You know…is this it?"

I caught the look on his face, the one that said I was going over the edge. I decided not to give up, not yet. "Honey, don't you ever want more than what we have now?"

He was eyeing me strangely. "I have everything I've always wanted, Mick. I thought you did too."

LET IT GO. I heard the inaudible warning, but chose to ignore it. "I'm not talking about material things," I said to my husband. "I'm talking about us, our spirits. I want to know what happens when we die. Is right now all there is? Were our lives predestined? Do we keep repeating lives until we get it right? I want to know what you think."

He smiled at me. At that moment he looked so much like the young boy I'd fallen in love with. The years had been more than kind to Larry. He was more handsome now than the day we married. Big beautiful brown eyes that sparkled with love and mischief, dimpled cheeks and thick brownish hair with red highlights that was softer than our grandchildren's. He cut an imposing figure with his six feet of male energy. He was still trim but more muscled. And he never failed to elicit looks from adoring women. That never made me jealous. I knew without a shadow of a doubt that Larry loved me.

"Honey, don't you ever wonder?" I persisted. I wanted just once not to be told that I was being silly. I wanted to discuss this and I wanted to discuss it with my husband.

Larry smiled at me. Then his smile turned into a full- fledged grin. That was one thing about Larry that I loved. His smile was always so wide and warm. It made me feel special when he turned it on me as he was doing now.

"You know I deal in evidence, honey. Show me proof that we've lived before and I'll let you know." He hesitated. "Don't tell me you believe in that stuff. You never have before. Why now?"

"How do you know I've never believed in it? Maybe I just didn't mention it to you." Thoughts of my dreams flashed before me. *Maybe I've always believed*, I thought, *and was just too afraid to admit it*. I was still too afraid to admit it.

"In all the years we've been together, I think I would know if you believed in anything so kooky."

He turned his attention then to his steak. "I talked to the kids today. Erica and Roy were wondering if we might like to keep the grandkids for a couple of weeks so they can spend some time alone."

"What did you tell them?"

I amazed myself at how easily I could switch gears. I still wanted to know my husband's opinions on reincarnation, but he'd effectively slammed that door. Now I supposed I was to pretend some sort of enthusiasm for caring for a spoiled three-year-old boy and an even brattier five-year-old girl.

"I told them we'd love it, but I needed to check with you, to see when you can take some vacation time."

"Why would I be taking vacation?" I stared at him with what I hoped was innocence in my eyes.

"To keep the kids of course."

"I don't recall your mentioning this to me, nor did our daughter call and ask me. She asked you, so I assume that you will be the one taking vacation time."

"My God, what's wrong with you?"

Larry slammed his fork onto his plate and then hastily wiped his mouth with a linen napkin before tossing it across the plate in disgust.

"Are you going through the change?" he asked.

"Why are you asking me that?"

I was so proud of myself for being able to sit there and talk in a rational tone of voice even though inside I was crying. I hated feeling guilty because I didn't want to keep two rowdy kids with absolutely no discipline. They were my grandchildren, but still.

"Well, look at you." He pointed a long slender finger toward my face. "You're talking nonsense about past lives and now, when I ask you to keep the kids, you behave as if I'm asking you to commit murder."

"I have a job, Larry." One look into his eyes and I knew what was coming before he spoke one word.

"That's not my fault, now is it?" Larry shouted. "I've never asked you to work. In fact, I believe I've asked you more than once to quit that damn job. It interferes with our plans too often. Every time we plan a trip to visit one of the kids, you have to work.

If I didn't know better I'd think you'd rather work than take care of our grandchildren."

"Have you ever thought that maybe you don't know me as well as you think you do? I would rather work than take care of those two spoiled, obnoxious kids." I smiled, then said, "You know what, I'm not going to. You volunteered, you take care of them. In fact why don't you go to Arizona and keep them there. I don't feel like rearranging my life."

"Don't tempt me, Mick. I'll do it."

I laughed out loud and felt my spirit soar. "You really don't hear me, do you? I'm not kidding. I'm not taking one moment of vacation time to baby-sit so Erica and Roy can have time alone. They created those little monsters, let them deal with them."

"They're our grandchildren, Mick. Don't you love them?"

"I'm not sure." I looked at the shock on his face and decided to go all the way. "I know I don't like them. They have no respect and they're destructive."

"They're babies."

I thought about that for a second. "You're right, they're babies. Maybe I shouldn't blame them, but their parents aren't babies. I don't like them very much either. Have they ever offered to pay for one thing those two have deliberately destroyed?"

"They don't have the kind of money we have."

I knew what Larry was doing. He was trying to play on my sympathies. He was working me, to get me to agree to do what he wanted. If his burst of anger didn't work, then he was going to try to guilt me into it.

Why not? It had worked for twenty-six years. I never wanted to make waves. I was forever treading lightly. I always gave in. But for some reason, not tonight. Maybe not ever again.

I stared at him hard before asking, "Larry, did either Erica or Roy ever once clean up the mess their kids made of our home? No, I'm serious. I don't want them here."

His smile that I loved was gone now. He was wearing his stern look as though I were one of the witnesses he was trying to intimidate.

"This isn't the way for you to have a good relationship with the kids. They need us. They need our help and the least we can do is be there for them."

"No, the least we can do is nothing." I took a sip of my wine, feeling unnerved now. I felt as if I were walking on a dozen eggshells, still trying to prevent a crack. Yet I felt a strength surging through my veins I hadn't felt in years. I knew I wasn't backing down. Something in Larry's eyes told me he knew it too.

"What am I going to tell them?"

"Tell them the truth."

"You want me to tell Erica that her mother doesn't want to help her, that she doesn't want the kids in our home because she doesn't love them? Would you like me to tell her that you don't love her either? Mick, she needs you. This is crazy."

"Tell her whatever you want." His jaw went slack. This was not the wife he knew. "Let me know when you plan to leave," I said. "I think I'll make plans to do something special for myself while you're gone."

Then I dug into my food with gusto. I wanted to laugh at my husband sitting there in disbelief.

I ate every bite on my plate, then ordered dessert and coffee. The tight band that had existed around my head and my heart was gone. I felt free and by God, it felt good. I was being reborn into the Michelle I wanted to be.

Chapter Four

I listened to the quiet as Larry got ready for bed. We had barely spoken since leaving the restaurant. Erica, our eldest, was now twenty-three and still daddy's little girl. At seventeen, she'd gotten pregnant and broken her father's heart.

As for me, it was the beginning of my countdown. I was glad when Erica married Roy and moved to Arizona. With only four more to get out of the house, I felt there was now an end in sight to my life sentence of motherhood.

Before I knew it, all the kids were gone. If only they would actually stay away. It seemed that every other week one or the other of them was coming to visit. Then they started having babies and began bringing them by, leaving them first for hours, then for days.

Larry cooed over the babies then went off to work. I was always the unasked, designated caregiver. Nevertheless, I had done it. Up to now, I had been forced against my will to repeat the caregiving part of my life.

I'd talked to Larry a dozen times about saying no to the kid's frequent visits and their dropping off their children, but each time he'd laughed off my words with kisses, telling me that I was being a grouch, that he knew I loved having them there. Well, I didn't.

I was thrilled when Shannon, our youngest, left home for college. Within a year she was shacking up with her boyfriend. She thought we didn't know. We went along with the deception because our agreement with Shannon was that we'd totally cover her college and living expenses, as long as she remained on her own. No live-in boyfriend.

When we found out, neither Larry nor I wanted to confront Shannon. She was getting good grades, and we wanted her to have an education.

"Are you coming to bed?"

Larry had reappeared in the door of the family room. I was not following my usual modus operandi. By now I was usually in our bed rubbing his back, not wanting to feel the silence building between us.

Larry's silence would generally break down all my defenses. He'd never shout, just turn away until I would turn to him, touching him, caressing him, making love with him. And somewhere between my first touch and his release I would utter my acquiescence to whatever problem had come between us.

I thought of the books Chance had given me. I didn't want to go to bed and be ignored until I came around. I wanted to remain where I was, within myself, knowing I didn't have to give up two weeks' vacation time to Erica, the spoiled daughter that believed it her due. She was not the monster of my making; she was Larry's.

"Are you listening to me, Mick? I'm going to bed. Aren't you coming?"

"No, I think I'm going to read for a while."

His legs moved apart and he squared his shoulders. "This is Wednesday, you know."

For the last several years we'd gotten into the habit of making love on Wednesday and Saturday. It didn't matter what was happening, or what plans had been made. Wednesday and Saturday were our high holy days, not to be messed with.

"I'm not in the mood."

If Larry had glared at me, I probably would have felt better, more justified. But as it was, he just stood staring at me, as if he no longer knew who I was.

"Fine. Goodnight."

He kissed the top of my head, his lips closed and cold. This was only the second time in our marriage that I'd stood up to Larry for what I really wanted. The first time had been when I was pregnant with Shannon.

Larry's anger over finding my secret supply of birth control pills had led to that particular pregnancy. I'd cried while trying to explain to him that I didn't want any more children.

I had not considered my actions a betrayal but he had. So for weeks I had turned to him in bed each night and initiated lovemaking without the benefit of any protection other than praying not to become pregnant. It didn't work.

When I found myself about to become a mother for the fifth time, I took a step even I didn't believe I was capable of. I went to an abortion/Planned Parenthood clinic, paid my money and three days later, I sat there crying, waiting my turn.

I was alone and afraid. Afraid of burning in hell and afraid of ending my marriage if Larry found out. I alternated between being sorry and making plans for my life alone. A part of me welcomed my husband's anger. I would be free.

Somehow Larry had intercepted a call from the clinic reminding me of the time and came before I was taken in. It surprised me that he wasn't angry, merely sad. He pleaded with me not to abort the baby. In exchange he talked with the doctor, took my appointment and had a vasectomy on the spot.

He never wanted to talk about what had almost happened. The doctor convinced him that I could still be in the midst of post partum depression from my last pregnancy. No one listened to me. No one believed that was not the case.

For once, I had taken matters into my own hands. My defeat, I had another baby. My minor victory, I would have no more.

Larry walked toward the stairs to go to our bedroom alone and I opened up the book, *Is This Your Only Life?* by William Davis Jr.

Four hours later I was still reading, engrossed in the concept of past lives. Even without regression therapy I believed. This surely couldn't be the life I was destined for.

I wanted to find my life. I wanted to feel what I'd felt in the arms of a stranger and it had nothing to do with sex.

I didn't want to go to bed. I didn't want to give in and I didn't want to feel my husband's silence. I couldn't remember a time that we hadn't slept in the same bed when we were home. We did everything in that bed, our reading, our fighting, the little that we did, and our making up.

Now we were in different rooms and for the first time I knew we were not on the same path. I had just taken a major step away from Larry and from our life.

A small part of me wanted to turn back, to beg his forgiveness, to be what he thought I was, but after reading that book I could no longer pretend that marriage to Larry was my destiny.

"Are you sure this is what you want?"

"Yes, honey, I'm sure."

"It's not too late for you to change your mind and come with me. You know Erica's pretty peeved. She mentioned the fact that you rarely visit and she thinks you don't want them to come here."

We were standing in the airport. It had taken nearly a month for Larry to believe that I was actually not going to be the one going. He was the one taking two weeks vacation and leaving for Arizona to care for two of our grandchildren.

He was making a last ditch effort to change my mind and if he couldn't do that, he was bound and determined that I would be miserable while he was gone. He imagined I would be consumed with guilt. He was wrong.

"Honey, believe me I do hope you have a wonderful time with the kids." I looked at him long and hard. "And please don't make any excuses for my not coming. Maybe for once you could tell them that their children are destructive and unruly and until they're older and have been taught how to behave, I would prefer they remain in Arizona."

He looked at me, his eyes filled with skepticism. "Will you go see Dr. Payne while I'm gone and have a physical?"

I couldn't help smiling at him. I had betrayed my husband for the second time by not playing my part. He was confused. He had every right to be.

"I'm not sick."

"Will you do it for me?" he asked.

This was a small thing he was asking. I almost said yes to his request. But this new me that had been evolving for the past two months wouldn't allow it. I no longer wanted to do anything, no matter how small, just because it would make someone else happy. I smiled at my husband but didn't answer.

"What are you going to do while I'm gone?"

"Oh, there's a lecture I want to attend." I left out that it was on past lives. "And I might go to the movies, or out to dinner. Who knows? I have two weeks. I think I'm going to look for something very important that I lost."

"Should I be worried?"

I noticed for the first time the tiny worry lines around his eyes. Something was bothering him that he'd not put into words.

"Mick, are you planning on having an affair while I'm gone?"

"I thought you believed me incapable of that?" I said, looking over his shoulder.

"I still do." He reached for me then stopped himself. "But you're not acting like yourself. You're beginning to scare me. I can't deal with the paranormal and I've noticed all the books you've been reading lately are about it."

"What do you want me to do, Larry? My reading isn't affecting your life. I still cook and clean for you. I'm there whenever you turn to me. What have I taken from you or from our marriage?" I noticed the hurt look that came into his eyes.

"We've always shared and this one time we can't." His voice was muffled. I was aware that he was uncomfortable talking about anything that couldn't be proven.

I was undaunted by his feelings, and elected instead to focus on his words. The fact that he wanted to share gave me hope. So I said to him, "We can share it. We can find out about it together, we can make the journey together." I smiled, feeling maybe this was the way things were meant to be. Perhaps Larry and I would explore this new avenue of interest.

"I don't want to make that particular journey. And I want you to be done with it when I return home."

"Excuse me?"

I watched as his jaw tightened. I listened as he spoke to me as if I were one of the children.

"I've never given you an ultimatum, but this is one time I must put my foot down. When I return home, I want this nonsense out of our home and out of your head."

I laughed out loud. "You want to regulate my thoughts? I only read when you're not around, or when you've fallen asleep."

"I know that, but I don't like waking and finding you not there. I want you to stay in bed with me, where you belong. I need you there. So whatever you have to do to rid our lives of this invasion, you have two weeks to do it. And that includes your dreams. I want you to go to a doctor, get something for them. I want them to stop. I know they have something to do with all of this nonsense."

I couldn't believe my husband's gall. I wanted to strike out at him, hurt him for his remarks and I knew just how to do it. If he thought it was an affair I was after, maybe I'd give him something to worry about. And since he was the one who'd brought it up, I couldn't help wondering if he was giving me his tacit approval to have an affair. It sure as hell sounded like it. It sounded to me as if he was giving me two weeks to do whatever I wanted, as long as I was done with it when he returned.

I looked away from him for a moment in disbelief. Surely I was hearing him wrong. "Larry, is that why you asked if I'm planning on having an affair? Did I hear you right? Are you giving me your approval? If so, why do you think two weeks will be long enough?"

He glared at me and walked toward the security line leading to the gate. He wanted to be away from me. "Two weeks, Mick," he said. He continued walking, looking back once over his right shoulder to repeat, "Two weeks." Even from where I stood I could tell his teeth were clenched in anger.

I drove to the only medical office I planned to visit for the next two weeks. I'd decided to take a two week vacation while Larry was gone.

This time my wait in Chance's office was much shorter. He came to the waiting room door himself and invited me in. I rolled my bag in, handed a stack of notepads to the receptionist on the way.

My knees were knocking together, and my hands were trembling. I knew why I was sitting across from Chance Morgan and he knew also.

"I've been waiting for you to come back."

It was simple when he said it. Yet his blatant assumption angered me. I wanted him to share the guilt for my infidelity and even more, I wanted to blame him for what we had not done, but what I knew we would do.

"I read the books you gave me," I answered at last. "I'm curious about what you have to say. I don't know that I believe you, but I want to hear more about it. I want to hear what you were going to tell me before. What happened, Chance? How do you know this is all real?"

I watched as he walked around to the front of his desk and peered at what appeared to be a work calendar. There was not the slightest doubt in my mind that he would make time for me regardless of his appointments.

"Do you have time for lunch? This is going to take a while to tell you."

He was trying hard to hide the wistful look. I saw it though it sent tremors throughout my body. I had been moving toward this moment long before Chance ever walked into my life.

Of course I hadn't understood what was happening to me, just felt a great apathy and an underlying knowledge that someone, somewhere was waiting for me. I needed to know more about regression therapy. I needed to know more about Chance.

Larry had ordered me to get 'it' out of my system and I was taking him up on it. Of course Larry never had in mind the things I was about to do. For the first time in my life I had someone to talk to about the feelings I'd had my entire life, someone who might have the answers, someone who didn't think I was crazy.

"Yes, Chance, I can have lunch."

Maybe it would turn out to be that after being married for so long I just wanted a change. But within my psyche I knew there was more. There had better be more because I was gambling my life on the slim chance that there was.

"Give me a minute." Chance smiled at me, then went out the door. I wondered briefly what he would tell his staff. Surely, they were curious.

He came back, then smiled at me from several feet away. Again, I knew he was sensing hesitation on my part, but I wouldn't change my mind, not now. I wanted to know why I felt an intense connection to him. Was he really my husband from a previous life, the dark-haired lover from my dreams?

"Are you canceling patients?"

"Of course not, I would never do that." He must have sensed my doubt because he continued, "Not even for you would I leave my patients hanging."

"What about the day we met? You said you heard me calling you and came. Didn't you have patients that day?"

"Michelle, I didn't cancel patients the day we met. It just so happened that my calendar was clear. I do take time off from work. I'm a cardiologist but I'm also human. I need down time."

That was the right thing for him to say. I wondered how he'd known just the thing to say that would allow me to release the last little bit of hesitation. It was a little spooky, as if he could read my thoughts. I peered at him, wondering if he could be psychic.

"Where would you like to have lunch?"

I looked in his eyes. There was no hidden meaning. "I want to see where you live. Is that possible?"

In a way I was challenging him. If he was lying about being unmarried, he couldn't take me to his home. There would be pictures. If his wife was working, there would be some sign to let me know. It was amazing that I wondered if he was married while my own marriage hung like an albatross around my neck.

"I would love for you to come home with me. I'm a great cook. My specialty is Chinese."

I stood, licking my lips. Okay, I'd come this far. I heard Larry's voice screaming at me in my head. Then I saw our daughter Erica with her disapproving nod and her unruly kids by her side. I thought of my husband's ordering me to be done with this foolishness. I was tired of taking orders. "I love Chinese food," I answered.

"Would you like to follow me in your car?"

For an answer I smiled, then followed him out the door saying a hasty good-bye to the receptionist. The woman barely glanced at me but I felt as if *Adulteress* was written across my forehead.

In the driveway of Chance's home I killed the engine and looked around. His house was not what I expected. Somehow he'd found Utopia in the midst of the Chicago suburbs. His home stood alone on a small manmade hill and looked to be very old. I glanced up and down the block. The other homes were lovely, huge, yet half the size of Chance's. They had lots of trees and thick well manicured lawns but they all appeared to be rather new, no older than ten years. In fact I knew the subdivision hadn't been there twenty years ago. I wondered if this was really an old refurbished house, or a modern dwelling made to resemble its predecessor.

I followed Chance through the widest, thickest pair of oak doors I'd ever seen. A rush of strong emotions hit me squarely in the chest and I stumbled and clutched my breast, suddenly afraid. Never in my life had I felt something so powerful. The energy in the room rapidly wrapped around me, enveloping me in warmth and love.

I knew this place, these things. I was overcome with the strangest sense of deja vu. I had never been here before, and even if it was as Chance had said that I had a past life, why would these objects in his house be so familiar to me?

"Are you all right?"

"Something's wrong, Chance. Your furnishings feel so familiar to me. This is spooky."

His hand reached out for me. "I searched a long time in antique shops for everything in here," he said, as though that explanation alone should suffice.

"I felt for the energy until it was right. There were some things I wasn't so sure of."

The pleasure shone on his face. I took the hand he offered and proceeded into the room. I ran my free hand over the furnishings, stopping in awe in front of an antique rocker covered in a beautiful brocade.

For several long moments I stood before the chair. Then my glance found Chance and I sat, closing my eyes. This was my chair. Flashes of me sitting there rocking, Jeremy kneeling at my feet, came to me, Jeremy's smile, his hand touching mine, his love. *Oh God*, I thought, *what's happening to me*? I was afraid. This was not a dream. I didn't know what it was.

I wanted to get up, take the chair, and run. I wanted to beg Larry to come home, to take me to the doctor for that physical he wanted me to have. And maybe I would spend some time in an institution. I believed now I needed it.

"Michelle, it's okay, take it slow." Chance's arms were around me, holding me simply to comfort me.

"I have to go," I said as I stood up. I need time to think about this." He stared at me. "I need to call my husband. I feel I'm losing touch with reality and you're the reason, Chance."

Larry sat in his assigned seat, surprised that Michelle had remembered to get him a window seat. The way she'd been acting lately, as though she didn't care, he half expected to find himself seated in the middle of two strangers. Instead, she'd gotten him a first class seat.

He didn't know if that was a good sign or not. He pressed his head against the glass. If he were not a forty-six-year- old man he would cry. Something was wrong with his marriage.

That was an understatement. Something was terribly wrong with his marriage, had been now for over eight months. Ever since Mick had hit the old lady with her car there had been a cloud hanging over them.

It was the first time in their marriage that they'd screamed at each other, saying hurtful things. Mick going to visit the woman had been out of the question.

He had been trying to protect her. But since then she'd looked at him with, if not hatred, intense dislike. He wasn't the enemy. He was her protector, always had been, and always would be. He hoped.

Larry could barely wait to be airborne. He wanted a drink. He could feel the fear eating away at him and needed something to dull the ache. He was aware that in first class he didn't have to wait, but to have a drink before the plane took off would be an act of desperation.

And he didn't want to admit to desperation. The most he would admit to was despair. He missed the easy relationship he'd always enjoyed with his wife. Michelle was his life. He loved her more now than he had the day he married her.

Sure, there were some things lacking in their marriage, but he'd done his best to ignore them and for the most part it worked. If only he were able to make his wife feel the passion for him that he felt for her, their lives really would be perfect.

He leaned back in his seat, grateful for the quick takeoff and the even quicker drink put into his hand. He downed the scotch in one gulp, the smooth liquid going down to the center of his pain and setting his stomach ablaze. He rang for another. The thought that his wife was falling out of love with him would undoubtedly require every ounce of booze on the plane.

When the second drink went down, he allowed himself to relax, glad that he didn't have anyone sitting next to him to disturb his train of thought. All he could think about was Michelle, the woman he loved, had loved for over twenty-eight years. He had no idea how he would live without her.

She was the only woman he'd ever made love to. He'd been too afraid as a boy. He'd been ridiculed and called names, shuffled from place to place, not wanted by anyone. That is, until he was in college and the beautiful woman with hair the color of warm cinnamon sat down next to him and stared.

"Hi, you have the most beautiful eyes," she'd said to him. *"I just wanted to tell you that."*

Those words were carved into his soul. He remembered he'd smiled at her, stunned, and immediately fallen in love.

"Oh my God, I thought your eyes were beautiful, but your smile would light up the world. My name's Michelle, by the way. What's yours?"

"Larry," he'd managed to stammer out, sure that this had to be a prank. Where had this beautiful woman come from and why the hell had she chosen to talk to him? "You have beautiful hair, I love the color," he'd whispered softly not daring to tell her how beautiful he thought she was.

"Thanks," Michelle replied. "I dye it. Since you love the color, I hope they never stop making it."

Larry closed his eyes tight against the pain he was feeling now. It hadn't been a prank. Later she'd told him that she'd been watching him and felt drawn to him. She'd told him he was meant to be in her life. He hadn't minded that one bit.

After months of dating, they'd made love. It was the first time for both of them, something that surprised them both. It ended so quickly that no one had to tell him Michelle had not enjoyed it.

He'd assumed it would get better for her with time. Hell, it had been all that he had hoped for, only magnified about a million times. For him it had only gotten better with time.

Even now, as angry as he was with her, the thought of her made him hard. He loved touching her, all the silky moist spots that he knew were reserved only for him. He loved the feel of the hot juices that flowed out of her body over his hand. He'd done every damn thing he could think to do to please his wife.

He could still see the look on her face when he brought home the porno tapes. She didn't object, she just wasn't pleased. And when he'd suggested that they try some of the things they'd seen, the look of disgust on her face had been enough to make him forget the idea. He was too afraid of losing her.

He knew that was the reason he'd never insisted on discussing their problem more fully. If it was said out in the open, she might stop loving him, stop touching him, not allow him to touch her.

No, for several years they'd both pretended that nothing was wrong. Who knew for sure? Maybe there wasn't. Neither of them had ever been with anyone else. Maybe that was the way it was with all married couples.

In every other manner they were in synch. They laughed together and had fun. After several years their lovemaking improved. Mick even began to enjoy his touches.

He could tell when his wife began to enjoy making love with him. She'd pulled him to her and begun caressing his body, teasing him, telling him to make love to her, to let her make love to him.

It should have been enough. It was just that he'd never been able to rock her world as she rocked his. He didn't just want her to enjoy making love with him, he wanted her pleasure to be so intense that she screamed out with it, calling his name as she came. He wanted that more than anything. No, that wasn't true. More than anything he wanted his marriage to continue. He wanted his wife to continue loving him as she always had.

He thought of Viola, the woman Michelle had hit and the look on Michelle's face after weeks of fighting. He'd put his foot down, demanding that she not go see the woman or get in touch with her in any manner. He was relieved when at last she'd acquiesced.

Larry took a slower sip of the drink in his hand. Had she really acquiesced? Her exact words had been, *"Do whatever the hell you want. You always do."*

He'd not thought about it at the time. He'd been too busy making sure that Michelle was protected, too happy to hear that she was going to listen to him, allow him to handle things. He'd been too busy to see how unhappy the decision made his wife.

He took another longer sip. She'd get over it. She had to. He thought of their latest argument. In the past eight months they'd fought more than they had their entire marriage. She was trying to hurt him deliberately, that much he knew. He just didn't understand why.

How could she say she didn't want kids? That would make her as bad as his own mother, and she was nothing like his mother. He remembered how much attention she'd paid to the kids, putting them in ballet and music lessons, baking cookies for them. She had been a wonderful mother.

She would have never taken their kids and just dumped them on the state, never bothering to look back. And regardless of what she'd said, he didn't believe she would have ever aborted their child.

A stab of pain hit him in both temples with the force of a two ton truck. After their second baby Mick had cried during each pregnancy and begged him to allow her to have her tubes tied. He'd always said no. He wondered what would have happened if this had happened now, when a woman no longer needed their husband's consent to do it.

He couldn't believe she'd refused to take time off from work and keep the kids for Erica and Roy to have some time alone. Now he downed the drink and rang for another.

He definitely hadn't believed she would send him to Arizona alone to care for two small children. He'd expected her to board the plane right until the moment the jet taxied down the runway. This was not the woman he loved. Michelle wouldn't do this. But she had.

Larry polished off his drink, the last he would have. Getting drunk never solved anything. He laid his head back against the soft leather and groaned. There was an ache in his heart as well as his head. The last place he wanted to be at the moment was flying away from his wife. He needed to be home. He needed to make things right.

Lately she'd started having the dreams again, the ones of another man, someone she believed she'd loved and lost, and she'd begun talking nonsense about past lives and willing herself to die.

A shiver froze his heart. Once started, he seemed unable to stop the chill that had crept around his heart from enveloping him, turning him into that same frightened boy he'd been when his mother had told him she was finding him a new home.

His heart had pounded in fear as he'd tried to remember what bad thing he'd done to make his mother find him a new home. He'd begged and pleaded with his mother, promising to be good. None of the efforts of a five-year-old had mattered. She'd not found him a new home. She'd turned him over to the state.

Larry had endured it, at first helpless, as one after the other of the caregivers he was entrusted to abandoned him also. Then he'd learned to survive. He'd learned to be strong, to harden his heart. Mick's love had been sudden and unexpected, the balm he'd needed to heal his heart and spirit.

Mick was his constant. She'd sworn to love him always. And until recently he'd never doubted that she always would. Now she was behaving oddly. He thought of the night more than two months ago when she had confessed to sleeping with another man. He'd laughed at her and she'd been insulted. She'd questioned whether he doubted another man would find her attractive.

He shouldn't have laughed. He should have told her then and there that the sight of her inflamed his senses. He thought she knew that. He had never meant to hurt her feelings, but the thought of her touching a stranger, making love with him…It wasn't possible.

His wife had taken years to get comfortable touching him. She'd been just as bad about him touching her. So he knew there was no way in hell she would allow a stranger to touch her.

Opening his eyes Larry looked around the cabin. Enough thinking about problems that didn't exist. Mick was probably going through the change. He'd heard women behaved strangely during that time. They would weather it as they had everything in their lives. He forced a smile to his lips. Mick was not his mother. She would never desert him.

I left Chance's home thinking of Larry, wondering what he was doing, wishing I had flown to Arizona with him. It seemed as if I'd tumbled headlong into a whirlwind. With shaking fingers I dialed the phone. I needed to talk to Larry. I wanted to tell him what had happened.

"Hello, Mother."

Erica's voice was cold and hard. Her use of Mother, instead of Mom, was her signal to me that she was angry. I smiled at the fury in my eldest child's voice. If I had cared that my actions would upset her I would have her kids right now and would probably be downing a handful of pills from the migraine they invariably gave me. No, I had no time for her histrionics.

"Erica, let me speak to your father." My voice was just as cold and dispassionate. I had given her twenty-three years of my life. I didn't owe her more. I had done the mom thing until I was sick to death of it. The plays, the games, the sleep-overs, the trips, the park, the zoo, baking cookies, helping with homework until finally it was baby-sitting. And all this while working fulltime.

Yes, I had done it all. No wonder Larry thought of me as the perfect mother. I had played the part and kept my feelings buried deep inside, but now, now I wasn't ready to give away the next part of my life caring for my children's offspring.

I sagged against a chair and slid into it as I heard Larry's voice on the other end of the phone.

"I decided to take some vacation time. I need you to come home." There was silence, dead silence such as I'd never known. Then Larry's voice talking to Erica.

"Honey, the connection on your phone's not that good. I'm going to go outside and call your mother on my cell phone."

"Is everything all right, Dad?" I heard Erica answer him. He replied to her, "Everything's fine, honey."

I could imagine him smiling at her. I wanted everything to be fine.

I realized the silence on the phone had turned into a busy signal. I knew my husband had hung up the phone without telling me of his intentions. Sure, I'd heard him tell our daughter, but didn't I count? I clicked the off button to stop the noise.

I was beginning to feel sorry for myself and part of me knew it was an excuse to run back to Chance, to experience him the way I wanted. I was dying of thirst and he was the long awaited drink of water I needed.

The cordless phone rang in my hand. The moment I clicked the button, Larry's booming voice was screaming at me, something he never did.

"What the hell do you mean, you need me to come home? Are you ill?"

"I don't think so." I waited.

"You don't think so? You don't think so!"

This time his voice was so loud that I moved the phone away from my ear. "Hon, I know this sounds crazy and I can't really explain it. All I can tell you is that I need you home. I can feel that I'm going to do something we'll both regret if you're not here to stop me. Please baby, come home now."

"What are you talking about?"

I heard the momentary fear in his voice. He was probably thinking I was going to swallow a handful of pills or something else equally as innocent. If only that was what I was thinking.

"Mick, when did you take this vacation time?"

"That doesn't matter."

"Like hell it doesn't. It matters. If you're on vacation, the kids could be there with us right now. I would be home with you and we wouldn't be having this absurd conversation."

I heard the sound of the ocean in my head. I was screwing this up. I wanted to make him understand. I wanted to make it painless. Tears were streaming down my face. I couldn't find the words to tell my husband the truth without making him want to commit me.

"I asked you a question, Mick. When did you take vacation?"

I ignored the question. To me that didn't matter, not as much as trying to make Larry understand. "I touched a chair today, Larry. It was an antique, at least a hundred years old. I sat in it and I felt it envelope me. It was my chair."

"What are you talking about?"

"I'm talking about past lives."

"Not that shit again!" he roared. "I warned you, Mick. No more. All you had to do was tell me anything else, you missed me, you loved me and I would have come home to you in a flash. But this…God…"

I heard the end of the profanity he muttered before he hung up on me. I wrapped my arms around my body and cried for the loss of innocence in my marriage. For sure we would never be the same.

Every nerve in my body tingled with awareness. I wanted Larry, but I needed Chance. I needed him to help me make sense of what was happening to me. My glance caught the recent picture of my husband smiling from the frame on the mantle. I loved him. With all my heart I loved him.

At two in the afternoon I made my way toward my bed, reaching to take my husband's picture from the mantle. I curled up in bed with it and cried, begging God for strength.

Three days later I made a decision. I had not talked to Larry again. He'd not bothered to call me and I'd not called him.

What finally made up my mind were the dreams I had for three nights in a row. Vivid dreams of another lifetime. Chance was there with me, holding me. He didn't wear the face he wore now and neither did I, but it was us. Of that I was sure. This time there was no blood, just the two of us laughing, loving, being happy. Again I saw myself sitting in my rocker, Chance staring up at me tenderly, only his name was Jeremy. "I'll love you always, Dimitra," he said. That was the name he'd called me that night in the hotel. I didn't know if I'd made myself hear that name in my dream or if this was what it felt like, a memory, a long ago forgotten memory.

This time as I dialed the phone I knew the man on the other end would have a different response. He would be there whenever I needed him. In my dream he'd made a solemn vow that we would always be together, that death would only separate us for a moment.

Larry sat glaring at the phone, willing it to ring. He'd not spoken to Michelle in three days. He was afraid to call her, afraid to hear her tell him that she'd awakened after twenty-six years of loving him and realized she no longer did.

Damn. The whole episode was crazy. They'd never handled their problems this way. He missed her with every fiber of his being. Maybe that was the reason the kids were getting to him. He'd never seen it before, but they could be rather obnoxious. As much as he loved his grandchildren, he had to admit that.

He'd only been there with them for one day alone. The other two days, he had taken a good long look at his daughter, the daughter that Mick always accused him of spoiling, of favoring.

Maybe it was true. He'd looked at her the day before thinking how much she looked like her mother. He'd been surprised that her resemblance to Mick did in fact create a bond. He had never dared admit it to anyone, least of all to himself.

But now he knew Mick was correct in her assessment of the situation. But how could he not love Erica a little more? She was the spitting image of the woman who'd given her life. Her birth had been the cement that glued them together as a family instead of a couple.

Larry looked around his daughter's spotless white kitchen, remembering how amazed he'd been not to see any clutter. The all white kitchen was new. Something they never would have tried with young kids, something Mick wouldn't try now for fear of their grandchildren's visits.

He'd walked around the house looking at Erica's collection of Lladros safely ensconced behind glass in a curio cabinet. Not one fingerprint marred the glass. He'd been the one to start his daughter's collection. From the day she was born he'd collected them for her. Not a one was broken-unlike Mick's meager collection.

He'd been standing there looking at his eldest daughter's collection when she'd come to stand behind him.

"How do you manage to keep the kids away from those?" He waved toward the curio.

"They wouldn't dare touch my things."

"Are you saying they've never tried?"

"They tried and I spanked them."

He watched as she turned smiling brown eyes on him. "These are precious, they're all from you. I would never let them destroy them." His mouth fell open in surprise.

"That wasn't the attitude you had with your mother's figurines."

"Daddy, you know Mom isn't as attached to her things I am."

"Erica, it was an anniversary gift. I gave it to her for our twentieth anniversary."

He had watched as Erica pouted, her face frowning, her eyes no longer smiling, but glaring at him.

"If it was that important to her, then why didn't she just let you buy her another one? Nooo, she had to take it out on me and my kids and make me feel guilty that they're so lively."

Larry looked at his daughter and saw the face of his wife a year before, crying amidst the ruins from her broken figurine, an anniversary gift from him to her. He hadn't given her many, preferring instead to take the entire family on anniversary trips. Now watching his daughter's angry face, he recalled every word. He got a shiver as he heard Michelle's voice in his head calling to him.

"Oh my God! Larry, look what they did."

"They're just kids, Mother," Erica had answered her mother, before he could say a word. *"If you didn't want it broken you shouldn't have put it out."*

At the time he'd ignored the fire in Mick's eyes when she answered Erica. *"It was on the mantle, Erica.* Maybe you should have better control of your kids and teach them to respect other people's property. They had no business climbing up there anyway."

"What's the big deal, Mother? Just go buy yourself another one."

"It was an anniversary gift."

"Then tell Daddy to buy you another one."

Larry could clearly picture the tears as they rained down his wife's face. He'd wanted so much to stop her from hurting, but he chose to stop the fight. "Erica's right, honey. Stop crying, I'll buy you another one tomorrow."

"If you do, I'll break it myself," she'd replied. He had watched, as she finished picking up the broken porcelain and dumped it in the trash without another word.

For the first time, looking at Erica in her uncluttered home with over twenty years of an expensive Lladro collection intact, he was beginning to understand. Mick was right, Erica was selfish.

Chapter Five

"Michelle?"

I dared to breathe, the relief evident in my bones. If I closed my eyes in a certain way I could almost see the string that connected me to the voice on the phone.

"Michelle, I've been waiting for you to call me. I've had time to get used to this."

A pause.

"I was so sure when I found you, that you would be ready for this. I'm sorry I didn't give you more time."

I couldn't believe it. Chance was apologizing to me for my behaving like a fool and running away from him.

"Chance, can we talk?"

"I'm swamped with patients until six."

"I could buy you dinner."

"Where's your husband?"

"In Arizona."

I heard the slow, even breathing from the other end of the phone. I shivered. I wondered how long Chance had been collecting these things to show to the woman he loved. Then it hit me. I was the woman he loved, the one he'd stored up treasures for.

"I could meet you at your house at seven...bring dinner fixings...and cook dinner for you."

"Do you remember how to get there?"

"Yes."

"Are you sure you want to come?"

"I have to."

"Then I'll meet you there at seven…only don't bring dinner. We'll order in."

For the rest of the day I moved through the rooms of my home cleaning and dusting, remembering my life with Larry, my children, my parents. I felt the way I had after having been given morphine for pain years before. Dizzy.

I was not quite sure that I wasn't in a dream. I concentrated harder, trying to stop the shadow that was now forming around my life. It felt as if I were living inside a board game. If I wanted, I believed I could pick up the pieces and move them about.

Call Larry. The sound reverberated through my head not quite reaching my soul.

I didn't want an attack of conscience. I didn't want to forgive Larry, to have him forgive me. I didn't want to hear him ask me one more time if I'd gone to the doctor, implying that I was crazy. I wanted something that I knew would be bad for me, and I knew that it would cause me problems later.

It was with that in mind that I pulled an invisible veil over my eyes to block out the pictures of my family, to block out my life. I was totally aware of what I was about to do. In that aspect, I have no defense.

By six my entire body felt as if it were wired into a circuit board and someone was shooting little jolts of electricity around and through me.

I walked into my bathroom, my hand automatically opening the drawer and pulling out a brand new toothbrush. This I stuck into my purse. A cold shiver ran through me and I thought of the saying that someone had walked over my grave. I now knew what that meant.

A few minutes before seven, I sat in the driveway of Chance's home waiting for something to happen to make me stop this incredible madness. Nothing happened. Not guilt, not a sense of loss, nothing. The door opened and Chance stood framed by the soft light from inside. Though he was smiling at me, my own uncertainty was evident in him.

I sensed he wanted to come to the car, but was holding back, waiting for me to make my choice. It seemed strange that all it would take for me to change my life was the simple act of getting out of the car.

My eyes fell on the door handle. I gazed at Chance then found myself walking toward him, not remembering actually opening the door.

"Hi."

I stood about a foot from him, the shuddering from within now on the outside. I sank my teeth into the flesh of my lips. His arms reached out for me, enclosing me in a circle of warmth.

"Welcome home."

I fell against his chest sobbing, knowing in some strange way I had indeed returned home, to this man.

"Chance, we need to talk. I have to understand what you're telling me. This all seems so romantic and so farfetched." I closed my eyes allowing a loud sigh to escape.

"How do I know I'm not just here with you now because I'm tired and want a change? How do you know I'm not angry at my husband right now and using you?"

I stepped away from Chance. Finally, my husband's face had managed to push its way into my brain, making me aware of exactly what I was doing by being here with this man. Even if I didn't sleep with him again, I'd crossed the barrier of trust.

Chance was caressing my face, the pads of his fingers warm and gentle.

"I can tell you why you're here if you really want to know."

"If I don't know the reason, why would you?" I asked, amazed that he had the guts to voice his feelings without hesitation.

"Because you've been searching for me, as I have for you," Chance purred. "You've been calling to me and I heard."

I was frowning. I'd thought I was ready to hear what he had to say, but I wasn't. "Chance, just for now, can we change the subject?"

Chance smiled in my direction. "Tell me about your husband," he said. "What does he do?"

"He's a lawyer."

"Do you love him?"

"Yes," I replied, noticing that Chance's eyebrows shot up at my answer.

"If that's true, why are you here?"

"I don't know."

"Ahh, but you do. You're a smart woman, Michelle. Why are you here?"

I looked at him, at his lips that I so wanted to kiss. I could feel the heat of desire rushing through my body. I was embarrassed as hell to tell him that for all my life I had wondered what true fulfillment was like and in one night he'd shown me. He'd managed to satisfy the cravings of my body and soul. I wanted it again.

"Are you here for the sex?"

I couldn't believe he'd asked me that. My mouth fell open. "I...I...yes," I finally admitted at last. "That is part of the reason I'm here."

"And if I told you there was going to be no sex, would you leave?"

I stared at him. "No, I wouldn't leave." I realized in that moment that I did mean it. "Are you telling me that you don't want to make love to me?" I found it impossible to stop the blush that began at my toes and continued to the root of my hair.

"That's exactly what I'm saying. More than anything we need to talk. You need to know why I feel so strongly that we belong together. You have commitments. I don't. And that, my dear Michelle, is going to be a bit of a problem."

He slid down to the floor, his arms reaching out for me. After my head was settled on his chest, we remained like that, not talking for a few moments, just enjoying being together.

"Tell me something," he whispered into my hair. "That day I met you, what had happened? Why did you want to die?"

"I don't know. I guess I was...feeling a little down."

"People don't want to die because they feel a little down."

I wondered if I should tell him about Viola. Larry had instructed me not to mention it to anyone. So far I'd followed his instructions.

"Several months ago I hit a woman with my car." There. I'd said it out loud. This was the first time I'd ever admitted this to anyone other than Larry and the police."

"What happened?"

He was still holding me, the pads of his thumbs gently drawing circles on the soft flesh of my arm. I looked at him. "I don't know. One minute I was driving, the next I saw this figure in front of me and I tried to stop. I hit her. Oh my God, I hit her!"

He held me tighter and allowed me to cry. I knew he couldn't understand what I was saying. I barely could, I just kept repeating, "Oh my God, oh my God. It was awful."

"Did she die?"

"No."

"Did you go visit her, make sure she was all right?"

I didn't turn my gaze from his. I wanted to witness the revulsion that I was sure would cross his face when I told him. "I never went to see her."

"Why? Look at you. I think you would have felt better."

"Larry handled everything. He told me not to go. He told me not to talk about it with anyone. He took care of all her medical bills and he made some sort of settlement."

"I'm sure he was generous with her," Chance offered. "Why are you carrying this guilt?"

"I told her I would come. I told her I would be there for her. I promised her, Chance. She was so afraid. You didn't see her, you didn't see all the blood." I started to shake uncontrollably.

I wished Larry had allowed me to tell him my feelings. Just saying the words out loud was a relief. The revulsion I'd expected to see in Chance's face never materialized. There was only concern for me. It was his understanding, his allowing me to talk that tore me apart.

"Michelle, it was an accident. Maybe your husband was right. I don't know. I'm not a lawyer. But I know you have no reason to blame yourself for an accident."

"What if I do, Chance? I don't remember what I was doing before I hit her. What if I was fiddling with the radio or daydreaming? Maybe I could have stopped. Why don't I remember that?"

He held me, rocking me as if I were a child. "It's going to be all right," Chance whispered. "You'll see."

He kissed my cheeks, stopping a millimeter from my lips. "You're hoping I can help you recall what happened, aren't you?"

"I wasn't trying to use you, Chance...but I haven't had anyone to talk to about this. Larry gets angry any time I bring it up. I thought if it's true, that there is really such a thing as regression therapy that maybe you can help me go back to before the accident."

"Why haven't you gone to a hypnotist?"

"I was so afraid. At first, I thought when it happened that it was just an accident. I felt horrible to have hit her, but I expected to see her through her recovery. I would be able to live through the nightmare.

"Then I called Larry and everything changed. I felt like a criminal, like I was running from the law. I couldn't talk about it with him, or the children, and I certainly couldn't talk about it with a stranger."

I felt his hands go still in my hair. I knew what he was thinking. "You want to know why I'm telling you, don't you?"

I lifted my shoulders in a shrug. "You asked why I wanted to die. That's part of the reason. I couldn't get that old woman out of my head. I couldn't get over my breaking a promise to her, or the feeling that I was cheating her somehow because she was poor. I lost respect for myself and…"

Chance tilted my chin upward, his dark eyes piercing my own. "You lost respect for your husband?"

I wrenched my chin from his hand. Closing my eyes I inserted the tip of my thumb in my mouth and began biting down. I refused to answer Chance's question.

"Michelle, why don't you go on your own to see Viola? I'll help you find the records. You know the hospital she was taken to?"

"It's been so long, so many months have passed."

"That doesn't matter," Chance retorted.

"What if I get Larry in trouble? I can't do that, Chance. Whatever he did, he was only trying to protect me."

"Are you sure you're not afraid that it will be you who winds up in trouble?"

I wasn't worried about myself, but still I thought about it before I answered. "I'm sure. I have no way of knowing what strings, if any, Larry pulled to make this go away. I don't know if he broke any laws. I'm worried for him.

Chance played with my fingers a moment before saying, "So, it's Larry you're worried about?" I heard the hesitation in his voice, his eyes turning even darker as he caught me in his gaze. "You really do love him, don't you?"

"Why should that surprise you? I told you the first night I loved my husband." I watched as his eyebrows quirked upwards.

"Well, you'll have to admit it's unusual for a woman who loves her husband to go to bed with a stranger she met in a parking lot…unless of course she was trying to punish him. Am I your husband's punishment, Michelle?"

"I'm not sure what you are, Chance. The day I met you, you were a lifeline for me. Now you offer me hope that I can remember thirty seconds of my life. Maybe I was in the wrong. Maybe I am only using you to make the pain go away."

He ran his fingers across my lips."If you want to use me, go ahead. I've been your husband and your lover. It could be that in this lifetime, I'm only supposed to be your friend. It looks to me like you could use one."

He smiled at me. "I will be for you whatever you need. Use me, my love. And do it without guilt. That will be my gift to you."

It would have been so easy then to fall into his arms, to kiss him senseless until he forgot about not wanting to make love to me, until he sank deep within my body making the pain go away. But I didn't. I eased my head to his chest softly and allowed the love I was feeling for this man to grow.

Chance ordered enough food to feed an army. I was stuffed. For the past several hours I had listened as Chance told me about his life, his family, his ex-wife. These were safe topics. Nothing dealing with the paranormal. He had yet to tell me of the incident that had changed his life.

It was late, after midnight, when I decided to leave. Chance had not indicated that he wanted me to stay. I stood. "I guess I should be leaving now." I watched Chance's lanky body rise from the floor.

"Stay with me tonight."

"I thought…"

"There's more than one way to spend the night together. I want to fall asleep with you in my arms and awake to find you still there."

"Is your bed one from a past life?"

He laughed out loud, my reactions to the rest of his home laid bare in my question. I couldn't take knowing that one more item this man possessed had been shared by the two of us sometime in the past. For tonight I'd gone as far as I could. Talking about Viola was more than enough for my psyche to handle at the moment.

"My bed is not an antique, but we are."

When I glared playfully up at him he swung me up into his arms and carried me toward his bedroom. I couldn't remember the last time Larry had done that. I blinked twice, realizing what I had done.

I had to distance myself from what I was doing. I had to forget about my marriage and I had to forget Larry, at least for now.

I lay shivering in expectation as Chance undressed me slowly, kissing my body in reverence. These were not the actions of a man that didn't intend to make love. I was finally in only my panties when he stopped. He pulled the covers over our bodies and spooned his muscular hard body around me.

"Goodnight, Michelle."

He kissed the back of my neck and before long I heard his soft snores. I smiled to myself, not feeling in the least bit let down. Instead, I pushed against him, wedging my behind into his crotch. This was enough for now.

I awoke from a dream feeling more at peace than I could ever recall being. I opened my eyes slowly and smiled. Chance was propped on his elbow staring down at me. Sometime during the night he must have taken off his shirt because his chest was bare.

I shifted to get a better look at him before searching for the clock. Five A.M. Something had awakened me. I thought it was the ringing of a phone, but wasn't sure.

"Thank you," Chance whispered.

"Why are you thanking me?" I absently ran my hand down the side of my body, going to the vee between my thighs, allowing my fingers to search for any telltale wetness.

"I'm thanking you for staying the night." His smile was broad. "What did you think I was thanking you for? Did you think perhaps I had molested you in your sleep?"

"Your bed is so comfortable," I answered, ignoring his comment and the reason for my blushing.

"You really think so?"

I blushed even deeper. Chance was looking at me in a manner that left no doubt in my mind that he wanted me.

"What time do you have to be in the office?" I asked, my voice husky with desire.

"I'm thinking of taking the day off, that is, if you can spend it with me."

He reached his hand toward me, touching my hair, caressing my face. I fell back on the pillows feeling wanton and wicked. I was on vacation from my life.

"I thought you said you'd never abandon your patients even for me?"

"And I meant it. There is such a thing as having another doctor cover your patients. I can easily have a cardiologist friend take over my office. God knows, I've done it for him often enough." He picked up the phone. "By the way how long will your husband be gone?"

"Another ten days," I answered and watch the wide grin that filled his face as he dialed the phone securing coverage for his patients. My breath caught in my throat and I swallowed.

"Michelle, you have a strange look on your face. What are you thinking about?"

"I'm thinking about how I want you to call me something else." I watched his lips curl into a smile.

"Are we playing let's pretend? Will this make it easier for you to be with me?"

"Yes. Do you mind?"

"Why should I? This is the first time I've known you as Michelle."

I'll admit, I was more than curious. I wasn't entirely convinced that I believed Chance, but I knew I wanted to. I wanted a reason for the fluttering of my heart. I desperately needed a reason for throwing my marriage down the toilet, for betraying Larry. I stopped myself. If I dwelled on my husband I would get up and leave and that I didn't want to do. Wrong or right I wanted to stay with Chance…for now.

"What names did you call me before?" The question slipped out without much thought. Now that it had, I waited breathless to see what he would say. I vaguely remembered the name he'd called me in the hotel the day we met.

"I've known you as several women, all beautiful with beautiful names. Brianna, Smaro, Dimitra…"

Dimitra. Yes, that was the name that seemed so familiar to me. "Dimitra, I like that."

I rolled the name around on my tongue relishing the sound of it. "Call me Dimi." I watched as he smiled at me, his eyes sparkling. "What?"

"That's what I used to call you."

"Chance, you're making this stuff up. Show me proof."

"I'll show you your proof if you'll give me a kiss."

With that he raced over to a cedar chest in the corner. I raised up on one elbow watching him.

"Here," he said, triumphantly handing me a sheaf of papers. I skimmed through what was labeled 'Regression.' I spotted the names Jeremy and Dimitra. My skin started tingling as distant memories began a slow crawl across my skin. I gave the papers back to Chance, not daring to voice what this all meant.

Chance threw the papers into the air and we watched as they fell and scattered around the bed. He was laughing. "I want my kiss," he said, menacingly coming toward me.

"Now?" I nearly screamed. "Before we've brushed our teeth?"

I couldn't imagine doing such a thing. In the entire twenty-six years of our marriage Larry and I had never kissed without brushing first. I found the idea revolting.

Before I could voice my objections I was in Chance's arms and his tongue was in my mouth. I pushed weakly at his chest, but that only caused him to deepen the kiss.

Within a fraction of a second his hand slid down the small mound of my belly and parted my thighs, his fingers slipping in, finding me moist and hot. In that moment I didn't give a damn if I never brushed my teeth again.

He released me from the kiss and I found myself moaning my disappointment. My eyes shut tightly. Then he began at my neck, kissing and licking my skin, the heat from his tongue searing me with a lust that I feared I would pay for later in hell.

He captured the nipple of my left breast between his teeth. I jumped, feeling the pressure that hadn't occurred. He was as gentle as a mama cat carrying her babies. Gentleness I was used to and frankly tired of.

Before the thought had coalesced in my mind, the pressure of his suckling changed. I could feel his own greed taking over, his body entwining with my own until I began to delight in the slight pain. It made me feel alive.

From moment to moment I couldn't tell where his hands or his tongue would be. He covered my entire body, three, maybe four times, kissing me, loving me, until I was weak with wanting him.

When I thought I couldn't possibly take any more I felt him again parting my thighs. When I felt his hot breath an inch or so from its destination I clamped my legs shut and pushed him away.

I had smelled the heat of my body rising up to my nostrils, carrying the slight musty odor from being in panties all night and the juices his ministration had caused to flow.

"No, Chance, I need a shower."

He pushed my hands away and opened my legs again. "You need me."

"Don't, Chance." It was too late. His tongue had slipped inside of me and he was lavishing me with pleasure beyond belief. I could feel him blowing his breath into my moist flesh. I heard his sharp intake of breath as he sucked it back into his body.

My body began a rhythmic convulsing, the likes of which I had never experienced, not even the first time we had made love. I heard a woman's high pitched screams and wondered briefly if she needed help, but the pleasure coursing through my body quickly took away any concern I had for her. Somewhere inside, I knew the screams were my own.

When at last only tiny quivers remained, I opened my eyes. My hands were twisted in Chance's hair and I was holding on so tightly I knew it had to hurt. I released him, ashamed of my actions.

His head remained where it was, making me wonder when he would expect me to return the delicious favor. Thing was, I hated fellatio.

Larry and I had tried it several times but mostly it was reserved for really special occasions like making up. And since we didn't have many fights we didn't do it that often. Our on-going feud over Viola hadn't warranted that kind of making up, not yet. However, Chance was different. He didn't know about my dislikes. He'd know soon enough. The very thought of taking Chance, in my mouth…he also needed a shower. And unlike him, I found I couldn't overlook that fact.

My body settled into a dreamy, relaxed after glow. Even if I was willing to give Chance what he'd given me in such abundance, I was too tired. Part of me felt like such a depraved pig for so greedily enjoying myself. It was this that prompted me to ask despite my reservation, "Would you like me to do you?"

Chance started laughing. He came toward me bringing the smell of my body with him. He kissed me and I tasted my juices on his lips.

"Dimi, the look on your face tells me you'd rather suck on a stick of dynamite or take a lethal dose of poison."

He continued laughing, his head landing with a thud on the pillow behind him. He pulled me close, his arms wrapped around me.

"Baby, this one was for you. You don't have to ever do anything with me that you're uncomfortable with."

I made a weak attempt at moving, not wanting to sever the connection of extreme peace. I had been truly made love to and I didn't want to do anything, not even make love to him in return, not then. The moment was too blissful to end.

So I took the time for myself, for Chance, the husband I'd left behind in another life. I practically lived with Chance while Larry was gone. I went home only to change clothes. I avoided looking at any of the dozens of pictures of the occupants of the house. I couldn't allow myself to be pulled into their world.

I would get the mail like a robot and toss it on the kitchen counter. It was all addressed to either Michelle or Larry Powers. I was sure one of them would take care of it. I was Dimitra.

"I've got a surprise for you."

Chance was grinning at me as I lay in bed contented. I stretched lazily, feeling like a hungry cat. I liked this woman Dimitra. She was comfortable in her body and she was happy to have the man who'd given her this freedom grinning down at her.

"What's your surprise?" I looked up at him, not caring that my time of being Dimitra was drawing to a close.

"There's a big seminar tonight in Elk Grove. They have this medium there, Blaine MaDia. I'm not familiar with the name, but I hear he's pretty good.

"He's rumored to talk to the dead. Tonight I hear he's going to do something different. He's going to delve into reincarnation."

My skin started to burn. I looked down to find the source. I ran my left hand over my right arm and pulled back from the heat coursing through me. I was afraid and my fear had come alive, burning my very flesh.

"Chance...," I began. "I don't know."

"Why not? He might be able to tell you what you were doing when you had your accident. What if he's the key to this prison you've put yourself in?"

I began to shiver. Everything in me was telling me to avoid this Blaine character like the plague. When I Looked at Chance, his eyes held such a mixture of love and worry that it began to melt my resolve.

Of course I knew what he was hoping for, some way to prove to me that this life he so vehemently insisted we'd shared was real.

"What if-"

"What if you find out I've been telling you the truth? Is that what frightens you so much? Are you worried that you're going to be forced into making a decision?"

"Chance, I only want to remember what I was doing before I hit Viola. It's hard enough living this life. I don't have time to worry about what I did or didn't do in another one."

I fell back on the pillows, flinging my arms over my face, trying to shut out Chance's penetrating glance. As always, he had known what I was thinking.

I felt him take my arm in his hand and massage the spot that was burning. A ripple of pleasure went all the way through me. "How do you always know what I need?"

"I listen," he answered me, "to your voice, your eyes, to your body."

"What if I tell you that I don't want to go, that I'm not ready?"

"Then we don't go. It's as simple as that."

He lowered his body until he was inches from me. I felt the warmth of his breath on my cheeks. His eyes bore into me. He had the most unusual expression on his face.

"Why are you so worried about my reactions? Is this the way you've lived this lifetime, worrying about someone else's feelings, ignoring your own?"

I looked away from him, from the eyes that gave me no concealment. I closed my eyes, ignoring him and his questions. The kisses on the back of my neck made me smile.

"You want to eat in?" he asked.

I could see the hunger in his eyes. His hunger was for me. I looked at him marveling at how easily he'd shoved his plans aside. He was so different from Larry. Larry would have harped on the subject until I gave in.

"You're too good to be true, Chance. There has to be some chink in your armor. I think you're humoring me."

I looked down my nose at him, the way I had at my children when they were small and I was grilling them. "Is this how you get what you want from me, Chance, by pretending you're happy with whatever I want?"

He laughed out loud, the sound sending warmth to my heart. I didn't join in. I was curious, wondering if perhaps this time I'd struck a nerve. Was laughter his cover? Why didn't I know him as well as he seemed to know me?

"Michelle, you're so damn suspicious," he laughed. "Why don't I try and find my ex-wife's address. She hates me for divorcing her, for what she said was an idiotic reason. But I do believe she'll tell you that I don't play games.

"I'm not trying to manipulate you. I got the tickets to the thing because I thought you might want to go. I made a mistake. I should have asked you first."

Oh my God. I thought I had died and gone to heaven. A man admitting he'd made a mistake. "What time is this thing?"

"Eight."

I looked at the clock. It was early, just a couple of minutes after six. There was plenty of time if we wanted to go, yet I had to test Chance, see if he meant it didn't matter.

"Why don't we order dinner and eat in?" I watched as a smile curled his lips and the hunger came back in his eyes. *He was telling the truth*, I thought to myself. *He wasn't trying to get me to go. It doesn't matter to him if I go or not.*

By eight-thirty we'd taken care of all our appetites. I lay in Chance's arm, satisfied. "Why don't we take a quick shower and catch the last part of that medium's act?" I intentionally said medium sarcastically.

He looked at me. "We don't have to do that," he muttered into my mouth. "In fact, I'm happy just where I am."

I gave him a quick kiss, then pushed him away and bounded out of the bed. "No, I want to go," I answered him, realizing I meant it. I really did want to go. Whatever the reason I was afraid to go it was the same reason propelling me to go. Strange but true.

"It's late. It will probably be over by the time we get there," Chance answered me.

"And if it is, it wasn't meant to be." I bent to give him a hasty kiss on the lips.

Damn, where is she? Larry had not expected Mick to be anywhere but home. If he'd had to bet money on it, he would have sworn she would call him back.

He knew his wife. She hated it when anyone was mad at her. She couldn't stand the silence. He knew she went crazy with boredom when he wasn't home.

That's what the old Michelle did. Larry wondered where those thoughts kept coming from. The old and the new Michelle. What the hell was that all about? There was only one.

Granted, she had become unpredictable. When he got home the first thing he was going to do was drag her to the doctor, kicking and screaming if he had to. He was going to get her started on hormones. That was what she needed. And if that didn't work? He hesitated, hoping to never have to deal with the possibility of the hormones not helping.

Larry tightened his grip on the phone. The damn thing had been ringing for ten minutes straight. Where the hell could she be? He'd been calling constantly since five A.M. It was now after eight P.M. Chicago time.

He knew for damn sure it wasn't that she was sleeping or showering. Mick could hear a phone ring in her sleep or when she had the shower going full blast.

Where could she be? He thought to call the cops and have them check out his home, but he stopped short of doing that. If his wife was in trouble he would surely sense it.

He didn't want to, but he could not help remembering what she'd said about having an affair. Larry smiled nervously to himself.

That had been a joke, something he'd planted in her head. She was probably sitting there looking at the caller ID and refusing to answer. That would explain it. It would also explain why she didn't have the answering machine on. As soon as he returned home he was getting voice mail and cell phones for them both.

Larry hung the phone up at last. Calling his wife every half hour wasn't doing him any good. He paced the rooms of his daughter's home feeling the dread build. He wanted to be home. For a moment he thought of waking his grandchildren and taking them home with him. To hell with Mick's demands that they not come.

When his eyes landed on his daughter's collection, an icy chill wrapped around his heart and traveled throughout his body until he was shivering from it. He could only pray that he'd not waited too long to open his eyes.

Chapter Six

I sat next to Chance in a jam-packed room twice the size of any banquet room I'd ever been in. We sat near the front, grateful for two seats together. I glanced around the room at the rapt expressions on the faces of the audience. Looking at them, a person would think that the Messiah had come again.

I focused my attention on the speaker. He was tall, at least six feet, maybe more, and he was pale. There was something eerily translucent about his skin. It almost appeared to glow. That had to be my imagination. I was not as enthralled with him as the rest of his audience seemed to be.

I looked around the room for the source of the light that had to be shining on his body. No one, but no one, had skin that glowed. My body began to tingle as I saw a current of electricity arc from the speaker's body. It rose high into the air. I watched as the current hit Chance, then me.

I fell back against my chair. Chance's arm was there. I could feel him rubbing my back as I fought for breath. What the heck had just happened? I sucked in the now electrified air and brought my head back up in time to see the electrical current retreat into the speaker's body.

I watched as he stumbled and fell halfway to the floor, bent over, writhing as though in pain. He lifted his face and looked around the immense room. I saw the same look of fear reflected in his eyes that was radiating through my bones.

"Chance, what was that?" I whispered hoarsely, feeling an unknown panic building within me. I wanted to run from the room, but this mysterious voice inside my head urged me to stay, to listen.

"I don't know what you're talking about," Chance whispered back. His eyes had darkened to a stormy blue with concern. "Are you all right? Do you want to leave?" he asked.

"Did you see the current, did you feel it? You had to, it hit you first." I could tell he had no idea what I was talking about.

I looked around the room. The only two people who seemed to be aware that something out of the ordinary had happened were the speaker and me.

The speaker was standing upright now. He scanned the room quickly, muttered an apology, stating he needed a drink of water, and left the stage.

If I wanted to leave, now was the time. I was holding Chance's hand so tightly that when I loosened my grip I saw the print of my sharp nails in his flesh. "I'm sorry," I offered.

He kissed my hand. "What got you spooked? What happened?"

"I'm not sure. There was this energy that came from the speaker. It looked sort of like lightning. It hit you, then me."

I put my hand out to show him how it had moved, and my hand hit an invisible force field. I touched the seemingly empty air, feeling a strange yet intense energy.

It was completely surrounding the two chairs where Chance and I sat. That much I knew. I got up and walked around first to the back, then to the front, putting my hand out along the way feeling for this energy.

Chance was watching me, a worried expression on his face. The other people in the room smiled at my odd behavior, making me wonder if we'd all been hypnotized. I went back to my seat beside Chance. "Pinch me," I begged.

"What?"

"Pinch me, damn it, pinch me now!" My voice was loud, too loud, people were starting to turn and stare at me. I didn't care. This was the moment I had known my entire life would one day come. I had gone completely insane.

"Pinch me, Chance."

He did, so gently that it wasn't giving me what I needed to awake.

"Pinch me harder," I demanded in a harsh voice.

He pinched me harder. I felt it. I put my hand in front of me, praying that the force field had moved away. It hadn't. I felt the tears coursing down my cheeks. I took Chance's hand in mine and placed it at the barrier.

"Don't you feel that?" I cried. "You have to feel it."

He was rising to leave. "Michelle, let's go. I don't know what happened, but I think we should leave."

"We can't," I said, convinced now that I had to stay. *Oh Lord, what has happened to my reasoning*? All these people only minutes before I had written off as being insane, thinking they would make the perfect cult followers, and now here I was acting the craziest of all.

The speaker came back out after a few minutes. I watched as he looked out into the audience. I knew he was searching for me. He closed his eyes, shook his head and began again going from person to person telling each about their deceased loved one.

I could feel the rapid pounding of my heart slow with each tale he wove. I now felt safe. This was hooey. I didn't know what had happened before, but I was no longer buying his act.

One after the other, the audience members cried out as he told them snippets of information. *Nothing important*, I thought. I would want to know where the treasure is buried, what the winning number to the million dollar lottery is, something that could help me.

I breathed a sigh of relief before turning to Chance. "It's okay, it must have been my imagination. This guy's a fake," I whispered in his ear.

Blaine MaDia turned from the person he was talking to and glared directly at me.

"Do you really believe that?"

Oh God, they must have hidden microphones all over the place. That had to be it. That's how he knew.

"There are no hidden microphones."

Blaine was answering a question I had not asked. I clutched Chance's hand tightly. "Let's go," I cried out, ignoring the voices telling me to stay. The speaker was now walking toward me.

"I wasn't going to do this," Blaine said. "Not like this. You forced me."

When he was directly in front of me, he reached his hand out to touch me and immediately fell away, bending down once again.

"It is you. You're the one."

"No, I'm not." I cried out my lie. "Chance, don't let him touch me."

The place became filled with noise as the audience attempted to adjust to what was happening. Chance was attempting to place his body between Blaine and me, trying to block off his contact with me, when he was thrown back by an unknown force.

"What the…" He looked at me, puzzled.

I looked at Blaine. My head was hurting from a fierce banging inside. I was about to lose consciousness. I could feel it.

"Mommy, don't go, don't leave me again," Blaine wailed in the voice of a child as tears fell from his eyes.

"Don't call me that." He gripped my arm as we both fell to our knees. I leaned into him for support. He opened his hand to me and I clasped it, not wanting to.

Immediately I was thrust into another realm. I was lying on the floor, my body covered in rags. I saw blood, bright red as it poured from my body. My hands were covered in it. I grimaced at the sticky feel of it on my thighs as it pooled around me. A burst of pain shot through my abdomen, then traveled the length of my spine, going to the top of my head and reversing until it went all the way to the tips of my toes.

I was reaching a bloody hand for more rags, shoving them between my legs. I could barely mutter the words, "Jeremy, save the baby."

It was only then that I noticed a man working frantically over my body. His sobs were so loud I don't know how I had missed him. "I want to save you," he moaned over and over, lifting my legs slightly, rubbing them. He was screaming for someone to get the mystic.

"It's too late for the healer," I wanted to tell him. "It's no longer any use." I could feel my spirit preparing to leave my body.

Jeremy was shaking me, only it was Chance's face I saw. I was confused. This man was known as Jeremy to me. He was my husband. He was shaking me, trying by the sheer force of his will to get me to stay.

"Dimitra, don't leave me, don't leave, oh dear God! I can't live without you. Please don't leave me. I love you."

"Hush, my love," I whispered to him, not able to speak more loudly. "What God has joined together, death will not put asunder. I'll wait for you in the next life. I promise."

"I don't want to find you in the next life. I want you here with me now. Don't leave me, Dimitra."

"Jeremy, I have no choice. Take care of our son."

"I can't, Dimi. How can I look at him? How can I love him? It's his fault that you're dying." He looked down at his bloody hands. "Oh my God, it's my fault that you're dying."

"Jeremy, don't blame yourself, I wanted with all my heart to give you a son and I have. Don't blame the baby. Promise me you won't blame the baby, promise me you'll love and take care of him until we're together again."

I felt the pain begin to leave my body. I knew I didn't have much time, but with my dying breath I wanted to extract promises from the husband I was leaving behind.

"Jeremy, we've never broken our promises. Promise me you'll love the baby."

"I promise," he sobbed.

"Promise me you won't let death cheat us of our love. Promise me you'll find me in the next life and the one after that."

"I promise."

"Good."

I felt coldness such as I'd never known. I shivered and Jeremy gathered me into his arms, rocking me gently against his chest, crying, covered with my blood. He was in agony. I wished with all my heart I could relieve his suffering, but it wasn't up to me.

I smiled weakly at him then. "Tell our son I love him." With my last strong breath I whispered, "I love you, Jeremy. I'll love you throughout eternity and I'll wait for you. I promise."

Then my cold lips closed over those of my newborn son and I breathed my last breath, into him, praying he would know how much I loved him, giving him his birthright, my gifts.

The moment I felt my spirit leave my body, I blinked. I looked into Chance's face and saw Jeremy. He was holding Blaine by the collar, shoving him away from me. His fist was thrust out, getting ready to strike him.

"No, Chance. Don't hit him." I looked at Blaine MaDia and though I pushed my body away from him, I could not tear my eyes from his face. There was so much sorrow in his gaze. He glanced at Chance, then back at me.

"You kept your promises. You've found each other again."

For a long moment I looked from him to Chance, not believing what had happened. Surely it had to be a trick. This couldn't mean what it seemed to. I thought about my own dreams of a man with Chance's face. I couldn't take any more.

"Chance, let's go."

"Don't go," Blaine pleaded with me. "I'm sorry for what I did. We need to talk, please. I've been hoping this would happen, but I never believed it would. I know who you are. You're my mother. I'm your son, the baby you just remembered. I know you know what I'm saying is the truth."

Blaine glanced at Chance and smiled. "He's my father. Mother, I can't believe we've found each other. Please wait until the program is over."

"I'm sorry, I can't." He attempted to reach for me. "No," I screamed, panicked at the thought of him touching me again.

I nearly ran out of the room, ignoring Blaine's calls for me to stay. My life as I knew it would never be the same. With every fiber of my being I knew this and I was terrified.

"Michelle, what happened back there?"

We were in the car. Chance was holding me in his arms trying to coax me to talk. My chest was filled to overflowing with grief which rocked me to my very soul. All I could do was hold on to Chance and sob.

I don't know how long we stayed in the car locked together in sorrow and confusion. I was sick to my stomach. The pounding that had begun in my head when I was hit by the bolt of energy continued. Only now it was worse.

"Tell me what happened."

Chance tilted my face toward him. I saw worry for me etched across his face. I didn't want to tell him what had happened. I worried he wouldn't believe me.

I gathered my courage at last. "When MaDia held on to my hand, I thought I saw something. I'm not sure." I looked down, away from Chance's eyes. I felt a bubble of hysteria trying to take over my thoughts. I fought to remain sane. Maybe if I said the words, if I told Chance, it would make sense.

"I saw a couple. The woman was dying in childbirth." Chance pulled back from me.

"What were their names?"

"Jeremy and…and…Dimitra."

I looked up to see Chance's eyes close. He had a rapt expression on his face.

"I knew it was you."

He began kissing me, crying, the salt from his tears falling onto my parted lips. My body started trembling. Nothing I did stopped it.

"What did he do to me, Chance? Why did I see those things?"

"I'm not sure. It sounds like it could have been a regression."

"I didn't ask him to regress me. Besides, I thought you told me it's usually done through deep meditation, or even sleep induced. I was doing neither. He just touched me. How could that happen?"

"I don't know." He pulled away slightly. "I'm not even sure that's what happened. It just sounds like it. I'm as much in the dark as you are on this one. What else did you see?"

"There was a baby. A boy, but I don't know for sure if he was alive. No one was helping him, he wasn't crying." My tears joined Chance's then as a monumental stab of pain pierced my heart.

"He said he's our son. I heard him. Do you think Blaine MaDia is…do you think he's our…?" Chance's voice held hope and his eyes were filled with love and longing.

"Don't, Chance. I don't want to think about this anymore or talk about it. The whole thing is too strange. Why me, Chance? Why didn't he do this with anyone else in the room? Why only me?"

"You know why."

"I don't know." I lied to him and myself. "When we went in there I felt sorry for all those people wanting to contact the dead, believing in all this. I thought they were all fools and he'd tricked them somehow. I'm just not sure what happened. What if this was staged?"

"How would he have known about Jeremy and Dimitra?"

I looked at Chance but I didn't answer. His head tilted away from me as his eyes probed me with an intensity that reached the core of my being.

"I can't believe you'd think I put him up to this," he whispered hoarsely.

I broke the connection of our eyes. I couldn't look at him and give him the answer that was swirling around in my head. "You have to admit the way we met is pretty strange."

"You think I'd go to such lengths to get a woman in my bed?"

His voice was low and guttural, anger fighting with pain. I wasn't trying to strike out at him. I was only trying to preserve my own sanity. "You got the tickets," I muttered under my breath.

"You're right, I got the tickets," he answered me. He rubbed his palms across his eyes, and then he licked his lips. He kept opening and closing his mouth and his fist. His head moved from side to side in agitation. I knew he was hurting. I also knew he hadn't done what I had accused him of.

"What about that electrical arc you told me about? You said that it hit me first, then you. I didn't see it. I've never seen anything like that or even heard of this happening. If there's a connection, I'd say it's between you and Blaine MaDia."

I wanted to forget about the arc of energy as I wanted to forget about the tremendous connection I felt for the medium. It was different than the connection I felt with Chance.

With Blaine it was love in its purest form. With this newest stranger to enter my life, I felt an overwhelming sense of loss and unbearable pain. And I felt something more. It was an all-consuming guilt. I felt guilt that I had denied him, shoved him from my memories and guilt now that I had left him once again. My heart felt he was my son, the baby I'd dreamed of since childhood. How could this be possible?

"Why don't we go back in? You can talk to him. If he can make you see things merely by touching you, perhaps he can take you back to the accident with Viola. Maybe he can show you what you were doing in the seconds before it happened."

I could feel the hysterical laughter as it bubbled up once again and made its way out of my throat. *Have Blaine MaDia touch me again? Not in a thousand lifetimes.* "Take me home, Chance."

He started the car, his eyes sad and his mouth tense. He glanced toward me, not meeting my eyes. "I'm sorry I got the tickets, sorry I asked you to go."

I turned from him to stare out the window. With the slightest effort I could still feel the pain and loss of my other self.

"*Mommy, please don't leave me again.*" The words rang out in my soul, each piercing me with pain. Was it really possible that Blaine MaDia was my son from a previous life?

Why not? I thought to myself. *If Chance can be your husband, Blaine sure can be the baby you gave birth to.* I felt my eyes fill with tears, wondering what kind of life my son had had. *My son*, I thought, *Blaine's my son*. I wanted to stop thinking about what had been. It hurt too much.

"Dimi, are you okay?"

I could clearly hear Jeremy calling out to his Dimi not to leave him, not to die. I clutched Chance's hand in my own, overcome with unbearable grief.

"Don't call me that right now. And don't ever mention what happened today." With that I closed my eyes and shut Chance and Blaine out of my world for the moment.

My time of freedom had come to an end. I knew I could no longer pretend to be Dimitra, the woman in Chance's past. In less than twelve hours my husband would return and I would once again have to go back to being a reasonably sane, responsible, mature adult. I could barely remember my years of being Michelle.

I lay next to Chance in his huge bed, caressing his flaccid penis. It was beautiful, all silky and shiny. I'd grown to love it almost as I'd grown to love the man. It was only the night before that I'd decided that I wanted to taste all of him.

He'd made no demands on me. He did as I had asked and never brought up our visit to Blaine MaDia. Instead he held me each night with a determination I could sense.

He was going to put a lifetime of loving into the time we had left. He'd continued to give, laughing away my weak objections until I no longer pretended that I didn't want him to do the things he was doing to me.

I wanted him. The feel of his hands, his lips, his tongue, but most of all the comforting familiarity he gave me nudged me forward. That and my own guilt over not talking to him about Blaine.

I wanted to give him something I'd never willingly given anyone. We had made love and showered together afterwards. We were just lying there, not talking, enjoying the silence.

The thought of slipping back into my old life depressed the hell out of me. How could I give Chance up? I moved my head to his abdomen and began kissing him, teasing little kisses, not meant to arouse.

His penis quivered and I smiled to myself at the power of my kisses on this man. I took him in my hand examining him, every bump along the ridge of his now hardening shaft. I felt the texture, the softness.

Then I noticed the glistening liquid that had formed around the tip. I touched it, not feeling revolted in the least. I inserted my finger in my mouth, licking away the fluid, wanting to taste that part of Chance.

Before either of us knew what was happening I slid down and took Chance in my mouth. He attempted to push me away.

"You don't have to do that," he moaned.

"I know," I answered him. "That's why I want to."

I found myself running my tongue up and down the length of him, not being able to get enough, quickly enough.

I was behaving like a child at play with a new toy. There was nothing I didn't like about it. The feel, the smell, the taste, the feeling of power as I learned what would bring him to his ultimate climax and what would slow it. I almost swooned with the sheer wonder of it.

A feeling of sadness began to mingle with the power and I felt a crushing sensation in my chest. This would be all that I would ever be able to give Chance. This was not my life.

I felt the beginning of his release. It began much as the rumble of a volcano. His grunts of pleasure, primal. His hands twisted in my hair trying to pull me up as he growled, "I can't hold it back any longer." I wanted so much to take his seed inside me in this manner.

I did attempt to do it, but the force of his release and the hot, thick, salty liquid caused me to gag and pull away. I did hold him in my hand as he came, stroking him as his body jerked toward completion.

When he was still at last, I slid into his arms and held him tightly, crying softly for what I had lost, for what I had found, and for what I would lose once again.

"Dimi, don't cry, it's not over. I won't let it be."

He was holding me so tightly I found it impossible to breathe. "You have no choice, Chance. I have no choice."

"Why? Haven't you ever heard of the word divorce?"

"I can't just walk away. We have a life together, five children, grandchildren."

"And you'll still have those things. Dimitra, I never lied to you. You've known all along that I was looking for you. For you, Dimi, not an affair."

He pulled away from me. He was right. I'd allowed him to believe I was willing to give him what he needed by my actions of the

past nine days. I had in essence abandoned my family. Why shouldn't he think I intended a future for the two of us?

I glanced at the clock. Seven A.M. "Chance, we don't have much time. Please, let's not spoil it."

He looked at me for a long time, not speaking, just looking. My stomach began to knot up.

"Shall I go back to calling you Michelle? Can you so easily forget who you really are? How are you going to get your answers, Michelle?"

I cringed a little at his steady attempts to incorporate our past and present. I knew it was a deliberate move on his part. I didn't want to be Michelle. For Chance I wanted to be Dimitra. The Dimitra of his past.

"Don't worry, I'll get the answers."

"How are you going to do that?"

Damn, I thought to myself. How am I going to do that? Chance had tried several times to introduce me to regression therapy. I'd refused, not wanting anything to get in the way of our stolen happiness. Somewhere within myself I knew the nine days we'd spent in heaven would never be duplicated.

I cringed inwardly. I'd wasted so much time, so many opportunities when I could have accepted Chance's help.

He could have helped me find out what I was doing in the few seconds before I hit Viola. For a moment I wished we had tried regression. But after that debacle with Blaine, there was no way I'd wanted him to even broach the subject.

Chance had introduced me to a love so powerful that I believed it could survive the ages. And he'd given me pleasure and by so doing taught me to give him pleasure in return. But leaving my life forever? That I'd never meant to do. I'd only intended to take a little vacation.

"How can you let me go?"

"I have to. I never meant this to be forever."

"But you did," Chance objected. "You made me promise to find you. You vowed you would wait for me."

I sat up then and returned his look. "The past nine days will be hard enough for me to explain. What do you think my husband would do if I told him I wanted to make it permanent?"

"He can't stop you. He doesn't own you."

"He doesn't own me, but I made promises to him also. He has a right to expect me to keep those promises. Besides, Chance, I'm a big part of his life. What would he do without me?"

I looked away from Chance. "Larry doesn't know the first thing about taking care of the house or paying the bills."

For the first time in weeks guilt assailed my conscience. I had sent Larry away to care for two small children alone. He was ill equipped for the job.

"You're thinking about your husband now, is that it, Michelle? He's coming home and now you want me to vanish into the background."

I watched as he climbed out of the bed, his back to me. He was wrong. I didn't want him to fade into the background. What was I supposed to do, meet a man I'd loved for more than half of my life at the airport with divorce papers?

"You don't have to worry, Michelle. I told you I would never force you to do anything and that includes loving me."

Ouch. "If you meant that to hurt, Chance, it did."

He turned and gave me the oddest look before asking, "Is this a game to you?"

I watched the differing emotions swirling across his face. I had been flippant on purpose. I wanted him to react as Larry would have. I wanted him to give me the silent treatment. That I would have been able to handle. I could have walked away from Chance and never looked back.

He walked toward me, a puzzled look on his face. He stopped only when there was no longer any space separating us.

"I promised to be your friend. That offer still stands. We've loved through many lifetimes and we found each other again in this one. That reason alone makes me happy."

He wasn't happy. We both knew it. He was hurting, but had decided not to burden me with his pain.

"Chance, Larry doesn't deserve this."

"I know he doesn't. Then again, neither do we. I wish I could say I'm sorry I didn't stop us, but it would be a lie. I'm not. I am sorry that you're now feeling remorse that you allowed me to love you, that you allowed yourself to love me. The last thing I want for you is to have you feeling guilty over leaving me."

I watched as he attempted a smile. As always, he was right about my feelings. I was consumed with guilt. In the back of my mind I'd known this moment would come. Still, I'd allowed him to shower me with love.

I'd devoured it and him, taking, hoarding it away to last me during my remaining years with Larry. I was no better than a common thief.

"Don't be sad." He smiled warmly at me. "At least I found you. I know now I'm not crazy, that the last twenty years I've spent alone has been worth it."

He touched a finger to my lips, his eyes locking with my own. "If you like, I'll still help you figure things out about Viola.

"That's as far as I think you should go with this regression. After you find what you need I want you to be happy with your life. At least we can still see each other as friends. I can still see you in my office. As for our being together, well..." He looked away. "As long as you're back in my life, I'll wait. I'm sure we'll meet again in another life."

"Chance." I fell against his chest sobbing.

"Shh. It's going to be fine," he crooned in my ear. "You'll see. We'll both do what we need to do."

"You know I can't see you again after today."

"What are you talking about? Of course we're going to see each other. What about your job? You have to come to the office."

"We don't have to see each other. You can sign the authorization and I'll leave the samples with the nurse. I could even mail them."

I watched Chance as he looked at me. There seemed to be pity in his eyes. *Why should he pity me?* I wondered. *Had I made my life appear so unbearable that he'd gotten love confused with pity?*

An image of the day we met flashed before me. I had been a mess that day. Yes, he would pity me, but that was not what I wanted from this man. And definitely not on the last day I would see him.

"Chance, I don't like the way you're looking at me. What are you thinking?"

"I'm thinking that life is so unfair. You're asking something of me that I don't know if I can give you. I've been searching so long for you and now you want me to forget I've found you"

He smiled then. It was my turn to take the bait. At least the veil of pity was lifting from his eyes and a hint of a smile was in evidence.

"It would have all been so simple if I had met you twenty years ago when I discovered that you existed."

"You forget I was already married."

"But maybe you wouldn't have felt so bound to your husband; maybe your memories of our life together would have been stronger. Life is so unfair. Why weren't we born remembering?"

I thought over what he was saying. I didn't want to think of my marriage as some cruel trick fate had played on us.

Before Chance came along I had thought that I was a wee bit crazy to think that I had lived before. I had only admitted to an occasional feeling of suffocation that had increased in frequency and duration with the passing of the years.

I couldn't really say what it was, but to think that I had wasted the last twenty-six years of my life, I didn't like it.

"I wanted to marry Larry. I believed then he was my destiny. I still believe it."

"You wanted to die, Michelle! Do you remember that? Why are you insisting that you have to stay in a marriage that had you looking for a permanent way out? I wonder what would have happened to you if I had not been the one you met that day in the parking lot."

"But you were the one I met."

He stared at me for a long moment, his eyes narrowing into slits.

"You don't really believe me, do you?" He smiled at my attempts to deny the truth. It didn't seem to bother him.

"I know you don't believe me. You don't even believe what you saw and felt for yourself. Yet you're here with me now. I can feel that you love me, yet you tell me that you're going to remain in a marriage that was killing you. In all the lives that I've known you, this is the first time I've witnessed you weak."

My face was burning from the shame he'd stirred in me. I swallowed several times, my mouth feeling twice its size, my tongue thick. "I'm not weak."

"I'm afraid in this lifetime you are. You've told me about your life. What do you call it?"

"Marrying Larry wasn't a wrong choice."

"No, but remaining with him is."

"Chance, you know nothing of our lives. You know nothing about Larry, the pain he's had to overcome." I was angry and defensive. Despite what I was doing I was bound to protect Larry from Chance's scrutiny.

"I've been watching you, Michelle. You worry too much about what others think, about pleasing people even if it makes you unhappy. Dimi never would have put up with an unhappy marriage for so many years."

"I'm not Dimi, Chance. My name's Michelle and my marriage is just fine. We're happy."

"Is that why you've spent the last nine days in my bed, because your marriage is so damn happy?"

Had he shouted or looked angry I could have at least pretended righteous indignation, but he did none of that. He was looking at me, saying these things with as much calm as one would ask for a cup of coffee.

I tried again. "Chance, Larry's a good man. He loves me."

"I don't doubt that. You're very easy to love. Yet his love didn't stop you from wanting to die, did it?"

I could see he wasn't going to let that go. "Chance, I can't just walk away from my life. I have..." I bit the words off; the reason seemed too flimsy even for me to say it.

He finished for me. "You have what, obligations? Commitments?"

"Yes." I looked away from him, knowing he was goading me into taking a stand. "You have no way of knowing how complicated my life is, Chance. Larry needs me."

He was staring at me. His dark blue eyes held the very secrets to my soul. I needed him to stop looking at me that way. It was making it damn near impossible to leave him.

"I'm the first woman Larry's ever loved. The only woman. He didn't chase me. I went after him. We made promises to each other. He's kept his promises."

I felt the sting of tears behind my eyes. None of this was any of Chance's business. He didn't need to know that Larry had been abandoned by his mother. How the hell was I supposed to abandon him too?

"He needs me, Chance."

"And you, Michelle, what is it that you need?"

I shut my eyes tight against the smart ass retort that I wanted to give. I couldn't remember ever asking me what I needed.

Countless scenes flashed in my mind of Larry's excited voice. "*Honey, this is just what you needed.*" I always wondered how he knew what I needed when he'd never asked. It would have been fine if the things he'd done were things I had longed for, but they never were.

So I thought over what Chance asked me. "I need to get over the feeling that I'm going crazy, that someone has taken over my body. I need to get over this strange connection I have with you. I need to get over this love I feel for you that's tearing me apart."

I sensed the beginning of tears. God no, I begged. I wanted to do this without turning on the waterworks. "I need to get over this fascination with reincarnation and regression. What does it matter anyway? It can't be proven."

"No? What about Blaine MaDia and the possibility that he's our son?"

I saw the color draining from my hand. The mere mention of Blaine's name was making me ill. "How is knowing it going to change my life? You really want to know what I need, Chance? I need to find my way back to my husband."

We sat on the bed staring at each other. I was so proud that I didn't cry. I would show him that I wasn't weak. When I walked away from him without a backwards glance he could witness my strength. I alone would bear the pain of knowing how much leaving him was robbing me of my spirit.

His head dipped to the side. He appeared to be studying me, making me feel like a specimen under a microscope.

"Then, Michelle, I suggest you go back to your husband. I can't give you what you want. I don't need you in my life. I don't need you to take care of me. I don't need you to shelter me from life. I want you. And I think you…need to be needed. So go back to Larry. He needs you."

I felt the tears sliding down my cheeks. I'd lost my battle not to cry. It all sounded so awful when Chance voiced it. I'd never thought of my marriage in that way. I didn't like what Chance was saying. It wasn't true.

One look in his eyes and I knew he meant it. He thought Larry and I had some sort of sick relationship, that we were somehow co-dependents in our pain. I didn't need to be needed, that wasn't true.

"Why are you crying?" he asked.

What did he expect me to say? He'd ripped my heart out and stepped on it and now he wanted to know why I was crying. I'd destroyed my marriage because of my desire to be with him and now…

I felt awful. I didn't want us to end like this. The past nine days had been what I'd unknowingly longed for my entire life. The words might have been easy for him to say, but they sure weren't easy for me to hear. Chance didn't need me in his life.

To feel pain hearing on him say that didn't make me an emotional cripple. It made me human. To hell with Chance Morgan.

He was looking at me with pity again and the very thought of him pitying me made me want to hit him over the head with a very heavy object.

He attempted to use the pads of his fingers to brush away my tears, but I angrily wrenched myself from his touch. He allowed his hands to drop to his side. He stared at me for a moment, shaking his head slowly, as if trying to decide what to do next.

"You're angry because I said I didn't need you. You're not listening. I said I wanted you. I want you in my life. I want you in my arms. I love you.

"You have no reason to cry," Chance continued. "Do you think I would have devoted twenty years of my life to finding you if I didn't love you? It seems what I found is an imitation of the woman who made me swear to find her, who swore she'd wait an eternity for me. I kept my promise to find you. Now it's up to you to decide if you want to be needed or wanted. It's not my decision. You chose. Are you Dimi, my wife? Or are you Michelle?"

Chapter Seven

Chance Morgan felt the beginning of a severe migraine coming on. He knew what it meant. For a few minutes he could cross over into another time.

He could be rejoined with the woman he'd loved through eternity. In that time they'd had no obstacles to overcome. He was Jeremy and she was Dimitra. They were man and wife. They were free to love.

He resisted the pull. The woman he loved was sitting on his bed in front of him. In the flesh. That was a thousand times better than having her only in his dreams.

He knew he was as bad as she was. He'd accused her of playing the martyr. He had needs of his own, the primary one being to see to it that she got whatever it was in this lifetime that would make her happy. He could only pray that what she needed was him.

If it wasn't, he would give her whatever it took to make her happy. If Larry was what she needed, he wouldn't stop her, but he damn sure intended to give it all he had before he threw in the towel.

It was a little after seven. Larry fed his grandchildren breakfast, cold cereal and fruit. In the middle of talking to the kids something pierced him from the inside. He found himself staring at the children.

He knew.

Mick, his Mick, was having an affair.

His decision was not based on the fact that for a week and a half he'd not heard from her. Nor was it based on the message he'd gotten when he gave in and called her job. She wasn't available. She was on vacation.

Larry had given into the fear and called a neighbor to check on Mick with a phony excuse that he didn't believe the phone was working.

The neighbor reported back that she'd tried several times to tell Michelle Larry wanted to get in touch with her but that she was in and out before she got a chance. Larry thanked the neighbor, telling her that Michelle had called him.

At least he knew his wife was alive. That he'd known anyway. He didn't doubt that if she was hurting, he would feel it, just as he didn't doubt that feeling that now came over him that Mick was with someone else.

She was loving someone other than him. He was blind not to have seen it before. All the signs were there, had been for some time now. Why else wouldn't she allow the kids to come?

He walked into the small bedroom he was using and began packing his clothes. The kids came from the kitchen and began running around his legs. Larry barely saw them; his mind was on leaving.

The three hours he had to wait for Erica's and Roy's return was like a short tour of hell. His hand kept moving toward the phone, stopped only by one of the kids yelling, "Grandpa." He was grateful for those interruptions. It allowed him a little longer to pretend that his life had not been shattered.

I drove home, thinking over what Chance had said, sure that mixed up in all of that were his desires. He was not any different than Larry. He wanted me to give up my life for a dream he'd carried for twenty years.

He knew nothing about the joy on my husband's face when Erica was born, of the tears he'd shed. He knew nothing about the love Larry felt for me. That was one thing I never doubted, Larry's love.

In some ways I did think he was using our lives to make up for his mother's leaving him. I knew his need for a family had to do with that, but

I had never pressed the issue. I'd wanted so much to wipe away all the sadness that the five-year-old I'd never known had endured.

There was something tragic in Larry's face from the first moment I met him. He carried around a sadness in his beautiful brown eyes. He didn't have any friends as far as I knew and his cool manner intrigued me. I thought he needed a friend.

So I'd set out to save him, to be his friend. I didn't know how badly he was in need of someone to love until after we'd made love the first time. Despite Larry's aloofness the last thing I expected was him to be a virgin.

The brevity of our encounter surprised me. It was nothing like I had imagined my first time would be. There was an awful, painful burning, much worse than the worst bladder infection. Then in about three seconds Larry fell on me in a heap. It took me at least five minutes to know that it was over.

Disappointment washed over me in waves. I had waited my entire life and given up my virginity for this. It wasn't worth it. After awhile Larry got off me and rolled to the side of the motel bed we'd rented for the occasion.

I remember the incident as clearly today as if almost twenty-eight years had not passed. For a long time we didn't talk. Larry turned his back on me. I felt my stomach knotting up. I hadn't pleased him either. I cringed at the thought that now I was no longer a virgin.

I heard sobbing. At first I couldn't believe it. When I touched Larry's shoulder's he turned and held me so tightly that I thought something was wrong. I didn't know what to do, but I was becoming afraid of his increasing emotions.

"Larry, what's wrong?" I attempted to console him by stroking his hair, wishing I was anywhere else but in the room with him. I didn't know how to comfort him. I worried that I was so bad that he couldn't handle it. Yet there was something else there beneath it all. I felt I had betrayed someone by making love to Larry. That thought scared me more than Larry's tears.

"I love you, Mick."

That was the first time he'd ever called me Mick. I liked it. I wanted to tell him that I loved him too, but I wasn't sure. I did like him a lot and I enjoyed being with him.

I loved the way he treated me. It was nothing like the way my parents did. He wasn't afraid of me. He didn't think that I was crazy. He always seemed in awe that I was with him, his face lighting up when he saw me coming toward him. It all gave me a good feeling inside.

"Don't ever leave me, Mick."

"Why are you saying that?"

"I couldn't take it if you left me. I need you, Mick. I need you to make my life complete. Promise me, Mick, promise me that you'll never stop loving me. Promise me that you'll never love anyone else, that you'll never give yourself to anyone else. Promise me that you'll never fall out of love with me."

I didn't answer him. I felt scared deep inside. Larry seemed so desperate that I began to pull away. I had never told him I loved him and yet he wanted me to promise him that I would never stop.

That was when Larry told me about his mother. As he talked, I saw the frightened little boy clinging to his mother's skirt. I saw him crying alone in the darkness, blaming himself, not knowing why he was abandoned. I now knew why he was such a loner. That picture of Larry struck a chord in my soul and for some reason I mourned the loss of another little boy who'd not had a mother.

Larry was right. He needed me. There was no way I could let him down. Yet I had a sudden urge to run away. I heard a voice clearly in my head urging me to do just that.

I looked into Larry's tear-stained face. What kind of person was I? He needed me. Then and there I swore I would love Larry always. I would not be the woman his mother was. I would make sure Larry could depend on me.

"Larry, I love you."

He pulled away to look deep into my eyes, searching for the truth. I knew that from the intensity of his gaze. "Larry, I love you," I repeated again. I ignored the voice that was now screaming in my head, telling me to run.

"Do you promise to love me always?"

I thought of his mother, of the five-year-old boy that he had been and my heart broke for him afresh. "I promise that I will love you always."

"You promise me you'll never love anyone else?"

"I promise."

"You promise you'll never let anyone else make love to you?"

I rubbed the tears from his face. I thought of our lovemaking. *Why would I want to repeat that with anyone else? It wasn't that big a deal.*

"I love you, and I promise I'll never love anyone else. I'll never make love to anyone else. I promise."

"Will you marry me, Mick?"

I gasped aloud. My head was swimming. I was so grateful that he wanted to marry me. I wouldn't have to feel ashamed that I'd given myself to just anyone. I would be his fiancée.

"Yes, Larry, I'll marry you." I wound my arms tightly around his neck even as a feeling of panic overcame me. Again, I wanted to run. If I didn't hold on to Larry I would. So I held on to him for dear life.

We made love for the second time. It lasted perhaps thirty seconds longer than the first time. I wondered about all the love stories I had read. For some reason I had thought it was real. I'd had dreams of making love to a tall, dark-haired man. Filled with passion, the dreams left me weak and wanting. Now I knew the dream was just that—a dream. Passion-filled lovemaking was a fantasy.

Our lives continued as we planned. Two years after we met, we finished school and got married. Larry went to law school and I went to work for a major pharmaceutical company. After a couple of years of blissful happiness as newlyweds I became pregnant. That was the moment I can look back on and know it was then when my fears began. Betrayal, pain and sorrow were my daily companion. My childhood dreams of a past lover, a son I'd not gotten a chance to raise came back with full force during my first pregnancy. I found myself grieving for my lost family yet pretending to Larry that everything was fine. I feared I was going insane and worked hard to control my dreams, my agony that was as real to me as Larry's love. Despite my occasional longings to be reunited with my lost family I'd kept my promises to Larry.

There were times when I would dream of the dark-haired lover and awake feeling I had broken my promises to my husband. I blamed myself for not finding more pleasure in my husband's touch. I thought I was crazy to feel that I was cheating on the lover in my dreams. I fought to get over loving a man that didn't exist.

I learned self hypnosis and taught myself not to cringe, to be more receptive. I found that just a small sip of wine heightened my desire, so I would take a drink. It almost worked. He almost touched me in the way I was craving, but I was afraid to say anything.

He needed a simple direction or two, but I didn't know how to tell him. I didn't want to do anything that might make Larry feel bad. I didn't want him to question where I'd learned about such things. How could I tell him that in my dreams I was loving another man?

I came to almost dread our lovemaking, my constantly being brought so near the edge, to be left there as he plunged toward bliss alone. I hid that knowledge deep within myself, afraid that it might be my inability to enjoy lovemaking to the fullest except in my fantasies.

I became adept at pretense. I learned what to do to give my husband satisfaction, what moves to make to make him think I, too, had reached the pinnacle of fulfillment.

How could I explain to Larry that somewhere in my memories there existed another man whose body I craved, whose touch set me on fire and whose very breath made me shiver with sexual desire? I didn't have the words necessary to explain that a phantom had claims on my very soul.

This man lived only in my dreams. I knew that. Yet I wondered why I knew instinctually that it was a different touch I craved. I repeatedly shoved my longings away from me. Larry and I had a good life. We rarely fought, we went out, we made love regularly, we had fun together and we were friends.

Slowly I saw my husband blossom in the knowledge that I would always love him, always be there when he returned home. He was a confident, loving man that always saw qualities in me that I didn't believe I possessed.

Chance was right. I needed Larry every bit as much as he needed me. Without him I would be forced to deal with the fact that I didn't believe I was a nice person inside.

I was a good mother because it was expected of me. I was a good wife because I'd promised. And I'd been a good daughter because I had thought it would make my parents happy, keep them together.

None of it worked. My parents got divorced, my kids were angry with me most of the time now because I was no longer at their beck and call. And my husband was confused. I needed Larry to retain my sanity. Damn my dreams and damn Chance for turning out to be the man in them.

He thought I didn't believe him. I had known from the moment he held me in the rain that he was the man in my dreams. My heart had lurched toward his. I'd called myself crazy when I felt it and him crazy when he spoke of it, but I had known. I couldn't admit any of this to Chance. What would happen to my life if I did? What would happen to the promise I'd made to Larry?

My life was spiraling out of my control. In time I'm sure I would have been able to push Viola to the back of my mind as I'd done with so many things. Being with Chance had changed things. I could no longer pretend, or keep things shoved to the back of my mind. I now knew it would be impossible for me to keep pretending to be the virtuous wife and mother my husband thought me to be.

Somewhere deep within I heard the same voice I had heard many years before telling me to run. It was now telling me it was time for me to live again.

Chapter Eight

I opened the door of my home and walked through it as if for the first time. I thought of when we'd bought it. Larry had fallen in love with the layout, with the many bedrooms and the huge backyard.

At the time I'd had no idea that all of the rooms would be filled with children. I was thrilled to be buying a home, happy with my wonderful, handsome husband. I would have agreed to live on an ant farm if he had suggested it.

Now I walked through each room remembering the years we'd spent there. I waited to walk in my bedroom last. I lay on my bed fully clothed, not bothering to kick off my shoes. I had spent most of my life here in this bed with my husband. I couldn't anymore. I knew that. But I also couldn't leave Larry. We needed each other.

I went to the closet and began removing my clothes. I hadn't known what I would do when I left Chance but I did now. It would be impossible for me to sleep in the bed with my husband after spending the past nine nights in Chance's bed, in his arms.

As I moved to Erica's old bedroom I felt a shudder of pain go through me. This was the second promise I'd broken in the past several months. It seemed since I'd broken the promise to Viola, everything else was happening in rapid succession.

I thought of the night Larry asked me to marry him, the promises I'd made to him. Well, those promises were now broken. I'd given my body and part of my heart to a man who claimed we were destined to love.

Larry would never understand that. If it had not happened to me, I wasn't sure if I would believe it myself. But my soul stirred within Chance's embrace, alerting me to the fact that he spoke the truth.

My dreams were confirmation that somewhere, sometime, this man and I had shared a life. We'd shared a love that apparently death did not and could not erase. Still, where did that leave me now? I didn't want to leave my husband, but I couldn't sleep in our bed and pretend that nothing had changed.

When all my personal possessions had been removed from my room, I calmly went to the store. I would make dinner for Larry's return, steak, the same as it always was when he returned from visiting the kids.

The only thing that would be different on Larry's return would be me. I would not be waiting in a flimsy gown.

Larry walked into his home, bone weary from the fear that had gripped him so tightly the past two weeks. Michelle wasn't home. Panic began a slow beat in his temples, then proceeded to his belly, churning the bitter acid upward toward his now closing throat.

He walked throughout the house, something telling him not to go into the bedroom. The hairs on his arms pricked with static electricity whenever he turned in that direction. Whatever was waiting for him lay in that room.

Icy fingers gripped his heart and squeezed. Fear such as he'd never known invaded his entire being. He stood for a moment remembering when he was a child and afraid of the dark. But he was no longer a child. He was a man. He had no choice but to face his fears.

Larry turned toward his bedroom and began walking, slow even steps, counting slowly to himself the many years he'd spent with Mick. He didn't want it to be over. *Where the hell was she? She knew damn well what time he was coming home.*

He was doing his best to direct the pain mounting in his chest to anger directed at his wife. He didn't like being reduced to the five-year-old old hiding inside. He didn't like the feeling of abandonment that was stiffening his bones with each step.

Larry stood inside his bedroom door and breathed in, trying to still the rapid beating of his heart. His eyes surveyed the room. Nothing was out of place yet the air felt charged with sadness and impending doom.

He reached his hand out, now knowing why, and swept it through the air. The hairs on his arm stood at attention. Everything looked the same, but something was different. He'd stake his life on it.

The attorney in him came out as he searched the room for the obvious clues before moving on to the less obvious ones. He didn't feel Mick's energy in the room. He shivered.

Where the hell had that thought come from? Now he was sounding as mad as she was. She was infecting him with all that energy and past life crap.

Still, as he stood in the room fighting to analyze what was before him, he could no longer deny it. The room no longer held the essence of his wife. Her smell was missing, her warmth. Her energy.

Oh hell, he thought and headed for her closet door. The sight of the emptiness slammed into him, with the force of a three hundred pound prize fighter. He sank to the bed trying in vain to recover.

Mick had left him. He sat there immobile, not seeing, hearing, or feeling. He stayed there until he heard the front door opening and the rustling of bags. He stood, not knowing which he feared most, wondering if his wife was gone from his life or looking into her eyes and seeing the truth.

The pain that was long ago buried began to take root and live again. It grew inside him, doubling, tripling in size. The anger was valid. It was real. But the source was no longer his mother, it was Michelle.

"How long, Mick?"

I walked through the doors knowing Larry would be waiting for me. I'd not meant to spend so much time in the store.

"How long?"

I stared at my husband, wanting to pretend I didn't know what he was asking, but over twenty-six years of being married made that impossible.

"Damn it. How long, Mick?"

"Are you asking me when was the first time?"

I headed for the kitchen. The pain in his eyes was masked only by his fury. He followed behind me as I had known he would. Anger and pain darkened Larry's features. I saw what I had done to my husband. And that alone almost stopped me.

I felt tears welling in my eyes, tears that I couldn't give in to. I'd known full well there would be consequences for my actions.

My throat was constricted. There were words I wanted to say to my husband, to make him understand why I'd done it. Why I'd chosen after a lifetime of loving him to destroy our marriage.

I needed to explain that I'd been dying inside, that I had needed something, anything to make the pain go away. Chance just happened to be more than I had bargained for.

I watched my husband advance toward me. For a moment in time the world stopped. My head filled with an incredible pressure and I felt a sudden rush of wind inside my kitchen. I turned toward the window. It was closed.

When I turned back toward Larry, I could swear he was covered with a fine silver mist. I heard a faraway tinkling of bells.

Then the mist surrounding Larry began to dissipate, carrying with it my own broken dreams. I could see now that the hope of my marriage to Larry lasting forever was gone. I stared into his eyes and saw my thoughts were mirrored there.

"It hasn't been long," I whispered to him, as though whispering would make up for the knife I'd just plunged into my husband's heart.

I watched as he continued toward me. He appeared to stagger, his hand reaching out to hold the countertop. Instinctively I lunged forward to help him. "Don't," he growled at me. "Don't touch me."

"Larry, I didn't plan this."

"The hell you didn't. Now I know why you were spouting off that crap about past lives and not wanting the children here. Tell me, Mick, did you fuck him in our bed?"

I closed my eyes tightly, reeling from his words as though they were a blow. My back was pressed against the sink. I needed to move. Larry was pressing his body next to mine. His hands moved roughly over my breasts. His left knee was shoved between my legs.

"Larry, stop," I screamed at him, at this stranger who had invaded my husband's body. I placed both my palms on his chest and pushed with all my might. He went back and in the same instant I moved.

"Someone else can touch you and I can't?"

I walked toward the living room trying to focus, to get words that I needed. "You can't touch me like that. You were hurting me. Why are you behaving like this? You've never touched me like that."

I watched as Larry gripped his head in his hands. He was clawing at his hair, his reddened face turning purple. "Honey, calm down, you need to sit," I said to him from a safe distance across the room. He glared at me, but sat. I moved to the sofa directly opposite Larry and sat down. I'd known this day was coming. I sighed, trying to decide how to start.

"I'm not going to see him anymore. It's over."

"Why? Because I'm home? It should have never begun, Mick."

"I tried to avoid it." I whispered

I looked away from him, then back. I was wrong for what I had done, but I found myself getting angry.

"I asked you to come home. I told you I needed you."

He stood up and came to stand over me, glaring with righteous indignation. The veins in his neck appeared to have swollen to ten times their size. Despite what was happening I found myself more worried about Larry's health than the unraveling of our marriage.

"If you can't keep your legs closed unless I'm at home to watch you, that doesn't say very much for either of us, does it?" he screamed at me.

He knelt before me on the floor. With his right hand he tilted my chin up so my eyes were looking into his.

"How many times have you done this?"

"This is the first time," I answered him before my breath caught on a sob. "I mean…this is the only man, but I was with him once before."

As I watched my husband's eyes, panic replaced some of my own anger. A shudder passed from his body into mine. It was revulsion. I could feel it.

I attempted to shrink into the sofa pillows, but my husband's fingers bit into my flesh, not allowing me to escape even an inch from his wrath.

"Larry, you're hurting me," I whispered to him, my eyes again pooling with unshed tears. I felt the immediate loosening of his grip.

"Tell me everything, Mick," he demanded, his voice low and dangerous.

"I told you two months ago." I watched his head as he dipped it lower, his mind a mental calculator trying to recall when I'd dropped such information in his lap.

"The stranger I met in the parking lot of the grocery store. Chance. I told you."

Larry stood then. "Are you telling me that you actually met some man and went to a hotel with him?"

"Yes."

I watched as he paced around the room throwing me looks of disbelief. I saw fear in his eyes, fear that I knew was for me before he constructed a mask and dropped it into place to hide his feelings.

He walked to the other side of the room and stood there looking at me, not speaking, just a puzzled little frown tugging at the corners of his mouth.

"You could have been killed," Larry whispered, his voice almost a moan.

His eyes closed. I watched his chest as it heaved up and down. He was trying to calm himself.

"What is wrong with you, Mick? You've been acting crazy ever since you…"

"Go ahead. Say it, Larry. Since I hit Viola."

"Are you doing this to punish me?"

"I'm not trying to punish you."

"It sure as hell feels like you are. I did what was best."

"For whom, Larry?"

"For you. I did what was best for you, Mick."

Larry ran his hand roughly over his face, his eyes red rimmed. He was no longer glaring at me. Instead, his eyes were a mass of confusion.

"So, you're fucking some guy, some stranger you met in a parking lot, because I was trying to protect you?"

I wanted to tell him he should be grateful to Chance, that if it had not been for him, I would probably be dead right now. I didn't. I didn't have a death wish and right then Larry looked as if he wanted to strangle me.

"It wasn't like that. I needed someone to listen to me and he was there."

"Why didn't you talk to me? I've always been there when you needed me. I've always listened to you."

"No, you haven't. I talk, but you don't hear anything I have to say. You always paint this picture in your mind of what you think I said, or what you think I want. You've never asked."

I stopped at the look of pain that literally desecrated my husband's face, leaving him looking old and beaten.

I gentled my voice. "Honey, you made me into what you wanted me to be. You wanted me to be this wonderful mother. You wanted me to want a house full of kids. When I said no, you didn't hear me. That wasn't your picture of me, so what I said didn't count."

"Why didn't you ever tell me you felt this way?"

"I tried, Larry. For twenty- six years I've tried. But you were happy...and I made a promise to you." My voice broke on a sob. "I couldn't break my promise to you."

I saw a look cross his face that was much worse than the pain I had already inflicted. I knew before he asked what he was thinking.

"Were you only with me all these years because of a promise, Mick? Did you ever love me?"

"Yes, I loved you, Larry. I still love you. This," I waved my hands around my body, "this affair," I could barely say the words, "had nothing to do with my not loving you. Things were happening to me, inside my head. I wanted to talk to you, but you wouldn't let me. I tried to tell you that I needed you."

"When, Mick?"

I could tell Larry was confused. Why shouldn't he be? I was doing a miserable job of telling him what I meant. A horrible thought hit me. What if he'd never understood me because I'd tried to tell him in the same garbled way I was doing now. For a long time neither of us spoke. Then I heard a strangled sound coming from Larry.

"That doesn't give you the right to destroy our marriage. And if you stayed with me because of a promise, I have to tell you, you failed miserably. You broke your promise, Mick."

I knew what promise he meant. "I've had practice. I broke my promise to Viola also."

He got up, throwing me a look of disgust. I sat on the sofa shivering as he stomped into the bedroom. The vibration of the slammed door caused me to jump. We'd settled nothing.

I sat on the sofa for over an hour, waiting for Larry to come back out. I couldn't fix our lives alone. I wondered if he was waiting for me to come and apologize, to tell him that Chance meant nothing to me.

I realized we had not really talked about Chance. I tried hard to remember what we'd actually said and for the life of me I couldn't remember.

Was this how it was when a marriage dissolved? The most important words in my life had been spoken by us and I didn't know what they were. *Dear lord, help us,* I prayed.

I awoke to the smell of coffee, surprised that I'd drifted off. I lay in the bed knowing that eventually I would have to face my husband and the decisions I'd made. There was no way I was going to get out of confronting Larry.

I threw an old robe around my shoulders and walked toward the kitchen. Halfway there I stopped. Larry was coming toward me, a steaming cup of coffee in his hand, sorrow lining his face.

He reached the cup out to me and I took it. "Thanks," I murmured. It felt peculiar standing before my husband as though we were strangers. Nothing in our marriage had prepared either of us for this.

"We need to talk."

He spoke softly before turning and walking back into the kitchen. He placed his cup on the table, then reached for mine.

"I'm ready to listen now, Mick."

The sound of his voice broke my heart. The thin wall I had attempted to erect for this conversation came crashing down with a thud. I was crying, wailing for the pain I was in and the pain I was causing.

"Mick, Mick, Mick."

Larry moaned and wrapped me in his arms. He held me tight to him, crying out my name. I clung to him, to the man I had lived with and loved for more than half my life.

He was the man I'd promised to love forever. My hands rubbed his back. When at last I pulled slightly away to look at him I was stopped by his pain. His eyes looked back at me so full of hurt. All I could see was that five-year-old little boy who'd been abandoned by his mother. Now his wife was the one abandoning him and I hated myself for it.

Larry lifted my chin upwards and kissed me softly on the lips. When he attempted to part my lips with his tongue, I gently pushed him away.

"Don't, Larry. Let's talk."

I saw his pain rapidly change to anger. I lowered my eyes, sat and took a sip of my coffee. Soon Larry calmed down enough to sit opposite me.

"I can't believe you're willing to throw away our marriage over some guy in a parking lot."

Larry was attempting to reason with me. He was being a lawyer, not my husband, and I resented it.

"He's not just a guy I met in a parking lot." I watched as his eyebrows shot up and hurried to continue.

"I was married to Chance in a past life. His name was Jeremy. My name was Dimitra. I died in childbirth."

Larry shut his eyes so tightly that they appeared to have sunk into his face. The chair he had been sitting in went flying across the room hitting the wall with a bang.

"This is crazy. You're crazy. That's it," Larry bellowed. "I've had enough. Get dressed. I'm taking you to the doctor myself." He stalked off for the bedroom.

"But, you said you were ready to listen." I followed him, my feet hitting the floor hard. I wanted to reach him before he had a chance to slam our bedroom door in my face. "Larry, I have proof."

"How can you possibly have proof that you've lived before?" He turned to face me. "Show me your proof, Mick."

I watched as he went to the closet and started tossing objects around the room. He pulled out a strong box that held all of our important papers. As he went to the dresser drawer to retrieve the key, I knew no explanation would be enough.

Larry was screaming as he pulled papers out and tossed them on the bed. I don't know what he said. This time I was the one not listening. He tossed our marriage license in my face.

"You want proof, Mick? I have proof that in this lifetime you're my wife. You want a divorce? I'll take everything. Try me. And what about the kids? Do you think they're going to be on your side?"

The more he talked the calmer he became. It was that calm that made me afraid. We lived a good life because of Larry's abilities as a lawyer. Now he was turning that gift against me.

I held the license in my hands. "I don't want a divorce."

"Then what the hell do you want?" he screamed. "Why didn't you just lie to me if it's over? Why didn't you just say you were angry and went out of town?"

"Because I've never lied to you."

"Now that's a laugh." Larry came toward me. "You've been seeing this guy for months and that wasn't a lie?"

"I didn't see him for months. I told you I met him two months ago." I looked past my husband's shoulder out the garden window. "I wasn't having an affair with him all this time. It only started when you left."

Larry cocked his head to the side. "I could swear that you think somehow this is my fault. Tell me, Mick, is it my fault that you've turned into a two-timing slut?"

I gritted my teeth, batting my eyelashes furiously to keep the tears away. "It's not your fault, Larry. It's not anyone's fault."

"Oh my dear wife, you have that so wrong. It is someone's fault and someone's going to have to pay." His voice was now cold. He made a melodramatic sweep with his arms, motioning me to take a seat.

"I believe in this state I can sue for alienation of affection."

"Who would you sue?"

"This Chance person. What's his last name? What are you going to do when I haul your lover's ass into court?"

"Larry, it's not Chance's fault. Can't you see it was fate? He was looking for me. He'd been looking for me a long time." I watched as a puzzled frown covered my husband's face, forcing him to sit.

"Mick..." He stopped, sighed loudly, and then shook his head. "Mick, do you really believe all this nonsense?"

An involuntarily shudder ripped through my body. "Yes, I do. But there's more. I went to a medium while you were gone. He touched my hand and I saw myself. I saw myself in another life. I was giving birth. I've told you about my dreams, about the son I couldn't find. You always thought I was talking about Derrick. I wasn't. It was always my son from a past life. I know you're not going to like this, or believe me but...the medium, I believe he's my son from that lifetime."

"Who did you go to this thing with? Was Chance involved with this?"

"Yes. He got the tickets."

"Can't you see what's happening, Mick? Those guys are probably in this together. They're using you. You've been vulnerable now for a few months. They saw this and concocted this elaborate scheme."

He slapped his forehead. "Damn. I should have thought of this before. Honey, you've been conned."

He was smiling, rising up from his chair to pull me with him. "Mick, it's not you, it's a scam. We'll put those bastards away." He hugged me to him. "God, Mick it's going to be all right."

"Larry, it's not a scam."

"Honey, it is. Think how ridiculous this sound. It's just a scam. They're after money."

He started laughing. "Your husband in a past life, your son." Tears were rolling down his cheeks. "You saw yourself dying in childbirth... Oh Mick... You're right. I didn't listen. If I had, I would have known sooner that you were being conned."

"God! I can't believe it. You're still not hearing me. They aren't conning me. I remember them both from my dreams. It's true. I believe the dreams are my memories."

"Think about it, Mick. You were never interested in this nonsense before this...this... Chance character came along. All this time you've been a sensible woman."

I watched as he heaved a sigh of relief. Just like that he'd forgiven me. I wished for a moment it could be that easy. I thought about it. This was how we'd always handled any disagreements that came up during the years. Larry would dig around until he found a plausible reason that he could accept.

My insanity was now his reasonable explanation. That, and his believing Chance to be a con man. So what would I do?

I looked at Larry, wishing that for once that he'd listen to the woman he'd married, not his version of who I was. I didn't want him to find a reason for my having slept with Chance. I knew why I'd done it. I'd wanted to.

"Honey, would you go with me to the medium? His name's Blaine MaDia. If you go with me you can see for yourself that he's not conning me. Will you go?"

"No, I won't go."

"How are we going to get past this if you're not willing to open your mind to what I'm telling you?"

"My mind is open, Mick. I don't have to go anywhere to know he's conning you. Look at all the junk mail that comes for us every day. We get stuff from so-called psychics all over the country. You think some kid you met is going to get me to change my mind?"

"He's not like that, Larry. There's something about him. He has this energy surrounding him." I was going to tell him about the arc, but decided not to. He was staring at me, no doubt deciding whether or not to have me committed.

I decided to try again. "Haven't you seen that show on television? You know the one I mean, where that guy talks to the dead."

"Yeah, I've seen it. I hope he's not the best you've got to build your case on. I also saw the show where this reporter did the same thing and got the same hysterical responses from the audience members.

"Those people want to believe, Mick. They're unhappy. Why do you need to believe this? I don't understand. Has your life with me been so miserable?" Larry asked.

I wanted to stop talking, to give in. There was no way the two of us would ever meet in the middle on this point. But this was the only time Larry had ever talked this long on the subject.

Granted, he was calling me crazy, but at least he was still in the room. "Honey, you know better than that. I've never been miserable with you."

I stopped in mid-sentence. I was going to tell him I'd been contented, but I knew he wouldn't want to hear that. He only wanted to hear that I'd been happy.

"If you haven't been miserable, why all of a sudden have you starting acting like this? You're scaring me." He frowned. "I thought it was a hormonal problem. Now I'm worried that it might be more. Stop talking like this, Mick. Don't make me do something I'll regret."

His words sounded like a threat to me. Could my husband be implying that he would have me committed? Did he think we still lived in the Middle Ages? Wanting to explain to him how I felt battled with my growing irritation at his mild intimidation tactic.

"Larry, it sounds like you're telling me that if I don't think the way you approve of, you might take legal action."

"I'll do whatever I have to, to protect you."

I smiled at him, hoping my sarcasm would show through in my words, if not in the smile.

"And exactly what means are you willing to go to? What hoops are you asking me to jump through? Exactly what do I have to do?"

"Well," he began.

I couldn't believe he was actually going to give me details. My blood began to boil over with anger as I listened to his solution to our problems.

"No more talk about having lived before. No more going to see any more psychics. No television shows, no books, no lectures, no talk of dreams. Nothing. And I don't want you to ever mention his name again."

He looked at me expecting that even after something as major as this I would eventually acquiesce. I leaned a little away from him, making my voice even. "So you don't want me to mention whom? Chance or my son?"

I waited for his response, watching as he clenched his jaw in anger.

"I want you back in our bed tonight."

Larry's voice was just as calm. I'd seen him use that tone many times in court when he was going for the jugular.

"Are these demands or requests?"

He blanched visibly before answering me. "Call it what you want. If you don't want me to file complaints against your," he cringed, "your husband and your son, I suggest you do what I say. And I'm well aware of what century this is. I can still have you hospitalized for your own protection." His voice was stern. He meant every word he'd said.

"Larry, let me tell you something you might not know. There are millions of people who believe in reincarnation and psychics. You can't have me put away for that." I laughed at him wondering how he had thought to frighten me with so weak a ploy.

"I can prove you're a danger to yourself."

"How can you do that?"

"You went away with a stranger you met in a parking lot. I'd say that makes you a woman who needs to be looked after."

"Touché," I muttered between clenched teeth. "I'll admit that wasn't the brightest thing I've ever done."

I watched as a small smirk of satisfaction crossed his face and I wanted with all my heart to wipe it away. So I stared straight at my husband, knowing full well that I was pouring salt into the wounds I had created.

"Do you really want to know why I went to a hotel with a stranger?" I asked. "It was something that felt right to me. When they start locking people away for having affairs let me know."

I reached for the cold cup of coffee, just for something to do. My hands were shaking so badly I could barely hold the cup.

"I'm not leaving you. I'm merely changing rooms. I'm also willing to compromise with you. I won't see Chance again. I already told you that. And I won't mention this to you again, but as for my interests, you can't legislate what I read, watch, or what event I go to."

"What about coming back to our room?" Larry asked his voice wistful.

"That's non-negotiable. I'm staying in Erica's old room."

"Forever?"

"Until I decide that I no longer want to be there. This is my decision to make, Larry, not yours."

"Mick," he pleaded with me. "I hate sleeping apart from you. Last night was hell. Oh hell, honey, what am I talking about?" He attempted to smile. "The last two weeks have been hell. Come back to our room. I need you beside me. I need you in my bed. Don't make me beg you, Mick. I need you."

"I know you need me, Larry. I need you also." My anger at my husband was draining away. "Our desperate needing of each other is killing me."

I turned from him and exited the kitchen, not stopping until I reached my new bedroom. I had to move quickly. The look on Larry's face was more than I could take. I sank onto the blue and white goose down quilt and cried.

I cried for my husband who had been abandoned twice, first by his own mother and now by me. And I cried for Chance and for the old soul of Jeremy. Then I cried for Dimitra and the son she'd never held to her breast to nurse.

At last I cried for myself. It appeared I was destined to keep hurting the people I loved no matter what lifetime I was in.

Chapter Nine

I stayed in Erica's room until my bladder could no longer take it. I had listened in silence as I heard Larry stomping around the house, making calls, slamming down the phone, only to hear him make another in a minute or two.

I wondered who he was trying to reach. I prepared myself for two men in white coats to burst through the door of my new bedroom any moment and haul me away. I wondered, would it look better for me if I went along peacefully or should I fight?

When nature's call could no longer be avoided, I opened the door as quietly as I could and hurried down the hall to the bathroom. I heaved a sigh of relief when I was done. No Larry.

I peeped in the kitchen. I was starving, but I couldn't chance another run-in with him. So I decided to endure the hunger a little longer. At least I was alone.

My eyes were focused over my shoulder looking for Larry. My plan was to rush back into the bedroom and close the door if he appeared. When he didn't I released the breath I was holding and stepped into the room.

I closed the door, sighing in short-lived relief. "Larry," I gasped as I finally turned. He was sitting on the bed waiting for me. "Why are you in here?"

An eyebrow shot up before he answered me. "Because this is my house. I paid for it. And you're my wife. I think that means I'm entitled to what you obviously don't mind giving away to anyone who asks."

I leaned into the door. Surely he wasn't intending that we make love. That would be ludicrous. Of course the entire situation was crazy.

Who would have thought in a million years that I, straight-laced, by-the-book, keep-her-promises Michelle, would ever be in the position I now found myself?

If it was not my life I would have thought it was a bad movie. Or at the least a very bad and unbelievable book. I knew better. It wasn't something I'd made up. It was real and it was happening to me.

Chance Morgan was real and so was Blaine MaDia. I would stake my life on the fact that I believed neither man was conning me. Hell, I'd staked my marriage on it. What did my life mean?

"I called the kids."

"You did what?"

I walked toward him no longer worrying if he was in the room to assert his marital rights. I had not thought that far ahead. I felt my stomach roll over. I wondered if he told them about the affair.

"What did you tell them?" I managed to whisper.

"I told them the truth," he answered me. He eased his body from the bed and began walking toward me. "They're in agreement. They think maybe you've been conned. If you keep insisting that this nonsense is true they're in agreement with me that I should take you in for an immediate psychiatry evaluation."

He was standing directly in front of me. He reached out a hand to touch my hair and I began to tremble. I wondered if there was any possible way Larry could carry out his threats.

"I want you back in our room, Mick." His eyes looked feverish; there was a thin film of sweat lining his upper lip. "I'm not going to allow you to destroy what we've worked so hard to build."

"Larry, why are you doing this? I told you the affair is over."

"It's not over until you're back in our bed." He ran his hand over my hair, then down the front of my gown, letting it fall and linger on my left breast. "I'm fighting for us, Mick, like it or not. I will protect you."

I wanted to push my husband's hand away, but at that moment I was afraid. I knew I needed to use my head to keep him calm. The last thing I wanted to do was make him go past the point of no return.

"You're not going to throw me away," Larry said. "You're not going to find me another place to live. You made promises. You're my wife. I'm going to make sure you honor those promises."

A sudden flash of awareness skittered across my soul. He was thinking about his mother. He was remembering her abandonment.

"I told you, I'm not asking you to leave. I'm not your mother. I'm not abandoning you. I'm still here, I'm not going anywhere."

He dropped his hands and stared at me for a long moment. "What are you talking about?" He looked confused. "My mother has nothing to do with this."

"You said I wasn't going to find you another place to live. Larry, that's what your mother said to you."

Now it was he who was backing away from me.

"Drop it, Mick." I heard the pain in his voice. "You know damn well what I meant. The woman always wants the man to leave and she takes the house. That's what I meant."

"It's not what you said."

"So now you're a shrink. Listen, I'm serious. You get this notion out of your head that we're sharing a house only. It's not going to happen. We're sharing a bed. If you don't come back to our room, I'm moving in here."

I moved to the opposite side of the room. "Can't you give me time to work through this?"

"How much time are you talking about?"

"I don't know. I want to go see..."

"Don't you dare say his name."

"Not him. I want to see Blaine."

"Why?"

"I think he can help me."

"Help you with what? How much money did this guy charge you? Do you think he's going to help you out of the goodness of his heart?"

"I want to see if he can help me with Viola."

Larry slammed the open palm of his left hand against his forehead.

"Damn," he muttered loudly. "That again?" Then he marched determinedly toward me, grabbed me by the shoulders and began shaking me.

"Do you have any idea how many innocent people have gone to jail for hitting a pedestrian? Don't you know how much juries hate people as privileged as we are? Just because you have money you could have had the book thrown at you.

"Do you think anyone would care that it was an accident? Did you think I was going to wait around and trust your life to the system?

"Hell no, Mick. I love you! I kept my promises to protect you. If that's what all this nonsense has been about, I'm getting sick to death of it."

He shook me one last time, then stalked away. I thought he was afraid of being so close to me. No matter the reason, I was just glad he moved away.

"You're not a stupid woman," he screamed at me from his new position across the room. "I gave that woman more money than she's probably ever seen in her entire life. I didn't cheat her, Mick. There was no reason why you should have gone to see her."

"But, I promised her, Larry."

He sighed loudly before throwing me a look of pure disgust. I was beginning to wonder if he didn't think me a backward child.

"Then you shouldn't have broken it, should you? Tell me something, Mick. Why is your promise to her so important, but your wedding vows you managed to break so easily? Did you enjoy sex with this man? Did you scream out his name? Did he rock your world? Or did you fake it with him also?"

It was finally out in the open. Hurt and humiliation claimed my husband's features. I bit my lips wishing to God I had never met Chance.

"I don't fake how I feel for you."

"Don't," he whispered. He put his hand up as though to ward off a blow. "Do you enjoy it more with him?"

"This isn't about him, Larry. We're talking about Viola."

"Then consider the subject switched. Did he give you what I haven't been able to give you in twenty-eight years?"

"I need to know if the accident was my fault. I want to know what I was doing before I hit her. I'm hoping Blaine can help me remember. It's important that I remember. You never saw her, the fear in her eyes, you never saw her blood or the groceries spilling in the streets."

I was crying. "You weren't the one who urged her not to worry, who promised to be there for her. I was. I promised her and I'm the one who broke that promise."

He glared at me then. "If it was that important, why didn't you go?"

"Because," I answered him, "from the moment we said I do and became husband and wife, for twenty-six years I've been doing what you wanted me to do. For twenty-six-years I've been trying to please you, to keep a promise I made to you. That's why I didn't go."

Larry's fists were clenched at his sides. "So you do blame me. Why in the hell don't you get it over with? Why don't you just tell me that you're angry with me?"

I don't know how it happened. It was as if his razor sharp glare released years of resentment. I found myself screaming at my husband.

"Yes, I'm angry with you, Larry, for acting as though I can't cross the street unless you're there to tell me the light is green.

"I'm angry that, as usual, you convinced me to do something I didn't want to do. I wanted to go visit that old woman and it's my fault for not going.

"I'm an adult. I should have told you to go to hell, but I didn't. Instead, I allowed you to convince me that it would be easier that way. I wanted our home to remain happy."

I started laughing hysterically. "Funny thing, about that. I'm not happy. I don't know the last time I've been happy. You've been telling me all these years how happy I am, but I haven't felt it."

The tears were running freely down my face now. I had no more to lose. My marriage was over. There was no longer any reason to keep my feelings damned up behind a façade, so I continued.

"Baby, I've been too busy walking on eggshells to be happy. I always wanted our marriage to work. I was afraid to fight with you. I didn't want to be like my parents any more than you wanted to be like yours.

"You always thought it was so wonderful that I was raised in a home with two parents. You never heard me when I told you how miserable my childhood was.

"I can understand how hard it was for you to have been abandoned, but maybe you were better off. Maybe you had a better life because your mother left."

A look I was unfamiliar with from Larry came into his eyes. It took me a moment to recognize it as hatred. He thought I was deliberately trying to hurt him but I wasn't. I was trying to make him see he'd painted a fairy tale world that had never existed.

Before I could say another word he'd stormed out of the bedroom and headed for the front door, pausing only long enough to retrieve his keys from the kitchen counter. I ran behind him, barefoot, screaming for him to stop.

"Larry, don't go. I wasn't trying to hurt you."

I banged on the car window. He ignored me and drove away, the screech of tires ringing loudly in my ears. I looked up to see a neighbor staring at me and realized how I must look. I was in my nightgown, my hair matted and uncombed, screaming at a now invisible car. Without a word I turned and walked back into my house.

It was three days before I saw my husband again. Three days of agonizing over where he could possibly be. During that time I cursed his mother for having left him. I cursed Larry for asking me to assume the burden and I cursed myself for accepting it and letting him down. Lastly I cursed fate and my dreams of a dark- haired man.

It was only my incredible guilt that kept me from cursing Viola. My hitting her was the catalyst for everything that had happened in the past eight months. I could only go so far in not accepting blame for my actions. My mind refused to travel down that path. Viola was not to blame. I was.

I could have said no to my loneliness and pain. I could have tried harder to make Larry understand what I was going through. But I had chosen to take the easy way out. Even I had to wonder what I was trying to prove by returning home to sleep in separate bedrooms. What was that all about?

I closed my eyes against images of Chance and more recently the invasion of images of Blaine. Blaine's face was a constant onslaught of pain. I shivered each time his face came into focus. I remained stunned at the images I'd seen when he touched me.

I'd meant it when I said the affair was over, but I didn't think I could so easily put Blaine into my past. I had to see him again. I had to talk to him. But not before I was sure my husband was fine. His safety was the most important thing to me at that moment.

For the first time in our marriage, I believe Larry heard me, but only the parts that caused him pain. Maybe Larry and Chance were both right. Perhaps I slept with Chance to punish Larry.

I thought about that for a long time. It wasn't true. I loved Chance. Our being together was meant to happen. If I only had a crystal ball so I would know what was coming next.

Blaine. The name whispered across my brain with an intensity that couldn't be ignored.

If I'd ever needed a psychic, I needed one now. Ironically, the only thing that kept me going those three days was Erica and her constant, annoying phone calls. The first dozen or so had been scolding calls. She was determined that I would know the error of my ways.

Initially I tried to hold my tongue. She was right, I was wrong. I had indeed hurt her beloved father. Finally I could take her sharp tongue no longer. I did what I had wanted to do for many years.

"Erica Jean." I spoke her name fully and loudly. I had to, for her to hear me.

"Butt out. This is my marriage. What happens between your father and me is our business, not yours. I would suggest you take care of your own husband and leave me to take care of mine."

There was an angry silence on the other end of the line. I knew the sound of it. I was used to it.

"Goodbye, Erica," I said at last. "Don't bother calling again unless it's to apologize for the way you've talked to me." I severed the connection feeling a lightness I hadn't felt in weeks.

A few hours later Larry walked through the door, his face unshaven and drawn. His clothes were rumpled; his entire demeanor reeked of a bone weary tiredness. My husband was grieving and I grieved along with him

I went toward him. "Larry, are you all right?" I moved closer to him, not liking the pasty color of his skin.

He lifted his eyes up toward me slowly. He didn't answer. Just turned from me and walked toward the bedroom. I followed him, ignoring the fact that he slammed the door in my face. I opened it up as he was shedding his clothes, dropping his expensive but rumpled suit on the floor.

I called his name again. "Larry, I'm sorry. I didn't mean to hurt you."

He had shut me out effectively, leaving me with nothing to do but pick up his clothes and put them in the pile for the cleaners. I went through the drawers and laid out fresh underwear on the bed.

I went to the kitchen. He looked as if he hadn't eaten since he'd left. When he was done with his shower he came to the kitchen, ate the food I placed before him and ignored my pleas for forgiveness. He refused to meet my eyes. It was as though I wasn't even in the room.

An involuntarily shiver touched my bones. My husband could forgive my infidelity, but he couldn't forgive me mentioning his mother. He couldn't forgive me for breaking the bubble that he wanted to maintain of my perfect childhood.

We co-existed like that for two weeks. Not once did Larry object to my sleeping in Erica's room. Not once did he say so much as good morning to me. He ate the meals I prepared, wore the clothes I laid out and ignored me. If he was watching television and I attempted to join him he would go into the bedroom and close the door.

It was a living nightmare. Every morning and every evening I would tell him I was sorry. I even left messages on his pager and his answering machine at work, after hours. Once I even left a message with his secretary, not caring that she would wonder about it. Still nothing.

I was at the end of my rope. My home life had gone straight to hell and my professional career was heading there also. I received a reprimand masked as a polite question. My boss had peered at me from behind his horn-rimmed glasses.

"Dr. Morgan called. He said his office is out of samples. He was wondering if we could ship him some."

The man smiled at me in an undertaker sort of way before reminding me that it was my job to service the doctors, that they should never run out of samples and have to call for them. He had smirked as he told me how the scripts the doctors wrote were our bread and butter. Damn. I wasn't a new rep. I was a senior rep. I knew that.

What could I say to him except that I was sorry and it wouldn't happen again? I wanted to tell him that the doctor had a ton of samples and there was no way he could have used them all but I didn't. I told him I would rectify the problem immediately.

I left my office and went immediately to the post office to ship off samples to Chance. If he thought I was bringing them, he had another thought coming. I would do that in a pig's eye.

I went home exhausted, not wanting to spend another night in silence. As Larry and I sat at the table I went for a bottle of wine in the fridge.

"Larry, don't you even care that I was unhappy until I met you? You changed that for me. I didn't mean to hurt you with that remark about your mother."

I watched as he propped his hands on the table and entwined them together. For the first time in weeks he was looking at me.

"Were you really unhappy as a child?" he asked. The look on his face was pleading with me to say no.

I answered honestly. "Yes. I've told you that many times. My parents fought constantly. I lived in fear that my father would kill my mother. He was cheating on her and we all knew it, but she stayed because of us." I sat down in the chair. "I don't think she made the right choice."

"You wanted your parents to get divorced?"

Funny, but in all the years we'd known each other he'd never asked me that.

"No, I wanted them to stay together, despite all my fears. I didn't want my father to leave home. I blame myself sometimes for my mother staying. I was a daddy's girl. She knew how much I loved him. She said she stayed for me. When it was finally over she said he left because of me, that he couldn't stand the thought of having a crazy daughter any longer. She said it was my dreams, my saying that I'd lived before." I stopped and looked at my husband. "They were both afraid that I really was nuts. The dreams that you call nightmares, I've had them my entire life. My father and mother fought because they couldn't decide whose side of the family I inherited my craziness from."

"I'm sorry, Mick. I just never understood. You had what I wanted. I wanted to believe that you were just talking. I needed to believe families can be happy." He looked down then, toward the floor.

"I was determined to recreate your childhood for our family. I guess you're right. I guess I didn't listen too well."

Larry looked me over then and I felt my skin warming from his gaze. "You've lost weight," he said at last.

"Yeah, I guess I have. Finally!"

"How much?"

"About twenty-five pounds."

Now I saw concern taking over. He didn't want to worry about me but it was a habit that wasn't any easier for him to break than it was for me.

"Were you trying?"

"No."

I started to smile at him then caught myself. Now was not the time for smiling. "It's been a rough month," I answered at last.

We continued our dinner in silence, but the tension was not as thick. This time when he started to watch television in the living room I walked toward my room. He called out for me to join him. When the news was over we shut the set off and headed toward our separate bedrooms. We couldn't have been more civilized.

In the next several weeks we resumed talking. Things were still not normal, but it was a lot better. Every evening one of the kids would call and talk to Larry for an hour or so. The most they said to me was, "Can I talk to Dad?"

Larry and I were sitting in a companionable silence watching a comedy. We were laughing easily together when he turned to me.

"My firm is having a party. It's expected that the partners will all bring their wives. Is there any way you would consent to go with me?"

He appeared almost apologetic in the asking. "Why would I mind, Larry? I'm your wife, that hasn't changed." I saw him heave a sigh of relief that he tried to pretend was a bored yawn.

"Thanks, Mick," he murmured.

"You're welcome."

We finished watching the show and went to bed. This time our goodnight was not so difficult.

"Mick, you're beautiful."

I felt myself blushing. I looked around the room at all the women in their sparkling gowns and even more sparkling jewels. "You're just saying that." I smiled at Larry.

He tilted my chin until my eyes were on a direct path with his. "I mean it. You're without a doubt the most beautiful woman in the room."

He pulled me into his arms and we danced to the slow beat of the mellow music. He was holding me so tightly I could feel the beating of his heart.

"I love you," he whispered into my ear. "I'll always love you, Mick."

I felt his breath, warm, sweet and familiar. I clung to my husband as tightly as he was clinging to me. "I love you too. I always have and I always will."

The music ended and we remained on the floor in each other's arms, afraid to break the magic spell, afraid that we would return home and once again be forced to endure the pain of our separate live.

"Larry," I whispered. "Forgive me for hurting you." I gazed into his eyes feeling the mounting tears wanting to spill.

"Hi, Larry, haven't seen you lately."

It was one of Larry's colleagues pounding him on the back and reaching around me to shake Larry's hand. He asked Larry if he could dance with me.

With my eyes, I did my best to plead with him to say no, but before either of us had a chance to answer, I was swirling away for another dance. My only salvation was that the tears stopped instantly.

We ate dinner, talking and laughing with the other couples at the tables. Once in a while I would look up to find Larry's gaze lingering on me lovingly. It was time we began the healing process. I was now ready to do whatever it would take to put us back together.

In the car heading home we laughed together about some of the things we'd heard, the same way we'd done hundreds of time in the past. It all seemed so long ago.

I leaned into the car cushion. "That was fun. I really enjoyed myself." I felt Larry eyeing me suspiciously. "Why are you looking at me like that? We always had fun together."

"When did it stop being fun for you, Mick?"

I sobered instantly. "Larry, I don't want to fight anymore."

"We're not going to fight. I really want to know. When did our life stop being fun for you?"

I watched as the knuckles on his hand turned white with the strain of keeping his emotions under control. He gripped the steering wheel. "Tell me, Mick, I won't get angry."

"We've been married a long time. I think our marriage is better than most. I have nothing to complain about, really." I sighed. "Can't we let it go?"

"We can, but I think that's part of the problem. I think we've let too many things go for too long. I don't think you would have turned to someone else unless you were unhappy. So tell me." He glanced at me. "How long have you been unhappy?"

"I don't know," I answered truthfully. "I've thought about that myself and I really can't tell you. I think at first I just missed having all of your attention to myself. You never seemed to need time with just me after the children started coming."

"What are you saying, Mick? Are you jealous of our children?"

I found myself moving away from him emotionally, then physically as I moved closer to the door.

"Don't."

"Don't what?"

"Don't move away." Larry said. "I want to know. I think you owe me that much."

I turned and stared out the window for a long time before turning back to face my husband's stony profile. "I don't think I was jealous of the kids, just the time it took from us. I think…I think…" I didn't want to say it.

"You think what?"

"I sometimes thought you used me to get the things you never had, the family. Then I think I lost importance to you as a person. I became just the mother of your children. I disappeared. You stopped listening to me. Whenever I tried to talk to you, you said I was imagining things, that we were happy. Whatever my problems, you had solutions. I never wanted you to solve all my problems, Larry. I just wanted you to listen."

"I don't understand what you're trying to say."

"Don't worry." I laughed softly. "Sometimes I don't know myself."

"Mick." I heard the panic in his voice. "Did you really not want to have a large family? Would you have gone through with it if I hadn't shown up?"

I heard the fear and the sadness. I knew he was thinking of the abortion he'd arrived within minutes to prevent.

"I don't know. It was all so long ago. I always thought that I didn't want them, that you forced me to have them, but I know now that's not true."

"Then why did you feel like that? Why did you try and… You know… with Shannon?"

He couldn't say the words. "I don't know. I think I wanted you to listen to me. I wanted not to just be a means of paying your mother back. I didn't want to keep having babies to fulfill a promise."

Larry was silent and so was I. What could we say? I felt the car being smoothly maneuvered to the shoulder. I looked at Larry, wondering what it was he wanted from me now.

He turned to me, his eyes filled with grief and tears and said, "I'm sorry I didn't tell you often enough how important you are to my life, not as the mother of my children but as just you. I love you, Mick."

I watched the tears rolling down the face of my strong husband, the man who was always filled to overflowing with joy, and I winced at the pain my acts had wrought. I had to ask him.

"Were you never unhappy, not even for a day of our marriage?"

"Not even for a moment," he answered, his eyes brimming with honesty. "From the moment you first spoke to me I became whole. I fell in love with you immediately. I've been happy since that moment."

"How could you have been happy all the time? What about the times we struggled, or when the kids were all sick at once?"

"I had more than I had ever dreamed of. I had you and the kids. I had a family. I was happy. The problems for me were just minor inconveniences. They never interfered with my happiness.

I was feeling about as big as a microscopic bug. "It bothered me." I corrected myself. "No, it made me angry that you were always so happy. Then I would become consumed with guilt for resenting your happiness and resenting the children. I held it in. I didn't want you to hate me for not enjoying your dream as much as you seemed to be. There was no good reason for me not to. I knew that. I was angry at myself a lot for feeling that way."

"Is that why you had the affair?"

"I don't think so."

I looked in his eyes. For the first time we were talking, really talking. I wanted to tell him as much as I could without hurting him further.

"The day I met Chance, I wanted to die. He made me want to live again."

"Did I do that to you? Did being married to me make you want to die?"

"No. It wasn't you. I felt I'd lost control of my life. I didn't know who I was any longer. I may have resented you for what I thought was your fault but it wasn't.

"You took care of me because it made you happy. You thought that was what I wanted. I know that now. But that day I didn't. I was thinking about Viola, and I kept having these dreams."

Remembrance flashed across Larry's face. "You're talking about the nightmares, aren't you? The ones that had you waking up in tears."

"Yes."

"It really bothered you that much not to go and see that old woman?"

"It bothered me that I broke my promise to her. She was depending on me. I let her down."

Larry looked away from me for a split second before his hand wiped at the moisture gathered in the corners of his eyes. He looked back and I saw the return of the pain in his eyes. I knew the question before he asked.

"Is that why you married me, Mick, because I made you promise?"

I'd given my husband enough hurt to last a lifetime, maybe more. I wouldn't continue to hurt him.

"I came to you, remember. I married you because I loved you. I've stayed married to you because I still love you."

He stared at me, not understanding that what I'd done had nothing to do with my feelings for him. It would do no good at this point to tell him yet again my feelings of connection with Chance, to talk about another life I'd led in the past. My husband had gone as far as he could go and much farther than I had imagined he would.

"Tell me what he did to make you happy?" I saw embarrassment coloring my husband's face despite his earnest efforts to find a way once again to solve my problems.

"I don't want to talk about that."

"I want to make you happy."

"Then let's not talk about this anymore. It's over. It's been two months. I haven't seen or talked to him and I don't intend to."

"Please."

"Larry, he listened to me. That's all."

My husband studied me, frowning in deep concentration. "I've always known I didn't satisfy you. Did he?"

"Like I just said, he listened to me. He made me feel the way you did before the kids came along. I had an opinion. That was important to him. That's what he gave me. As for the rest, sex is just sex. And for the record I do enjoy our lovemaking."

"I know you enjoy it…but… I've always wanted to make you scream out in pleasure. You really rock my world, Mick. And I've always wanted to rock yours. I can't help it, I don't want to think about it, but the thoughts won't go away. I want to know if he rocked your world. Did he make you scream out with pleasure? Did you scream out his name?"

"Please, don't go there, Larry. I'm not with him. I'm with you. I love you."

"Are you over him?"

God, how I wanted to end this conversation. How was I supposed to keep answering my husband's questions? I'd done my best to reassure him, to downplay the magnitude of what I'd felt in Chance's arms. I didn't want to keep lying to him yet I wanted an end to the pain.

So I said, "I can never forget him or what he gave me. He reminded me of who I am. I'm grateful. If it weren't for him, we would not be having this conversation. Neither of us would be really listening to the other."

"Do you think there's a chance we can repair the damage? Do you even want to?"

"Yes," I answered him, not stopping the tears that were falling. "How about you. Do you want to try again?"

"I love you, Mick. I don't want to live the rest of my life without you in it." He paused. "I'm tired of the silence and the wall between us. I'm ready to tear it down."

Oh, Larry," I managed to sob before my husband crushed me in his arms, his lips on mine. This time when he slid his tongue between my lips, I opened wider to give him entry.

"Will you stay with me tonight?" His eyes were pleading.

It had been long enough. If we could continue talking we could make it work. I would forget the man in my dreams. I would forget Chance Morgan.

"I'll stay with you."

Chapter Ten

The remainder of the ride was peaceful. I laid my head on my husband's shoulder and whispered a silent prayer. "Lord, please help us to find our way back. When we're home let us continue talking."

Every few seconds Larry would kiss me on the forehead. We didn't talk. I knew both of our hearts were peaceful. We'd said enough for now.

Larry pulled into our driveway. I sat up, stunned to see our home ablaze with lights. "Larry, someone's in—"

"That's Erica."

I saw the small frown that pulled at his mouth. "I forgot to tell you that she was coming. It's okay, honey."

"Why is she here?" I don't even know why I asked the question. I knew the answer.

"She came to help us work things out."

"She's our daughter, Larry. She's not a marriage counselor. I don't want her advice. Besides," I looked at my husband's face, "we're going to work things out."

"I know, Mick. Maybe we could just humor her."

"Why? Why can't we just tell her thanks, but we'll handle this problem ourselves?"

"It will hurt her feelings. She came a long way to help."

"I didn't ask her to come."

We sat for a couple of minutes in the car not wanting to go inside. *So okay*, I thought, *you said you were going to give this marriage another chance. Now's the time.*

"Turn the car around. Let's go get a hotel room for the night and make love. We'll come back in the morning." I smiled at Larry thinking he would agree.

"That would be wrong, Mick. She'll probably be worrying about us, wondering where we are."

I could feel the stiffening of my spine. "It's your call, but I think we need to do this for us. I think for once we need to come first. What do you think?"

"I think as much as I want to make love to you right this moment, I won't be able to, for worrying that our daughter is awake all night worrying about us."

I looked at him. "You need to work with me, Larry."

"We have a perfectly good bed waiting for us in our home." He smiled then. "We don't have to do anything but go in the house, talk to Erica for a few minutes and go to bed."

I leaned away from him and looked at my home. I felt a tremendous impulse to flee once again, but then I'd decided to give up running.

"Why don't we go in, talk to Erica for a few minutes, tell her we're going to spend the night in a hotel. Would that be all right?" I asked. "She won't worry then."

He kissed me quickly on the lips. "Sure, honey. We'll do that."

He bounded up the stairs not bothering to wait for me. *Don't think about it*, I told myself as I followed him. I prayed again, that this time she was alone, that she had found someone to keep the kids or had left them with Roy.

The moment Larry turned the handle on the door I knew that was one wish that wasn't coming true. The screams of my grandchildren vibrated throughout the house. I glanced at my watch. It was one A.M. They should be in bed.

We stepped into the living room to utter chaos. The sofa pillows lay on the floor and drawing paper littered the room. I took another step and felt a crunch under my shoes. I looked down. Cereal. That surprised me. We didn't have any in the house, or we hadn't when we left.

Erica spotted us the same moment as the kids. The kids ran for us screaming, "Grandpa, Grandpa." Erica's lips were thinned in disapproval as she eyed me.

"Hello, Mother," she said to me as if I were no more than the crushed cereal under my feet. "Dad, are you all right?" She went to Larry and kissed his cheeks.

Larry's face was alight with joy. He held one of the kids in each arm, looking down at them with total adoration, oblivious to the mess they'd made of our home in our absence.

He glanced at Erica. "Hi, honey, nice to see you."

I interrupted their little reunion. "Why is there cereal in the entryway?"

"You had no food they wanted. I had to go to the store and buy it," Erica said in an accusing tone, as though the mess wouldn't be on my floor if I had not been so thoughtless as to not have it in the cupboards.

I sighed loudly, looking over at Larry. "Erica, your father and I are staying the night in a hotel. We'll come back in the morning. I would appreciate it if by then our home is in the same condition that you found it."

She ignored me and turned instead to her father. "Dad, I just flew 1500 miles with two grumpy kids, find you gone, no food and you're going to leave?" I watched as she turned away. "I came here for you, to support you. If you didn't want me to come you should have told me."

I smiled inwardly at my daughter's maneuvering of her father. Surely he wouldn't fall for such an obvious ploy. I reached for his hand to hold it, stroke it, my insurance that he wouldn't, that he would remember what we'd planned

Mindy, our granddaughter, wrapped her arms even tighter around Larry's neck. "Grandpa, don't leave, please…," she wailed. Her big brown eyes filled with tears and I marveled. She was even better at this than her mother.

Larry turned to me. "Mick, it's up to you." I watched as three pairs of eyes turned to glare at me.

Okay, so I would be the bad guy once again. "I think we should stick to our plans." I ignored the pleading look my husband was attempting to give me. I knew without a doubt we needed to be alone, now more than ever.

The words were barely out of my mouth when little Larry, named after his grandfather, knocked a vase of flowers to the floor. My husband released my hand as I stood there watching the water spill on my new carpet.

"Mick, we can't go now. Why don't you get ready for bed? I'll join you in a little while."

He walked away to clean up the mess. Erica never made a move toward the kitchen for a mop or towel. She ignored it and gave me a smirk.

"I put your things back in your room. I'm sleeping in my bedroom."

"So you're flying home tonight?" I answered and walked past her to my newly claimed room.

I calmly took her things and put them outside the door. She was staring at me as if I'd lost my mind. What difference did it make now? I knew that's why she was here anyway. She thought her mother had finally lost her marbles.

Larry came from cleaning up the mess just as I was tossing the last of Erica's belongings on the pile. He looked from the pile to me, then toward the stairs leading to our bedroom door.

"I'll be in as soon as I read the kids a story and put them to bed."

He smiled at me, not doubting that I would be waiting. I went into the room, locked the door, fell into bed and instantly fell into a dreamless sleep.

I was awakened by a tapping on the door and Larry calling my name. I looked at the clock. Four A.M. I turned over and blocked the knocking out of my mind.

Larry stood knocking softly on the door. He knew without a doubt Mick was awake, just as he knew there was no way in hell she was going to let him make love to her now.

He looked around his home in dismay. They'd only been gone a few hours. How had two kids managed to totally destroy every room in their home in that amount of time? Why had his daughter allowed it?

He thought for a moment of her sparkling home in Arizona and he cringed. He knew he needed to tell his daughter that she'd crossed the line. But all it took from her was watery eyes and he couldn't scold her.

He walked back to his own bedroom, his hunger for his wife a deep ache within his soul. He had not touched her in three months. He had not caressed her creamy flesh, or felt himself buried deep within her. And now he was left with a painful erection the size of Montana.

If only he hadn't spent the last two hours cleaning up the mess his grandchildren made, maybe Mick would have let him in. He groaned at his lie. The time wasn't the issue.

It was his not leaving with her. He was hoping the somewhat cleaned house would soften Mick in the morning. If she woke and looked at the mess in the kitchen and bathroom he didn't doubt that she would toss Erica and the kids out on their butts. So he'd cleaned when all he wanted to do was make love to his wife.

He slid beneath the covers thinking of all the wasted time. He'd given Mick the cold shoulder to force her to give in. She hated his silence. For twenty-six years that had worked. Now she fought against it. He knew it bothered her, but not enough to make her come back to their bed, to his arms.

He thought about the party, how beautiful she'd looked, how right she'd felt in his arms. He thought about the kisses they'd shared. His erection swelled until he found himself rubbing his own flesh, thinking of his wife.

She should be here with him now, lying beside him, her head on his belly or his on hers. She should be in his arms, touching him, loving him. She'd said she still loved him. Larry shut his eyes tightly, the urge to cry fighting with the need for physical release.

He'd blown it once again. This time he didn't need his wife to point it out to him. He wasn't completely dense. If only he could tell her the real reason he always gave in to the kids.

Larry stopped his self manipulation. His hand was not what he wanted. He was disgusted with himself. Mick had almost hit on the truth he'd kept hidden from her. That little kid that he tried to keep buried kept turning up at the oddest moments.

That crack Mick had made about him being better off without his mother had hurt. When he ran out the house, he'd gotten a hotel room and stayed there until he could face her again. He knew she thought he was angry but that wasn't what drove him away or kept him away for three days.

It was having to admit to the weakness. He hated the fact that just the mention of his mother could still cut him like a sword. He was a lawyer, for God's sake. A damn good one at that. He was in his forties, too damn old to carry around the baggage from an abandoned runny-nosed five-year-old kid.

He hated that the memory haunted him and had the power to drop him to his knees. Mick had suggested several times through the years that he get counseling for it. He could never do that. She would think he was weak. No, damn it, she would know he was weak.

He liked that she looked up to him, that she respected him. He didn't want her feeling sorry for him. Hell, what kind of man would he be if the only emotion his wife felt for him was pity? No, he had to remain strong for her. How would she ever look to him for protection if she saw him fall apart?

So he'd gone to the hotel and he'd stayed there until he felt he could safely return home. When he saw her, all he'd wanted to do was fall in her arms and cry, have her hold him and comfort him. He couldn't do that. He had to be strong for her. All that he did and had done for the last twenty-six years was for her, for her and the kids.

He thought a moment about the kids. He wished he had told Mick of his own promises. There in the car, when she said she thought he'd used her to get the family he wanted, he could have told her, but he didn't.

The day they'd married he'd promised himself and her that he would love her forever. When Erica was born he remembered whispering in her ear that he would never leave her, never make her feel the pain of abandonment. Never would he ever want her to go through the emotional hell he'd been forced to endure.

With each child he'd promised the same thing. He would have loved to have more kids, but he'd gotten the vasectomy.

Mick had no idea how hard that had been for him to do. He'd never told Mick, because he loved her. He didn't want her worrying about him. It was his job to worry about her.

When the kids starting giving them grandchildren, some of that hurt of not being able to have more babies went away. He made the same promise to them as he had to his own kids. He would never abandon them.

His promise to love Mick forever? Hell, that one was easy. He loved her with every breath he took. It was that second promise that caused him the problems. He was no more happy with his daughter's behavior than his wife was. He just didn't know how to discipline her and not make her feel abandoned.

He'd never been any good at discipline with any of the kids. He loved them so damn much it hurt at times. Mick had no way of knowing that there were plenty of times he wanted to yell at them to go away, but the image of that five-year-old haunted him and he couldn't do it.

When he saw his trashed home, he had almost sent them away, until Mindy wound her arms around his neck and pleaded with him not to leave. He'd fought against the image of the little boy tugging on his mother's skirt crying, *"Don't leave me, Mommy, I'll be good."*

Now he was in bed alone, wishing he had some remedy that would banish that memory from him forever.

The only thing that gave him a semblance of peace was that Mick had told him she still loved him. Yeah, she was angry now and hurt.

That was preferable to her losing respect for him. That he couldn't handle. Just knowing she hadn't stopped loving him gave him the strength to stay in bed and not break down her door.

She would come to him. It would take time, but she would come. He fell asleep hoping Erica's visit would be short. Maybe after she left he'd take Mick on a getaway. *Just a few more days. She doesn't need to know that I can't make that little boy go away.*

I woke a little after six. I groaned from the weariness I was beginning to feel. For a time last night I had been Michelle.

And Larry, Larry had once again been the handsome boy I'd married. In fact my husband was even more handsome than the day we'd married. His dark brown hair was thick and soft. I loved it and I loved the huge dimples in his cheeks when he smiled down at me. My stomach twisted thinking of the many things I loved about my husband. I'd been so sure he'd heard me at last. Then the daughter from hell had shown up on our doorstep, unannounced.

From shortly after Erica's birth we had been like oil and water. I think after awhile she even preferred a bottle to my breasts. I sighed with the forgotten memory that it hadn't always been like that. Initially Erica had been as happy to accept breastfeeding from me as I was to have her suckle at my breasts. My baby, my firstborn. The memory was fleeting but it was there. I'd been happy with my new baby. What had happened to change that? I couldn't for the life of me remember what it was.

Larry said we had the same temperament. If that were true Larry and I would have been divorced ages ago. Erica was not passive, not like me. She spoke up for what she wanted, demanding more than her fair share. I'd often wondered how Roy could stand her.

Larry's refusal to stand up to her angered and puzzled me. I had been married to the man for twenty-six years. Of course I knew the baggage he carried. How many times had I attempted to get him to confront his pain?

I knew deep in my gut his unwillingness to punish the children, even with a mild scolding, had to do with his mother.

My attempts through the years to get him to acknowledge this had met with stony resistance. The mere mention of her and his eyes would fill with pain.

If I ever met the woman I swore I would strangle her with my bare hands. Of course she'd probably be in a nursing home by now, preventing me from carrying out my plans. She'd inflicted scars on my husband that I had been unable to heal. I knew firsthand that pain doesn't go away with time.

When thoughts of Chance flitted across my mind, I pushed them away. My decision was made. I felt the ache begin in my heart. I knew how easy it would be to succumb to wanting him. He fulfilled things in me that I had not known I needed.

Enough, I reprimanded myself. *You can't think of him, not when you're this angry at Larry.*

I slipped out of the bed, my thoughts turning instead to the medium, Blaine MaDia.

I could see him again, I thought. *Seeing him would not take anything away from Larry. And I didn't give my word not to see him.*

The moment I opened the door a loosely formed thought turned into a concrete idea. Erica's things scattered about told me that I would spend my morning out of the house. Hopefully, I could find enough to do to keep me away until bedtime.

I felt like a thief sneaking down the hall to the shower, running the water at half force, not wanting anyone to wake up. It wasn't out of concern for them, but because there was not a one of them that I wanted to see.

I would make coffee, only enough for myself. I couldn't help smiling at the rebellious thought, knowing that I wouldn't follow though.

The smell of soap followed me out of the bathroom, to be replaced by the scent of fresh brewed coffee. Larry was awake. God forbid that it would be Erica who would be thoughtful enough to start the coffee. I headed for the kitchen. I might as well get it over with.

I glanced at Larry sitting at the table with a cup of coffee in his hands, waiting for me. I took a cup, turning to the counter determined to block him from my view.

"Mick, do you really want to start the silence all over again?" he asked. There was not a trace of sarcasm in his voice. I turned toward him. I didn't want to live in silence. He knew that.

"I'm sorry about last night, Mick. I knocked on your door."

"I know." I answered. If he was looking for an explanation he would have to keep looking.

"What was I supposed to do?"

"You were supposed to be my husband. You should have demanded Erica clean up the mess she allowed her kids to make. You should have gone with me to a hotel, any hotel. You should have been a man."

I was trying so hard not to cry. I saw the glint of anger come into his eyes as he squared his jaw and stared at me. He was right to be angry. I regretted the words the moment they came from my mouth.

"Are you saying I'm not a man?"

"I'm saying you sure as hell didn't act like one last night."

I wanted to stop saying things to my husband that I didn't mean, but I couldn't seem to stop myself. I knew Larry's problems came from his childhood. I knew his mother was to blame. But I was angry also. I wanted to push him into admitting the truth, if not to me then at least to himself.

He had a menacing look in his eyes. "I've been a man to you for over a quarter of a century. Now what? You get bored with our life and blame me. You find a lover and now I'm not a man."

"I'm sorry, Larry. I shouldn't have said that."

"But you did. Maybe that's what you really think of me. Is it, Mick?"

His voice was the controlled steel he used in the courtroom, yet he was unable to mask the pain my words had caused him. I had gone much farther than I wanted or had ever intended to go.

"No. I'm angry with you. I only said it… Oh, forget it. I didn't mean it."

"I can't forget it that easily. Why did you say it?"

I decided to stop the escalation of our argument before it became even more hurtful. "Last night was wonderful." I stopped. "Before we came home, that is. I wanted so much for us to be together to make love. I wanted to fall asleep in your arms and wake in them. I've missed you."

"Then you should have opened the door."

I stood looking at my husband, my eyes rolled to the top of my head, shaking my head back and forth.

"I don't believe it. You really don't hear me, do you? What's wrong with you, Larry? Why did we have to even come in the house? Why did you let Erica talk you into letting her come here? You know she and I don't get along. Why pretend?"

"Let's get something straight, Mick. You're the one who had the affair, not me. Erica came to help out. I don't think you have any right to talk to me the way you are."

I shook my head while glaring at him. "I thought you were finally getting it." I laughed. It was a harsh, brutal sound to my ears. "What I did had nothing to do with sex. It had everything to do with my getting my needs met for a change."

"Yet you had sex with him."

"AHHHHHHHHHHHHHHHHHHHHHH." In mid scream I realized what I was doing, but I couldn't stop the high-pitched sound from coming from my throat. Larry's mouth was open in shocked horror. He was staring at me, as if he thought I was a stranger, a crazed stranger.

"Larry, stop being an attorney for once. Stop looking for clues. There's no need. I'm telling you what happened. It had nothing to do with sex."

I regretted briefly my self-indulgent scream as I heard the mumble of voices. I'd awakened the demon kids.

For a long moment I stared at my husband before I spoke. "Why can't you be honest with yourself? Why do you always freeze up when it's time to discipline the kids? You're such a strong confident man. I've seen you in the courtroom. You're brilliant, you don't take any crap off of anyone. Your one weakness is the kids. They're not going to stop loving you if you discipline them. You're their hero. They're always going to love you.

I was pleading with him. Maybe there was something more than his mother abandoning him that was at work here. Maybe she'd beaten him and he'd never told me. There had to be something that made my husband, whom I knew without a doubt loved me, shove me aside time and again for our kids. I hesitated a moment, made another decision. I couldn't continue to live the same life I'd led. I was going to heed the advice of the voice. With or without Larry, I was going to learn to live again.

I shut my eyes for a moment, the remnants of a sob long dead filling my chest and coming out as a sigh. "Baby, help me, please. Tell me what's going on. Why the kids, Larry? Why are they more important to you than I am? Why are they more important than our marriage?"

I looked away, darker thoughts filling my mind, thoughts that I knew were not true, but still they came.

Larry saw the look on my face and knew what I was thinking. "Don't go down that road, Mick," he warned. "What is it that you want me to tell you?"

"Tell me the truth."

"What truth?"

"Why are you so willing to throw our lives away? The children are grown. You've fulfilled your obligations. This time should be for us."

"That's just it, Mick, you see them as obligations. They were never that for me. They were gifts, precious gifts, just as you were. Are you faulting me for loving my children, for loving you? You never talked like this before...before..."

I saw his confusion and it saddened me, permeating every cell in my body with sorrow. "Before what? Before Chance? If that's the case I think we both owe him our thanks. If we salvage this marriage it will be because of him."

I turned on my heels to go and get dressed. We were not getting anything accomplished. We were merely going around in circles.

"*If*, Mick? *If* we salvage our marriage?"

His voice was so forlorn that I almost changed my mind. This life I was leading was not what I wanted, yet I didn't know how to go back and be the same woman I'd been before I met Chance. I didn't even know how to be the same woman I'd been before I'd hit Viola. Neither woman was me. They'd merely been occupying my body in my absence. Well, I was back now to lay claims on my life.

"Yes, *if*, Larry," I said loud and clear. Then I went to get dressed.

In less than twenty minutes I was dressed and about to head out the door. Larry was standing nearby watching me. I saw him glance at his watch, then avert his eyes. We both knew I wouldn't be calling on any of my clients at this ungodly hour. Even the office wouldn't be open for two more hours.

"Mother, why were you screaming? You woke me and the kids. I think that was very inconsiderate of you."

It was Erica, who else? I went to my firstborn, kissed her on the cheek, smiled at her and said, "Good morning to you too, dear." Her eyes widened in surprise as did Larry's.

I rolled the bag I used to carry my samples to the car, opened the trunk, and was about to put it in when Larry did it for me.

"Thank you."

"Mick..."

"That's okay, Larry. Nothing's going to change. I know that now. You can't help how you feel and neither can I."

"Where are you going?"

"Not where you think."

"Then where are you going."

"I'm going to go treat myself to breakfast, and then go do my job."

"I can come with you."

I looked at him for a long moment, and I raised my hand to his face to touch his cheek. It was too little, too late. "No, I don't think so," I answered him. "It wouldn't do any good."

I got in my car and drove away, leaving Larry standing in the drive looking after me. He would be fine. He had Erica and the kids. He had the family he'd always yearned for.

I could barely wait until nine A.M. to call Blaine MaDia, though the last thing I needed in this life was another kid. Maybe a child from a past life wouldn't be as mouthy. I smiled to myself as I listened to the ringing of the phone.

"Hello."

His voice was smooth and refined. I felt a sharp electrical jab, amazed that even the sound of his voice was having such an effect on me.

"Hi, this is…hmm…hmm." I had to stop to clear my throat. "I'm sorry. I came to see you a couple of months ago, and I…I… Well, I…"

He laughed, the sound a musical tinkle. "I know who you are," he answered me. "I was wondering how long it would be before you called."

"How did you know that I would?"

"I'm a psychic, remember?"

"I don't quite know if I believe that."

"Then why are you calling me?"

He had me there. "Something strange happened to me at your lecture and I want to know what it was."

"What do you think it was?"

"I think you're very good at your job, that you seem to be asking all the questions and wanting me to supply the answers."

I was just a little irritated. I had pictured the conversation going a lot more smoothly. I don't know if I expected him to tell me how he'd been searching for me as Chance had, but I didn't expect his evasiveness. He was as mouthy as the kids I had in this life.

"Thank you."

"What are you thanking me for?"

"For saying that I'm good at my job. But I can't take the credit." He laughed softly. "It's a gift."

"Listen, I have my doubts about you. Matter of fact, my husband thinks you're a con. He's a very high profile attorney. If that is the case, I mean, if you're going around conning people, he can make things very rough for you."

"Excuse me, but are you threatening me?"

I could feel myself blushing because that was exactly what I was doing. "Listen, let's start over. I want to make an appointment with you. How much do you charge?"

"I'm very expensive. I have to be in case I need to defend myself against a high profile attorney."

I found myself laughing then. "That just came out. I'd never been to a psychic before your seminar. I didn't know what to expect and never in my wildest dreams did I expect what did occur. I just want to talk to you, see if you got the same impressions I did."

"What were those impressions that you got?"

"You're doing it again."

"Oh, am I? I guess I was fishing for information, probing, as it were. You know that is a method that... what did you call me before, a fake? Well, that is a method used by fakes."

I listened to the sound of his voice. He wasn't angry or hurt, but simply amused. "Mr. MaDia, would it be possible for you to be serious for a moment? This matter is very important to me."

"I'm sorry, go ahead. I sometimes go into my sarcastic mode when I'm nervous."

"Why would you be nervous?"

"The same as you."

"Can you see me?"

"Of course."

"When?"

"Anytime you say."

"How about in an hour?"

"I'll be waiting."

"One more thing. I need to know this. How much is the charge?" I heard his musical laughter once again before he answered me.

"Because of the family connection, this one's on me. See you in an hour." He laughed and severed the connection

My entire body tingled. He'd been toying with me. So it was true. He had seen the same images I had. Did he truly believe he was my reincarnated son? I held onto the phone looking at it.

Was it possible that I was this Dimitra and that this man I was going to see was a son I had lost? *I must be crazy*, I thought.

Suddenly I felt a tremendous lift to my spirit. The dark cloud that had enveloped my spirit for such a long time was lifting. I felt energized, as if I was finally going to get a chance to right a wrong.

"Come on in."

Blaine was ushering me into his inner office. He was about to touch his hand to my back. I cringed and moved away. He smiled and stepped back, allowing me to enter the room untouched.

I felt stupid, childish. The thought of this man being able to touch me and make me see things was so amazingly terrifying, that I marveled at his gift, yet a part of me feared it.

He sat across from me lacing his hands together. His fingers were long and slender. I watched him, awed at the tenderness that flowed through me.

I felt strongly that this man facing me was a good man, not a con. He was someone I could easily care about. He felt more like my child to me in that instant, than the daughter that was waiting at home.

There was a moment of awkwardness that evaporated the moment he spoke.

"I know you're nervous."

He smiled at me and I watched the dimple in his cheek. He was a handsome man, if perhaps a little too pale. He had wavy almost white blond hair and eyes that I couldn't tell if they were blue or gray.

"What's your name?" he asked.

"Michelle," I answered barely above a whisper. "Michelle Powers?"

"That's a nice name, Michelle." He appeared to roll my name around on his tongue. "Would you mind if I call you Michelle? Or would you prefer that I call you Mrs. Powers?"

"Michelle's fine, Mr. MaDia."

I watched him smile more fully this time, his eyes barely crinkling. Laugh lines dotted his features.

"If I'm going to call you Michelle, you may as well call me Blaine."

"Okay, Blaine." I snuggled into the seat and stared at him. "What do we do now?"

"What would you like to do?" He stopped and laughed. "I'm sorry, that's a habit. I'll try and stop when I'm with you."

When I'm with you. The words played in my head. He was making it sound as if he expected an ongoing relationship.

"Michelle, I'm sorry for the way I approached you at the seminar." His eyes probed my face. "I know you've come here to me for answers to what happened, but I really don't have any. I can only guess."

I stared at him. This was not what I had expected. I thought in a matter of minutes he would be able to answer every question I'd ever had about my life, about my marriage, about Viola and about Chance.

He held his hands toward me as if he wanted to touch me, then thought better of it and drew back

"Listen, this has never happened to me." He stopped. "Or to anyone I know, psychic or otherwise."

"You want to touch me, don't you?" I grinned at him.

"Why do you ask?"

"Because it's obvious. Your hands are twitching and you seem ready to spring out of your chair."

He laughed and I joined in. "Are you curious to know if it will happen again?" he asked cautiously.

"Yes, but unlike you I don't have the gift. I don't know what to make of all this. You seem to be adjusting to it much better than I am."

"Ah, that's just what I wanted you to think. I've talked to a ton of people since the day I saw you. I've read everything I could get my hands on and nowhere did anyone ever mention anything like what happened between us. I'm not altogether sure you're not psychic though."

"Believe me I'm not. What did happen, Blaine? Tell me what you saw."

"So you want me to go first. You're still a little skeptical, aren't you?" He laughed off my objections. "Don't...don't worry about it. I'm glad that you're cautious.

"Here goes. I was standing on my stage minding my own business, trying my best to get a bead on all the voices that filled my head. I was trying to focus the energy on just one person in the audience. It didn't matter who. But I had to still the voices to allow just one to come through."

"Did I interfere with that?"

"I believe you did." He smiled. "But it wasn't your fault. For the first hour of the lecture nothing unusual happened. I was about to give a reading when I felt an electrical current begin in my toes and work its way toward my groin. I tried to ignore it, but then it reached my belly and kept moving until it reached my chest.

"It took me so by surprise that I remember dropping to my knees. I didn't know what was happening. The voices in my head were no longer clear. I couldn't focus. I looked up and saw a thin stream. It was silver in the beginning but it turned to a blinding white light. I saw it leave my body and rise up in the air and shoot out into the audience.

He stopped talking for a moment, breathing hard. "The whole thing was so damn freaky it scared the hell out of me." He paused, looking embarrassed. "I'm sorry for the language."

"Don't worry about it, continue."

"I didn't have time to think about what was happening before this stream of energy came back and hit me in the chest. It seemed to go inside my body. I could do nothing for a few moments.

"When I went off the stage I could barely stand. I thought it was perhaps just someone from the other side that was pissed at being ignored. I didn't know.

"When I came back out I kept hearing your thoughts. They were louder than any of the voices of the spirits I was trying to reach. That's another thing that had never happened to me.

"At first I thought you were another psychic trying to ruin my lecture. That's why I was so rude to you. That's why I came to where you were. I never would have done that otherwise. It wasn't until I touched you that I knew you were the source of the phenomenon. You were the voice in my head, the voice I've heard my entire life saying, "I'm sorry. I love you. Forgive me. Your voice was the voice of the mother I'd known only in my heart."

He stood, clearly agitated, and began moving around the room. "I touched you, Michelle, and I was in another place. You were there and the man that was with you, the high profile attorney, I presume."

"No," I answered, feeling my face flame with my shameful knowledge. "He's a friend. He's not my husband." I looked down, biting my lips.

"I'm not judging you, Michelle."

"Thanks."

"Do you want me to continue?"

"Yes, please. What happened next?"

"I saw myself as a baby wrapped up and off to the side in a heavy towel. I was cold, very tiny, covered in blood and having a difficult time breathing. I saw you and the man beside you.

"I heard you call him Jeremy and he called you Dimitra. I saw you bleeding. You were crying and asking him to take care of the baby. He didn't want to. He blamed me for your dying, but you made him promise to love me. Then you made him promise to find you in the next life."

He looked at me hopefully. "Is that what you saw?" he asked finally.

"Yes. That's it exactly. Am I crazy?"

"If you are, then so am I. I've talked to a lot of people about it, other psychics," he answered my questioning look. "I also talked to other people I trust, people who are experts in regression. I've helped others with regression thousands of times. In fact I'm quite good at it," he stated proudly. "But this, it had me stumped.

"I tried to find you. I put an ad in the paper; I talked about it on the radio. I hoped you would call. It was beginning to feel as if you weren't, but I knew you would eventually."

"Is there a way to find out if this really happened?"

"Only one that I know of."

"What's that?" I asked, suspicious that I already knew the answer.

"Everyone I talked to agreed with me, that we should try it again."

Suddenly I wished Chance was by my side. He'd gotten me into this. If I'd never met him I would not be sitting here now trying to make sense of a vision, trying to find out if it was real.

"You're thinking about him, aren't you…the man you were with?"

"Yes." I had decided lying would be impossible with a person who could so easily read my thought.

Blaine laughed at me. "Your thoughts come through loud and clear. Also, you wear your feelings on your face. Even if I weren't a psychic, I think I would know what you're thinking." He smiled. "You love him, don't you?"

"I have no right to love him. I'm married."

"But you're unhappy in your marriage."

"It doesn't take a gift to figure that one out. If I weren't, I wouldn't have been with Chance, now would I?"

"So that's his name?" His eyes became veiled, shutting off the hint of something. I was aware he was trying to hide something from me. Something to do with Chance. "Are you ashamed of loving Chance, Michelle? He's not ashamed of loving you."

I looked at him.

"I could tell. He was so protective of you."

I saw the way Blaine's eyes darted around the room before focusing on my face. There was something going on with him.

I could only solve one mystery at a time. The one concerning information Blaine was hiding from me would have to wait for another time.

"Chance has nothing to lose, Blaine. He doesn't have a family. I have a husband. I have five children."

I looked at him seeing a tiny twitch around his lips. "I have five children this time around. I also have grandchildren. I have responsibilities. I can't just run off and forget all of that."

"You're making a great defense. But I'm not a lawyer. You don't need to defend yourself with me. Seems like you may have picked up some of your husband's skills."

"I'm sorry I'm ranting. It's just that I got into this fight with my husband this morning. This thing with Chance really hurt him. I'd never cheated on him before, never thought I would."

I laughed then. "You could have bet me a million dollars and I would have taken the bet. That's how sure I was. I knew I would never cheat on my husband."

"How did it happen?"

I closed my eyes tightly and held my face in my hands. "He picked me up in a parking lot."

"Just like that?"

"Just like that."

"There's not more to this story?"

"Nothing that will justify it. I wanted to die that day. I was crying in the rain. He came over to me to help. He held me in his arms and the next thing I knew I'd destroyed my marriage and hurt my husband beyond belief."

"You were destined to meet, Michelle. You made him promise. If you had not met this time you would have met in the next life."

"Do you really believe in reincarnation? I mean, the whole thing sounds so far out." I attempted a lighthearted shrug. "My husband threatened to have me committed if I don't stop talking about this stuff."

"And you came anyway." He opened a small compact refrigerator he had tucked away and offered me a bottle of juice. I took it, careful not to touch him. He laughed at me and took a long swig from his own bottle.

"Larry would never do anything intentionally to hurt me. He loves me."

"Do you love him?"

Now I was offended. "Of course I love my husband." I bristled, stopping at the look on his face. "Just because of what happened with Chance doesn't mean I don't love my husband."

"I didn't say anything."

"But you're looking at me." I ignored his indulgent smile. "Your look says I'm lying. I'm not. I love my husband."

"So, what's the problem?"

I took a long drink. "I feel like you're a shrink. I don't know, I guess I feel unnecessary to his life. He's accomplished his goal and now I'm dispensable."

"What were his goals?"

"To have a family."

"Aren't you a part of his family?"

I stared at Blaine. Those were Larry's words. "I guess I am."

"So then, it has to be more."

I thought about it for a moment. For some reason things were spilling from my lips that I had never uttered aloud. I don't think I'd even thought them.

"I feel lost," I said in a small voice. "Swallowed up, as if I've been playing a part for so long to make everyone happy that I no longer know who I am. It feels that I've awakened from some long nightmare. I'm frightening my husband and myself because usually I keep the peace. How does the peacemaker repair the damage she's caused?"

"Sometimes there are things that shouldn't be repaired. Sometimes you have to let things go and start over again."

"If you believe everything you say, that I'm your mother in a previous life and Chance is your father from that same lifetime, couldn't you perhaps be just a little biased?"

We both laughed then. "Yeah, I suppose you could be right," Blaine admitted. "It seems like such a romantic story to have the two of you find each other again, that maybe I did get a little carried away."

I looked at my watch. "I have to go. I have clients I have to see." Blaine stood.

"Will I see you again?" he asked.

"You can count on it. I want to hear all about your life. But I do have to run now." I glanced quickly at him. There was something so familiar in his eyes. "I want to give you a hug."

"Then why don't you?" he teased, knowing I was still afraid of touching him.

"Maybe next time. I'll remember to wear rubber, that should insulate me." I stood, smiling at the tall man who'd given me so much just by listening to me and not judging. "Thanks, Blaine. It was nice talking to you. If you'd like to bill me for this…"

He stopped me. "Thanks for coming, Michelle. Please come back soon."

As I drove away from Blaine's office I couldn't help smiling. Only death would prevent me from seeing him again and again and…

Chapter Eleven

My soul had taken wings. With each step I took I could feel the cleansing release. I sailed through my appointments, not minding for once the nurses that kept me waiting, welding the power they possessed, cajoling more supplies from me than I should have given.

It didn't matter. I gave it all joyfully, for joy was the only emotion left within me. That and a great need to share that joy with the one person that would understand. I wanted to share this with Chance.

My last call finished, I sat in my car talking myself out of just driving to his office. I wondered if I was still bound by my words to Larry. I'd told him and Chance that it was over. Now the need to connect with Chance gnawed away at me like a deep hunger. There was only one thing that would abate the intense craving.

Retrieving my cell phone from my purse, I rapidly punched in Chance's office number and asked for him before my courage failed me. I heard his muffled voice before he spoke into the receiver.

"Hello."

"Hello, Chance. How are you?"

"Dimi? Dimi, is that you?"

"It's not Dimi, Chance. It's plain old me, Michelle." I clutched the phone to my cheek, my heart feeling as if it would burst from my chest at any moment. I missed him. The sound of his voice, the touch of his caress, his love. I remembered and I missed his love the most.

"Why are you calling, Michelle?"

His voice was cold yet I detected no anger. "Are you upset with me, Chance? Did I catch you at a bad time?"

"You can't keep doing this, Michelle. You're killing me."

"Doing what?"

"Dropping in and out of my life. I don't think I can take much more."

I heard a long sigh from the other end of the phone, his voice stilled by sadness. I shivered, my mouth opening voluntarily as if to capture Chance's pain in my body.

"Would you like for me to hang up?"

"Everything in me is demanding that I say yes, tell you never to call me again. God help me, I can't. I've been so damn worried about you, nothing, not a word, for two months, not one word. How could you do that to me?"

"I didn't know you were going to be worried."

"How could you not know that? You were going back to your husband. We both knew you were going to tell him that you'd been with me. I tried everything to find you. I had to know that you were safe. I've never been so afraid and felt so helpless in my entire life."

His voice broke on a sob, wrenching my heart in two. This was not the reason for my call. I didn't want to hurt him. I didn't want to feel his pain. I only wanted to share my joy with the one person who would understand. I searched my mind frantically for something, anything, to lighten the dark mood.

"So that's why you called my boss?" I asked at last.

"Of course. Why else would I do it? I had no way to reach you. I thought this would make you call me even if you were angry." He paused. "I was wrong. You sent a damn cavalcade of drugs and still not a word."

"I was trying hard to work on my marriage, Chance. I couldn't do that and keep seeing you at the same time. Larry would never stand a chance. Too much has happened between us. You have my husband at an unfair advantage. I had to even the odds."

"And have you?"

"Have I what?"

"Have you repaired your marriage?"

"For a short time last night, I thought I had. Then it all fell apart again."

"Is that why you're calling me, you're angry at Larry and I'm the one you run to, to soothe your bruised spirit?"

"Chance, I thought you said you would be my friend." I squeezed my eyes shut, doing my best to keep my own pain inside. I would not use tears against Chance. "I just need a friend. I'm sorry I called. I won't do it again."

A split second before I severed the call I heard Chance call my name. The mournful sound stopped my fingers.

"Michelle, why are you in such desperate need of a friend?"

"I have wonderful news and you're the only one I can share it with." The excitement was bubbling up in my throat, pushing away the pain of only a moment before. I knew he would allow me to share my joy with him.

"I went to see Blaine MaDia. Oh my God, Chance. It was wonderful." I was all but gushing now. "He's so nice. He talked to me for the longest time, and guess what? He didn't even charge me. He didn't want my money. Can you believe that?" I laughed. "Chance, he's not a fake. I know he's not."

"I thought you were afraid of him, that you never wanted to mention his name again."

"I know, but I haven't been able to stop thinking of him. I had to go see him again."

"You went to see him, but you didn't think to contact me?"

"Chance, Blaine poses no threat to my life. Besides, I only got up the nerve to do it today. It's still today," I tried to placate Chance. "You're the only person I wanted to share this with."

"Chance, stop pouting for a minute and listen to me. Blaine was wonderful. I felt this energy surrounding him. The connection I felt this time was much stronger than before. You would like him. I know you would."

"You're right. I do."

I stopped then, my joy dying a slow death in my chest, turning my joy into ashes within my spirit. "Are you saying you've been back to see him."

"Yes."

"And you told him about me? What a fool I was. I believed him."

I heard Chance shushing me. "Calm down, Michelle," he said. "Blaine didn't ask revealing questions about you. He refused to allow me to tell him anything. He said you were going to come and see him and he wanted there to be no doubt in your mind about whether I had supplied the answers."

I needed badly to believe Chance's words. Still, the seed of doubt Larry had planted earlier reared its ugly head. "You wouldn't lie to me about something this important, would you?"

"I would never lie to you about anything, important or not," Chance answered, sounding slightly miffed.

"I'm sorry for saying that. I know that you wouldn't lie to me... It's just...I haven't felt this good in a long time." I stopped to think about it.

"I don't know if I've ever felt this way. I don't know, Chance, just talking to Blaine seems to have freed me somehow. Did you feel like that when you saw him?"

"No." Chance laughed. "I went there to knock his block off. I thought it was because of him that you were too afraid to even think of a future for us."

"You didn't hit him or anything, did you?"

"No, I wanted to and he knew it. He did nothing to stop me. He sort of sat there looking at me with a smile on his face. He told me if it would make me feel better to hit him, to go ahead.

"He asked me where my wife was and if you were coming to see him. I told him no. I never told him we weren't married. He said to me, 'I'm glad to see the two of you were able to find each other again.'

I heard the change in the tone of Chance's voice. "He called me Jeremy. He thinks that's my name. How could I want to hit him then?"

"Did he touch you?" I held my breath in anxious anticipation.

"Yes, but nothing happened, if that's what you're asking me. He was hoping it would happen with me. Actually, so was I." I heard his disappointment in the words he didn't say.

"How many times have you seen him?"

"I've been seeing him every week, sometimes two or three times a week. He's been to the house several times.

"If he thought we were married, didn't he ever wonder why I wasn't there?"

"The first time he was there he said, 'She's not here, is she?' I answered, no, she's not. Then he said, 'She doesn't want anything to do with me.' He had a sad look on his face. I felt sorry for him, so I told him that you were afraid of him.

"That was enough to satisfy his curiosity?"

"That coupled with the fact that he could feel your energy there. So he didn't question me further on it. He never came uninvited. I assume he thought you left home for his visits."

"Chance, didn't you find it strange to have him there? I mean...none of this bothered you at all about his being there?" I shook my head to clear my thoughts. "Chance, his saying he's our son, that didn't disturb you?"

"No. I enjoyed his visits. In fact he reminded me of you on your first visit. He felt the energy also. He actually sat in the rocker and cried."

"Oh Chance, what did you do when he cried?" My heart was breaking for the young man who had become entangled in my life, but his presence I felt as a blessing not a burden.

"I left the room," Chance said in answer to my question. "I let him cry in peace. When I came back we both pretended nothing was wrong."

I found myself laughing. Here Chance was telling me of Blaine's tears and I was laughing. "You men are so strange. You can deal with the tears of a woman, but let a man cry and you fall to pieces."

We laughed together for a few minutes. I knew eventually we would get around to more serious matters. But for now this felt good. This connection with the other man in my life was what I needed in this moment. Too soon I heard the shift in Chance's voice.

"I want to see you, Dimi."

"Michelle, Chance."

"No. Dimi loves me. This Michelle's too afraid to say who she loves. She stays in a marriage out of guilt and commitment.

"I want to see the woman who lay in my bed for two weeks. The woman whose most secret taste haunts my tongue. I want to see the woman I love. I want to see Dimi."

"Are you saying you don't love me as Michelle?"

"I would love you, if you were Mike, as long as you loved me too. But it seems too hard for you to do that, so I want the woman you pretended to be. She had no problem loving me."

"You know I can't, Chance."

"So what am I supposed to do, wait around another two months until you become sad or filled with pain? Or when you have something you can't share with anyone but me? Is that what you want me to do, Michelle, feast on the crumbs from your table, take whatever Larry leaves and say nothing?"

"I thought we were okay."

"Why? Because you distracted me by talking about Blaine? It worked for a moment. But seeing him is no substitute for my loving you. There is only one thing, one person who will satisfy that particular craving. It's you."

"Chance, don't."

"Don't what? Tell you how much I love you, how much I want you? Michelle, I'm no different from Larry. I need you. Tell me you don't need me, need my love and I'll let this drop."

"I told you I needed a friend."

"Michelle, you're evading the question. Tell me you don't love me and I will never try and be anything to you but a friend. Tell me that."

He knew as well as I did that I would never be able to tell him that. I did love him. I loved him with an intensity I couldn't describe, and he was right. I was committed to Larry. I'd made promises to myself, to him. As disappointed as I was with Larry I didn't want to leave him. I wanted to love him. I wanted to feel this all-encompassing love I felt for Chance, for my husband. I sighed loudly, wanting Chance to hear me, but also wanting the cleansing breath that sighing provides on occasion.

"Chance, I called you because I was happy. I wanted to share that with you. Please don't take that feeling away from me. I don't want to fight. If you do, let's continue this when I'm down and depressed."

To my amazement, he started laughing. Then I started laughing. "Dimi, I love you," Chance said.

"I love you too." I answered him. Why not say it? He knew it and so did I.

"Will you call me again?"

"I will," I promised as I said goodbye and ended the call. If only I could be two people, Dimi the woman who loved Chance, and Michelle, the woman who loved Larry.

I turned into my drive and waited a moment. I thought I would have at the very least pangs of guilt for having called Chance. I didn't.

I was riding high, elated because I'd done what I wanted. I'd talked to two men, who, regardless of what anyone believed, had a place in my life and in my heart. I wouldn't flaunt it, but then again neither would I deny it to myself.

Screams of Mindy and little Larry greeted me as I opened the door. I walked in, looked at the mess the horrific twosome had made of my home, and made another decision.

"Mindy, Lars," I yelled above the din of their shrill baby voices. "Would you two like to go to the park with Grandma?"

The house became so quiet you could hear a pin drop. Mindy eyed me suspiciously, refusing to answer. Little Larry or Lars, as I called him, looked to his sister for guidance.

"Why would you want to take them to the park, Mother?" Erica voiced her suspicions out loud, her voice sarcastic. I swiveled my head around my destroyed home and leveled my daughter with a look before answering her.

"Because I think they need more space to play. Outdoors in the park sounds like a good solution to me."

Erica's mouth was hanging slightly open. I laughed in amusement. I saw the fear enter her eyes as I continued to laugh.

"Really, Erica, I'm not going to kill them. "Lars, Mindy, go grab your jackets. Maybe you should both go potty," I called after them. "Remember to wash your hands."

I turned to see Larry coming toward me. He was eyeing me in an almost identical fashion as our daughter. He attempted to pull me away from Erica's hearing.

"What's this about, Mick? You've never done anything with the grandkids."

I thought about it. He was right. "Maybe it's time I start doing something constructive to keep them from destroying our home. I can't think of a better way to do that than take them to play in the park. Can you?" I challenged.

"Let me get a sweater, I'll join you."

"No, Larry, you stay here. This is for me. I'm not doing it for you."

"It's just the park."

"I know."

"What are you planning? Why don't you want me to come?"

"Do you think it might have anything do to with the fact that we haven't resolved our argument? And maybe, just maybe, I'm not ready to share this with you. For God's Sake, Larry, I don't have any sinister plans. I'm not going to murder them or run away with them, so just relax and stay here with Erica."

I looked away, then back, not able to resist just one little dig. "You didn't want to be with me last night, why now?"

The kids ran up to me before Larry had a chance to answer. "We're ready," they screamed in unison.

"Then let's go," I answered them in my bad imitation of their sing-song voices.

The door had almost closed behind us when Erica whipped it open and looked at me, curiosity getting the better of her. "Mother, will you be back in time to make dinner?" she asked.

"No, I don't think so. I'll treat the kids to dinner out. Why don't you make dinner for your father and yourself?"

The look on her face was so amusing that I leaned over and kissed her, the shock on her face making me regret not having done it sooner.

My eyes connected with Larry as my lips caressed Erica's cheeks. He looked so frightened and alone that I started to tell him to join me. In fact, I opened my mouth to do just that, surprised at the words that came out instead of what I'd intended.

"Erica, while I'm gone this will give you more than enough time to return my home to the condition you found it when you came last night."

I ushered Mindy and Lars into Larry's car and the car seats he had already put in. Once they were safely buckled in, we waved goodbye to Erica and Larry. They both wore puzzled expression and their looks amused me.

I watched the kids playing at the park, running until they were dead on their feet, screaming in joy until they could scream no more. I wanted to kick myself for not having thought of it sooner. They would be much too tired when I returned them home to create any further damage.

The plan worked much better than I would have thought possible. Both kids were so excited about being out, they behaved like perfect angels when we went to eat. I didn't push my luck by taking them to an adult establishment. McDonald's was the voted choice. Their bellies filled, we started home with promises from me that if they were good we would do this again.

Why not? Nothing else had worked. Bribes were my last options. Besides, they would not be here forever, and I didn't have time to modify their behavior. I could only work on the way I reacted to them.

I went to see Blaine twice in the next week. Once we had lunch. I found him an extremely engaging young man. I allowed myself to care for him. His easy manner and quick smile were contagious.

The only thing that was stopping this time from being truly happy was Erica. She never stopped looking at me when I was home. She never said anything, but for some reason her suspicious looks caused me to have suspicions of my own. I had had the distinct impression that I'd been followed but had shrugged it off. Erica's manner made me wonder.

I continued to take the kids out to play a couple of hours a day when I returned home. And miracle of miracles, my home stayed cleaner.

One night after a visit with Blaine, I was feeling extremely peaceful and thought again that with talking perhaps Larry and I could cross the great divide that existed between us.

I showered in the small hall shower, missing the comfort of my huge shower in my bedroom, missing my Jacuzzi tub and missing my comfortable bed. Part of me was missing my husband.

On this particular night, I climbed the stairs to my bedroom instead of going into my newly commandeered room. I walked inside the door and closed it.

Larry stared up at me, his face curious. He watched me as I made my way from the door to the bed. I ran my hand across the thick mattress, missing it even more now that I was not lying on it.

"Hi," I said to Larry. "Mind if we talk?"

He put the book he was reading down on the nightstand. "What is it you want to talk about?"

I was wishing the strange way he was looking at me would change with my words, but I wasn't holding out much hope. I saw the hunger come into his eyes. I knew he wanted me. It had been months since we'd made love. He couldn't hide the fact that he was horny. I saw the covers rise ever so slightly. Denying it would have been futile.

"Larry, I was thinking, maybe we should try marriage counseling." I moved closer to him and allowed my hand to accidentally touch the bulge under the cover. I felt him shiver before he moved away from me.

He looked away toward the door. "Is that the reason you've finally come to our room?" He looked back at me, at the nightgown I wore and I could see him struggling with his lust and his desire to see me give in.

I recognized it in the slant of his jaw as he tilted his head back and gave me the look that said, *So you give in, you're tired of fighting.*

Funny thing, if he'd said that to me I would have readily said yes. I was tired of fighting. I wasn't ready to give in, but I was ready to compromise.

"Tell me something, Mick. What have you been doing this week?"

He was looking at me as though he knew something and he was only waiting for me to admit it. I thought about the two times in the past week I'd seen Blaine. Surely Larry had no way of knowing about that.

"I've been working as usual. What does that have to do with our seeking some help with our problems?"

"Mick, I don't think it's *us* with the problem. I think it's you. You've changed. I used to know without a shadow of a doubt that I could trust you with my life. Now it seems as if I can't even trust you to keep your word."

Larry's eyes fell on my lips and I knew he was using tremendous will power not to kiss me. For some reason he wanted to be angry with me.

"What else did you do this week, Mick? Please give me enough respect not to lie to me again. Tell me the truth."

I knew then that somehow he was aware I'd seen Blaine, but how? "Larry, I haven't lied to you. I never promised you that I wouldn't see Blaine."

"I told you not to, I told you to forget this nonsense."

"You're my husband, Larry. That doesn't give you the right to tell me what to do, and whom I can and can not see.

"Have you been following me around, Larry, waiting for me to sneak away to see Chance?" I wondered if that was what he was doing, because surely it couldn't be Blaine that he was worrying about.

"Is this easy for you, Mick?"

"No, it's not easy for me."

"What did I do to make you stop loving me?"

He ran the pad of his finger down my arm. "I haven't stopped loving you."

"This is the first time you've been in our bedroom in over three months, other than to clean. That sure as hell doesn't feel like you love me. It's been months since we've made love. Most of the time, you won't even come close enough for me to touch you."

His fingers were trembling as he ran them more easily down my arm. His breathing was becoming heavy and I knew that in a matter of seconds the conversation would take an entirely different turn. I didn't move away from him, but I made my voice as firm as I could. I was a bit trembly myself.

"Larry, my not sharing your bed doesn't mean I no longer love you."

"Then what does it mean?"

"It means you refused to listen to me until I took that step."

"Are you saying you're not here in our bed where you belong in order to teach me a lesson?"

He was moving closer to me. He captured my head in his hands; his eyes bored into mine.

"Are you playing games with me?" His voice broke then before he asked, "Are you putting me through hell for no good reason?"

"The fact that you're asking me that is the reason I'm not back in our room. I've been trying to tell you. I'm not happy." I pulled in a deep breath before continuing. I wanted to do this right. I didn't want to hurt my husband or make him angry. I just wanted him to listen to me.

"Honey, please listen to me," I pleaded. "I'm sick and tired of giving in just so we don't have any fights. I'm tired of taking a backseat in your life to our children. If you think I'm attempting to do this to punish you..."

His lips captured mine. His kiss was rough and demanding as he shoved his tongue into my mouth. He pushed me back into the pillows, crushing me beneath his body, his hand searching beneath my gown.

Tearing my lips from his I whispered. "Honey, stop, we need to talk. This isn't going to solve anything."

He was beyond hearing me. His breathing was raspy, and his hands were moving rapidly up and down my body. He pulled away for a moment to pull down his pajamas.

I thought of giving him what he wanted. It had been so long that I knew it would be over in a matter of minutes. All I had to do was lie there, give in, and then maybe he'd be more willing to listen, willing to go to a marriage counselor.

I felt Larry's hand reaching between my legs to guide himself into my body. He didn't care that this wasn't what I wanted. It was what he wanted, what he intended to have.

Just as he moved his hand to begin his descent, I rolled away. "No, Larry! Not until we talk."

My husband froze. He was holding his penis in his hand ready to enter my body and I wasn't there. He made a strangled sound and his hand fell away from his body. The confusion he felt was reflected on his face and in his eyes.

"Why are you even here, Mick?" He rolled away from me, pulling his pajamas back up.

"I want to talk. Do you want to save our marriage? If you do, we need an unbiased third party. We need counseling."

The anger was evident in his voice as well as the hurt when he answered me. "Who told you this, Blaine MaDia? If he's such a hot shot psychic, he should have told you my answer." Larry was out of the bed now, pacing back and forth.

"He hasn't given me any readings. I haven't asked him to. He's just being my friend."

Larry turned, his eyes glaring. "What about Viola? I thought that was the reason you wanted to see him. Weren't you concerned about what you might have been doing right before you hit her? You said you wanted to know why you hadn't seen her. Was that a lie, or are you screwing him too?"

The sound of the slap reverberated throughout our bedroom.

Larry's hand went to the cheek that I'd hit. He was staring wide-eyed at me, surprised. So was I. The sound of the slap was still echoing in every nook of our bedroom.

"You hit me." Larry sounded dazed. "I can't believe you hit me for some guy you're screwing."

I threw my hands up into the air. "Everything comes down to sex with you, doesn't it? Why am I even trying?"

I didn't know if I was asking Larry or myself. I stood in front of my angry husband, bracing myself for the worst, remembering my parents and how their fights always escalated to the point of violence.

Our fights never had, because I had never allowed us to fight. Now, in the middle of our fight, I thought about my mother. Maybe she hadn't been so weak after all. In the end she'd had the guts to end it and get a divorce.

"Larry, you've never listened to me. In the two years we were dating and the twenty-six years we've been married, you've never listened. Anytime I tried to tell you there was a problem, you thought kissing me and telling me everything was fine would make it so.

"It won't work anymore. Your kisses won't stop me from hurting, they won't make the problems go away and your telling me that I'm happy doesn't make it so. I'm tired of promising you things I can't deliver. I can't give you a perfect life."

"Before him…before Blaine, it was perfect."

He couldn't say Chance's name. He could barely make himself say Blaine's. "Maybe for you, Larry. Never for me."

We stood staring at each other. For an instant I almost laughed. All those years I'd walked on eggshells. Now look at me. All the damn eggs were broken and we were still standing. We hadn't struck out at each other in anger. Well, I had slapped Larry, but he'd deserved it.

But other than that, our fights, and this was the worst one we'd ever had, didn't involve blood or trips to the emergency room.

We were not my parents. I looked around our bedroom. It was still intact. We had fought, no broken bones, no broken furniture. In the midst of all this I felt a tremendous relief.

"Baby, we're not our parents. Let's stop being afraid. Let's begin again. Let's do it right, the way we should have years ago."

Tears were running down my cheeks. "We're fighting, but it doesn't mean we don't still love each other. It just means we're human. I don't have to be afraid anymore of what's going to happen to us if we fight."

Larry was staring at me, fear in his eyes. "What are you talking about?"

"I'm talking about us. All these years I've given in to you because I've been afraid of what would happen if I didn't. I thought for sure we'd get divorced if we didn't kill each other first."

I started laughing then. I felt so good, so free. "Honey, let it go. It's time you release your fears also. Believe me, it feels wonderful." I sank down to the bed.

"Mick, what's wrong with you? How can you laugh about our fighting? What is it you want me to release?"

"Your feelings about your mother, about her abandoning you."

He started to pull away from me, but I grabbed his hand and held on. "No, Larry. It's time to admit it to yourself and to me. It's part of the reason for both our pain."

He stood and I stood with him. "You don't have to beat yourself up about being a good father. You are, you always were and you always will be.

"It doesn't mean that you have to let them walk all over you or us. I know how much you love the kids, but it's time they were on their own.

I'm tired of them dropping in on us whenever they want. I want them to give back their keys."

He was looking at me as if I was insane and I was. I was insane to have put up with this crap for so long.

"Please," I whispered. "For once would you listen to me? They come into our home whenever they want and they take things without asking and never return them. I can't stand it. They're driving me nuts."

I had stopped laughing and was now crying again. "You're not your mother. You didn't abandon your kids."

I walked closer to him. "But I feel that you've abandoned me. It wasn't so bad when they were babies or even before they moved out, but they're all out and adults now. It's time to let go. It's time for us to be the center of each other's life."

"You're asking me to choose between you and our kids. How can you do that, Mick? You know how I feel about that."

"Yes, I know. That's why I've kept silent so long. But I can't any longer. What we have is not enough anymore. You're not your mother. And I'm not mine."

"Keep my mother out of this."

"I can't. The scars from what she did to you are still with you. They're the reason that you are the way you are. You need to talk to someone about it. Let it go. I'll help you."

"Shut up, Mick, shut up about my mother. I don't give a damn about her. This isn't about her anyway. This is about you. You're the one who broke up our marriage, you're the one who had an affair and you're the one who's sneaking behind my back to see a fucking psychic."

It hit me then, something I hadn't thought of. It was so obvious. I should have asked him in the beginning of the argument.

"You never did tell me. How did you know I saw Blaine?"

He looked away. He didn't need to tell me. It was Erica. I remembered the looks she had been giving me. I couldn't believe it. My own daughter had been following me. My feelings that I was being followed had turned out to be right after all.

A crushing sadness overtook me and I stood in surrender, shivering from the pain of total loss. "I think I'll answer the question you've been harping on for months. Remember this, you asked for it.

"You really want to know about the sex with Chance? You've been asking if I enjoyed it. I'll tell you now. Yes, it was incredible." I looked up into my husband's eyes that were beginning to cloud over with pain.

"Do you want to know why it was so incredible? He gave himself to me completely. He didn't hold back. There were no memories, no pain to stop him from loving me. There was no one who he found just a bit more important than being with me. And do you want to know what else? He listened when I talked."

I turned to walk out of the bedroom. I had one more person to confront. I knew I'd twisted the knife in my husband's heart. He was crying and so was I.

"I love you, Mick," he said as I walked down the stairs.

"I know you do," I answered him, "just not enough."

Chapter Twelve

Every step I took was laced with determination. It was time I put Erica in her place and sent her packing. If her father couldn't do it, then I would have to.

I pounded on the door to the bedroom she was sleeping in, oblivious to the noise I was making, or to Larry's voice coming down the stairs after me.

"Mick, she's asleep. You're going to wake her."

"Do I look as if I care?" I asked him, amazed that he would even say that to me.

"What about the kids? They're asleep also. Do you want to wake them? They're just babies. This can wait until the morning, Mick."

"Larry, why don't you just go back to bed and leave me alone? Your precious daughter will never blame you for my actions. Don't worry, you'll still be the perfect father."

I was being nasty. Part of me wanted to stop, but the other part of me wanted to lash out at Larry, to do anything that might make him actually open his ears and hear me, not what he wanted to hear, but me.

"Erica." I pounded on the door. "Wake up." The door opened to her glaring, sleep-filled eyes. I marched in the room, Larry right on my heels.

"Mother, why are you banging on my door in the middle of the night? I was sleeping."

Erica glared at me before looking over my shoulder to glare at her father. "Dad, why didn't you stop her?"

I answered her before Larry had a chance. "Erica, I want you out of here. Tomorrow morning you get your things and go to a hotel until you leave. I'm serious. I also want the key to this house back. I don't want you coming here letting yourself in anymore when we're not home."

"Why are you so anxious for me to leave, Mother? You think that Daddy doesn't know what's going on? You want to continue having your affair, don't you, Mother? Daddy may believe you that it's over. I don't. It's too late to send me home. Tomorrow, everyone's coming."

I looked first at Larry, then at Erica with the permanent sneer on her face, ignoring that she was being so proper in calling me Mother instead of Mom. "Who's everyone?" I asked.

"Your other children, Mother. Shannon, Derrick, Beth and Brigid. They're all coming to support Dad. We're going to have a little family meeting."

"Who arranged this little meeting?"

I held myself in check, finding myself for the first time in my children's lives really wanting to hit one of them.

With Larry the slap had just happened. With Erica, I could imagine the feel of her skin on my hand, the imprint of my fingers on her cheek. I could well imagine doing this, so I stayed as far away from her as I could in the small bedroom.

"I called them, Mother. You've been acting strangely ever since I came. First you didn't want me or the kids here. Which was normal," she said with a smirk.

"But when you decided to play grandma, I knew something was wrong. So the next day when you were supposed to be going to work I followed you." Her chin jutted out in defiance.

"You've been going to see that psychic, Blaine MaDia. Daddy told you not to. You won't sleep with Daddy, so you must be sleeping with someone."

She said this as though that justified her spying on me. My voice was quaking with emotion, sadness laced with anger. "Larry, did you tell her to do this?"

"No," he answered, his voice low. He wasn't being completely truthful. It only took one lifetime with him to know he was hiding something from me.

"But you knew about it, didn't you?"

"I knew," Larry said. "I thought you would tell me. But when you went to lunch with him and still didn't tell me I'd say I had reason for concern. You have to admit, Mick, you have been acting weird. You haven't been yourself in a long time."

I laughed hysterically. "You don't know how right you are. Since I was born, I haven't been myself."

I turned from him to Erica. "This doesn't change anything. Tomorrow morning I still want you to leave." I smiled at her. "Your brother and sisters can all leave with you."

"Mick," Larry called out to me.

"Don't say anything, Larry. Don't make me lose whatever respect I have left for you. This was wrong. Much more than what I did."

I walked to my room. So, Erica had arranged a little family meeting. Well, I had news for all of them. The free ride was over.

I was sure the money they were using to come to my home to scold me as though I was a child was financed no doubt by their father, who'd never heard the word no, let along uttered it.

I awoke that morning to more voices in the house than Mindy and Lars' excited screams. I heard Derrick asking where I was. It was time for me to get up and put in an appearance.

Derrick and Shannon were standing only a couple of feet apart. They were talking and looked up quickly when I came into the room.

"Hi Mom," Shannon almost whispered, glancing once at her big sister Erica, to see if her talking to me was permitted.

Derrick glanced at both of them, then came to me and hugged me. He pulled away from me, looked me over and whistled.

"Wow, Mom, you look good. You've lost weight. How much?" He angled his head for a better look, not giving me a chance to answer, before he commented on my hair. "You cut your hair too. I like it."

"Didn't you know, Derrick, that's the first sign of a woman having an affair? She loses weight and gets a makeover."

"What are the signs of a man having an affair, Erica?" I looked at my daughter. "If I were you, I'd worry that the first step could be when he doesn't care that his wife and kids take off so frequently to visit her parents without him. I'd worry that maybe my husband was glad I left."

My daughter's face flushed a bright red as she huffed and stomped angrily away. I heard her dialing the phone. Larry was sitting in a chair in the family room. I hadn't noticed him at first.

"Was that really necessary, Mick?"

"No, it wasn't," I admitted. "But it wasn't necessary for her to make that crack either."

"You're the mother, the mature one." He paused. "You're supposed to be the mature one. I wouldn't know it by your actions."

I went and sat across from Larry. "And you're supposed to be my husband. But then again, I can't tell it by your actions."

This time I wasn't trying to goad Larry. I meant it. I was tired of the spineless act he pulled when our children were around. I wanted him to be the confident man he was in the courtroom.

"Mom, why don't we go for a drive, just the two of us?"

I looked up at my son. Only then did I wish I had not spoken to Larry in such a manner. My son's expression mirrored his father's confusion and pain. God!! For a moment I wanted to die. In all the years of our marriage Larry and I had taken great pains to never speak to each other disrespectfully in front of the children. Actually, until my accident in now more than twenty-eight years we'd never spoken in disrespectful tones to each other. I didn't like it. If only there was a way to make it stop without me having to completely give in I'd gladly take it.

I looked again at Derrick, my only son and the child with whom I had the closet connection. Erica had just re-entered the room, frowning. Derrick rolled his eyes at his sisters.

"Mom," he said, "we didn't come to condemn you. We only want to help. I want to help, Mom. Can we take a ride someplace?"

I think I knew then what I was going to do. I followed Derrick out to the car. Surely there had to be a better way to end a marriage.

"Mom, is everything that Erica's been telling us true?"

"I don't know. I don't know what she's told you."

"Did you have an affair while Dad was in Arizona watching Mindy and little Larry?"

My son looked so young in that instant, his eyes moist. He was trying to be strong. I could only imagine how he was feeling.

The mother that had raised him would never do the things I had done. I saw a look come into his eyes. He wanted me to call Erica a liar, to say it hadn't happened, so he could pretend that nothing was wrong.

I wished momentarily for him that I could. But the pain I was in was the result of years of pretense. I didn't wish that on my son.

"It's true," I said at last.

"You met him in the parking lot of the grocery store?"

I was surprised that Larry had filled them in on all the details, and that aspect made me feel ashamed, but still I refused to lie to him.

"Yes, Derrick, that's true also."

"Erica said you think this guy…she said you think you were married to him in a previous lifetime."

He wasn't looking at me now. He was embarrassed to be asking me such an intimate question. I was aware of that.

"It looks as if your sister has all of her facts straight."

"All of them, Mom?"

"What else did she say?"

"She said you claim this Blaine MaDia is a long lost son. That he's the child of the man you had the affair with."

Derrick laughed nervously, too macho to admit that he was worried that I was attempting to replace my entire family with a new husband and son.

Derrick glanced over at me. I saw the hesitation in his eyes, heard it in his voice.

"You haven't answered," he said to me. "Are her facts accurate on that one also, Mom?"

"Derrick, are you worried that I'm trying to replace my family?"

"You have to admit, it kind of looks that way to all of us. Are those your plans?"

Derrick's voice was breaking. I saw the tears welling up in his eyes. I had an irresistible urge to pull him into my arms, but knew what he needed was a straight answer.

"She's only partially right. No one could ever replace you. Any of you. Not even Erica." I smiled and Derrick smiled also, some of his burden lifted.

"But you still think this guy is some baby you had years ago and that you died after it happened?"

"Yes, I believe that." I folded my hands across my lap, feeling nervous. "Do you think I'm crazy?"

"No, Mom. I don't think you're crazy. If you say you believe it, then there must be a very good reason for it."

The tears fell down my cheeks. I gripped Derrick's hand in my own as I looked out the window. It felt so good to hear someone beside Blaine and Chance tell me that I wasn't crazy.

It felt good to have this son that I knew, whose birth I fully remembered, whose pictures proved it, tell me that he didn't think I was crazy.

"Derrick, would you like to meet Blaine?"

Derrick hesitated. I could tell he was wondering if by meeting Blaine he would be disloyal to his father. "You don't have to go, I was only wondering."

"I don't want him telling me my future or anything like that."

"He would never do that without your permission. He's not like that."

"Dad's not going to like it if I go with you, is he, Mom?"

"You're right, Son. He's not going to like it."

We were quiet for a few minutes, driving aimlessly, neither of us talking. I knew my son's thoughts were the same as mine. He was thinking about Blaine.

"Give me his address, Mom."

"Blaine, this is my son Derrick. He wants to ask you a few questions. Do you mind?"

Blaine looked from Derrick to me, then smiled at Derrick and held out his hand in greeting. Derrick glanced away and Blaine pretended not to notice the snub as he brought his outstretched hand down to his side.

"Ask away, Derrick," he said.

"How much money have you taken from my mother?"

Blaine turned toward me, amused. "Is your entire family hung up on money?"

I gave my shoulders a tiny shrug.

"I give your mother the family discount."

"She's not your family."

"That depends on how you look at it."

"She has one son, that's me. What kind of discount are you giving her? Erica said you charge her anywhere from five hundred to one thousand dollars an hour."

My mouth dropped. I noticed Blaine only smiled in amusement before he answered Derrick.

"Your sister Erica came in here yelling at me, calling me a charlatan, telling me I overcharged. She was convinced of it, so I told her what she wanted to hear."

I watched the two of them, Blaine so confident and sure of himself and Derrick so young, jealous and determined to protect his mother from the only friend she had.

"How much are you really charging her then?" Derrick wasn't going to let it go.

Blaine stood. I wondered if he was getting annoyed. First I'd threatened him, now here was my son. As far as Erica's visit, I didn't know everything she'd done or said to Blaine, but knowing my daughter I knew her visit wasn't a pleasant one. I started to intervene but caught Blaine's eye. He would handle it. So I allowed him to do just that.

"Derrick, I'm not charging your mother anything."

"Okay, I know how this works," Derrick replied. "She's giving you gifts or donations. How much?"

"Nothing. No money has exchanged hands between us."

"My sister said the two of you went out to lunch. She said she even saw you going to the mall."

I watched as Blaine closed his eyes. He was shaking his head from side to side, most likely in disbelief.

"I took your mother to lunch, Derrick. I treated, she didn't pay and yes, we went to the mall. I wanted to buy your mother a present, so I did. Didn't your sister stay around long enough to see who paid the bill? Jeez."

Blaine sighed, "How old are you, Derrick?"

"You're a psychic, you tell me."

Blaine starting laughing. "Michelle, he is your son. The family resemblance is uncanny."

I laughed, too. Derrick looked nothing like me. Blaine was referring to our distrust.

I decided to interject something into the conversation or the inquisition. "Blaine, how did you know Erica?"

Blaine smiled at me before glancing at Derrick. "She's the spitting image of you. She has a temper, doesn't she?"

I glanced at Derrick, who was eyeing Blaine with anger. It wouldn't take much to ignite the powder keg I'd brought into Blaine's office. I saw my son weighing Blaine's words to determine if his sister had been insulted.

"Derrick, are you about done with your questions?" I studied my son. "Blaine probably has clients to see."

Derrick looked at me, his eyes taking in the looks that passed between Blaine and myself. I thought we'd been there long enough.

"Just a couple more questions, Mom, if Mr. MaDia doesn't mind."

"You can call me Blaine."

"Thanks, but I'm not looking for any new friends. I'll call you Mr. MaDia.

"My parents' marriage is breaking up. Were you aware of that?"

I saw Blaine attempt to look in my direction.

"Don't look at my mother," Derrick instructed him. "Look at me unless you're hiding something."

"Your mother and I haven't discussed her marriage, but I had assumed there were some problems in her personal life."

"If you're her friend why are you encouraging this?"

"Derrick, I didn't introduce your mother to anyone."

I heard the hesitation in Blaine's voice. He didn't want to say Chance's name, in case Derrick didn't know.

"But you think this man my mother is involved with is your father? That's true, isn't it?"

"Yes, it's true."

"Is that the reason you don't charge my mother? You want to recreate this perfect family for yourself?"

"I'm sorry to tell you this, Derrick, but there is no such thing as a perfect family." Blaine looked directly at Derrick, holding his gaze. "But then I never had a family, so any kind would be perfect to me."

I'd never known this. Blaine was right. We hadn't done much talking about important things. I'd wanted to put them off. I thought that at least this time around Blaine had two parents who loved him.

I wanted to cry for him for having to go through his life without a mother, or father, to love him. I found myself walking toward him, but his gaze found mine and he shook his head no.

I looked from Blaine to Derrick, grateful that Blaine had stopped me. My first instinct was to finally touch Blaine, to hold him in my arms, to make up for the times he'd spent alone without a mother. I no longer feared what visions I would have on touching him. I only knew that I wanted to, needed to.

I wanted to wipe away his hurt, but not at Derrick's expense. Blaine was talking to Derrick. I forced myself back to the present to listen.

"Derrick, I'm not a threat to you or to your family." Blaine said. "I'm not trying to hurt your mother. I give you my word on that."

He walked toward Derrick, his words soft and calmly spoken. "I can't help that I feel a connection to her. I didn't go looking for her. And even if I had, I would have never expected to know without a shadow of a doubt that she was my...my...mother...before."

Blaine looked my way, trying to hide the pain, for the first time totally serious, the amusement gone. "Derrick, I'm not trying to take her away from you. And you're right. You're her only son. I could never take your place."

"I thought you believed you were her son also." Some of the hostility was gone from Derrick's voice.

"Most people don't believe in reincarnation," Blaine explained. "It's taboo. But for several hundred years it was thought of as natural. People died expecting to meet their loved ones in another life. Some even made their loved ones promise to find them. This is the only case I've heard of where I believe that it happened."

"If you really believe that, why are you saying I'm her only son? You think you are too, don't you?"

Blaine turned his back to Derrick and walked toward his desk. "We can live only one life at a time, Derrick. It doesn't matter what I believe. I have no birth certificate. You do."

Blaine looked in my direction. "I'm sorry, Derrick, your mother is right. I have clients waiting. If I'm giving out discounts, I have to make my living on someone."

He stood smiling to usher us out of the room. This time he didn't extend his hand to Derrick. We walked out the door. Moments later I was back to retrieve my purse I'd left on purpose.

"Blaine, I'm sorry for the inquisition. Thanks for talking to him." I walked closer to Blaine. I had to hold him.

Blaine laughed. "You didn't expect him to like me, did you?"

I didn't answer. I stared at him, tears filling my eyes. I saw him back away, knowing what I intended.

"What if it happens again? I thought you were afraid."

Blaine's eyes belied his words. They were wistful, full of hope to at last feel his mother's touch. I knew his feelings as surely as I knew my own and I was no longer afraid. Blaine's pain erased my fears. I wound my arms around Blaine and pulled him tight to me. Again the visions assailed my senses, so vivid that I could smell the flesh of my newborn son buried beneath the stink of the blood.

I pressed Blaine's head into the curve of my shoulder holding him even tighter, not pulling away as I saw my baby lying there waiting for someone to pick him up. I caressed the back of Blaine's head as I attempted to feel the soft baby skin of the child in my vision.

I felt the volt of electrical current enter my body and pass through to Blaine. In that moment I was able to touch the skin of the baby I would never be able to see grow up.

I could see the spark of energy go from mother to baby, from Dimi to her son, just as it was doing now. My heart lurched with love for the child, this now grown man that I held in my arms.

If there had not been an insistent knocking on the door I don't know if I would have ever released him.

"It's really true, isn't it?" Blaine said to me, his voice awed with the wonder of it.

"Yes, it's true." I ran my hand down the side of his face. I didn't want to stop touching him. He was a lost part of me.

The knocking became louder. Both of us wanted to ignore it. We couldn't. This was Blaine's job.

"Can you meet me for lunch tomorrow around two?" Blaine asked.

"Yes," I answered. "Where?"

"Brookfield Zoo."

"The zoo?" I almost laughed.

"Yeah, that was always what I dreamed as a kid. That I could have a mother and she would take me to Brookfield Zoo. Corny, huh?"

"No, it's not corny." I answered. "Brookfield Zoo it is, tomorrow at two." I gave him another quick hug and left.

Derrick and I drove in a companionable silence. We had not spoken since we left Blaine's. Every once in a while I would catch him looking at me.

I decided to breach the tranquility. "Derrick, since neither of us ate would you like to stop and get something?"

"We can just go home, Mom, get something there."

I tilted my head back against the seat, my eyes focused on the stubborn lean to Derrick's chin. "I just thought it would be nice if the two of us had lunch."

He swiveled his head toward me, his mind half on the traffic. "Mom, if you're doing this because of your going to lunch with that guy, don't worry about it. I'm not a kid."

I smiled inwardly. That was exactly why I was doing it. That and the fact that I knew the moment we entered the house, this family meeting would begin.

"Derrick, this has nothing to do with Blaine. I never thought about it. I just thought you might want to get something to eat. No pressure. Besides," I tapped my son on the shoulder, "I'm enjoying your company."

"We've never gone to lunch before, just the two of us," he answered at last. "It might be nice."

Chapter Thirteen

Derrick and I spent several hours in the restaurant. I got the feeling he was in no more of a hurry to go home than I was. But we couldn't stay out all day. Eventually we would have to return home.

Derrick was being a gentleman. When he came to open the door for me, I put my hand on his shoulder.

"Don't put yourself in the middle between your sisters and me, okay?"

He tried to avoid my eyes. He was in the middle, and I didn't want him to be. I was pretty sure of the outcome of the meeting my children had arranged before I walked up the drive. I didn't want anything to spoil what Derrick and I had shared.

"Derrick, I'm serious. Whatever happens is not your fault. Remember that."

Beth and Brigid were there. They both came up to me and gave me lukewarm kisses before they fell on Derrick, giving him kiss after kiss.

Derrick was definitely the middle child. Two girls, him, then two more girls after him. He was doted on by his older sisters, adored and worshipped by his younger ones.

I watched the love my children had for each other, then glanced over at Larry. He was the one who'd given them that. I could take no credit for their bond. I thought of Blaine and was saddened that he'd never had a chance to experience either the love of parents or siblings.

I walked over to Larry and whispered, "Did you have to tell them everything?"

"You said you weren't ashamed of what you had done. I saw no reason to lie."

I stared at my husband, wanting to shake some sense into him. Yes, this was a major problem, but we'd never had that many. I truly had thought in the beginning we would be able to put it behind us. I was beginning not to recognize either of us.

We were both deliberately trying to hurt the other. If nothing else, I had hoped that no matter how this turned out Larry and I would at least remain friends, that we would at least be left with respect for each other.

"Mother."

It was Erica. It was evident she was in charge of this meeting.

"Mother," she repeated, "you know why we're here. We want to help you and Daddy." She stopped to smile at her father before glaring back at me.

"We've all talked this over and we've come up with the solution."

I turned from Larry to face my accuser head-on. "What is your solution, Erica?"

"Mother, this whole thing is your fault. How could you have an affair? Daddy's always taken care of you, given you everything you wanted. I don't understand how you could hurt him like this."

She looked around the room at her brother and her sisters. "They all want to forgive you, to understand. They think maybe you're going through a mid-life crisis."

She actually had the nerve to sneer at me. "I don't think it's that at all. I think you're just one of those bored housewives that don't know how good they've got it."

I sat down. I didn't think I could handle this load of crap standing up. I glanced at Larry. He refused to look at me.

"So this is what we think you need to do," Erica continued. "Quit your job and go to see Dr. Payne. Get him to start you on hormones. We don't want you to see that psychic any more. He's crazy and he's fooling you."

She looked disgusted. "Really, Mother, at your age to fall for something like that." She frowned as if she had a bad taste in her mouth.

"We also think it would be beneficial to both of you to have family around for the next few months. We can stay in shifts," she offered. "That way you can get to be a real grandmother, do the things you're supposed to do. And no more not coming to visit when Dad comes."

I ran my tongue back and forth over the roof of my mouth. This had to be a bad joke. "Erica, let me get this straight. My baby-sitting and quitting my job will help my marriage?"

I watched them in amusement as all five of them shuffled their bodies. I could only assume they'd thought if they confronted me as a group, I would go along quietly, make no protests. They were wrong.

"Well, Mother, it's a start," came Erica's huffy voice.

The audacity, I thought, but decided to play along for a few more minutes.

"What about counseling? Don't you think that might be more helpful?"

"No. Besides, Daddy doesn't want to go to counseling and why should he? He's not the one with the problem. You are."

"In a marriage if one person has a problem both people are involved." I looked over at Larry. "Especially if it's something that could destroy the marriage."

"Mom, you lied."

"And you've never lied, Shannon?"

"Mom, we're talking about you. We're trying to help you and Daddy save your marriage. We don't know what happened. You always had such a perfect marriage."

I smiled at her. "Shannon, if it were perfect we wouldn't be having this discussion, would we?"

"I don't believe you, Mom," Shannon said. "It was perfect. If you had not, not…you know, then lied about it, everything would be all right.

"Daddy said he would forgive you, but you don't want it. Then you lied to him again about going to see that psychic. Just stop all the lies, Mom."

"I'll stop when you agree to stop, Shannon."

I watched as she tried to pretend she didn't know what I was talking about. She glanced hastily at her sisters, wondering if I knew, if one of them had told me.

I was extremely familiar with Shannon's guilty looks. My baby who almost wasn't. I felt the most guilt for her and probably gave into her more than I did any of the others, with the exception of Derrick.

I had never had to force myself to behave in any particular way with him. It was more natural, more easily achieved.

"Shannon, we know that you're living with Sam. We've known about it all along. Since you're so big on people living by a certain standard, I suggest you learn to do just that. As per our agreement." I glanced over at Larry.

"The beginning of next month you will have to figure out how your bills are going to be paid. We'll still pay for your college and your dorm fees." I smiled at her. "We'll even continue to buy your meal tickets, but if you want to play house, you and Sam pay for it."

Shannon was almost in tears. I did feel sorry for her, but I wasn't budging.

"Mom, I only want things to be the same between you and Daddy, that's all I meant."

"Shannon, don't you understand? That's what this whole thing is about. I don't want things to be the same."

"Mom, maybe you and Dad can go away somewhere together, talk, relax, get to know each other again," Derrick piped in. "Maybe we can all come with you like always, bring all the kids, all the spouses, make it a real family vacation."

I smiled at my son's innocence. He really did think it would be that easy. A family vacation was the last thing I wanted.

I looked toward Beth and Brigid. They still had not said anything. They were watching Erica for directions. I wondered how long Erica had had control of my family. When had she begun intimidating her sisters and brother?

"If you girls have something to add, go ahead. You don't need Erica's permission to talk to me."

I felt Erica's glare without even turning toward her. I regretted that I had allowed her to grow up into such an unlikable person.

"We're only trying to help."

Erica was shouting, her voice angry. She didn't like that I was attempting to usurp her authority with her siblings. I turned in her direction. It was time her reign of tyranny was brought to a halt.

"Stop it. Damn it. All of you stop this nonsense now. Erica, I don't appreciate how you're talking to your mother. She's right. None of this is any of your concern. I was wrong to have involved you kids in our problems. I'm sorry about doing that, Mick."

Larry had been sitting on the sofa watching his life disintegrate. He felt as if he had been in a coma. He didn't know how long he had sat there, not hearing the conversation.

He'd been lost in his own thoughts, his memories. He sat watching Mick, wondering what had happened to his dream.

He saw the anger in Mick, something that had not been there often in their marriage. The one thing he'd fought to save was her respect; now that was gone. He looked at her, unable to read her.

"Larry, don't bother, I can fight my own battles."

This couldn't be happening, Mick couldn't mean any of this. "There shouldn't be any battle, Mick. They're our children." The words pained him as much as the agony in Mick's eyes.

It was crazy, but he had always thought there would be only one way that he would lose his wife's respect. He'd thought it would be if he ever gave in to her pleas to get counseling. He'd held out against that. Men didn't need to do things like that. They only needed to be strong and provide for their families and love them.

Well, he'd done all of that. Where had it gotten him? He should not be here, not in this predicament, on the brink of disaster, not after twenty-six years. He fought to concentrate on her words. She was speaking yet he couldn't hear.

"Why are you trying so hard now, Larry? Neither one of us is happy. Admit it."

He didn't believe Mick. It didn't matter what she said. There was no way she had not been happy. He loved her, he was her husband, he would have known.

She had to be doing this to hurt him, but why? He could think of no good reason. And this nonsense about a husband in a past life and her dying in childbirth to find that child in this lifetime... It was simply absurd. There was no way she could expect him to buy that. No sensible person would.

He saw Michelle watching him as were their children. The look in her eyes told him he'd waited too long to say something, and even now his words were not in defense of her beliefs.

"Let her go, Dad. If that's what she wants, you'll be better off without her," Erica bellowed.

"Erica, shut up." Derrick moved toward his sister. "Let Dad handle this."

"But he's not," Erica retorted.

"Both of you just shut the hell up, let me think. Mick." Larry turned pleading eyes on his wife. "This wasn't supposed to happen like this. Everything's moving too fast, everyone's saying things they don't mean."

He stopped and glared at his firstborn, daring her to speak.

"I didn't do anything, Daddy," Shannon moaned. "Why's Mom taking it out on me? How am I going to pay my rent if you don't help me?"

His world was crumbling around his feet and he could think of no way to fix it. His children yelling at his wife. His Mick yelling at them, telling Erica to go and leave the keys. Now this, her threatening not to support Shannon. They'd agreed on not mentioning this.

"Mick, can't we hold off on Shannon?"

"See what I mean, Larry? You don't listen."

Mick was shaking her head slowly, a look of great sadness making him want to comfort her.

Larry searched his memory vigilantly. Mick was accusing him of not listening. He was trying to fit the pieces together when he noticed the worried looks on the faces of his children.

He'd become lost in memories, lost in thinking about how much he loved his wife. He licked his lips. "Leave us alone. Your mother and I need to talk."

"Dad, we want to help."

Erica moved toward him and he held his hand out pointing his finger at her.

"No, Erica. Get the kids and go, take them to the park."

"But, Dad."

"No buts, Erica." He was screaming now. "It's time for you to butt out. It was wrong for me to have involved you kids in the first damn place. It was none of your business. It was wrong for me to do this to your mother. This was a betrayal of my love for her, of our marriage. I was wrong."

He turned to Mick. "I'm sorry. I needed someone to talk to. I didn't have you any more. This thing," he pointed toward Erica and the rest of the kids, "kind of snowballed. I'm so sorry. It was a mistake to have involved them. I wish I could take it all back."

Mick wasn't talking to him. She was looking instead at their children. None of them had made a move toward the door.

Larry looked first at his wife, then at his kids before he stormed over to the door and snatched it open. "Get the hell out. Now," he ordered them. "And don't come back until I say you can."

"How will we know?" Beth attempted to ask, but Larry stopped her.

"Call, I'll tell you if you can come back."

Larry stood in the entryway until Erica had gathered the kids. He slammed the door after them, turning back to face his wife.

"You're leaving me, aren't you, Mick?"

"Yes."

"Is there anything I can say to make you stay?"

He didn't know if he would be able to stand there and talk to his wife calmly. All he wanted to do was tie her up if he had to, lock her in the basement until she loved him again.

"Larry, I've said everything. There's nothing left."

"What if I agree to get counseling?"

His entire world was crumbling. He felt hands on his shoulders, cold hands shaking him until his body began shaking of its own accord.

His chest was burning and a searing pain was running rapidly up and down his left arm. He couldn't breathe. It felt as if an elephant was sitting on his chest. His body suddenly became cold and clammy.

From out of nowhere, Mick was handing him a glass of cold water and asking if he was all right. Hell no! He wasn't all right. His dreams had all been turned into a pile of ashes. He would never be all right again.

He took a long sip of the water, willing his body to cooperate. He didn't want her to see him like this. He felt the tears coming to his eyes and try as he might, he was thrust backwards into time, forty years in the past.

He saw himself as a little boy crying and pleading with his mother not to leave. He watched her leave with him screaming out her name. And she never looked back.

Now it was happening again. Only Mick meant so much more to him than his mother ever had. This time he would not scream or cry out in pain. He attempted to suck the tears back into the aching void that had become his body. If she was going to leave him, he would not hold on or beg her to stay.

"You're leaving me for him, aren't you?"

"No," Mick answered. "I'm leaving you because what we have is not enough anymore. I can't make up for all the hurt in your life and I was wrong to try."

He looked at her, wishing his heart would stop thumping a mile a minute. How the hell was he ever going to be able to pull off pretending she wasn't killing him?

If only he could make the pain go away. She was looking at him with worry. The last thing he wanted from his wife was pity.

A week ago to keep her he would have accepted even that. Now with resurfacing memories of the little unloved boy he'd been, he couldn't accept pity.

Not from Mick, the woman he adored. Not the woman he'd loved from the first moment she spoke to him. No, if he couldn't have her love, he damn sure didn't want her pity.

"Do what you have to do, Mick. I won't try to stop you."

He took another drink of the water, noticing the trembling in his hands. A clear image of the child he'd been came to him. If only he could erase the look of fear and pain on the face of the boy he'd been.

Larry sank into the chair, his strength ebbing. Whatever Mick was going to do he wished she would do it quickly, so he could be left to bleed in peace.

He closed his eyes, sending mental commandments to his heart to slow its pace. He listened to the sounds of Mick moving around. He heard her going down the stairs to the basement for luggage.

He thought about it being high on the shelf and her not being able to reach it. He almost got up to go to her, to get the luggage down. But that was too damn civilized. Besides, he was nauseous. He had to sit to let it pass.

It seemed to take forever for Mick to pack. And at the same time, it seemed as if she did it in the blink of an eye. It was over. It was really over. How the hell would he ever be able to say goodbye to her?

Larry watched as Mick struggled with the two large pieces of luggage and her bag she kept her samples in. To not help her now would be just plain mean. His heart had finally slowed down. The pain had receded to the feel of only a very heavy adult male sitting on his chest instead of an elephant. He thought he would be able to handle lifting the bags for her.

Without a word, he took the bags from her hands and carried them to her car. He placed them in, turning back to face her with the key to her trunk outstretched in his hand.

She took it from him, her fingertips brushing his, melting away his resolve, his brave front. As hard as he tried, he couldn't stop himself from crushing her in his arms. He held onto her for the longest time.

"Oh God, I love you, Mick. I don't know how to say goodbye to you."

"Then don't say good-bye, Larry."

"Just let me hold you a little longer."

He resisted the temptation to kiss her. He felt the trembling in her body and knew it wouldn't take much to change her mind. She would stay if he pressed the commitment. He no longer wanted to use that. Maybe he'd heard her after all.

At last he pulled away. "Take care of yourself, Mick. Remember that I love you. I always have and I always will."

"I love you too, Larry."

"Just not enough," he murmured as he let her go. She was crying and she stopped the car three times to look back at him.

He never would have believed it, but he wished she would just do like his mother had done when she abandoned him. Just leave and never look back. Every time Mick got out of the car, she killed him just a little more.

We were being so polite about everything, about my leaving. Larry took the luggage from my hands, helping me as he always had.

From the first moment Larry had told me he loved me, he'd been there to do things for me, maybe even before that. I looked into his reddened eyes and wondered why I was leaving my husband for loving me too much, for trying to protect me? I had a mouth, I should have spoken up sooner, told him what I wanted. I hadn't and now here we were. There was no turning back.

Larry held me in his arms. I could feel the heavy pounding of his heart, his ragged breath, his clammy skin. I wanted to hold onto him forever, never leave him, never say another mean word to him again. I wanted to be for him the Michelle I'd promised to be, but I was no longer her.

I caressed my husband's back and face, kissing his stubble cheeks, breathing in the smell of his aftershave, ingraining the prickly feeling of the coarse hair on his chin.

This man was a part of me, a part of my life. What would I do without him? I pulled away, finally aware that to stay with him would do us both more harm than good. Now we loved each other. We had that.

If I stayed, our love would eventually turn to hate and despair. I didn't want that. I knew without Larry asking me that he wanted me to stay. I also knew it would kill him for our love to turn completely sour.

As I pulled away from Larry, my heart was breaking for both of us. I knew he thought it was easy for me, that this was what I wanted all along.

I knew he hadn't believed me when I said I wasn't leaving him for Chance. I had not spoken to Chance other than to tell him about my seeing Blaine. I had not seen him once since Larry's return from Arizona. He had no idea I was making this move. This was done on my own and for me.

Easy to leave my husband of twenty-six years, my comfort zone, easy to break another promise? No. It was the hardest thing I'd ever done.

As it was, I could barely make myself drive away from him, from our home, from our life. I stopped twice maybe three times, I wasn't sure.

Anyway, each time I stopped, I got out of the car and looked at my husband standing there, pretending that it was alright, that he wasn't hurting.

The last time I got out of the car, the realization hit me like shock waves rolling through my body. I didn't want to leave my husband.

As much as I thought I wanted this, needed it in order to save my very life, I didn't want to leave. I could feel the tears beginning again as Larry and I stared long and hard into each other's eyes. As much as I didn't want to leave I knew I had to for both our sakes.

When I was probably two blocks from my home, I pulled the car over to the curb and bawled like a baby. I don't know how long I stayed there. I was paralyzed by the pain I'd caused Larry and myself.

I was free, free to do whatever I wanted. I didn't have to hide or pretend, yet I felt more bound to Larry in that moment than I ever had. I didn't want the last thing we would share to be pain, but I had made the decision.

I drove to the same hotel I'd first gone to with Chance months before. I had a little over a hundred dollars and a couple of charge cards. I hadn't made concrete plans for my life. I hadn't thought about the financial aspects.

I thought of Larry. He hadn't written a check in years. I knew he wasn't stupid. He was a lawyer, for God's sake! Still, I worried about him.

I checked in, remembering the pasty look on Larry's face. I worried about him, his health. I couldn't stop that. Regardless of my need to leave, Larry was a part of me. If no one but me believed it, it didn't make it any less true. I loved him.

I picked the phone up several times to call my husband, to tell him I was sorry, to tell him I was coming home, to ask him to join me.

I did none of those things. I stripped all of my clothes off and climbed naked into the bed under the covers. Then I cried myself to sleep.

Larry stood outside for several minutes after Michelle drove away. He walked to the curb and saw her when she pulled over. He stood watching her, wondering what she was doing, wanting to run all the way to her car to make sure she was fine, to beg her not to leave.

When the urge to do so became so strong that he'd taken a step toward her, he felt the burning pain once again flaring up in his chest, constricting his diaphragm, making his breathing difficult.

He took a half step forward toward Mick before stopping himself and turning back toward his now empty home and broken dreams. He had to let her go. He had to let it be over.

Utter despair weighed heavily on his shoulders, washing over him in waves, sapping away the little remaining strength he had left. He walked slowly up the drive, into the house, first to Erica's old room that Mick had taken as her own for the past months.

He took the pillows from the bed, and then he walked up the stairs to his bedroom. He stripped away his clothes and climbed naked beneath the covers. He clutched Mick's pillows to him. Breathing in her scent, he prayed for death.

Chapter Fourteen

I woke feeling slightly disoriented. Then I remembered. I was not in my bed, not in my home. I was alone in a hotel room a few miles from my house. My marriage was over.

I lay there in bed looking around the room. I had what I wanted, what I had at last demanded. I was free to start my life over again. I felt like hell.

I couldn't resist knowing if Larry was okay. I dialed the number to my home. *It's not your home any more, Michelle.* The words came to me on a gentle breeze from somewhere in the room. I shivered and pulled the covers up around my neck.

The revelation filled me with terror. This was no longer my home I was calling. I wondered which of my children would answer the phone, what I would say to them. I waited with bated breath for someone to answer. I heard Larry's voice and let out the moan I hadn't known I was holding.

"Leave me alone, Erica, I'm fine."

He hung up. He was hurting, that I had expected, but he was alone. That came as a shock to me. I'd expected all the kids to be hovering around Larry, trying to insulate him from the pain.

It sounded as if he didn't want them there. That was strange. It had never happened before. Even when I begged Larry to go on a second honeymoon to Hawaii, he had gone behind my back and changed the plans, telling my mother after I'd had to beg her to keep the kids, that it wouldn't be necessary, that we were taking them with us.

I thought about how happy he'd been on that trip, how happy the kids were. No one had noticed that I spent half the time alone in the room eating and watching television.

I swallowed, wanting to forget, not wanting to place the blame any longer for my unhappiness on Larry or the children.

I thought about all of them. Erica, my eldest and the hardest for me to get along with. It wasn't her fault that she was a spoiled, obnoxious brat. We were her parents. It had been our job to teach her. Larry had adored her while I ignored her and her behavior.

I thought about the client calls I needed to make. I didn't want to but I no longer had the luxury of not going in when I didn't want to. I needed to get my finances in order. I needed to work.

I forced myself to shower, skipping breakfast, but ordering a strong pot of black coffee. I knew I was going to need the caffeine to get me through the morning. I dumped the nearly melted ice from the ice bucket, placed it in a towel and put it over my swollen eyes.

At two P.M. I was parking my car in the Brookfield Zoo parking lot. I had planned on getting there earlier, to be at the gate waiting for Blaine. I didn't want to have him worrying that I might not show.

Blaine was waiting inside the gate for me. I forced a smile to my lips and marched toward him. He deserved one day not to worry about other people and their problems.

"Hi."

I kissed him quickly on the cheek, no longer afraid of the visions I saw when I touched him, but not wanting one now.

"Hi," he answered.

I stopped for a moment, taken aback by the unaccustomed shyness from Blaine. He was definitely uncomfortable. The light-hearted banter that generally existed between us was missing.

"What's wrong?" I asked.

"I was going to ask you the same thing," he smiled at me, "but I know what's wrong. You left your husband." He cast his eyes downward. "Listen, I know how hard this has to be for you. We can leave, do this another time."

"Please believe me, Blaine. There is nowhere in the world I would rather be than here with you."

"Do you want to talk about it?"

"No. I want this day to be for you. I want to do whatever it is that you dreamed of doing when you were a little boy and wishing for a mother."

He laughed. "Michelle, you do know I'm thirty-two? You're looking at me as if you want to diaper me and maybe burp me."

"You remind me of someone I used to know. You're an expert at changing the topic when the conversation gets serious."

"I remind you of yourself, don't I?"

I reached for his hand and held it, laughing, glad for once that the only thing I felt was the warmth of his skin.

"You do so much worrying about other people you have no idea of how to just relax and not try to take care of people. Believe me, Blaine, you can't fix my problems. I know. My husband tried to do it. Only I can take care of them."

"Is that why you left him, because he wanted to take care of you, or is there some other reason?"

"You think I left because of Chance, don't you?"

"Didn't you?"

"No."

"Are you so sure that you didn't? I know how much you love him."

"I never said I didn't love him. I said I didn't leave my husband for Chance."

"No, that wasn't exactly what you said. You said you didn't leave because of Chance. There is a difference."

We were heading toward the monkey cage. I stopped without warning, almost causing a group of school children probably there on a field trip to collide with me. Blaine pulled me to the side and over to a bench.

"Blaine, didn't you hear me? I said I didn't want to talk about this."

I huffed and attempted a frown, wanting to make him believe I was annoyed. The problem was that Blaine didn't annoy me. I realized that there might be some truth in what he'd said.

"Michelle, just a couple of questions and I'll let it go. Why are you so hesitant to accept the help of a friend?"

I thought about it seriously. "Well," I said to him. "I've always been the person doing the helping. I guess I just don't know how to do it any other way."

"How old are you, forty-one, forty-two?"

"A tad older," I laughed. "Why?"

"I was just wondering, in all that time, no one ever helped you?"

Blaine was stubborn, I gave him that. "My husband, sometimes too much. Blaine, I want to find out about you, how you became a professional psychic, find out about your life. I don't want to heap my problems on you."

"I have an idea. Why don't we compromise?" Blaine offered. "You ask me a question, then I ask you one."

I contemplated what Blaine had in mind, not sure how he was going to do it, but sure that he was going to get more information out of me than I wanted him to have.

"Have you ever heard of astral travel?"

I shook my head and got off the bench, heading in the direction of the peanut stand. I glanced back at Blaine. He had a huge smile on his face.

"I thought you were going to ask me something else. Why that question?"

"Michelle, I can see you haven't played this game very often. I get to ask a question and you have to answer it. You can't ask me a question until you do."

He was looking at me in an odd manner. He had me wondering why he had skipped to this particular subject.

"Yes, I've heard of it." I stopped there. I wasn't giving more information than he asked for. Two could play this game. "Why are you asking?"

"Very good." He smiled at me. "I'm just curious. I want to know if you believe in it. And this, Michelle, is a two part question. Do you believe you've ever done it?"

"Easy," I retorted, "no to both."

He stopped walking to look at me. "You're really good at shoving things to the back of your mind, aren't you?" He caught himself and put up his hand. "Never mind, don't answer that. That's not my question."

"Then what is your question?"

He tilted his head to the side, giving me an '*it's not your turn look.*'

"Has Chance ever told you why he began the search for you?"

I should have known the talk would eventually lead to Chance. I didn't want to talk about him, not right then. "Blaine, ask me something else."

I shelled a peanut and popped it into my mouth, offering the bag to him.

"Why don't you want to talk about him?"

"It seems inappropriate. I just left my husband. I shouldn't be here discussing another man with you the day after."

"I'm sorry." Blaine handed the bag back to me. "I didn't realize there were rules of conduct as to what one should talk about after separating from their spouse."

He went and stood near the bars, looking in at the baboons. Oh, he was good, he was very good. I walked over to him, tugged on his sleeve and watched as he ignored the sign not to feed the animals and tossed several peanuts into the area, watching the baboons fight over the bounty.

"Okay, lets have this conversation and get it over with. I haven't seen Chance in months and I've talked to him only once.

"In answer to your earlier question, no, he wanted to tell me why he began searching for me, but I didn't want to hear it." I stopped.

"Why?" Blaine asked.

"Just having the information that I did was almost more than I could handle. I couldn't accept any more knowing. I guess Larry has rubbed off on me. I thought I was crazy to accept all of this without proof."

Blaine was shaking his head and smiling as if he knew something that I didn't. It was obvious he wasn't about to volunteer the information. He forced me to ask.

"Okay, Blaine, do you know why Chance got divorced and started looking for me?"

"Yes."

"And are you going to tell me?"

"No. That's something I think he should tell you himself."

Ahh, so that was his plan. He wanted as I had suspected to see me reunited with Chance, his father.

"This isn't going to work. I'm not going to go running to Chance."

"You don't have to run. All you have to do is make one call and he would come running to you."

"You know, you sound much more like a matchmaker than a psychic. It also sounds as if the two of you have been discussing me in great detail."

I watched as Blaine forced himself to turn from the bars to peer at me. "Not as much as you might think. It seems you haven't shared very much of yourself with either of us. Why?"

I smiled into his eyes, amazed that not long ago all I wanted was to stay as far away from him as possible. Now I found myself wanting to touch him, to remember what I wasn't supposed to. I ran my hand down the curve of his wrist, feeling the familiar tingle. I stopped. This wasn't a game.

"You're stalling," Blaine said as he captured my hand in his. I could tell he too was amazed at the connection we shared.

"Answer one question for me, and I'll answer yours." I took the lift of his brow for a yes, so I began. "All those years when you longed for a mother to take you to the zoo, did you ever imagine it would be to grill her about her love life?"

He started laughing hysterically. Before I knew what was happening, he lifted me from the ground and began twirling me around.

"You're right. Let's enjoy the zoo."

Several hours later Blaine and I were beat. We'd ridden the train three times and walked miles. My God, did we walk, covering every square inch of the zoo at least twice.

For the first time in a long time I enjoyed it. There were no kids fighting, no one wanting to go to the bathroom every ten minutes. It didn't feel strange at all that I was sharing something I'd done with my children dozens of time with this adult son I'd never had a chance to know. It felt right. We had fun.

When we walked to the parking lot, I felt myself not wanting to let go of the day. Blaine and I had reverted to our usual good natured jousting.

We reached my car first. I stopped, my key out but not ready to get in, not wanting to admit how hard it was for me to see the day end. I thought some of it might be my not having a home to go to, but mainly I wanted to be with Blaine.

I put the key in the lock. "Well, Blaine," I turned toward him, "is this what you had in mind?"

"Yes," he answered, his eyes turning serious. "This was exactly the way I dreamed." He looked away toward the street at the traffic.

"Michelle, would you like to have dinner with me? Then we can talk," he offered. "It's just that I don't want to see the day end."He turned toward me, a hopeful look on his face.

"That's perfect," I confessed, "I was thinking the same thing. Instead of going out somewhere, why don't you come back to my hotel. That way we can have a long private talk. I want to hear about your life."

"And I want to hear about yours," Blaine replied

We got in our cars and drove back to the hotel. After ordering room service we sat on the sofa and began to really talk for the first time.

"Blaine, tell me when you first knew you were different, that you had some strange…gift, I guess."

I didn't know what to call it. I wasn't sure if I thought of what he did as a gift.

"It's a gift, Michelle. At least that's how I look at it, and all the people I've helped think of what I do as a gift."

He poured himself a glass of water. I saw the slight trembling of his fingers. I'd insulted him. That surprised me because he was so good at hiding his feelings.

"Blaine, I'm sorry. I didn't mean to insult you. I just didn't know what to call…what you do." I took a drink from the glass he had poured for me and waited.

He appeared to be thinking over something as he continued drinking. In an instant his mood transformed and he was once again smiling, the lines around his mouth softening. He gazed at me and I realized what he was about to reveal to me would be something very important so I remained quiet and just listened as he began to speak.

"It took me a long time to think of this as a gift. I shouldn't be so touchy."

Blaine looked away from me, his mouth working, no words coming out. Something I'd said had struck a nerve.

"Michelle, you would have no way of knowing…" He turned his palms upward, toward me. "It's just, I guess, I thought with everything that's been happening between us, you would automatically know how hard it was for me to have this particular gift."

I felt terrible. I should have thought before I blurted out my insensitive words. I should have remembered my own childhood and the difficulty my parents had in raising a daughter who claimed to have lived in a previous life, who declared she'd lost her husband and son. "It was probably hard for you as a child, wasn't it?"

"Let's say I wasn't the most popular kid around. But who can blame kids for not wanting to play with someone who was always talking to someone who wasn't there? Someone who could tell them every bad thing they'd done."

"How old were you when you started--when you became aware of your gift?" He smiled at me, making me feel that I was probably the first person he'd shared this with.

"I was three," Blaine answered, his face turning pensive. "At least that's the age I remember. Who knows what I did in my crib?"

I thought of Larry and the lonely five-year-old boy he'd been.

"What happened to your parents?" I tilted my head to better observe him. "If it's not too painful for you to talk about I'd like to know."

"No, it's not painful at all. The girl they told me was my mother was a teen who gave me up for adoption. My adoptive parents gave me back." He smiled, "So you see, maybe I was a strange baby."

I wanted to touch him, but held back. I didn't feel I had the right to act as though I was privy to his pain, though my heart carried a deep sorrow.

"No one else wanted to adopt you?"

"Would you have? Think about it, a strange little kid that stands around claiming to speak to the dead, that asks husbands about the girlfriends they were out with, that tell mothers that the fathers of their babies are not the husbands."

"Did you do all of that?"

"Yeah, in several foster homes, until I learned that it was the reason no one wanted me around."

"What did you do then?"

"For a while I tried to stop talking with them when they came. The spirits," he explained."I tried not to hear their voices. I tried not to see things I wasn't supposed to see, but it didn't work. Still, no one wanted me, it seemed, except the dead, so I continued talking to them."

I gave a tiny smile once again, remembering my own childhood. "I never had psychic gifts, just dreams."

He smiled at me, as if I were a child innocent in the ways of the world.

"When I was five, I began hearing your voice. No psychic gifts, Michelle?"

His eyes took on a dreamy quality, and he appeared to be going into a trance. I called softly to him. "Blaine, are you alright?"

He opened his eyes. "Yes, I'm fine," he answered. "I was just remembering."

I felt cold suddenly, shivers of remembrance racing up and down my torso. "How did you know?"

"I don't know." He looked at me strangely. "I just remember your voice, your touch, your love and…your giving me my birthright. My gift." He smiled.

I watched as he closed his eyes and ran his hand over his face before continuing. "I guess that's why it bothered me a little, what you said before.

"I always knew I'd lived before. I've been searching my entire life for you, hoping you'd kept your promise, that you were here somewhere looking for me. You'd made a promise to find both Jeremy and me. It was a promise I always believed you would keep. I thought when I found you you would know all of this without my telling you. I wanted you to know it."

So that was it, I thought. I got up and walked away from him. I wasn't ready to delve into the promise I'd made in a past life. If I'd had gifts, I no longer did. I'd passed them on to my son. I groaned inwardly thinking of the childhood Blaine had told me about. He'd had a life of loneliness. I wasn't sure if I'd given him a gift or a curse.

"I can't imagine how your life has been. I don't think I would have been able to do what you're doing. You're putting yourself out there to be judged by millions of people, having millions more think you're a fake or crazy or both."

I turned back. "I don't like people thinking I'm crazy, Blaine."

"And I don't care what they think about me," he answered. "Hell, it's how I make my living. The very people who shunned me years ago now come to me for information. Can you believe it?"

I glanced at him, not detecting any bitterness in his voice. "It doesn't bother you?"

"Why should it?"

"Blaine, how did you get involved in all of this? How did you start making a living at it, I mean?"

"When I was almost eighteen, I realized that the state would no longer be responsible for me. A few people here and there were asking me for readings. The first time I jokingly told someone to pay me, they did, with no hesitation. I knew then I'd found my calling."

"About this reincarnation, how did you become comfortable with it?"

"It was never a matter of me accepting it. It was a part of me. I always knew I would one day meet my true parents in this lifetime, but of course my mentors never thought it was possible.

"I got into regression therapy to recapture lost memories. I became an expert at it, hoping that one of my clients would be the mother I was looking for."

He stood and began walking toward me. "Love never dies, Michelle. You must have really loved me. That first time in the auditorium after I touched you, I felt your love, for me, for Chance."

He reached out his hand, tilting my chin upward. "You're the key, Michelle. You're the reason we found each other. Your love for us was so powerful that it reached out across time, ignoring death, to find us."

"But that's not my life." I was shaking like a leaf. "I believe this happened because I can't begin to put any other name to it, but still I feel this Dimitra had her time. I don't think I can be her again. I can't complete her life."

"You're the one who called out to us."

"How? I don't have any special gifts."

"You do."

"What?"

"Love, Michelle, perhaps a bit more. The rest I'm not certain of but as for your love, I'm positive about it. You called out to both of us with your love. Do you think my touching you and seeing the past is something that happens every day? Do you think it happens with Chance, with anyone else? No, it's you, Michelle. You're the key. I figured it out."

I didn't want to hear any more. I wanted the room service guy to interrupt us, the phone to ring, anything. I attempted to move away from Blaine, but he wouldn't allow me to escape.

"Don't you think you've been running too long? You wanted this to happen, you're the one who brought us together."

"I didn't. I met Chance in a parking lot. It was just coincidence that we came to see you."

He grabbed my hand and held it in his. "Try and remember. In your dreams you went to Chance for many years. You're the reason he got a divorce. He heard your voice. He recognized it, he remembered. Chance never once thought he was going crazy. He researched what was happening to him and then, Michelle, he began looking for you."

A knock sounded on the door. Blaine was still holding my hand, his eyes burning with memories that he wanted me to share.

"Get the door, Blaine."

He dropped his hands reluctantly, going for the door, his hand reaching into his pocket for his wallet.

"No, Blaine, I'll sign it to my room."

"And have another member of your family accuse me of taking advantage of you?" He laughed. "I don't think so."

I took the few seconds that he was paying the bill to remember the dreams that I'd had through the years of a dark-haired lover.

Could any of this be true? I did remember many times waking up from the dreams crying, 'I can't find you,' and Larry comforting me, thinking I'd had a nightmare.

It was then I remembered Chance's words to me when we first met. *"I've been waiting for you."* And my answer to him, *"And I've been trying to find you."*

God in Heaven. Blaine was right. I felt the smog lifting from the memories I'd kept submerged through the years. Poor Larry, he'd never had a shot. How was he supposed to have a happy marriage with a woman who in her dreams traipsed off to be with the family she'd lost?

I felt the jolt of what surely had to be more than ten million volts of electricity running through every cell in my body. It was all true. I remembered.

I sat stunned as Blaine paid for our meal, watching as he closed the door and came to sit at the table preparing to eat.

I couldn't believe it. How could he possibly eat at a time like this? He'd just delivered a bomb, and now he was calmly lifting the covers and sampling food.

"Blaine," I called to him. "How can you possibly think of eating?"

"I'm hungry," he answered and continued chewing. "Come and join me. You may as well eat."

I stared at him, wondering if I had imagined the conversation of a few moments before.

I sighed, looking at him exasperation. "Blaine, let's finish our conversation."

"No," he said.

"No?" I repeated. "You're the one who brought it up."

"I know. I shouldn't have. Chance wants to talk to you about this himself."

"I'm not calling him."

"You will eventually."

I couldn't believe him. He was eating, not bothered about what he'd said. He didn't even know that I believed him, that I remembered. I looked again at the amused expression on his face. I was wrong. He knew.

"Michelle, you may as well eat. I'm not saying any more."

I sat down opposite him, my hand ready to still the next bite he attempted to take.

"Let's talk," I demanded, trying to ignore the look in his eyes that told me he wasn't going to budge.

"That's fine with me, only I think we should change the subject." He shook his head, smiling. "Why don't you ask me for help?"

I looked at him, puzzled, wondering what he was getting at. Finally he stopped eating, and his eyes fixed on me waiting for something from me. I stared back at him.

"What? What do you want to help me with?" Then I knew. Chance had told him.

"I've invaded your life enough. While that was my original objective, now it would feel as if I'm using you...you know, taking advantage of your gift."

"Michelle, you're very good at giving but you're lousy at accepting help. What about letting me help with Viola?"

I couldn't believe I'd almost forgotten Viola. In the past weeks, my life had become so hectic. And to think she was the beginning of my voicing my displeasure. How could I have forgotten her?

I sighed, closing my eyes and rubbing away at my temples. "I just need to know what happened in the seconds before I hit her, if I was distracted. I want to know why I didn't see her."

"Say the words and I'll take you back to the accident. You just need to tell me what you want."

Fear invaded my body for a moment but I'd already decided I was done with running away. I gave Blaine a weak smile before saying, "Let's try."

"Good," Blaine said softly, his admiration for my agreement showing in his eyes.

"So what do we do first?"

"Your guess is as good as mine."

"You're kidding, right? You get me to agree to this and you…you…"

"Michelle." He laughed, holding up his hand as though in defense. "I do have an idea. I can hypnotize you, take you back to the accident."

He pushed the table away after sneaking another bite, prepared to begin. Too many things had happened to me in the past months, things that I felt I could verify at least to myself. I didn't want to be put under.

"You're a psychic. Why don't you just tell me what happened?"

"Because you wouldn't believe me. You require more proof."

"Blaine, isn't there any other way? If you hypnotize me, I still won't know for sure."

"You will. I won't put you in a deep trance. You'll know. I've done this a thousand times."

It wasn't that I didn't believe him; it just wasn't the way I wanted to do it. "No," I said firmly.

"I don't understand," Blaine frowned as though trying to figure me out. "Why are you saying no?"

"Because I don't want to be hypnotized."

"Do you have a better suggestion?"

I felt myself smiling, me who had run in a panic from this man just a few short months before. I couldn't believe what I was about to propose.

"Try touching me, just a little, while I think about Viola and the accident."

"Michelle, I'm not a crystal ball or a genie. My touch can't give you the answers to your questions."

"How would you know? You admitted you don't know why we have this thing between us. Maybe it can work." I was insistent. "We can at least try."

"Are you the same woman who didn't want to touch me without rubber gloves for insulation? I can't believe it; surely you have to be someone different." He laughed softly. "Is this what I missed by not having a mother, being coerced and manipulated by your wonderful smile?"

I knew then he was going to give it a try. "Mothers are famous for that, Blaine." I gave him a grin. "I'll bet you're thinking now that you didn't have it so bad."

He turned serious. I saw it in his eyes, in the slight change of his body, his jaw tightening. "I'm glad to have you in my life. I hope no matter what happens you're here to stay, Michelle."

I didn't answer. He was asking me for a promise and I couldn't give any more of those. In my heart, I knew I would never be far away from Blaine, but the memory of the promise I'd given to Larry years before our marriage wouldn't allow it. I had not been able to keep my promise to him. I didn't want to break another one.

Blaine frowned slightly apparently having decided to let go of the fact that I'd not answered about remaining in his life.

"You know there's no guarantee. So far we've only seen images of us, of our past. I have no control over this, Michelle," Blaine offered, "But we can give it a try if you want to."

My heart felt as if it had wings. It would work, I knew it would. Staid, stilted, responsible, traditional Michelle Powers was asking a psychic to help her have a vision. Wow, what a transformation.

We sat close together, our knees touching slightly. Blaine held out his hand. This was my show; I would decide how to do it. I reached the tips of my fingers out toward his, not quite touching him, yet I could feel the magnetic force. I closed my eyes and thought of Viola and the accident.

I could see it clearly. I was driving, my mood cheerful. I saw myself look down to push the number on the CD player in my car. Number seven of the Police. I listened as the sounds of Sting singing 'Every Breath You Take' came through my speakers.

I saw myself singing along with the music, checking the rearview mirror occasionally. I glanced over at the sidewalk, heard my voice saying, "*Oh no*," as I realized that an elderly woman was stepping out in front of me.

I pressed my foot on the brake as hard as I could, but it was too late. The woman flew up onto the windshield of my car and fell back down.

I watched her groceries fall in slow motion, the cans of tomato sauce, the eggs as they broke.

I looked to the other side of the street and saw the city bus. The elderly woman had walked out into oncoming traffic to catch a bus. I had forgotten that.

I pulled my fingers away from Blaine and opened my eyes. I didn't need to see Viola lying there sprawled on the ground. I didn't need to see the blood, or feel her touch. I would never forget it.

Blaine looked at me with concern. "You have your answers?"

"More than I ever imagined. I did see Viola and I tried to stop but there wasn't time. It was very important to me to know if I'd not been paying attention. I was. The accident really wasn't my fault but my breaking my promise to her was. Blaine, I know now why I cried so hard in the parking lot. When my groceries fell, I thought of Viola."

I closed my eyes and saw myself in another life, as Dimitra covered in blood, my life ebbing away. All that blood surrounding Viola had made me subconsciously remember Dimitra.

I looked at Blaine. "You're right. I am the key. Chance knew me because the moment we met, I was remembering my death."

Chapter Fifteen

"Michelle, It's time to face him. You've waited a lifetime for this."

Blaine ran the pads of his fingers down my arms. "He deserves to know that you remember."

I raised my head from Blaine's chest, where it had been resting since I discovered I had not been at fault for hitting Viola. That guilt was gone.

Still, I felt bad that I had not kept my promise. Now I knew why promises were so important to me. Jeremy and Dimitra had made promises that had not been forgotten, through death or another lifetime.

Breaking my promise to Viola had started a chain reaction which made me fully remember my past. I might not have remembered had it not happened. Blaine was right. I had to see Chance, the husband from my past that I'd called out to in my dreams.

"Blaine, leave it to me, allow me to tell Chance in my own time that I've left Larry. Promise me."

"No, Michelle, I won't promise."

I looked into his eyes, puzzled. "Why?"

"Because your promises are binding. Chance is hurting and I don't know that I want to be a party to his pain. He's stayed away from you out of respect for your marriage. You've ended it. There's no reason you can't be with Chance."

I reached out my hand to touch his face. "Blaine, I wasn't a very good mother this time around. I know what you want. You're a psychic, you tell me, is it in the cards for me to finish out this life with Chance?"

He turned away. "You have the power to do what you want, to love whom you choose."

"That wasn't my question. I know how miraculous this all is, that we found each other. But what about my family? I've cheated them out of so much. I didn't want children."

"I don't believe you."

He was watching me closely, trying to read something that I wasn't saying. "I didn't. I did the things for them that a mother is supposed to do, but I always felt removed from them. The only one of them able to break through my reserve was Derrick." I remembered my eldest. For a short time after her birth love for Erica had been overpowering. I had no idea when or how it left.

"I still don't believe you," Blaine said softly.

"Only because you don't want to. You want to see me with Chance, here and now. You want us to be the family we didn't get the opportunity to be before. Blaine, I'm not a saint. I'm a woman who's made a lot of mistakes in her life, and who's hurt a lot of people, probably more than I was even aware of."

"How could a woman who had so much love for her baby that with her dying breath she told that baby she loved him, not love her children in this life?

"That woman's love lived on through death and found that son. Don't deny that you love me. I know you do, I feel it in your energy, I see it in your eyes and I feel it in your touch. Love doesn't die, Michelle."

"Then why didn't I feel that with my kids? Why did I feel so distanced from them, why didn't I want them?" I sobbed.

Before I knew what was happening, Blaine grabbed my hands and held on really tight. "I don't know, but I'm damn sure going to find out," he said.

"No, Blaine. I've been through too many memories today." He ignored me and held on.

I fell against him as both of us relived his birth. I heard Blaine ordering me to focus only on Dimitra, on her thoughts, her feelings.

We'd never done that. I didn't know if I could. It was hard to not focus on the infant, or on Jeremy who was in agony over the death he knew he couldn't prevent.

"Focus," Blaine shouted at me. This time I attempted to push my mind past the blood, past the poverty of the couple in the room. I concentrated only on Dimitra. I became one with her, allowing myself to enter not only her body, but her mind.

It worked. I heard the thoughts she didn't utter to her husband or child. I heard her crying out to God, asking him why he would give her a baby only to take her away. I heard her thinking, *"In the next life, I'll never love another child, because you'll only take it away from me."*

"Oh God, oh God, oh God," I moaned over and over again. Blaine released the grip he held on my hands and gathered me in his arms, letting me cry until I felt cleansed.

"I knew it," he said to me as he patted my hair as if he were the parent comforting the child. "I knew it all along. A woman with love strong enough to defy death couldn't not love her children. Michelle, because of your fear and your wanting to keep your children safe you buried your love so deeply into your subconscious that you wrongly thought it didn't exist."

As I stared into Blaine's eyes the memories came rushing back, the love for Erica, the pride in the miracle of her birth. He was waiting for me to speak to give him some profound wisdom. I had none. I had more questions than anything else. He was the one I was seeking out for knowledge.

"Blaine, it would have been so much easier if I had known. I've carried this guilt around since Erica was just a baby."

I looked up at him. "But I do think I understand what you're trying to say. My soul was trying so hard to convince God that I didn't want my children, didn't love them, so he wouldn't snatch them away, that I convinced myself."

"Exactly. The mind is a very powerful instrument. Now that you know, how do you feel?"

"Grateful and relieved. To know this within myself, that it's not just your telling me but my knowing that I love them has freed me." I couldn't help smiling.

"I've always loved them. I was too afraid that if I admitted it, or allowed myself to feel it, they would be taken away. What kind of karma do you think I've created for my kids?" I shook my head.

"I've only met two," Blaine sighed. "Derrick loves you. It's not too late to start over with all of them. Bad things happens, people die, that's all a part of life. But if it happens," he tilted my chin to look into my eyes. "Sometimes we're lucky enough to see each other again."

For the next week I worked, going to Blaine's office as soon as I was done. It was his suggestion. He freed up his calendar in order to have dinner with me each evening.

He'd stopped asking me to call Chance, for which I was appreciative but surprised. On this particular Friday we'd decided to take in a movie before dinner. I was looking forward to it. I knew Blaine was trying to fill my hours to diminish the pain of my failed marriage.

I walked into Blaine's office saying a cheery hello to his secretary whom I'd become quite comfortable with. I found it odd that she didn't look at me as she usually did, but instead looked away and told me to go ahead in the office that Blaine was waiting for me. He was. So was Chance.

"Chance." I looked from him to Blaine. "What are you doing here?"

As he walked toward me, I attempted to tell him not to come any closer. Before I could, I was in his arms and my world was spinning.

"You said you were going to call," Chance whispered into my ear.

"I couldn't. I wanted you to hold me much too much to try a phone conversation."

"Michelle."

He moaned my name over and over. I felt the solidity of my bones changing, melting, and flowing forward to combine with him.

An instant before his lips claimed mine, I saw Blaine leave the office. Chance moved his mouth closer, hesitating a nanosecond to gauge my resistance.

How could I resist him, this dark-haired lover I'd vowed to love throughout all eternity? I gave in to the desires of my heart as his lips, warm and inviting, melded into mine, his tongue plumbing the depths of my mouth, my tongue battling his.

He was holding me tightly against his heart. I couldn't tell where the beating of his heart began and mine ended.

"You're free now, Michelle."

"No, Chance, I'm not."

"I'm not going to lose you again," he declared. "I'm not going to let you go."

I felt my energy combining with his and everything that I thought existed in this life, in my sane, sensible world, faded away. I was whisked away with the speed of light across time after time. Each time, I was with Chance, in his arms, loving him, always his wife, always.

Each life had been lived joyfully and ended as a natural cycle of things, until the last time we were together. That was the only life we'd not completed.

It felt as if I were going to fall. My strength gave way and I could feel my body begin to fall. I was in Chance's arms. His face was wet and covered with tears, his and mine combined. He was kissing my checks, my neck, my throat and his love, so pure, so real, wrapped me in a cocoon of safety.

I had found the other half of my soul. I could only hold him without speaking, knowing that I was in his arms again and he was safe. I felt that I had just completed something, a circle. That was it. The circle was now complete.

Blaine re-entered the room and looked to the floor where I was cradled in Chance's arms. "What happened?"

Chance looked up at him. "I thought you were going to give us a few minutes."

My eyes followed Blaine's, as he looked at his watch then gazed back at Chance. "I've been gone over an hour. What happened?" he repeated.

"She fainted."

I blinked twice. I didn't remember that. "I had a vision," I told Blaine. "I saw Chance and me living out our lives, time after time."

"That wasn't a vision you saw. Those were memories."

Blaine helped Chance raise me from the floor. I felt a little woozy. "That's never happened with Chance. I thought it was just between us."

Blaine glanced from one of us to the other. "Did you feel the same burst of energy that you feel when we touch?"

Though the words sounded innocent enough I knew in my heart Blaine was hoping that particular connection was only between the two of us. "No, nothing like that," I finally answered. "It was just when Chance kissed me…" I stopped, blushing with embarrassment."He kissed me and suddenly all of these scenes flashed before me. It was almost as if I were in a movie observing myself in different bodies, different times. Yet I knew it was me, and always the man was Chance."

Chance was smiling at me. "We were destined to be together from the beginning to the end of eternity. Our lives were always preordained. That's why you called me. That's why I looked for you and that's the reason I found you."

I knew the words Chance spoke were true but there was something missing. Something had short-circuited in this life to prevent us from finding each other before we had a chance to hurt others.

"While I agree with you, Chance, in all the other lifetimes, we were young, in our teens, early twenties when we found each other. We lived our lives fully, we grew old together. Never once did I sense that we had hurt anyone to be together. We were always born knowing that the other existed."

"Why didn't it happen this time?" Chance asked. I couldn't help noticing a puzzled look on his face.

Blaine looked at us both. "I don't know the answer to that. Maybe you both chose not to know. Maybe in this century you didn't want to endure others' disdain. In earlier times it was okay to believe. Now it's not. Even if they believe in reincarnation most people don't admit it."

Chance held my face in his hands. "It doesn't matter, we've found each other. I'm not going to let you go."

"Chance."

"Don't. I see it in your eyes, but don't say it. Not now," he pleaded.

I looked to Blaine for help. My emotions were tumbling around inside me. Yes, I loved this man madly. My heart, soul and spirit belonged to him, but I had the niggling doubt that this lifetime, for whatever reason, was not meant to be spent in his arms.

"Chance, I have to go with Blaine, we're having dinner."

"I don't think so."

Chance lifted me in his arms as though I was nothing but feathers. I guess I was. I'd lost twenty-five pounds, the twenty I'd gained and an extra five.

I buried my lips in his neck. I knew where we were going and what he wanted. I wanted it too.

In the blink of an eye, or so it seemed, we arrived at Chance's home. "Chance, don't," I protested as he once again lifted me in his arms, prepared to carry me through the door.

"Shhhh," he answered softly. "This is what a man does with his new bride."

"But I'm not."

I wanted to protest, but the look in his eyes prevented it. No words have yet been invented to describe that look, something so much more than love and adoration, something purely spiritual. For this moment in time I could deny him nothing.

This time in his home, I welcomed the energy of our combined souls that had called out to each other. I felt the warm embrace of the rooms enfolding me in supreme love. Crouched beneath my feelings of joy were the first pinpricks of sadness. I pushed it away from me. There would be time to deal with whatever it was later. For now, this time, this moment belonged only to Chance and myself.

He kissed my hands one at a time, then walked to the middle of the room. I watched him push the buttons on his tape player, not in the least bit surprised when Sting's voice came on, singing, "Every Breath You Take."

How appropriate. It was so true. With every breath, I was closer to Chance, loving him more, remembering more, no longer running from my many pasts with this man, but capitulating to the inevitable.

I was in his arms spinning around and around believing that Sting had written the song so that when Chance and I found each other it would speak for us, saying the things we didn't say. It did the job beautifully. *Thank you Sting, for the song.*

I felt the fire beginning in the big toe of my left foot, the burn scorching me with its fervent power. It wasn't long before the flames of desire filled my entire being, rushing over and through me like a giant tidal wave. I succumbed to the lust raging in my soul for this man I loved.

Together we sank to the floor, the music having cast a spell over us. We could not take another step. The bedroom was too far away and our hunger, our need, too intense, too close to be denied. Chance's lips touched me all over, as mine did him.

I loved him with every cell in my entire body. I was his and he was mine.

He entered me and I looked in amazement into his eyes, seeing clearly every moment of every life we'd spent together.

Then something strange happened. As we began the exquisite climb together toward total bliss I saw us together in the future, blissfully happy and free to love. Chance was holding me in his arms. Suddenly a sword materialized out of the air and with one quick swipe, separated us.

I saw myself crying out for Chance, screaming, "No God, no." And a faceless voice answered me. "You stole one lifetime. This one I take back."

I saw myself crying, desolate, begging God for another life with the other half of my soul. I grew old, unloved, barren, always searching for Chance, always. I opened my eyes, fighting back the tears.

This time Blaine couldn't tell me it wasn't a vision I had, for I knew it was. I closed my eyes, giving in to the lust of my soul, knowing within my spirit what the vision meant. This lifetime was not meant for me to be with Chance.

Somehow we'd broken the plan. We'd found each other when it was never meant to be. I wondered what would happen if we accepted our stolen love now? Would we be denied the full and complete love I saw waiting for us in the future?

I felt the urgency in Chance's body pushing me toward completion and I allowed my thoughts to disperse. Nothing would stop me from making the total journey with Chance.

Together we climbed each peak and mountain, our spirits, our souls entwined. I knew without a shadow of a doubt that this man was the one whom God had created for me. Our love was everlasting.

As we began to spiral down, I felt an intense hot electrical energy coursing through my body. I could feel it in Chance's body also.

I listened closely, sure that I heard a low hum of energy around us. I lifted my hand to touch Chance's face. The same energy that had surrounded us the day we first found Blaine was there with us now. We'd found our way home.

We made love the entire night and into the morning, sometimes at a feverish pitch, our hunger for each other getting the best of us. It was as though for this lifetime we'd been starved and we now wanted nothing more than to feast on each other.

At times, we made love slowly, Chance kissing his way up my thighs, his lips, his hands, his heart branding my very soul.

I held nothing back. I gave him all that I was and all that I ever would be, because I knew what my vision meant.

When we were done with this night it would be our last. It would be over. This lifetime had not been meant for me to be with my husband, my love, the other part of my soul. This lifetime was meant for me to spend with Larry.

I kept this knowledge from Chance. I wanted nothing to mar the perfection of our loving. This one night, my love unhampered by any other love, was my ultimate gift for my beloved.

In the wee hours of the morning, Chance lay sated, his head across my abdomen, his hands caressing my naked flesh, the bed that we'd finally made it to soft and warm beneath our bodies.

"I had a vision," I said to Chance.

"I had it too. You don't know that's what it means."

It surprised me that not only had he had the same vision, but he also knew the meaning and denied it.

"Chance, we weren't meant to find each other. This lifetime, we were not meant to be together."

"I don't care. We did find each other."

"But how? Did we break some cosmic law to do it? I can feel it, that we've crossed some great divide we were never meant to cross."

"You came to me, Michelle. For years I had these dreams. When I met my wife they stopped for a time. I thought they were wishful fantasy but they weren't."

"What happened?" I asked, knowing in my heart that I probably already knew.

"You started coming to me more frequently, asking me why I wasn't looking for you. You were always so distraught, telling me you were lost, that you couldn't find me. I can remember the sound of your voice saying, 'Jeremy, find me. I'm looking for you. Remember your promise. I need to know that you're alright, I need to know our son was loved.'"

I felt his tears hot and wet falling between my legs where his head still rested. "How did you know I wasn't just dreams?"

"Because it felt so real," he answered. "I awoke one night crying out to you saying that I would find you, that I did remember my promise. My wife woke and asked what I was dreaming about."

He stopped then and raised his head to look at me before continuing, his hand sliding along the smooth surface of my abdomen. He moved slightly, burying his tongue in my navel, sending sensations of warmth spreading through me.

"Chance, tell me what happened. What did you say to her?"

"I told her the truth, that my wife Dimitra was calling me, that she was worried and trying to find me. I told her I had to find you."

I looked at him in disbelief. "How could you just say something like that?"

"Because it was true. I knew it. I had dismissed the incidents for too long as dreams. The moment I spoke your name to my wife, I knew none of it had ever been a dream."

"Is that when you got a divorce?"

"Shortly after. She wanted to go to counseling and I wanted to find someone to help me with regression, someone to help me find you. She thought I was nuts. Until I spoke your name I'd thought that I loved her. After that first revelation I knew I had to find you. Making love to her would have been wrong."

He looked at me. "I would have only been using her body. It would have been you I was making love to, so I told her how sorry I was, but that I had no choice but to find you."

"Was she bitter?"

"No, I think she was relieved in a way. I think for a time she thought she would be stuck with having a husband in the loony bin. She didn't think my career would ever get off the ground, not when I was chasing, as she refers to you, a figment of my imagination. Tell me something. Did you ever have those dreams?"

"Yes," I answered truthfully. "They began in early childhood. My parents were a bit afraid of me. They thought I was crazy. Around the time I met Larry, I thought maybe he was the man I'd been dreaming of."

"You didn't wait for me."

"I didn't know."

"When did the dreams start back for you?"

I thought about it for a moment. I knew exactly when. "Erica was two months old. I was holding her, breast feeding her."

I could picture the moment, the extreme joy I felt on nursing my baby. The love for her that filled my heart. I saw Larry's face, proud and oh so happy.

He had kissed me while I nursed Erica and whispered into my mouth, *"I promise, I'll never let anything happen to you, I'll love you forever.*

I felt a cold shiver ride up the small of my back. The same shiver I'd felt that night when I'd been happy with my husband and my baby.

I could still feel the sense of dread that crept in and laid claim to my happiness, a dread that told me not to hold on to the two of them so tightly, that they would be taken away.

I was determined that wouldn't happen. Whatever I had to do to stop it I would. If it meant loving them less, I would do that also.

I felt the sting of tears. "Chance, finding both you and Blaine has been a blessing in so many ways for me. It's cleared up my dreams. Blaine has helped me in ways I never believed possible. He helped me to see why except for a short period of time with Erica I never felt what mothers are supposed to feel. I've always felt so guilty, so damaged inside for not having maternal instincts. I will always be grateful to Blaine for releasing me from that emotional prison. Thanks to him I now know that I only wanted to protect my babies. I was afraid they would be taken away. I couldn't remember Blaine or you, except in my dreams, but I remembered a deep sorrow. I wanted to prevent it from invading my life again."

"I know what you're doing, what you're leading up to. All of this talk isn't as much about your children as it is your husband. I know what you're planning to do. You love him," Chance said in a surprised tone.

"Yes, Chance, I do. But I told you that from the beginning. I've never lied to you about my feelings for Larry. You and I, we've had forever together, and we're going to be together in the future, but this lifetime now doesn't belong to us. My life this time was meant to be spent with Larry."

"How can you leave me after all we've been through to find each other?"

"To safeguard our future. I have to give Larry the one thing I have held from him all of these years. I have to give him all of me, free from my past, free from my dreams of you and Blaine. He deserves that, and my kids deserve for me to try and be a better mother. Chance, you'd been looking for me for over twenty years. Why do you think you found me when you did?"

He sat up on the side of the bed, looking away. Then he looked back at me, as if having made his decision. "The night before I found you, you came to me. You told me you were going to die."

"I don't understand. How did that help you find me?"

"Because I made contact with you. I asked you to help me find you, to lead me to you. I asked you to hold on. The thought of your dying filled me with panic. That was the only day I've ever canceled patients."

"I thought you said you'd never cancelled patients and never would, even for me."

"I lied." Chance smiled slowly. "What choice did I have? I had to find you so I emptied my mind and made a connection with you, asking you where you were. I drove until I came to the store. I heard your voice saying, '*Jeremy, I'm here.*'

"I don't remember doing that."

"You wouldn't. You were in denial. It was your soul that was leading me to you. So I sat in the car waiting, wanting to have you come to the car and say, 'H*ere I am.*'

I smiled at him. "Instead you got caught up with me in a downpour."

He smiled back at me. "Yeah, I was annoyed in the beginning. You were distracting me from the reason I was there, but I couldn't resist helping you. The moment I ran to help you I lost contact with Dimitra. I remember saying, 'D*amn that woman standing there crying in the rain.*'

"When I held you, I swear I heard Dimitra in my head saying, '*Thank you, Jeremy. Thank God that I found you.*' And when I asked you where you'd been, you answered you'd been looking for me. That was my proof."

"It didn't dissuade you when I thought you were a mental patient?"

He laughed, remembering. "No, but I was surprised that with the frequency of the dreams, you had not sought out the meanings. Besides, you never really thought I was a mental patient. You just didn't want to believe what you knew to be true. You never wanted me to tell you. You weren't ready to know or to believe. I had to let you make that part of the journey alone."

"Chance," I moaned, reaching for him, feeling his arms lock around me. "Thank you for finding me."

"Why thank me if you're planning on leaving me?"

"Because, Chance, I had to know. I suppose my spirit couldn't rest without knowing you and Blaine were alright. I couldn't love the people in my life fully without feeling I was betraying you somehow, that I would lose them as I'd lost the two of you."

"But you've found us. Now we should all be thankful. Besides, Michelle, you weren't happy. You wanted to die."

I held him tighter. "You're right, I wanted to die."

"Then how could you ever consider going back into that? I don't care that you think we've broken some kind of cosmic law. I can't allow you to torture yourself, and for what? Honor, commitment, a promise you made?"

"Chance, it's none of those things, yet it's all of them. I love Larry. I always have. I was just afraid. This lifetime I'm meant to spend with him."

"In hell? Because that's what you were in. If not, your spirit would not have been in such agony."

"My life was hell because of me, Chance. Because of my actions, not because of Larry. I never demanded anything different of him. I allowed him to think I was happy when I wasn't."

I looked at Chance. "It wasn't Larry's fault that I was missing you, that I was suffering over losing Blaine, that when I nursed Erica, somewhere within my spirit I thought of the other child I loved and I mourned."

"But you've left him. Why go back?"

"Because I want to."

"Deny your love for me."

"You know I can't do that. Our hearts and our spirits are one. For the rest of my life and the next, with every breath I take I'll love you more."

"Then how can you leave me? How can you even think about it? I won't let you. I don't care about the next lifetime. I care about the here and now.

"Don't you see how wrong that is? Not caring about the future will insure that we'll never have one together. We'll only build a tremendous karmic debt if we remain together in this life."

"Is that why you're doing this?" Chance screamed at me. "To insure a future for us, you want to sacrifice our present?"

"No, Chance, I want to finish this life the way it was meant to be. I'm not going to return to Larry as a sacrificial offering. I love him."

"What about him? Are you going to tell him that you plan on being with him for the time you have left, that you never expect to spend eternity with him?"

"He has no need to know that," I answered. "He doesn't believe in this anyway. He only cares about here and now."

"How do you know he will want you back?"

"Because he loves me."

"I love you too."

"I know you do. I have faith in you, Chance. I always have. I know that you will do the right thing when the time comes."

"And when the time comes, will you ask me again to let you go? After you've haunted my dreams on a constant basis for twenty years, you want me to just let you go?"

"You have no real choice in the matter, Chance. It's my decision to make."

He paced around the room, his manhood hanging heavy between his legs, swaying with his body movements. I observed him, filling my senses with the sight of him because I knew I could no longer allow him to own my dreams.

"Chance, I wish I could tell you that I'm sorry you found me and mean it, but I can't. I can't tell you what it means to know that you and Blaine are here."

"What good does that do either of us?" He turned with fury in his voice. "We lose."

"Not both of you." I lay back on the pillow, waiting for him to come to me.

"You're telling me that Blaine can remain in your life, but I can't?"

"Chance, Blaine is my son, you're my husband, my lover, the man who haunted my dreams. How can you remain in my life?"

"How can I not? Forget Larry. Get a divorce. Marry me." He fell on his knees. "Michelle, I love you. I always have and I always will. Will you marry me?"

He didn't give me a chance to answer. He began kissing my throat and nibbling my lips, touching me at the very core of my being with his infinite love.

I pulled away from him to moan out my answer. "Chance, I want to complete this lifetime as it was meant to be."

"Why? Because he needs you? He'll learn to live without you. It's no more than you're asking of me."

"There is a difference, Chance. You know we'll be together again. And you know this lifetime is not for the two of us."

"So what?" Chance roared, his voice filled with anger and with pain. "I say we take it. Fate has handed it to us. Who are we to argue with it? You love me more than you could ever possibly love Larry."

I had no scale on which to measure love. I only knew that my love for Larry in this life was just as great and just as real as my love for Chance.

I wanted to be with Larry. That revelation surprised me because it was so unexpected. I wanted to be with Larry not out of need or commitment or even because of a promise.

I wanted to be with him because I remembered the look on his face as I breastfed Erica. And I remembered the love in my heart in that instant that I had for my husband and daughter and I wanted to return to them.

I held Chance tightly in my arms, accepting his love, accepting his body. "Make love to me, Chance," I whispered, "so that I'll never forget you."

Hours later, when Chance could no longer woo me with his body, he continued arguing, stating the many reasons I couldn't return home.

"Chance," I finally told him, exasperated, "it's not like I'm going back tomorrow. I can't return and live the same life I did before. I've changed. I have to give Larry the opportunity to change also."

"He's not going to forget that you left him for me."

"That's not what happened."

"Do you think he's going to believe that?"

I thought about it. Maybe Chance was right. Maybe I'd never be able to convince Larry that Chance wasn't the reason I left him, but that it was for my own soul.

I looked at our naked bodies, slick with sweat, stained with the fluids from our many hours of making love.

"If he saw me now, no, he would never believe you're not the reason I left."

"What if he doesn't change? What if he doesn't want to?"

It was a bit disconcerting to say the least that everything I was saying to Chance was spoken with some greater knowledge. There was a lot more going on with me that I knew I was going to need to explore. There was a wealth of knowledge buried somewhere inside of me and I needed to bring it out.

As gently as I could I stroked the face of the husband of my dreams trying my best to assure him of my love. "This still is not our time, Chance. I will wait for you like always and like always we will find each other."

"Even if I agree to that, how can you be so sure? How can you not grab what we have today and hold on to it?"

I ran my hand across the man it seemed I had loved forever and who I was destined to love in the future. "I love you, Chance, with all my heart. And as unbelievable as it may sound to you, I love Larry also. The last thing in the world I want to do is hurt you. You can call it guilt because I'm not certain that it isn't a part of my decision.

"But loving you now, here in the present, remembering that I've loved you in the past and knowing that I'll love you in the future gives me strength. I don't have to be afraid of loving my husband, my children, of showing them that I do. I need to give that to them and to myself."

"Then it is guilt."

"Call it what you will, but I saw our love. We never hurt anyone, Chance. I'm not going to start now. I've done enough damage to my family. I can only hope I have time to repair some of it."

I looked sharply at Chance. "Do you want them to carry my indifference around with them and drag it into their next life?"

For an answer, he held me and I held on him to him. Yes, maybe I was willing to let go of the man in my dreams because of my commitment, my guilt, my promises, but weren't those all a part of love?

Chapter Sixteen

I stood at last looking toward the huge oak doors. I had walked over every inch of the house, touching everything, imprinting it on my soul.

For the last hour Chance had stopped talking to me, though his eyes followed me around the rooms pleading with me to reconsider.

I saved the rocker for last. Going to it I sat and closed my eyes, touching the well worn wood that Chance kept polished, allowing the luster to shine through. It was an extremely well made chair to have survived the ravages of time.

I must have sat there for fifteen minutes before I opened my eyes to find Chance only a foot or two away staring at me. Chance's eyes were dark and piercing. He had no need to tell me what he was feeling. I knew. I was feeling it too.

I didn't know how to utter the words goodbye. I thought of saying, 'We'll meet again, but it didn't seem right.

I took a step toward the door. *Just a few more*, I thought. *I can do this.*

"Dimi."

Chance's voice called out to me, filling me with utter despair. I felt a breeze blow through the room though the windows were closed. The winds of change. I'd always thought it only a figure of speech, but not any more. I felt it on my face.

I turned to face Chance, watching as he seemingly glided toward me on a pillow of air. In an instant he was beside me.

I reached out my hand to caress his cheek. "Jeremy," I said to Chance. "Although this is my decision to make, you hold the power to make me stay. Please don't use that power against me. Release me, my love. Let me go."

I brought my hand slowly down the plane of his face, lingering on the slight stubble before I turned again toward the door.

"Dimi," he called again.

I waited for the wind to come through again. I waited while I felt the razor sharp pain of Jeremy's heart breaking.

"You know that Blaine doesn't have a family in this life. I want to ask a favor of you."

He hesitated. I felt his hands on my shoulders.

"Will you help me give him a family just for one day?"

It was an excuse, we both knew it, but it was an excuse my heart could believe. "Yes," I answered Chance, allowing my body to sag into his. "I should have thought of this myself. He's helped me so much."

"I'm glad he was able to help you see that you had been paying attention to your driving when you had the accident with Viola. That was unwarranted guilt. I'm glad you no longer have it."

"So am I."

"Are you planning on visiting her?"

"I thought of Larry and his need to protect me. "I'm not sure. Right now that isn't the most important thing I have to do. Repairing my marriage, making amends to my children and finding a way to rid myself of this huge karmic debt in preparation for the next life are the things I have to concern myself with." I looked at this man whom I had loved more than life. Hurting him wasn't what I wanted but being with him in the next life was.

We were finding words to fill the space, to lessen the pain. The task was futile, but still we tried. I felt the electrical current making its way up my legs and moved away from Chance. "Do you want to call Blaine or shall I?"

"I'll do it," Chance answered, moving away from me also. I went back to my rocker to listen to the call. I heard Chance's end of the conversation.

"Blaine, Michelle and I want to spend the day with you, together."

"No." I heard his voice breaking at that point before he continued. "It's not her destiny."

"I tried."

He glanced toward me, then lowered his voice. Still, I heard.

"I didn't force her, Blaine. It is not emotional blackmail. She wants to do this for you."

Chance looked at me again, and he gave a snort of disgust apparently to something Blaine had said. He held the phone out to me. "Blaine wants to talk to you."

Taking the phone from Chance I tried looking at him but he refused to hold my gaze and looked away. With great sadness I turned my attention to my other son. "Hi, Blaine," I said knowing the reason he wanted to speak to me.

"Michelle, this isn't necessary. You don't have to let Chance force you into this."

I smiled in Chance's direction before answering. "He's not. I want to give you a day with us as your family."

"You're not going to stay with Chance?"

There was the same sadness in Blaine's voice that was in Chance's and in mine. "I can't," I answered him

"You love him."

"Of course."

"You believe he's Jeremy," Blaine protested.

"One hundred percent," I didn't hesitate to reply.

Blaine didn't answer. He probably was trying to figure out how his predictions hadn't come true. I had known all along what he thought was going to happen.

"Blaine, psychics are not right all the time, even very gifted ones. Only God is."

"Do I fall under the very gifted?" he teased.

"That depends," I teased right back. Our relationship would remain intact. We'd just proven that. "So where do you want us to meet?"

"Michelle, are you really sure about this?" The worry had crept back into Blaine's voice.

"I'm sure." I laughed at the little boy longing I'd sensed in Blaine "Just tell me where you want to spend the day. Whatever you want to do, wherever you want to go, we await as your humble servants to fulfill your wish."

"Anywhere I say?"

"Anywhere," I answered.

"In that case," Blaine hesitated, "don't meet me. I'll come there. If you really mean it and you think you can handle it, I'd love to spend the day with the two of you surrounded by your things from the past. That would make me feel we're a family."

I should have known. Either I'd walked right into that or he'd set me up. I wasn't sure which.

I turned to Chance. "Jeremy," I called to him, surprising him and myself that I'd once again used that name. Blaine wants to spend the day here, with us. Can you handle it?" I asked, not seeing how either of us possibly could.

He stared at me, his gaze forcing me to turn away. It felt like forever before he answered.

"Yes, that would be perfect."

My face felt as if it was on fire. I had no idea why I should be blushing. A thin film of sweat beaded my upper lip which I wiped away. Chance stared at me as I did so. I saw the hunger in his eyes, felt it in the electricity that vibrated between us.

Then I heard Blaine calling me. I was unaware that I had dropped the phone from my ear as I stared back into Chance's heated gaze.

"I'm here, Blaine, sorry. Here would be just fine. Chance and I both want it."

"Good. Then give me two hours and I'll be there."

"Two hours." The whine in my voice was part cry, part plea.

He heard it and understood. "I'll be there as soon as I can. I have something for both you and Chance and it's not here. I have to go and pick it up."

"Okay. See you when you get here." I wanted to urge him to hurry, but Chance was staring at me.

"Is there a problem?" he asked.

"Not really," I answered, wanting instead to say, yes, there's a very big problem. But I didn't. "It will be a couple of hours before Blaine can come. He has an errand he has to attend to first."

The heat in Chance's eyes became stronger. "I'm sure we'll be fine for two hours."

Oh yeah, right. I was barely holding on by a thread. Two hours more to delay the inevitable. Even now that magical current that always surrounded us was snaking its way toward me, tweaking my cells with its vibrations.

Stay here for another two hours with a man who could turn me into a towering inferno of molten passion and undeniable love? I didn't think so. I damn sure wasn't made of stone. I looked into his eyes. And neither was he.

I walked past Chance, almost running in my haste. "I'm going back to the hotel to shower and change. Blaine knows I had this on yesterday."

"He doesn't care," Chance answered, coming toward me.

"I know," I shouted over my shoulder as I ran out the door.

"You can shower here. I'll give you a shirt. We're adults. Nothing will happen that we don't want to happen."

That's just what I was afraid of. There was no way I was going to be in the house alone with that man and have nothing happen. If either of us believed that, then we both could make a fortune writing fairy tales.

"Coward," he called after me.

Exactly two hours later, I returned to Chance, showered and dressed in fresh clothes. I heaved a sigh of relief at the sight of Blaine's car sitting in Chance's drive.

I knocked on the door knowing I didn't have to. It wasn't expected that I would. I hoped that by doing so it would send a subtle message to all three of us. I did not belong here.

Blaine opened the door, leaning only close enough to kiss my cheek. He smiled at me, ushering me in. The instant I stepped over the threshold, I knew something was different.

My eyes scanned the room. My rocker was gone. "Where did you put it?" I questioned Chance forgetting that the rocker really belonged to him and as such, he could do with it what he pleased.

Chance looked at me from hooded eyes. "I'm giving it away."

His face and voice were both serious. I wondered why Blaine was wearing an amused smile. Didn't he know what the chair meant to me?

"If you were going to get rid of the chair you could have told me. I would have bought it from you."

My tone was haughty, but I didn't care. I glanced at these two men that I was going to spend the day with. One with a sullen face, the other amused.

Okay, Michelle he's trying to get back at you. Ignore him. This day is for Blaine, to give him a family for the next few hours.

I walked toward the kitchen. I'd almost forgotten I hadn't eaten. Whatever Chance was cooking smelled delicious. My stomach rumbled as I came closer to the source of the delicious aromas.

"I thought you only cooked Chinese?" I said to Chance as my hand reached over his for a taste. The delicious morsel in my mouth, I stopped, tilting my head slightly as I caught sight of a huge packing box in the family room. There was an enormous lavender bow perched gingerly on top, looking as if it might fall at any moment.

At the same moment Chance reached for my wrist, holding me in place. He narrowed his eyes into slits, spearing me with his gaze.

"What did you think I had done with your chair? It seems like you forgot more than the fact that I love you. If you're that forgetful, how are you ever going to remember having loved me at all?"

Blaine stepped between us. He took my wrist from Chance's grip. "I think I have something that might help," he said as he led me to the family room and my gift-wrapped chair.

I watched as he pulled a heavy black velvet bag from his pocket. He dumped the contents on the coffee table. "Chance, come on in," he called to Chance, who was still in the kitchen watching us.

There were two men's bracelets and one old-fashioned locket on a sturdy gold chain.

I picked the locket up in my hand. "This is beautiful, Blaine. Where did you get it?"

"Oh, I didn't buy this for the beauty or those." He pointed toward the bracelets.

"I don't understand. Is there something special about them?"

"I hope so."

Blaine took the locket from my hand to show me the intricate details and the different stones. He pointed out to me that the stones in the bracelets were perfect matches. The locket had one huge diamond in the center. It looked to be a perfect cut, two carats.

"I've never seen stones like these."

"I'm sure you have seen them in a past life. Blaine stared at Me then smiled. "I've chosen each of these stones for the properties they emit. They are all good stones for recapturing lost memories. The Brandburg quartz crystal will help us rediscover our past life. The purple fluorite, spiritual growth and channeling of information.

"This one, he said pointing to another stone, "is unakite, it helps in past life healing. The rainbow obsidion, is for karmic healing. It will also relay to you your purpose for being in the next incarnation. The azurite is for psychic travel and connecting with other psychics and loved ones. The green calcite is used as a bridge through time. And the amber is for healing, love and so many things that I will teach you later, Michelle."

"You're planning on teaching me. Why."

"You're a psychic, Mother, and it's time for you to remember that."

"Mother?"

Blaine and I stared for a long moment into each other' eyes. "And the diamond," I asked, letting go of his calling me mother.

"Michelle, this diamond symbolizes purity. This bond of purity always exists in true love."

He looked toward Chance, who was now walking into the room. He picked up one of the bracelets, telling him the same thing.

"The stones are said to be magical. They've been used to transport from the past to the present."

"You're kidding," I said to him, glancing toward Chance to see what he thought. "Are you saying if we chose to go back in time we could relive the life we didn't get a chance to finish before?"

"It's conceivable, but this lifetime would be altered. Your entire family would cease to exist. Besides, I think it would break the laws of nature to try and change things. We'll just have to wait for our next incarnation."

Blaine was confusing the heck out of me. "I don't understand. You said the stones can take us back and forth in time. How will it help us find each other?"

Blaine smiled at me. "The stones will emit a signal, an energy, ours. That is, after they've been charged with our energy. Over a period of time I'm told they become magnetized, each pulling toward the other, leading us to each other. When the three of us are reunited, our full memories will be restored.

"All three of these have been psychically charged by a powerful mystic friend of mine. Wear these always and when the time comes, we'll be led to each other."

"Are you serious?" I couldn't help asking. His face was awash with hope and love. Still, this was stranger than anything we'd done thus far.

"I'm serious. My friend has great powers. I've witnessed it myself or I wouldn't have consulted him. He swears he's lived many incarnations and that each time he knows who he was and who he had to look for by having an amulet."

"Did he ever find anyone?"

"Not for the past few lifetimes."

Blaine looked apologetic. I couldn't help smiling at him. "Then how in the world is this supposed to help us if he couldn't even help himself?"

"He believes that since you and Chance have managed to find each other several times in the past and to find me this time, that you have the psychic ability necessary to make this work. He believes the special preparation he's done will help make it easier for us, if we always wear them. We each have matching stones and a diamond for love and purity."

He stopped to smile at me. "Yours just happens to be a lot bigger."

"That's all we have to do?"

"Well," he said, "it would help if one at a time we wear all three for seven weeks for the final, sealing, then pass them on to the next person, so that our vibrations would be in them all."

"You're talking twenty-one weeks?" I inquired of Blaine. "I don't think so."

"I know. I told him so. But when I told him we were spending the next twenty-four hours together. He said if we could spend it in a place that already contained strong vibrations, it would intensify the powers. He suggested we each wear them for seven hours. Though he couldn't guarantee it would work, it couldn't hurt."

Famous last words, I thought.

"So, who wants to be first?" Blaine looked from one of us to the other.

Chance took the locket from Blaine. "This will help us find each other again?" He looked directly into my eyes. "This will enable us to be born remembering the ones we love?"

"Yes," Blaine answered. Over time the properties in the stones will be transmuted to our cells. By the end of this incarnation the stones themselves will no longer be necessary."

"What if one of us changes our mind, decides our destinies lie in different paths?"

"That's why the taking and wearing of these symbolize a pact, an agreement. We will all meet again and it will be our destiny to live and love together as a family."

"I'm game," Chance said as he put the locket around his neck and slipped a bracelet over each wrist.

"All three of us have to agree." Blaine looked at me. "Do you agree?"

"What do we have to do besides wear the jewelry? That seems a little too easy."

"I just say a few words, we hold hands and that's it."

"Are we casting a spell, an incantation? I mean, is this some form of witchcraft? Blaine, we don't want to damn our souls to hell."

Chance looked at me. "I don't care what it means. If it will give us a chance at a life together I'll take it."

Blaine looked first at Chance, then back toward me "Michelle, you don't have to worry. It's nothing that drastic. It's barely more than the promise you made Jeremy give."

"Okay, let's hear it," I said suspiciously.

"We hold hands and say, 'I pledge here and now, always and forever, my love to the two souls gathered here with me. My soul will know your souls from the moment of rebirth and will seek out no other. My soul will wait and only your souls will make me whole. This I vow through all eternity.'"

"I can do that," I said to Blaine. He repeated the words. Chance and I repeated them with him. Chance's hand tightened on mine.

When we were done the three of us embraced until Blaine's arms fell away. Chance and I stood alone embracing and vowing in a whisper once again to each other that we would wait for our time.

"Blaine, I thought..."

"Yeah, I know what you thought." He grinned at me. "I may be a psychic, but I'm also human. I wanted you to remain with Chance, but I saw that there was a strong possibility that you wouldn't."

He touched Chance's arm where he had the bracelets, then touched the locket around Chance's neck. "I took out a little insurance, just in case." This time he laughed out loud. "So Michelle, am I now a great psychic?"

"You're the best." I reached my arms out to him to bring him back into our circle. "Blaine, I'm so glad we found you."

"So am I, Mother," I heard him whisper into my hair as he embraced me. "So am I."

Chapter Seventeen

Larry packed the small bag he used for overnight trips. He threw the items in haphazardly, not caring that they would be wrinkled when he needed them.

He surveyed the mess in his bag before deciding to dump everything and start all over. Damn, how hard could it be? He'd watched as Mick had packed his bags a thousand times. She'd always made it look so easy.

He felt the now familiar stab of pain run from his heart down his shoulder into his arms as well as an unbearable weight pressing down on his chest.

Larry had mentioned to several of his friends the physical discomfort he was having. They all assured him that it was stress from…from… He couldn't even think it.

God in heaven, Mick was gone, had left him. Why the hell wouldn't he be stressed? Even now he could hear her voice prattling around in his head, saying, "*Larry, do any of your friends have a medical degree? Stop being a baby and go see a doctor.*"

Well, he was through listening to her. Instead, he chose to believe his friends. The only time he ever felt the pain was when he was thinking about Mick, like now.

Just the night before, he'd felt the pain even stronger than now. He'd been arguing with the counselor he'd decided he needed to deal with the stress.

Actually it hadn't been so much him deciding he needed it as it had been Derrick. When Mick left, he'd refused to allow the kids to come back. He'd packed all their bags and put them out in the drive.

Derrick had called him several times telling him that they were all worried about him, that maybe it would be a good idea if he got some help.

He could clearly remember his son's words. *'Dad, you don't have to agree with Mom to go for counseling. It's obvious you're miserable without her. Think about it. Maybe you can still save your marriage.*

Larry had listened to his son, but saving his marriage wasn't what finally pushed him to get, he hated the word, *help*. He only needed an avenue to vent. He had gone on the slim chance that talking would stop the crushing pain to his chest.

It hadn't. He was the one paying the money and the therapist was siding with Mick. He couldn't believe the woman had the gall to tell him that his wife was probably right, that the odds were that he didn't listen. She'd even had the nerve to tell him that most of the entire male population didn't listen, that they heard only what they wanted to hear.

The woman had to be an idiot. She knew damn well he was an attorney. He could sue her ass for sexual discrimination. He wondered if she ever gave her female clients the load of bull she was giving him.

That's when he'd made his decision. He was not going to just lie down and play dead. He was going to that hotel and he was bringing his wife home.

If it wasn't for the trip he would be headed over there now, but the trip was important. Tomorrow night he would go to the hotel and bring her home.

Her even being in a hotel angered him. He popped several antacids in his mouth. It was taking more and more of them to dull the pain now.

He couldn't believe Mick had not told him where she was staying. If he'd not checked the caller ID to see if she'd called when he was out, he wouldn't have known.

There had been only one call from a hotel, the one that came the day after Mick left. He remembered answering the phone and telling Erica to leave him alone.

He hadn't known it was Mick, but he was glad he'd not talked to her in that moment. He was hurting far too much.

Larry took another look at the jumbled mess on his bed. He wanted to be angry with Mick. God, how he wanted to be angry with her.

But more than that, he wanted to find a way to repair the damage. He wanted to learn how to listen.

Our time together was drawing to a close. I'd fallen asleep for a little while and had awakened to hear Blaine and Chance talking softly in the other room.

I remained still, wondering why they had chosen not to wake me. This time was for the three of us. They knew that when the morning came I would leave.

"You have to let her go," I heard Blaine saying to Chance. "I'll help you get through this."

"I don't think you can. I keep having these awful thoughts, wishing that something would happen to Larry."

"Don't," Blaine said, "that's very bad karma."

"I know. Besides, I don't mean it. I just don't want her to leave."

I wished I had not eavesdropped on their conversation. I made some noise to alert them that I was awake and heard the immediate shift in conversation as I got up from the sofa and went to join them. I would not mention what I'd heard.

"So why did you two let me sleep?" I glanced at the clock. Six hours and it would be over.

"You were tired," Blaine said. "Besides, you didn't really sleep that long."

I noticed that Chance wouldn't look in my direction. He stared out the window into the darkness, his face giving nothing away.

I went and knelt beside Blaine. "How clear are your regression memories?"

"Very clear."

I had wanted to ask him a question for weeks, but had been unable to.

"Can you tell me what kind of life you had, if...if you were happy?" I glanced toward Chance and Blaine did likewise.

"I have several images of me playing as a child and feeling extremely loved by my father." He looked again at Chance.

That was what I needed to know, that Jeremy had found it in his heart to love the child that he and Dimitra had created. "Good. I'm glad to hear that."

Chance turned then, eyeing me with curiosity. "Did I ever break a promise to you, Dimi?" he asked.

It was the first time he'd called me Dimi in front of Blaine. When he used that name I was instantly back in the past.

"That's not it. I just wanted to know."

"You wanted to know if I was able to love our son. He was the only part of you that I had left. I worshipped him."

Chance's demeanor metamorphosed. I knew he was also in the past remembering.

"I was loved," Blaine interrupted us, "but there was a constant sadness that permeated our home. My father talked to me constantly about my mother. He lived only to see me to adulthood so that he could join her."

Chance and Blaine exchanged glances. "I adored my father and was in almost as much agony as he over the loss of my mother. The moment my father thought I could sufficiently care for myself, he called me calmly to his side, lay down on his bed, told me he loved me and that he was now going to find my mother."

"He was not ill," Blaine continued. "He had a long life ahead of him. He willed himself to die. Being without one parent was hell. To lose them both was unbearable."

Blaine stood and walked over to Chance. "I hope I never have to go through that again."

I watched while father and son participated in a silent communication. Blaine would see to it that Chance would make it through.

The rest of our time together went so fast that it was almost as if we'd just begun. We each wore the jewelry Blaine had bought for us, for seven hours each. Then our twenty-four hours were up. It was noon. In unison, the three of us turned toward the grandfather clock as it chimed out the end of our time together.

"Dimi, I know I have to let you go. I know what the vision means, but it's so damn hard."

I watched Chance through the tears in my eyes. He was trying so hard to be brave, but the look of betrayal on his face remained.

"Dimi, give me just a few more hours, please. The time went by so fast." He attempted to smile. "Surely a few more hours will not affect our future."

"What are we having for lunch?" I asked. The time was up, but I wasn't ready. I wanted more and like Chance, I wondered what it would hurt. I was more than willing to take a few more hours for this family I'd found.

Without missing a beat Blaine answered, "Anything you want for lunch you can have."

For the next several hours we talked, laughed, told stories, everything we could think of to put a lifetime of living in such a short amount of time.

It seemed only minutes later that the clock was striking seven P.m. It seemed impossible for that much time to have passed.

It was time for me to leave. I'd gone way past the agreed upon twenty-four hours. I stood at last, smiling at them and walked over to the box containing my chair.

"Chance, I don't have anywhere…"

Blaine stopped me. "I'll keep it until you…" He glanced at Chance. "Until you find a place to live." No one wanted to admit that in time I would be going home. No, it would not be tonight, or tomorrow, but it would happen.

I walked toward the door not wanting to touch either of them, no last embrace, no hugs, just yank, the same way you did with bandages to make it quick and painless.

"Don't lose any more weight," Chance called out softly to me.

"I didn't think you noticed," I answered without turning around.

"I noticed."

I willed my body to keep moving toward the door, but it refused to obey. My head swiveled around. Chance was standing there watching me. I saw the agony in his eyes, the same agony I'd seen in Jeremy when Dimitra was about to die.

"Don't come outside," I whispered to him before running out the door and to my car. It was over, done. I felt like hell, yet there was a knowing that what I was doing was right.

I surprised myself that I was able to drive to the hotel without bawling like a baby. The constant threat of tears I kept away by ordering up the images of Larry and Erica as an infant. That moment in time was the reason I was able to sever my love for Chance. I had to complete my life as it was meant to be.

An hour later I lay on the bed numb from the emotional havoc I'd put my body through. I knew that I should begin making plans for home, but I couldn't think.

I didn't know how to get Larry to listen to me when he never had. But I knew I wasn't as ready as I thought to give up on him, on us. I would have to find a way, just not now. I was too tired.

I heard a knock on the door and a voice calling my name. I opened the door to Chance.

How was I to ever end this if I kept seeing him? Didn't he know it was hard enough to leave him? Didn't he have any idea what he was doing to me? I looked in his eyes. Didn't he know he was prolonging his own pain?

Chance came into the room closing the door behind him. "I forgot to give you this." He held out a small package. I took it, opened the bag and took out the tape. It was Stevie Wonder.

"It's the only song I know that says I'll love you for a million years.'" Chance's voice broke. "I will, Dimi, I'll love you for a million years."

"Chance," I moaned, "don't."

It was too late. I was in his arms holding him, knowing we'd already had too many last hugs, last embraces, and last kisses.

Still I clung to him, feeling his lips, tasting him, loving him. He kissed me softly, slowly, deeply, not with the fevered pitch of passion, but like a man trying to fill his senses with what he was losing.

He was the one who broke away. "I had to hold you one last time."

"I know," I answered. I ran my hands over his face, over the long strands of his hair that he'd allowed to grow. "I know."

He backed out of the room leaving me there in tears. I fell on the bed. This was never meant to happen. I should not have met Chance, not known that he existed in my heart, or was connected to my soul. I lay there with my heart breaking.

When a second knock sounded on my door less than twenty minutes later, I could take no more. He was killing me.

"Chance, no," I said while opening the door.

It was Larry.

"Larry," I sputtered. "Larry, what are you doing here?"

He came into the room, his face red, a scowl deepening what had been a smile when I first opened the door.

"You didn't leave me for him, Mick?"

"Larry, this isn't what you're thinking. I know what I said makes it look bad but I promise you there's a good explanation."

"How do you know what it looks like to me? I come into your room, the room of my wife, and…" He looked up at me.

"You've been crying. You thought I was him. You sure as hell didn't think it was me. I heard you call his name. Now please tell me what it looks like."

"Larry, I didn't know you were coming."

He laughed a harsh angry sound. "You didn't know that I was coming. I'm sorry. Forgive me if I didn't make an appointment."

I saw him looking around the room. I knew he was looking for evidence that I'd just made love. God, I was grateful I had my clothes on. Still, that didn't seem to matter to Larry.

"How many more have there been, Mick, how many men?"

"Larry, listen to me, please. There's never been anyone else. I've tried to tell you. This wouldn't have happened except with Chance, only with him."

Larry was advancing toward me. "You think that's going to make me feel better?"

"I know him, Larry. I was married to him." Larry swept the glasses off the small table.

"Stop it, Mick, I don't want to hear this nonsense. Do you think you're the only one who's been hit on since we got married? Do you think that you're the only woman I could have slept with?

"There have been dozens of women, dozens of them, who have come on to me, who wanted to go to bed with me. I said no. I was never tempted, not once.

"I thought I was married to the most wonderful woman in the world. We'd made promises to each other, promises to love each other always. Not once, Mick. Not one damn time did I ever think of cheating on you."

"I was married to him, Larry."

Now that excuse sounded crazy even to me, but it was the truth.

"I don't care," Larry shouted, his voice getting louder and louder. "I'm only interested in this life here and now, our life. In this life, you're married to me, not him. Me, Mick. And what you did is called adultery in this time period. You've been whoring around and I'm expected to accept it, to say, 'Oh well, he's my wife's husband from her past life.'

"That's bullshit, Mick. That's bullshit and you and I both know it. If I'd given you this load of crap, you would have filed for divorce before the words were out of my mouth."

Larry stopped. There was that damn pain again. He looked at his wife. His Mick. He'd come there with such hopes, only to have them dashed in his face. He wasn't the one she wanted, the one she'd been waiting for. She'd been waiting for Chance. He'd heard her clearly.

For a moment the words froze in his throat. He could think only of the pain that was rapidly enveloping his entire body.

He was fighting for every breath, his jaw tightening now as never before. The elephant was back sitting on his chest, only this time he had brought a trainload of friends.

He gasped, saw the instant concern cross Mick's face. Oh God no. This wasn't supposed to happen. The last thing he wanted was for her to see him have a stress attack.

The pain increased, bringing him to his knees. *Damn,* Larry thought, *this is not a stress attack, this is the real deal. I'm having a heart attack.* Another wave of pain shot through him with the speed of a bullet ripping through flesh. He fell and his world went black.

One minute Larry was standing in front of me. The next, something was happening to him. I saw him pause in front of me, his mouth opening and closing, no words coming out. I watched his red angry face suddenly turn a pasty gray. I saw him clutch his chest a second before he fell to the floor.

"Larry," I screamed out at him, dropping to my knees beside him. "Oh God, Larry. It wasn't what you thought. I was coming home. I love you."

Think, Michelle, think. It will be time for that later. I ran to the phone guided by the clear thinking voice in my head giving the orders.

"This is room 915. My husband just had a heart attack. Get someone up here fast."

I ran to open the door, screaming out for help to anyone that might be listening.

I ran back to Larry's side, trying to remember the CPR I'd taken several years before. Oh God, I couldn't remember.   Was it five compressions and two breaths, five breaths and fifteen compressions? Ten? What? I couldn't remember.

I just began breathing air into Larry's mouth, trying not to think. Then I'd do compressions, no idea of how many of either I was doing. I only knew that I kept shouting to him to breathe.

I heard the clang of the elevator and running feet. *Thank God*, I thought, as I continued to breathe into Larry's lungs.   With the next compression, I was sure he was breathing, but I refused to stop until the stretcher arrived in the room.

I backed off as they began working on Larry, checking his vital signs, starting an IV, giving him oxygen, asking me if Larry had any allergies and relaying all the information by phone to the hospital, I assumed. When they spoke of my husband's condition, to me it was all jargon, code. Then they picked up Larry's limp body and moved it to the stretcher. His head lolled to the side, but yes, there it was. His chest was moving up and down on its on.

I raced behind the stretcher. "Which hospital are you taking him to?" I screamed, pushing my way onto the elevator they were trying desperately to keep me off of.

"Ma'am, we're taking him to Edward hospital, but you have to follow in your car." I saw them eyeing me warily. "Maybe you should call someone to bring you. You shouldn't drive alone."

Hell no! I raced from the elevator and to my car. I would not wait in a hotel for someone to take me to my husband, no damn way. I thought of Viola. I would be there with Larry. Nothing would keep me from him, not even my own panic. I commanded my body to calm down.

I was out of the parking lot and roaring down the street before the ambulance. I had to pull over to allow it to pass. "Come on, come on, move it, move it," I shouted to the vehicle. "That's my husband you have in there."

I grabbed for my cell phone. "Oh God, Blaine, Larry's had a heart attack.   He's on his way to Edward's. Do you think you could meet me there? I'm so scared."

"Of course. Michelle, be careful. He's going to be alright."

I hung up the phone and began praying, remembering Chance's words from earlier in the day when he thought I was sleeping. "God, please save Larry. I have to tell him how much I love him.

I was in the emergency room only seconds behind the ambulance. Blaine was in there when I ran through the door, stopping me and holding me back from getting in the way. I wondered how he'd gotten there so fast, but didn't ask. I was only grateful that he'd come.

"Blaine," I cried out, wanting to dissolve into tears, wanting to faint. Anything to escape what was happening. "It's all my fault."

I looked up from Blaine's chest to see Chance running down the hall. No God, no, not Chance. I ran to him, putting out my hands to stop him.

"Not you, Chance, get another doctor. I don't want you taking care of my husband. I heard you talking to Blaine. I want my husband to live."

For what seemed an eternity, Chance stared at me. He lifted my chin so I was looking into his eyes. Then he caught my wrists in his strong grip.

"Dimi, look at me," he ordered. "If you want Larry to live, you want the best. You want me. Now I don't have time to argue and convince you. You have to trust me."

He let go and continued running toward the cubicle into which Larry had disappeared. "I'll take care of him, Dimi," he shouted as he ran.

"Blaine." I fell against him knowing Chance was calling me Dimi to tell me he would do nothing to harm Larry. Using Dimi was his way of making me a promise.

I stared into Blaine's eyes. "You're a psychic. Is he going to make it?"

"Chance is with him. He's going to do everything he can to save Larry. Don't worry."

I pulled away from Blaine, looking at him. He didn't have a clue. "I have to trust Larry's life to a man who only a few hours ago wished him dead. And you tell me not to worry? That's rich, Blaine. If it wasn't so sad I'd laugh."

"Stop it, Michelle," Blaine scolded me gently, rubbing my hands with his to take away the sting of his words. "You know Chance is going to do everything in his power to help. You know he didn't mean what he said."

"But he said it." My voice was a worried whisper. "Now I have to sit here and wait for the outcome." I saw Blaine cast a worried glance toward the enclosure before he asked, "Shouldn't you call your children, tell them about their father?"

I had forgotten about the kids. I didn't want to fight with them in the midst of worrying about Larry, but I'd imposed on Blaine enough. I was taking advantage of him. I closed my eyes and leaned my head on the chair.

"I'll call them as soon as I know anything."

"Give me Derrick's number. I'll call him and he can call his sisters."

I stared at this son I'd not had an opportunity to love before. My heart swelled with love for him now. I'd taken so much from him.

For a moment I wished I had not called him to meet me at the hospital. But then I felt his hands on the back of my neck, massaging away the tension, and I was glad he was there with me.

"Blaine, I'm so sorry that I've turned your life into this big melodrama. I've taken up far too much of your time. I've come to depend on you too much. I can't ask you to do more."

"You didn't ask me. I asked you, remember?" For a moment he looked sad. "Michelle, do you really consider me a part of your family?"

"I do," I answered, not sure where the conversation was leading.

"Then please allow me to feel a part of you, of your pain. Let me help you. I've wanted to be a part of your life for so long. I like being needed by you." He smiled, shy, hesitant. "Please."

I was sorely tempted to do just what he'd asked, but I could only imagine the resentment my children would feel if I gave this job to Blaine. This was one I would have to take care of myself.

I touched his cheeks. "Blaine, this is something I have to do myself. I would very much appreciate it if you would stay right here. And if anyone needs me, please come and get me."

With that I rose to find a pay phone, accepting the handful of change Blaine was holding out to me, ignoring the hurt in his eyes that I wouldn't accept his help.

My first call was to Derrick. I talked quickly trying to keep the panic I felt to myself. I gave my son the number of my charge card and instructed him to charge the airline ticket to me. I was touched when his concern for his father reached out to embrace me also.

"Mom, he said. "Are you alright? You shouldn't be alone."

"I called Blaine," I told him. For a few seconds there was silence on the other end, then Derrick's voice saying, "That's good, Mom, I'm glad he's there with you. You need someone there who loves you."

It took me a moment to compose myself before calling Shannon. Derrick had put aside the fact that I'd called Blaine before I'd even called him. I never expected his understanding.

Calling Shannon was also easier than I expected. She was so worried about her father that her voice was soft and once again that of my youngest, not a member of the tribunal that had come for my sentencing.

"Mom, Dad's going to be okay, don't worry," she reassured me.

"Shannon, do me a favor please, I don't want to stay away too long. I've called Derrick. Would you please call your sisters, give Beth and Brigid my charge card number."

I was about to hang up the phone when a picture of Erica's baby face nursing at my breast flashed before me. The all-consuming love I had had for her in that moment resurfaced.

"Shannon, give the number to Erica too. I want all of you to put your airline tickets on my charge card." With that I said a hasty goodbye and raced back to wait at my post.

Blaine was eyeing me worriedly. "It's okay," I said as I hugged him to me. "Thanks for everything."

For hours I sat with Blaine, waiting for the slightest sound from the room. We saw people running in out and out. The bells, whistles, everything that was meant to throw the family into a panic attack worked.

No one looked in my direction or came to say, 'As *soon as we know something we'll tell you.*' Not one person acted as if the man they were working on was of any importance, and I was less. *Well, he is important*, I wanted to shout to them. *He's important to me.*

At last Chance walked toward us, a puzzled look on his face. He was dressed in all green, something he'd not been wearing when he went into the room. Surely they could not have performed surgery on Larry. They didn't have my consent.

"Michelle, Larry's fine," Chance told me softly, standing away from me as if he were afraid to touch me.

I looked at him. "You mean he's stable?"

"No, I mean he's fine. Everything resembled a massive coronary." He looked at me. "I would have sworn he had a heart attack."

He explained things to me in simplified language. "Every symptom he had mimicked a heart attack perfectly. He even went into cardiac arrest and we had to defib him."

Again I looked at Chance for a simpler explanation. For some strange reason everything I knew or should know about the medical profession had vanished. I knew I should know what Chance was talking about but for the life of me the meaning escaped me for the moment.

"We used the defibrillator. We had to shock him to get his heart going again. But, I swear, I've never heard of this. There is nothing wrong with his heart. The arteries are fine, there is no blockage, nothing, no tissue damage, the heart is fine."

"How can that be?" I asked the question several times, puzzled.

My hands were trembling. I'd seen the pasty look on Larry's face, seen the profuse sweating, the look of pain in his eyes. I'd breathed air into him when he'd stopped breathing.

This was hard for me to fathom. I'd seen my husband in the very throes of what could only have been a heart attack.

"I don't know." Chance was looking back toward the cubicle he'd left, his face drawn, and an awed expression in his eyes.

"Chance, you're the cardiologist."

"Michelle, I'm telling you, it took me so long in there because I wanted to be sure. I've done a complete cardiac work-up. We even did a cardiac cath.

"Michelle, we looked at his heart from every possible angle and there is nothing wrong. I have no idea why he stopped breathing. I have no idea why his heart refused to beat. There is nothing wrong with Larry."

"So what are you going to do, just send him home?"

"Of course not, he's sedated now and we're giving him oxygen as a precautionary measure. I'm having him admitted for a few days to repeat the tests. I'm sure they're going to all be the same, but in this case I want there to be no doubt in anyone's mind that Larry received the best of care," he said a bit pointedly. "And of course I'll turn his case over to someone else."

"I'm sorry that I...I...." I was attempting to apologize.

"Don't be. Why should you be sorry that you accused me of wanting him out of the way? I did say it. I'm sorry I said it and even more sorry that you heard it."

I knew Chance meant it. His eyes were filled with the same guilt I felt.

"When can I see him?"

"Give them about ten minutes to get him settled. I've already instructed the nurse that she's to get you as soon as they've done that.

"I'm the cardiologist on duty tonight. I'm covering, I'm sorry," Chance apologized again, "but in the morning he'll have someone else."

Chance took a seat on the opposite side of Blaine to wait with me until the nurse came for me. When she did I nearly ran after her.

My concern was for Larry. I barely heard Blaine and Chance's comment as I ran away.

"Chance, what happened?" Blaine asked, speaking low to prevent me from hearing, but I heard.

"I swear to God, I don't know," Chance answered. "Either a miracle was performed leaving him with no damage, or he was so convinced that he was having a heart attack that his body mimicked one."

"Is that possible?" Blaine started to ask, and stopped. "Chance, you do remember that Jeremy willed himself to die? Is it possible that Larry did the same thing?"

I wanted to tell them both that I knew the answer to Blaine's question. It was possible, both things. I had prayed for a miracle from the moment Larry fell.

I raced to Larry's side shuddering with guilt. Did he love me enough to will himself to die? I believed he did.

Chapter Eighteen

Larry lay deathly still on the bed. Mick was sitting beside him, stroking his arms, telling him she loved him. The sensation of having her close made him wince inwardly with pain.

He had what he wanted. His wife was once again by his side, pledging her love and loyalty. All he had to do was open his eyes and accept what she was offering, forget everything that had happened. He'd won. But he'd won by default.

When he could no longer take her whispered words of love he opened his eyes. He was glad for the oxygen mask; it partially hid his rampant emotions.

"Mick." He reached out a finger and stroked her hair. He was surprised that the incredible pain was gone.

For a second he wondered if he'd died, if Mick really was there at his side. Then he felt the wetness from her tears falling on his face, his hands. It was not a dream.

He opened his eyes more fully. He saw the fear in his wife's eyes and he saw something that he didn't like. He saw guilt.

"Oh my God, Larry," Mick cried.

With that she fell on his shoulder. He couldn't resist. He allowed himself to breath in her essence. This was the closest he'd been to her in weeks. He brought his arm up to stroke her, shushing her, telling her that he was fine.

"So I had a heart attack?" he asked. He felt her head slowly leave his shoulder to peer at him.

She was gazing into his eyes, her own darkening even more with some untold guilt she appeared to be feeling.

"The doctor said that you didn't. He can't find any evidence of it."

Larry held Michelle's chin in his hand, some of his strength returning. "What are you talking about? I felt the pain. If it wasn't a heart attack, what did he say it was, my imagination?"

"He doesn't know, Larry."

Larry watched his wife as she turned away feigning untold interest in his IV tubing. "He thinks maybe you convinced yourself that you were having one and so you had all the symptoms."

"Are you trying to say the doctor thinks I'm crazy? Where is he? I want to see him."

Larry noticed in that moment that Michelle's look of guilt intensified and he wondered why. "Mick, call the doctor, I want to talk to him."

"Maybe you should rest first, wait until morning. Then you can talk to the doctor."

Larry looked at his wife, at the confusion clouding her face. Did she believe a stranger over him, over what she'd seen? Did she think he was nuts? Was that why she was here, offering herself once again to him out of pity?

He looked along the side of his bed for the call button. It was time he found out what the hell was going on. "Either you go get him, Mick, or I ring for the nurse."

Larry adjusted himself in the bed while Mick went for the doctor. He gingerly touched his chest. It was sore. Was this too his imagination? He pulled at the oxygen mask covering his nose, then at the IV tubing. Were all these things done to him to appease his imagination?

His attention was drawn to the door and the inset glass window. He spotted Mick talking to a tall man in a lab coat. It had to be the doctor.

Larry stared harder at the two; they appeared to be arguing. Larry felt a coldness slither up his spine. This wasn't a stranger Mick was talking to. He knew that as he watched his wife's face inches from the doctor's. He wished he could read lips.

Mick walked back into the room and brought with her a feeling of foreboding. The hairs on the back of his neck stood at attention, alerting him to the fact that his pain was not yet over.

A moment later a doctor strolled in. Larry noticed the stiffness with which the man held himself, almost as if he'd rather be anywhere else but in the room.

He watched as the man's eyes slid over to Mick. He pulled his glance away quickly, but not quickly enough. Larry saw the flash of guilt in the doctor's eyes, but he'd seen something else also. He'd also caught the way Mick looked back at the man, the look so brief he should have missed it. But he hadn't.

Icy fingers danced over Larry's body. With a certainty, the knowledge came to him. This man was the one whom Mick was in love with, who loved her, the one Mick claimed to have been married to in a previous life.

Larry couldn't believe it. He gulped in the purified oxygen. This was the man Mick had entrusted his life to—her lover.

"Dr.—? I didn't catch your name. What is it?"

Larry eyed the tall, muscular man standing before him. He could almost feel Mick holding her breath. She wasn't looking at the doctor which was odd in itself. Usually she was such a take charge person when it came to the family's health. Now she was uncommonly silent.

It seemed for a time that the man wasn't going to answer. He finally croaked out. "I'm sorry, I'm Dr. Morgan."

"And your first name?" Larry inquired while he watched the man's gaze quickly swing again to Mick.

"I don't use it much." Chance attempted a half-hearted smile. "You know how it is, some names you just don't like."

Larry stared straight into his eyes, refusing to let him off that easily. He should have known it would be a doctor Mick was involved with. Her work involved so many of them. This was Chance.

And now it made sense, more than that cock and bull story she gave him about meeting a man in a parking lot. He'd always known that had to be a lie.

"The C. on you lab coat, what does it stand for Dr. Morgan?"

"Mr. Powers, if you like, you can just call me C. Morgan. I won't be the one permanently on your case. In a few hours another doctor will take over. Your wife told me you had questions for me. Would you like for me to answer them?"

Larry eyed the man, trying to decide what he wanted to do. One thing was for sure. He had no intention of allowing the good doctor to know how much pain he'd caused him. He'd focus instead on what had happened to him.

"Did I have a heart attack?"

"I'm not sure."

"What do you mean, you're not sure?"

"Well…"

Larry watched as once again the doctor visibly restrained himself from looking in Mick's direction.

"Your arteries are clean, there is no blockage, none, and there is no damage to the heart." Chance brought his eyes up finally to meet Larry's. "The scenario is highly unlikely. I have no medical explanation for it."

"So what happened to me? I had this tremendous pain in my chest. I've been getting it now for a couple of months." He looked toward Mick, who refused to meet his gaze or even to look up.

The rest of what the doctor had to say went by in a blur. Larry could barely keep from closing his eyes against the pain of seeing the apparent love for his wife in another man's eyes.

He knew for sure if he went home with his wife it would be by default. He didn't want that. He decided to stop asking questions of the doctor. He didn't want the man in his room any longer. He couldn't keep up the pretense.

For several seconds after the doctor had exited the room Mick and Larry remained silent. Larry turned toward his wife. "That's him, isn't it?"

She looked at him, her eyes large and watery. That did it. Larry closed his eyes and waited.

"Yes, it's him."

"Do you trust him, about what he said about what happened to me, I mean?" He wanted to say so much more, but this was safer. He couldn't hid behind his closed lids so he opened his eye and met his wife's gaze.

"He knows how worried I am about you. Believe me, he did everything possible to find out what happened." She looked into his eyes. "He thinks it might be a miracle."

"Yeah, right, I can imagine he'd be a big believer in that. I guess he's gotten you convinced of that theory already, hasn't he?"

He watched her squirm, wishing she wouldn't, wishing she would look him in the eye and tell him that the tall handsome doctor meant nothing to her.

"Larry, Chance is not going to do anything to harm his patients, even for me."

"I saw the way he looked at you, Mick. I'm not so sure of that." He took a deep breath. "I also saw the way you looked at him."

"Larry, it's over between us."

"Is it because of me, because of what happened or didn't happen?"

"No, Larry, we'd ended it already. I was trying to tell you that at the hotel, but you never gave me a chance."

Larry studied his wife for a moment, his Mick. "Tell me you don't love him."

He held his breath waiting for her to deny what he felt in the very marrow of his being, what registered in her eyes.

"That has nothing to do with us. I love you, Larry. I think if we talk, and if we both listen, we can work this out.

"Do you think it's going to be that easy?"

"I know it's not going to be easy, but I want us to give it another try. Larry, we've got a lifetime of loving each other on the line."

Larry thought about what she'd said; her words echoed those of his therapist. She wanted to live up to her commitment, and yes, he knew she felt some guilt for his heart attack, or whatever the hell he'd had.

He felt the pain starting again in his heart. He looked to the side of the bed and watched the spikes on the monitor go up.

Maybe the good doctor was right. Maybe loving his wife was killing him.

"Mick, I don't think we should be talking about that right now. I'm tired, I just want to rest." He closed his eyes and turned on his side.

"I'll stay until you wake up," Mick offered.

"Why don't you just go home?" Larry realized what he'd said. "I mean, why don't you just go back to your hotel? I'm in a hospital, I have everything I need."

Like hell, he thought. The one thing he needed was Mick, but he was through begging her to love him. It would have been so much easier if he'd never seen the man, but he had. What had happened was real.

"I want to stay, Larry."

"Suit yourself, Mick, but I really don't need you here."

He sensed the moment she left his side. He pretended to start snoring, anything to get her to leave. He was surprised that it worked. Then he felt the pain begin again. He had to think of something else.

I walked out of Larry's room feeling dejected. What had I expected, that he would instantly welcome me back with open arms?

Then I remembered he had done just that in the first seconds he opened his eyes. He'd held me to him.

I walked up to Blaine and Chance who were talking together, obviously waiting for me.

I glanced at Blaine, before looking directly at Chance. "He knows."

"Yeah, I could tell," Chance answered. "From the moment I entered the room, there was a certain look in his eyes. His voice held such hostility that I knew he knew."

"What did you expect? I'm sure he thinks you're trying to help me kill him."

I started laughing hysterically, unable to control myself. "Just think about it, Chance," I said between laughs. "He has this terrible pain, falls to the floor, he's brought to a hospital where his wife's lover just happens to be the cardiologist on duty. Where anyone else would have been diagnosed with a heart attack, what does he hear? No such thing, no heart attack, it didn't happen. He has to think we're all in this together. He already believes we're crazy."

Chance was looking at me as if at any moment he would be the one to call up to the psychiatric unit for me.

Blaine was glancing at me, at first worried. A moment passed and a smile touched his lips and he too began to laugh. "You're right. You throw in a husband from the past, a son, and now you tell him he's received a miracle."

I looked at Blaine because Chance was not appreciating the humor in this. "Try having the husband from the past for your surgeon. Poor Larry."

I felt the tears of laughter running down my face. "He has to think he's gone to sleep and landed in a different universe."

"This isn't funny," Chance admonished us both. "I don't know about the two of you, but I personally don't want my patients thinking I'm in a scheme to do them in."

I sobered instantly as did Blaine. "Chance, I have to laugh at the absurdity of the situation or I would be bawling on the floor, kicking my legs like a child. I know it isn't funny."

I sat down. Gazing up at Chance, I whispered, "I'm sorry. I just don't know what's going on. I was there with Larry. All of this is so unbelievable, from my meeting you, then Blaine, now this. I think I've reached my limit for the unexplained. I'm ready for this to end. I want my sane life back."

"Do you want me to leave?" Blaine inquired, no longer laughing, no longer seeing the humor in the situation.

"That wasn't what I meant." I watched him trying to read my emotions, hiding his eyes when he realized I'd caught him.

"Blaine, don't take this the wrong way, but I think I can manage now. You should go home and get some rest. I'm going to be here for a very long time."

"I thought you said Larry was sleeping." Chance glanced once at Blaine, spotting the same hurt that I did. "You may as well get some rest yourself." He looked at me, the grief in his eyes, touching my soul.

I fingered the locket around my neck Blaine had given me. "It's time I return to my life. I'll wait until Larry wakes." My response was to them both.

I went to Blaine and kissed him on each cheek. "I'll call you later. To Chance I said nothing. There was nothing to say.

Larry kept his eyes closed. He'd completely shoved Mick away, given her every reason to run back into Chance's arms. He refused to look out the window in his door. He didn't want to see Mick talking to Chance, didn't want to see the way they looked at each other longingly.

He heard the click of her shoes as she came back into the room, smelled her scent. Still he kept his eyes closed. Maybe she'd forgotten her purse. When he heard the soft whoosh as she sat, he held his breath. She lifted his hand and squeezed it in her palms.

With his head turned from her he felt his own tears slide beneath his closed lids. He gave her fingers a gentle squeeze in return, without speaking.

Larry had no way of knowing how much time had passed. He knew he had fallen asleep holding Mick's hand. When he woke she was sleeping, still holding tightly to his palm.

He brought his other hand over and ran his fingers through her cinnamon curls sprinkled with a little bit of gray. Maybe what had happened to him wasn't so strange after all. He remembered the night Mick left; all he'd wanted to do since that moment was die. He'd almost gotten his wish.

Mick started to stir. Her eyes opened, sleepy and sad. She looked at Larry. "How are you feeling?" she asked. He noticed the guilt was still there, hiding in the depths of her eyes.

"What happened, Mick?"

"Chance isn't sure."

"No, I mean what happened with us?"

He sighed, closing his hand over hers, and shut his eyes for an instant. "I swear, I thought you were happy. I never knew. Why didn't you ever say anything to me?"

"I did."

"When? I don't remember."

Larry watched his wife's face for signs that he must have missed before. "Was it because I didn't satisfy you? Is that why you had an affair?"

Michelle pulled her hands from Larry. "Larry, none of this has anything to do with Chance. You need to really hear me. Even if we're never together again, I want you to listen to me for once."

"But I..." he started to protest before Mick stopped him.

"No, Larry, you don't listen, you assume. And it's my fault for not demanding to be heard."

He watched her lips moving. He decided to be quiet; maybe he didn't listen. Now he wanted, no, he needed to hear her.

"Honey, it was not all your fault. I brought a lot of baggage into our marriage, baggage that I was unaware of. I was trying so hard to live the perfect life that we both wanted that I didn't know what to do when I found myself unhappy.

She laughed then, and he watched in silence until she began to speak again. "I thought I was so different from my mother," Mick continued.

"She never said anything to Dad about how she felt. She only told us kids. She told us repeatedly that she stayed there and took dad's cheating and his abuse because of us.

He watched as the tears rolled down her face. "She told us that so often that I began to believe her." Michelle looked away. Her pain was breaking his heart.

"Larry," she began again, "I really wanted you to have the life you didn't have, the life you thought I had. I really thought that in some way, it was my fault that my mother stayed, that life was so miserable, that my father cheated, and that he hit my mother. Larry, my dreams of having lived another life started when I was a kid. My mother took me to a psychiatrist. They all thought I was crazy. They didn't know what to do so they blamed each other for what they believed was wrong with me.

"I always thought that maybe, just maybe, if I was a good girl, pretend I wasn't having the dreams, it would be fine, that we'd have the happy home my mother said she was trying to give us."

She was crying fully now. "God, how I tried, Larry."

"I always thought you had such a good life." Larry's hand went out to rub his wife's cheeks."

"I know you did," Mick answered him. "I kept telling you how it was, but you never heard me."

Larry pulled his wife to him. "It was just that...," He bit his lips. He hated talking about his mother, hated admitting that even now the image of her leaving him bothered the hell out of him. It hurt like the blazes.

All at once he realized that the pain of his mother's abandonment didn't hurt with a billionth of the force that Mick's leaving him had. Maybe he could get over it.

"Mick," he said, holding her, "I couldn't listen to you. Your parents didn't divorce until you were out of high school.

To me you were the luckiest girl on the planet. I was so awed by the fact that you were raised by your mother and natural father." He smiled.

"Baby, I thought you had it so good, that you just were unaware of how lucky you were. You were raised in a home with two parents, and neither of them was a stepparent. You know how rare that is nowadays. There's always a stepparent around. Your life was magical to me. I would have given anything to have had even a foster parent that kept me for more than a month or two."

Larry looked at Mick and felt her sadness. "I wanted to recreate your life for you. I wanted to give you the happiness that I thought you'd grown up with."

"That's the problem, " she all but whispered. "I didn't want to relive my childhood. I told myself I had so much to be thankful for. You didn't cheat and we didn't argue, and you…you were so very happy."

"But you weren't?" He asked, saddened, hearing her for the first time in twenty-six years.

"No, I wasn't."

"Mick, you should have said something, anything. You should have hit me over the head with a lamp to get me to listen."

"That's just it," she answered him. "I was too afraid of fighting, afraid that we'd be just like my parents, that you'd take lover after lover, that you'd come in one night and not like something I'd done, that I'd purposefully do something to anger you and that you would hit me."

"I would have never hit you, Mick."

"I know but that was my secret fear, so I pretended to be happy, pretended that yes, we were the perfect couple. Larry, it wasn't the sex. That wasn't the reason I was unhappy."

His gut knotted. He noticed she'd not said that he satisfied her. He pulled his errant thought back, determined to listen to every word she had to say.

"Larry, I was so afraid of having children, of putting them through the same things, of blaming them for my own unhappiness, and here I did the same thing anyway.

"I got angry at you for being so happy. I couldn't understand it. The kids never got on your nerves, you never got upset with them, you kept wanting more and more and I felt with each pregnancy that I was being bound by a life I didn't want."

Larry cringed. *Here it comes*, he thought.

"Only that wasn't the case." Michelle paused. "I know you don't want to hear this, but the issue with me and the kids, I don't think it was what I always thought it was. I think now it was something entirely different."

He was staring at her, the words on the tip of his tongue. He was about to tell her that if she was going to tell him any more psycho babble to can it. He didn't want to hear it.

He realized that's exactly what he'd done to her in the past year. He'd told her that he knew what was best for them. He felt the pain in his chest again, only much milder. God, she was right. He hadn't listened.

"What is it, Mick? What changed your mind?" he asked at last.

"Are you sure you want to hear?" she asked, a little uncertain. "I don't have a scientific explanation for it."

"Yeah, I want to hear it." He gave her fingers another encouraging squeeze. "Tell me."

"It was because of Blaine."

He watched her eyes. When she looked downward, almost embarrassed, he lifted her chin. He saw the smile that appeared on her lips and was happy that he was finally listening. Was this what it took to make him hear her, an almost heart attack?

"This other life," she began. "It was real, Larry. I lived it. I saw it and I do remember it. I remember the anguish I felt when I knew I was going to die leaving an infant son whose father might not love him because he blamed him for my passing.

"I took that sense of loss into my spirit and I became afraid to love my children, afraid that if I did they would be taken away."

Larry felt his wife's shiver, heard her voice breaking. She couldn't have told him any of that before; surely he would have recalled.

"Mick, I don't remember your ever saying anything about this. You never told me you didn't think you loved the kids."

"How could I? We were the perfect couple leading the perfect life. How could I tell you I didn't want what you thought made us perfect? I didn't want you to think I was like your mother."

For a long time they stared at each other, trying hard to read the other's expression. Larry didn't want to ask but there might never be another time.

"Is that why you wanted to abort Shannon? You didn't love her?"

"I thought I didn't. I was afraid to love her or any of them except maybe Derrick. Somehow I couldn't stop myself from loving him."

"Mick, was there ever a time during our marriage that you were happy?" He watched her eyes.

"Yes," she answered. "Before the kids started coming, I was happy. Then for a short time after Erica was born. I think it must have been at that point that the fear took hold. I remember feeding her as a baby and you sitting there watching the two of us. You loved us so much, and I felt the same. I loved you and Erica with all my heart."

"What changed, what made you stop loving me, loving our family?"

"I never stopped loving you, Larry. As for the kids, I think I was just too afraid of losing them to allow myself to fully love them."

"But you were a perfect mother."

"Never perfect. I played a part to perfection. There's a difference."

Larry sucked down on his top lip. Where had he been all these years? How could all this have gone on without his noticing it?

"I still don't get it, Mick. Why now? Why this year?"

"Because I got tired of you telling me that I was happy when I wasn't. And the thought that you were going to force me to take care of our grandchildren for the rest of my life…I couldn't handle it."

She stopped and looked at Larry and he gazed back at his wife, knowing whatever she was about to say was the real reason for her leaving.

"There was the promise." Larry nodded for her to continue. "You made me promise to love you always, to never leave you. I knew why it was so important to you, so I did it. I respected you."

"But?" Larry supplied.

"But you didn't give me the same respect. When I gave my promise to an old woman, you ignored it as though it was nothing. I thought you were such a hypocrite."

Larry cringed. Michelle was right. He'd never looked at it from her point of view before. "I'm sorry, Mick. I just wanted to protect you."

He watched as she licked her lips then flicked her hands across her face to wipe away the tears that had gathered in the corners of her eyes.

"You never objected before when I made the decisions."

"They never involved me going back on my word before."

He looked at her thinking of all the fights over the past months, almost a year now.

"If I'd agreed to allow you to see Viola, none of this would have happened?" He waited while a strange look spread across the face of his wife.

"Eventually it would have happened anyway. That's one of the problems, Larry. We both thought you had a right to give me permission."

"I didn't mean it like that, Mick. You're twisting my words."

He had an urge to tell her she was mistaken, that the way she told the story was not the way it had happened at all. Something in her eyes stopped him. She had a questioning look on her face.

"Can I ask you something, Larry?"

He looked at her suspiciously. He felt a lurch in his heart. He knew she was going to ask about the one taboo they had--his mother.

"Do you remember your mother? I mean, really remember her? How she looked, how she smelled, if she ever hugged you? Do you remember anything?"

He attempted to look away from her, but this time it was Mick who pulled his face back to her. "Mick, why are we talking about this?"

"Because this is the first time I've felt you were capable of doing it, of listening without telling me you didn't want to talk about it.

"You need to face this, Larry. What happened when you were a child has had a huge impact on our family. We both have pasts, and we both came to our marriage with baggage. It's time for us to let it go."

"I don't want to talk about her, Mick. What is there to say? She abandoned me."

"Did you ever think that maybe she had no choice?"

That surprised Larry. Mick had always hated his mother for what she'd done. Now it sounded as if she was defending her.

"Mick, how can you say that?"

"Because it just occurred to me that I may not be so different from her."

Larry pulled away, not wanting to hear anymore. "That's a lie. You were never anything like my mother.

"That's just the point. We don't know what she was like. Maybe she was some young girl with no money, no family, and no way to provide for you. Maybe she was doing the best she could."

For a long moment he glared at her. Was Mick determined to hurt him to the quick? Her fingers caressed his cheeks and she smiled softly at him, making him catch his breath.

"I want you to stop hurting," she said.

"I don't know if I can."

"I'll help you. If there's one good memory that you have, maybe you can hold onto that. Maybe that will take some of the pain away."

"Mick, I was five-years-old. How am I supposed to go back and recall all of this? All I can remember is me crying, begging her, telling her that I would be good. And still she left. She didn't even look back to wave. That's what I remember, Mick."

"Have you ever thought, Larry, that maybe she didn't look back because she couldn't? Maybe she loved you so much that it was killing her to give you up.

"I don't know." Mick continued. "Maybe she was just an awful woman whom we've both wasted too much of our lives and our energy on hating. I just think it's time to let it go, maybe get some help."

He frowned. She was talking counseling again. Well, he'd started and as far as he could tell, it wasn't having the least effect.

He saw the familiar flash of light in her eyes that told him she had an idea he wasn't going to like. Then he knew. She wanted him to talk to Blaine MaDia. Hell no!

She stared at him and he sat mute. He couldn't do what she asked. He didn't have any happy memories with which to replace the one that was burned into his heart, and he sure as hell wasn't going to give some psychic license to poke around in his head.

"Let's change the subject…just for now. Okay?" he added gently. He watched as she bit down on her lip and knew that he wouldn't like her next question any more than he had her last one.

"That's fine." Mick answered him. She paused for a fraction of a second. "Larry, don't you ever find Erica's behavior rude and condescending? Don't you ever mind that she treats us both like her personal servants?"

He looked at Mick and found himself speaking words he thought he'd never say. "Perhaps I tolerate Erica's shenanigans just a tiny bit more because she looks so much like you. And her birth made us a family. I love her, I love all the kids. I'm their father."

"I didn't ask if you love Erica or any of the kids. That goes without question. I just want to know…can't you see how she behaves? Are you blind to that?"

Mick was looking at him once again with pity. He didn't like it. Why should he be on trial here for being a good father?

"No, I'm not blind," he answered. "And yes, sometimes her attitude does annoy me."

"Thank God."

Larry blinked twice. His wife had a huge smile pasted on her face while he felt like crap for admitting that his daughter's behavior annoyed him. He was speechless.

"Then why do you let her and the others get away with so much? When I've asked for your help in saying no, in setting rules, why did you always say for me to let it go?"

"Because...Mick...because..."

"Because what?"

"Because I made a promise to each of the kids that I would never abandon them, never let them down. I promised I would be there for them always."

"You've kept your promise, Larry."

"That's just it, Mick, I don't know if I have. I've wanted to say no, but I couldn't. The only time I've ever not wanted them around was the night you left me."

She reached for his hand, holding it tightly in hers. "I never wanted you to make a choice between me and the children. I just didn't want to come in sixth all of the time."

Larry thought for a minute. "Can you tell me then why all the animosity between you and Erica?"

"Think about it, Larry. She's spoiled, they all are, but Erica thinks it's her right to use us. She drops her kids off on us whenever she chooses. She allows them to destroy our home, our possessions."

She moaned then and he knew she was remembering her broken figurine. He couldn't stop the inward wince of pain. He remembered also. In fact, he would never forget.

Mick was eyeing him strangely. "Doesn't it ever upset you that Erica borrows thousands of dollars from us on a whim and never pays it back?"

"That's what parents are for." His voice was low. He wasn't so sure anymore. "I just thought you were...you know...a little..."

"I know," Mick answered him. "You thought I was jealous."

"Were you?"

"It may have seemed like that, but after Erica was born, I began to feel like this giant uterus that had no other function. You had your mystical perfect family. You all knew your roles. I didn't fit. And part of the reason I didn't fit was nothing you could have helped. I carried a grief constantly inside of me and I mourned the loss of my son from my dreams. Only I couldn't really express that grief not even with you. Whenever I tried to tell you about my son you wanted me to be quiet, you told me always that Derrick was my only son, that he was well. Until I met Blaine I had no proof that you weren't right, that I wasn't perhaps a little bit crazy. But it didn't matter, I still felt the grief, and that you couldn't have helped me with."

I closed my eyes feeling the need to swallow before continuing. "That wasn't your fault. I just didn't know how to live, how to be happy not knowing what happened to the family in my dreams. And I had no one to talk to about this. I loved you so much, Larry, and sometimes I thought all you wanted me for was to be a mother to our kids."

Larry swung his legs over the side of the bed, ignoring the loud beeping of the monitor. From what Mick and the doctor had said he didn't need the damn thing anyway. He gathered his wife in his arms, pulling her close to him.

"You were never that to me, Mick. I loved you so much that I guess I just forgot to tell you as much as I should have. I always thought you knew."

She was holding him, her words spoken between broken sobs. "I really wasn't jealous, Larry, at least I don't think so, but some time alone would have been nice. We haven't gone any place alone in the last twenty years. The vacations were always with the kids. Now that they're gone our only vacations have been to see the kids."

"I thought you enjoyed it."

"I told you I didn't."

For the first time since they'd started talking a memory brought him up short. He remembered her begging him to go away, just the two of them.

He could hear her voice saying she didn't want to visit the kids. He had never thought of that when she began making excuses, not going, doing anything else. He wondered if she had been with Chance during those times.

"Mick," he spoke into her hair. "Are you telling me the truth about Dr. Morgan? Did this only begin a few months ago?"

"Yes," she whispered into his ear.

"You didn't really meet him in a parking lot, did you?"

"I did."

"You must have really been hurting."

Before she could answer the door burst open and Erica all but ran into the room. Larry watched as his daughter glared at her mother. Mick pulled back to allow Erica to embrace him. He wanted nothing more than to continue holding Mick in his arms.

By the look of things, that wasn't going to happen. The room became abuzz with people, nurses, and doctors. He had no idea why they were even there.

Apparently they all wanted to see him, the freak, the miracle patient. The man whose body had had a heart attack with no evidence it had ever happened.

He glanced over Erica's head toward the door where Mick waited, seemingly pushed farther back into the corner as one after the other of their children arrived.

He noticed that all but Derrick hugged Mick timidly. Derrick was the only one who held his mother as if he meant it. The others looked at the glare on Erica's face and backed away.

For the first time since marrying Mick, Larry asked God for something. For twenty-six years he'd begun his day giving thanks and ended his nights the same way. Now he prayed for a way to make it up to his wife.

Outside the room and down the hall, Blaine and Chance kept vigil. Chance was not leaving until the oncoming cardiologist arrived. No one would be able to blast him out.

Chapter Nineteen

Larry's eyes narrowed as he zeroed in on Mick. She seemed to be shrinking into the background. He blinked before looking away from his children. Something was wrong.

He felt a coldness gripping his heart. How had the woman who was at the very center of his life been relegated to the outer fringes?

He smiled at her, hoping to convey that he was now aware of what was happening. He watched his wife's face. She tilted her head a slight bit toward their children, and slowly a tiny smile appeared at the corners of her lips.

Erica's frowning face caught his eyes as she turned toward the back of the room to glare at her mother. He watched in silence as she shifted position to block Mick from his view.

His mouth fell open. He stared at his eldest, his firstborn, the child who had made them a family. Larry cringed inwardly. This was the child who looked so much like Mick that he had literally imbued her with Mick's generous, loving spirit.

How in hell had he missed it? His daughter was nothing like his wife. His gaze fell on his other children. None of them were anything like Mick. If he had to hazard a guess, Derrick came closest.

He stared at his son for a long moment. He too played the role of peacemaker. He wondered if his son was happy in his marriage or unhappy the way his mother had been.

Larry closed his eyes as shiver after shiver overtook him. He almost wished for the squeezing pain he'd had around his heart. That would have been preferable to knowing he'd played a part in his wife's misery.

She was right. He'd been blinded by love, rendered sightless, unable to see what was happening in his family, loving them all so much, that in his eyes they could do no wrong. Oh God, what had he done?

"Dad, are you sleeping? I'm talking to you."

He heard the harsh tone of Erica's voice and felt her hand tugging on his arm. He opened his eyes slowly. "Mick," he called to his wife, feeling Erica's glare hit him with the force of an atomic bomb.

His eyes settled on his wife a moment before all hell broke loose.

"Why is she here anyway?"

Larry watched in disbelief as Erica rose from the side of the bed to stop Mick's approach toward him.

"It's your fault, Mother, that my father's in here. You've put way too much stress on him."

Larry looked from Mick to Erica. Did his daughter really think her mother was the source of stress now?

He watched as Mick came toward him, reaching Erica and gently but firmly pushing her aside to stand at Larry's side.

"You don't belong here, Mother."

"I have every right—" Mick started to say.

Larry gave her hand a quick squeeze. "I've got it this time."

One by one, he began pulling away the sticky round disks on his chest, ignoring the cardiac monitor going crazy, ignoring the nurses telling him to lie still. He ordered them out of the room, reminding them he was the miracle patient, that he'd not really had a heart attack.

Larry stood and went straight to his eldest child, the one he'd showered with so much love he'd become blind to her rudeness.

"Don't you dare ever talk to your mother like that again." He lifted his daughter's face so her eyes were glaring into his.

"She shouldn't be here," Erica screamed at him.

"She's my wife."

"She left you, Dad. Did you forget that? She had an affair. Why would you want her here?"

"Because I love her, Erica, and she's my wife." Larry's voice softened as he reached out to touch his daughter's cheek. "When did you turn into this nasty, disrespectful shrew? I always thought because you looked so much like your mother, that you had her sweetness."

He shook his head in sadness. "You're nothing like your mother."

"I don't want to be," she retorted.

"That's too bad. It's too bad for you, the kids, and for Roy. You're cruel, Erica," he said at last, an awareness suddenly filling him. "You're cruel and you're selfish."

"If I was selfish, I wouldn't be here now," she answered haughtily.

Larry looked toward Mick. "Who paid for your ticket, your mother?"

"Why shouldn't she? It's her fault. If you'd rather she stay, then I can just go home."

"I suggest you do just that. Go home to the kids and Roy, and pray that he loves you one tenth as much as your mother loves me."

"You're a fool, Dad. If she loved you, she wouldn't have slept around."

Larry could feel his blood began to boil, so he backed away from his daughter.

"First, that's none of your business. I'm married to your mother, not you. Second, I don't blame her. If it had been me, I would have tossed me out on my ass years ago for subjecting her to this kind of behavior."

His daughter was glaring daggers at him as well as looking over his shoulder at her mother. "Where did you learn to be this way?"

Erica started crying, covering her face with her hands, a move that for over twenty-three years had always managed to bring him to his knees. "It won't work this time, Erica."

Instantly the tears stopped. Larry felt the touch of Mick's fingers on his back, urging him to return to the bed.

"Don't, Larry, don't worry about it. It's not worth it to get you this worked up."

He turned from Erica to face Mick. "It's worth it. If I die in the next moment it's worth it. I should have done this a long time ago." He looked at Mick, then at the hospital bed.

"I can't believe I never saw it. This is what it took to open my eyes?" he whispered in amazement. "I'm sorry, Mick."

"Why are you apologizing to her? What about me? You asked me to leave. Aren't you going to say you're sorry, Daddy?" Erica wailed as though she were still a child.

"No," Larry said forcefully. "I meant every word. Go home all of you, to your own homes. And if you can't give your mother the respect she deserves, don't bother coming back."

Before anyone had an opportunity to respond, Dr. Chance Morgan came back into the room, accompanied by two nurses.

"What's all the commotion?" he asked. Larry observed the man's eyes scanning the room for Mick.

She'd seen it too. She glanced quickly up at him and shook her head no.

Larry watched the two of them. The doctor evidently thought Mick was in some danger. His movements quickly took him to her side.

He glared at everyone in the room with the exception of Mick. When his eyes came to rest on Larry this time there was no guilt. There was only anger.

"She loves you, you know," he said to Larry between clenched teeth, before turning directly to Mick and ignoring the fact that his staff was watching him, as well as Larry and his entire family.

"You don't have to do this, Michelle."

Larry turned as if in slow motion toward Mick, hearing her answer to Dr. Morgan.

"I'm not doing this because I have to. It's what I want. I love my husband and I want to be with him."

For about the space of a breath Larry wanted to throw the good doctor out on his white coated ass. He remembered his prayer.

He wanted to make it up to his wife for all the years of pain. He might not be able to give her the fantasy childhood he'd thought she had, but he could give her a new start. He could free her so she could find the happiness she didn't have with him, with Chance, the man who loved her as much as he did.

He would never have thought it possible that anyone could love his wife as much as he did, but the protective stance the doctor had taken against him and his entire family told the story.

There was so much love and longing in the man's eyes that Larry knew instantly what he was going to do. He was going to release Mick from her promise.

He loved her enough to want her to be happy. She was right. He did have a lot of baggage he hadn't dealt with. It might take him the rest of his life to settle it.

He didn't want Mick to go through any more. *No more*, he thought. Now he wanted her to be happy. But this would be something they would do alone, not here now in front of everyone. It was none of their business.

"Chance, I'm all right. Go." Mick's hand was on the man's sleeve tugging, urging him toward the door. It was obvious he didn't want to leave her.

Larry watched her eyes fill with tears. He'd made the right decision. She loved him too. He could see it, had seen it several hours ago.

Chance left reluctantly, taking the nurses with him while seven pairs of eyes stared at his back as he walked away.

"See, Daddy, what did I tell you?" came Erica's smug voice.

It would have been obvious to a blind man that the doctor was the one Mick was involved with. His children were adults and they were by no means blind or deaf. Mick had called him by name.

"Erica, shut the hell up. Like I told you before, my marriage is none of your damn business."

He watched his daughter's face color with anger. He glanced over at Derrick, who was trying hard not to smile. Larry smiled at him instead. His son gave him some kind of hand signal that told Larry he approved. So it seemed everyone had seen but him.

"Listen," he began, his eyes first on his son, then on each of his other children. "I do appreciate your coming, your being here for your mother when she needed you." He saw Beth and Brigid swallow but ignored it and continued.

"I didn't have a heart attack. The doctor said I'm going to be just fine. They want to keep me here for a couple more days just to be sure. I know you guys have come a long way, and I know you're tired. So go to the house now."

He'd purposefully not said for them to go home. Mick was right about that also. It was no longer their home. They'd each made homes for themselves elsewhere. They'd always be welcome, but it was no longer their home.

"I think it best that you all give me some time to rest. Go now, get some sleep and leave tomorrow. I'll call all of you in a few days."

One by one he embraced his children. Erica, stiff and cold, barely touched her cheek to his. He noticed that the others came to their mother and hugged her close to them before leaving. He heard Mick tell Shannon, *"Don't worry, I'll take care of him."*

This time he would take care of her. Still, there was time before he told her that. Several minutes after the children left, Mick smiled shyly at him.

"Since you want to rest, I guess I'll go too."

"I didn't mean you, Mick. Unless you're tired," he amended. "I want you to stay."

I sat staring tongue-tied at my own husband. He was smiling at me in that way he had that told me in no uncertain terms that I was very special to him. It had been so long since he'd looked at me that way.

His eyes were glowing with love. I looked at him and he literally took my breath away. I became aware of the slight tingling at the base of my spine. Oh my God, my husband of over twenty-six years was taking my breath away, making me tingle and reminding me why I fell in love with him in the first place. I couldn't believe it.

Larry hadn't looked at me in that particular way in almost a year. And I hadn't felt this way about him in just as long.

Since Viola, I realized with a start. *So I hadn't lied to spare Larry's feelings and I wasn't deluding myself. This hadn't been about Chance.*

I held my breath as Larry caressed my hand. I was waiting for him to tell me that he wanted us to try again. He had to. His touch, his eyes, told me how very much he loved me, wanted me. I sat patiently and waited to hear the words.

"I release you."

I blinked. "What did you say?" I asked, my tongue barely able to move.

"I said I release you, Mick."

He was talking calmly, massaging my hands, bringing them to his lips, kissing them tenderly.

"Larry, I don't understand."

He smiled at me indulgently, as though I were a child and he wanted to explain something really bad by smiling, as if that would take away the horrendous pain.

"Mick, I made you give me a promise when I proposed to you. It wasn't fair. But I thank you for giving it, for honoring it until you no longer could."

"Larry," I started, but he stopped me.

"No, Mick, it's alright. I'm not angry at you. In fact, I probably love you more at this moment that I ever have before."

"Then why?"

"Because I don't want you living out the rest of your life because of a promise. I don't want us together because of one, so I'm releasing you from it."

"Larry…"

"No, Mick, I've made up my mind. I think I'm beginning to believe you…you know, about you and Chance and a past life. He loves you too much for it to be only a few months."

I couldn't believe what was happening. No, I didn't expect Larry and me to just walk away arm in arm and for Larry to just forgive me.

But this, Larry giving me away? What the hell was wrong with him? I thought of the look that had passed between Larry and Chance when they'd held their mental pissing contest. Was I the prize in their macho game?

"Larry, you have no right. You can't keep making decisions for my life. It's up to me who I want to spend the rest of my life with."

"You're right. You decide on who and what you want, and so do I. I wanted to tell you, I believe now that a person can will themselves to die. It's beginning to look as though that's what I did."

I looked at him grateful that he'd finally heard me. "Don't do this, Larry."

"Tell me you don't still love him, Mick, tell me that. Tell me he doesn't love you. I saw the way he looked at you, the way you looked at him."

I fell silent, pulling my hands away from Larry. He brought them back.

"We've been together twenty-eight years, twenty-six of them married. I don't think that's so bad, do you? Lots of people don't make it that long."

I was sobbing as I stared at my husband who was trying so hard to be brave, believing that sending me away was the right thing to do. I knew it wasn't. I wanted to, needed to plead with him to change his mind.

"Larry, it doesn't matter what you do. It's over between me and Chance."

"Your seeing each other might be over, your love isn't. It is your choice, Mick, like you said. I'm only telling you that I'll understand. He loves you and you love him and as someone else who loves you with all his heart, I'm hoping you'll go to Dr. Morgan and be happy."

I had to try again. "Honey, you've been through a lot. You don't know what you're saying."

"That's where you're wrong, Mick. My heart stopped working and my brain begin to function. I know exactly what I'm saying."

"What about us, Larry?"

"I'm hoping we can be friends in time. But I will need time, Mick."

"What about when you go home? What if something happens to you?"

"What if it does, Mick? Then it does."

For several more minutes I attempted to change Larry's mind. I noticed that the now re-hooked machine was beginning to sound an alarming noise.

I decided to stop. At least Larry had said we could be friends. I could only hope that he meant that. In time he'd see that I did want him.

I sat beside him feeling an ache in my heart. God, I did want to be with my husband. I wanted to spend the rest of this life loving him. I wanted us to be like kids and demand a do-over.

Three days later Larry left the hospital alone, not even allowing me to accompany him home. He'd stayed an extra day until the children had all returned to their homes. He said he needed time alone. Surprisingly, the doctor and the insurance company had agreed.

As he stood outside the hospital about to get into the cab, he held me in his arms and I held on to him tightly. "Larry, let me come with you."

He pulled away and smiled. "No."

"You said we could remain friends."

"I also said I needed some time."

"Can we have dinner?" I asked, grabbing at anything, just something to hold on to.

"Call me, but give me a couple of weeks, okay?" He kissed my lips gently and got into the cab and rode away.

I stood there staring after him, knowing how he'd felt when I'd driven away from our home just a few short weeks ago. That old saying was right. Payback is a Bitch.

"Blaine, you're absolutely no help." I wrung my hands in disgust. "You claim to be a psychic, so tell me. Is Larry ever going to forgive me?"

It had been almost a month since Larry had left the hospital. I'd called him three times and each time, he'd said it hadn't been long enough, that he needed more time.

He was friendly, but not willing to see me, asking me instead to respect his wishes. So I did. But I was making a pest of myself with Blaine, wanting him to look into my future and tell me what he saw.

"Michelle, you're the one who's been married to Larry for more than a quarter of a century. What do you think?"

"Oh, so here we go again, back to the games?"

He actually had the nerve to laugh at me before he came to where I was standing.

"Come on, Michelle, what does your heart tell you? Use your instincts."

"I don't want to. I want you to read your tarot cards or read my palms. Whatever you have to do, do it. I don't give a damn if you conjure up the dead."

"Temper, temper," he smiled. "The dead can get mighty testy. Listen, I'm not going to do it. I didn't do it for Chance and I'm not going to do it for you."

"Chance asked you about me and Larry?"

"Yes, and that's all I'm saying on that subject also."

"Blaine, you know you're not any help at all, don't you?" I looked at him and glared, miffed that he might possibly have the information I sought and not give it to me.

"Okay, Michelle, what do you want me to say?"

"Tell me he's going to give in eventually."

"I'll tell you that he loves you so much that he didn't want to live without you."

"Yeah, that I already know, except now it seems he's finding a way to do that." I flicked my hair behind my ears feeling a little annoyed with Blaine and with Larry.

"He tried to give me away. Did I tell you that?"

"Oh, I don't know, maybe about a thousand times."

I glanced at Blaine. "Are you getting sick of me?"

"I'm getting sick of your pissing around. You know the answers to your questions and you're doing nothing to find them."

I was a bit taken aback. It was the first time Blaine had ever spoken to me in that tone of voice.

"I've done everything I could think of," I told him. "What else am I supposed to do?"

"If you don't know, don't ask me," Blaine replied and turned his back on me.

"Keep your information, Blaine. I don't need it. I'm going home. I have a key and I'm moving back in." I stalked angrily toward the door.

Blaine's voice stopped me. "I told you that you knew the answer."

I stood for a long moment staring at him, blinking in total surprise. Of course. He was right. It was what I should have done weeks before. I gave Blaine a quick hug and hurried out to my car to go home.

I pulled into my drive, trepidation filling my heart. I'd not been home in almost two months. I took time to look around, knowing I was stalling for time. It was now or never, I thought as I got out and walked toward the door.

I spotted Larry's car in the garage a second before I began to dig in my purse for the key to my home. I stuck it in and held my breath as I turned it.

I twisted the knob, nothing. I brought the key away and looked at it. Again I inserted it and this time I shoved at the door with quite a bit more force. Again nothing.

I must have tried my key a dozen times before a light went off in my befuddled brain. Larry had changed the locks. Maybe I'd made a mistake after all. Maybe he didn't want me back.

I thought to turn and leave, but I'd come this far. I wasn't leaving without seeing my husband. I rang the bell and waited.

Larry answered, a look of surprise on his handsome face. He smiled warmly at me. As he stared at me his smile grew even wider. I held out the key toward him, my body trembling in anticipation.

"My key didn't work," I said.

"I changed the locks."

"I thought it was something like that," I mumbled stupidly, "you know, that you changed the locks or something." God, I sounded dumb.

"Come on in, Mick."

"So why did you?" I pointed toward the door. "You know, why did you...?"

"I thought it was about time I made some changes in my own life. This time there are only two sets of keys to the locks."

I looked at him biting my lips, not knowing how to handle this. I felt awkward, but there was warmth in Larry's eyes and in his voice. He was glad to see me. I wasn't mistaken about that.

"You know, Mick, I'm a slow study. It took me twenty-six years to hear you. I waited until it was too late, but finally I did. I want you to know that. I did hear you, Mick."

"It's not too late, Larry," I whispered.

I looked at my husband, trying hard to remember the exact words I'd spoken to him when we first met. "Let's start over," I said as I walked closer to him.

I stopped inches from him and looked up at him. "Hi, my name's Michelle. My God, you have the most beautiful eyes."

Larry looked at me. Then his gaze fell to the floor before coming back to rest on my face. His eyes were filled with tears.

"Do you still love him?"

"Yes, I have no control over that. He's a part of me. He's a part of my past. But I love you too. And you're the only one I want to spend the rest of my life with."

"Not because of any promise?" Larry said, his voice breaking.

"Not because of any promise," I answered, my own voice breaking as well.

"Not because of your sense of commitment?" he almost whispered.

"Not because of my sense of commitment."

I reached my hand out to touch his cheek, my heart bursting with love for my husband. This was right, this was meant to be.

Larry held my hand to his cheek. "Not because you pity me?"

"No, Larry, not because I pity you."

"Why then, Mick?"

"Because I can't imagine living the rest of my life without you in it."

I watched as he closed his eyes and swallowed several times, seemingly having come to some conclusion.

"There will have to be some changes, Mick."

"What kind of changes?" I asked.

"I want us to go to a sex therapist—" he started to say when I interrupted him. He was embarrassed as hell to say it and I didn't want him to be.

"We don't need…"

"We do," he continued. "I want to learn how to please you. I want to rock your world and have you screaming out my name. I want us to reach the peak together. I don't want you thinking of him when you're with me. I want to know you're not faking it."

"Larry, I didn't."

I stopped when I saw the stubborn set to his jaw. He was mentally pulling away from me. So I stopped myself from the answer I was going to give and said instead, "Okay, if that's what you want."

"It's not only what I want, it's what we need," he said with authority.

"What about everything else?" I asked, "Our past baggage?"

"I've already started going to counseling," Larry answered.

"Larry, I'm sorry for everything that's happened to us. I should have spoken up, said something. I'm as much to blame as you are."

I felt my body begin to tremble, this time accompanied by the same tingle of excitement I'd felt in the hospital. These feelings were for my husband.

"Larry, I love you, I always have. I guess I forgot just how much for a while. Do you think you'll be able to forgive me?"

I watched as he walked toward the mantle and reached for a set of shining new keys and handed them to me. They had a gold name plate that said, *Mick*.

"I've already forgiven you," Larry answered one second before his lips closed over mine. I felt the beat of his heart against my own.

Regardless of what had happened in the past, that was not where I was, or where I belonged. I belonged here, now, in this time, with this man, in his arms. He was my destiny.

I thanked God as Larry twirled me around, both of us crying. It seemed we stood like that forever before Larry let go of me.

"One more thing." He went across the room and flipped through a bunch of papers. "I got this for you," he said with a smile.

"What is it?" I asked, holding out my hand for the rumpled paper.

When I looked down and saw Viola's number and address, my eyes filled again with tears.

"I got that for you. I thought you needed it. Mick, I just want you to know, I didn't cheat her."

"I know you didn't," I said knowing in my heart that he hadn't. I'd never thought that he had. I clutched the paper to me. "Thank you."

"Can I ask you a favor now?" He smiled hesitantly at me. "I want to go with you to see Viola."

"Larry," I moaned, going once again into his arms. "Oh, Larry, thank you."

"I'm sorry, Mick. I should have tried harder to listen to you. I should never have forced you to break a promise."

"Its okay now, it's in our past." I glanced toward the stairs. "Let's forget it for now."

His eyes followed mine and I watched as his filled with raw longing, making my toes curls with desire.

"I think as much as I want you right now, that we need to excise all our ghosts first. Let's visit Viola."

"When?" I was looking at him, totally awe struck.

"How about now?" he replied.

I made the call and within a couple of minutes we were heading for Viola's. Once there we walked hand in hand up the rickety stairs to ring Viola's bell.

A feeling of absolute peace filled my spirit. For the first time in my life I was truly happy. This was indeed my destiny. I was home. And it was time for both Larry and me to live again.

Epilogue

Today is my twenty-seventh anniversary. I awake and my arm snakes over to the opposite side of the bed seeking my husband's warmth. He's not there.

That's only one of the changes we've gone through in this past year. We no longer wake at the exact moment every day. Sometimes, but not every day. Perhaps this comes from the months of sleeping in separate beds alone.

I have the feeling I'm being watched. I open my eyes slowly and smile at Larry. He's sitting in a colorful chair, the kind Hawaii is famous for.

We're on vacation—just the two of us, on the beautiful island of Oahu, Hawaii. "Hi," I say sleepily to Larry, watching him, his love for me evident in his eyes. "What are you doing?"

"I've been watching you sleep and thinking how much I love you." He smiled. "I was also thinking how very lucky we are. For a while there, I doubted that we would make it."

He moved toward me. I adjusted my body so he could lie beside me. He kissed me gently, and then with a sense of urgency, the kiss deepened. I tasted the pineapple he'd been eating.

That's another thing we've changed. We've relaxed the rules on our sex life. We no longer have to brush our teeth or shower before we make love.

I also quit my job. I thought it was best to keep myself out of the path of temptation and our marriage didn't need the extra strain. As for Jeremy and Dimitra, they know their time together will come again.

My relationship with the children is slowly changing. Larry and I have been to see Derrick twice for a couple of days. We also went to see Shannon, just to check out her living situation.

I relented and am now sending her boxes of food each month, no extra money, but I don't want her to go hungry either.

Beth and Brigid call often and always speak with me for a couple of minutes before asking for their father. As for Erica, that's going to take a bit longer.

Blaine has been spending a lot of time out of town on speaking engagements. He calls often and when he's in town we see each other.

Larry has met with him twice. While I can't say that he likes him, he doesn't hate him, so that's a start. I think the fact that they were both abandoned by their mothers and shuffled from foster home to foster home gave them each a better understanding of the other.

As for the counseling, we're making tremendous progress. The sex therapist hasn't hurt either. Now more times than not when Larry climbs the peaks, I'm right there along with him.

I feel Larry's hand sliding beneath the flimsy gown I'm wearing. I turn to him trembling with want and need. I'm so amazed at what I almost lost. I bury myself in my husband's love, determined not to ever forget the things I've learned this past year.

The Beginning

*Here's a sneak peek of the second book in
the Undying Love trilogy,
The Gift
by Dyanne Davis
Coming 2011 from W.D. Publishing*

Blaine sat on the jet, his eyes closed behind the dark glasses he wore so often now. It had taken him less than a week to survey the damage in his San Francisco apartment and start the rebuilding process. In the meantime he needed a place to live. So he was heading to his spacious suburban home forty minutes west of Chicago

Funny when he'd flown to San Francisco he'd had thoughts of staying. Problem was, even with a psychic, life didn't always turn out as planned. For assurance he'd even drawn Tarot cards for himself. Too bad he hadn't asked if he would be burned out of his west coast apartment.

Blaine lifted the glasses a tiny bit from his face to swipe at the sweat that had beaded between his brows. He didn't want to take the glasses off because for the past week he'd taken quite a bit of ribbing, some of it good-natured, some of it mean spirited. Mostly people questioned if he were a true psychic, why didn't he know his apartment was going to catch on fire?

In all honesty he'd answered, 'I'm not God.' Now he was tired of the questions, tired of all the answers. He just wanted to go home undisturbed. If he didn't wear the glasses, strangers would be pestering him with requests for readings. He accepted that as a price for his fame.

On most occasions he handled those requests with a modicum of dignity and humor offering the person asking his card. He couldn't chance it now; he was in too weak of a state psychically. The fumes from the smoke had wrecked havoc in his body. He needed time to heal.

Right now he could ill afford strangers pulling at his energy field. It was all that he could do to keep the barrier of energy surrounding his body, keeping out the thoughts of his fellow passengers.

Sleep was pulling at him when Blaine sat up with a start. He rubbed at his temple feeling the beginning of what promised to be one doozy of a headache. He closed his eyes in order to better focus his powers, to see who was having such an effect on him. Not since the first time he met Michelle had he felt such a dramatic reaction. Blaine wanted to know who it was and what was happening.

As he focused his energy the feeling became stronger until at last he was on his feet, standing, moving forward without wanting to, yet drawn to someone's pain. His hand moved unobtrusively through the air. Since finding his mother he was discovering new powers he'd never known he possessed.

He smiled to himself, the thought that he had only to put out his hand and connect with someone else's energy surprising. After a lifetime of dealing with the unexplained, Blaine was comfortable with his gifts of clairaudience. He didn't have a name for this newest emerging gift.

The best way he could explain it was mining for energy. He used his hands much the same as he used his mind when speaking to those who had departed this life and were waiting. He focused.

Blaine stopped, his eyes landing on a woman of petite stature. Even from a sitting position he could tell she was short. He stood over the woman perusing her body in a quick perfunctory manner. She was slender also. His gaze fell on the woman's curly, dark brown hair and a lump formed in his throat.

Blaine stepped back as an irresistible urge to reach out and touch her clutched at his throat. It took all his psychic energy to resist the pull. A tightening began in his groin. Good Lord, not now. He panicked and moved backwards down the aisle. No woman had ever affected him so quickly.

"What is it that you want?"

Blaine stopped his backwards descent and looked down into the biggest pair of chocolate brown eyes he'd ever seen. For a moment he thought his heart would stop. Despite the woman's cold stare he felt drawn to her.

The sadness that had emanated from her to bring him to her now washed over him in waves. He clicked his tongue against his teeth trying to feel the woman's energy.

Damn. That had never happened before. She'd placed a block to keep him out.

"I'm sorry," he stammered. "My name's Blaine MaDia."

He smiled at the woman while his skin began a slow crawl of awareness. It wasn't so much her looks as her aura. In looks she was beautiful true enough, but he'd met more than his share of beautiful women. The exception to this woman was her eyes. Staring at her for a moment something pulled at him more than her physical appearance. It was the woman's spirit that held an intense fascination for Blaine.

"I'm sorry, Mr. MaDia. Am I supposed to know you?"

Blaine tried again to probe gently at the woman's thoughts. When that didn't work he tried more aggressively, but still she held out against him blocking any entrance. This stirred his curiosity making Blaine wonder what it was the woman was hiding so possessively that she'd thrown up a shield against a stranger.

"Mr. MaDia, did you want something?"

Now he was standing there feeling like a fool, his own psyche open for probing, his defenses weakened. He knew better than to continue with his questions, yet he felt compelled to press on. Never in all the years since Blaine became a professional psychic had he ever used that gift to seek out females, or to impress. He was now embarrassed and could feel the flush of that embarrassment with the next words he uttered.

"I'm Blaine MaDia, the psychic on television."

He gulped. The woman appeared unimpressed. "I was just walking, I didn't want anything." Blaine continued.

Still nothing. The woman simply stared at him, her deep-set chocolate eyes turning to liquid cocoa. Now besides wanting to touch her, Blaine wanted to stand there and take a long drink from her eyes.

"I don't know you, Mr. MaDia and I don't mean to appear rude, but I'm very tired. I paid for two first class seats so that I wouldn't be disturbed." She tilted her head slightly letting Blaine know she wanted him to leave.

"Sorry I bothered you," he murmured and turned to walk back to his seat. He paused and stuck out his hand toward the woman. "Nice to meet you Miss…Miss…"

He waited for an acknowledgment and a name, but the woman looked at him with mere curiosity, ignored his outstretched hand and cast her gaze back on the book in her hand.

Surely the woman had to be a psychic, Blaine thought. At the very least, she was familiar with psychic gifts because she was using them so effectively to keep him out. And he wanted in.

Author's Information:

Dyanne Davis is an award winning author. She lives in a Chicago suburb with her husband Bill, and their son Bill Jr. An avid reader her love of the written word turned into a desire to write. She retired from nursing more than a decade ago to pursue her lifelong dream.

Dyanne has been a presenter of numerous workshops. She has a local cable show, The Art of Writing in her hometown to give writing tips to aspiring writers.

When not writing you can find her with a book in her hands, her greatest passion next to spending time with her husband Bill and son Bill Jr. Whenever possible she loves getting together with friends and family

A member of Romance writers of American she served in many capacities for her local chapter, Windy City, including two terms as president.

Dyanne Davis loves to hear from her readers. You can reach her at davisdyanne@aol.com
You can write to her at
 P.O. Box 1218 Bolingbrook IL. 60440

www.ingramcontent.com/pod-product-compliance
Lightning Source LLC
Chambersburg PA
CBHW030912120626
46554CB00001B/121